R. Barri Flowers is an award-winning author of crime, thriller, mystery and romance fiction featuring three-dimensional protagonists, riveting plots, unexpected twists and turns, and heart-pounding climaxes. With an expertise in true crime, serial killers and characterising dangerous offenders, he is perfectly suited for the Mills & Boon Heroes series. Chemistry and conflict between the hero and heroine, attention to detail and incorporating the very latest advances in criminal investigations are the cornerstones of his romantic suspense fiction. Discover more on popular social networks and Wikipedia.

Katherine Garbera is the *USA Today* bestselling author of more than one hundred and twenty-five novels. She's a small-town Florida girl whose imagination was fired up by long hours spent outside sitting underneath orange trees. She grew up to travel the world and makes her home in the UK with her husband. Her books have garnered numerous awards and are sold around the world. Connect with her at katherinegarbera.com and on Facebook, Instagram and Twitter.

D1322829

Also by R. Barri Flowers

The Lynleys of Law Enforcement
Special Agent Witness

Hawaii CI
The Big Island Killer
Captured on Kauai
Honolulu Cold Homicide
Danger on Maui

Chasing the Violet Killer

Also by Katherine Garbera

Destination Wedding
The Wedding Dare
The One from the Wedding
Secrets of a Wedding Crasher

The Image Project
Billionaire Makeover
The Billionaire Plan
Billionaire Fake Out

Discover more at millsandboon.co.uk

CHRISTMAS LIGHTS KILLER

R. BARRI FLOWERS

BODYGUARD MOST WANTED

KATHERINE GARBERA

MILLS & BOON

First Published in Great Britain 2023
by Mills & Boon, an imprint of HarperCollins*Publishers* Ltd
1 London Bridge Street, London, SE1 9GF

www.harpercollins.co.uk

HarperCollins*Publishers*
Macken House, 39/40 Mayor Street Upper,
Dublin 1, D01 C9W8, Ireland

Christmas Lights Killer © 2023 R. Barri Flowers
Bodyguard Most Wanted © 2023 Katherine Garbera

ISBN: 978-0-263-30747-4

1023

This book is produced from independently certified FSC™ paper
to ensure responsible forest management.

For more information visit: www.harpercollins.co.uk/green

Printed and Bound in the UK using 100% Renewable Electricity at
CPI Group (UK) Ltd, Croydon, CR0 4YY

CHRISTMAS
LIGHTS KILLER

R. BARRI FLOWERS

To H. Loraine, the love of my life and best friend, whose support has been unwavering through the many wonderful years together. To my dear mother, Marjah Aljean, who gave me the tools to pursue my passions in life, including writing fiction for publication; and for my loving sister, Jacquelyn, who helped me become the person I am today. To the loyal fans of my romance, mystery, suspense and thriller fiction published over the years. Lastly, a nod goes out to my wonderful editors, Allison Lyons and Denise Zaza, for the great opportunity to lend my literary voice and creative spirit to the successful Mills & Boon Heroes series.

Prologue

His seemed like a friendly enough face. She could maybe even call it handsome. The eyes were crystal blue and a good fit above a Greek nose and a slightly crooked mouth. His triangular face had a square jawline and a dark chinstrap beard. Dark brown or black hair was in a messy, tapered style that seemed to suit him. Like her, he was casually dressed for winter weather in early December, wearing a blue hooded parka jacket, tech jeans, black leather gloves and brown steel-toe boots. The fact that he just happened along in his black Ford Bronco Sport Big Bend didn't faze her. How could he have known that her own red Honda Insight would just conk out on the side of the road, leaving her few options, given that she couldn't seem to get a signal on her cell phone.

So, when he offered her a ride to the nearest service station, JoBeth Sorenson threw caution to the wind and accepted graciously. The fact that it was Christmas time and most people in the town of Carol Creek, Indiana, seemed festive and in the holiday spirit gave her further reason for believing that accepting a ride from a total stranger would bring her no harm. After getting into the front seat and buckling up, JoBeth grinned at the man who never identified himself, but offered her a generous, toothy smile. He was playing some Christmas music, which again made it seem like he was anything but a grinch out to ruin her holiday. She wished the same were true for her ex-boyfriend, Aaron Heathcote. They'd broken up two weeks ago, after he confessed to cheating on her, validating what she had suspected for a while but chosen to ignore it till she couldn't any longer. Being single again right before Christmas wasn't exactly her idea of jingle bells ringing. But she supposed it was best that she knew the truth before the new year, giving her the opportunity for a fresh start as a suddenly available high school English teacher.

They drove down the snow-covered road for a full minute with neither uttering a word, as JoBeth was totally wrapped up in her thoughts. Only when she noticed that they had passed by Walker Street, which would take them toward the service station, did she face the driver with mild concern. "I think we missed our turn," she said, flipping her long, multilayered blond hair to the side.

"Really?" He glanced at her and back to the road. "Sorry about that," he claimed. "Don't know what I was thinking. I'll turn around up ahead and we'll go back."

"Thank you." JoBeth breathed a sigh of relief. Maybe he really was a nice guy after all. And not her worst nightmare. She even imagined that, judging by his looks and seemingly not much older than her twenty-seven years of age, he might even be good boyfriend material. Assuming he too was single and available, once they got past her current predicament.

"No problem," he said.

She smiled. "So, any big holiday plans?" she asked, if only for effect.

"Not really." He glanced at her. "How about you?"

JoBeth considered that her parents would be spending Christmas in Hawaii and her younger sister, Dana, had decided to go skiing with her boyfriend at the Paoli Peaks alpine ski resort in Orange County, Indiana, nearly one hundred miles away. That left JoBeth's best friend, Mariah O'Sullivan. But she had other plans that didn't include her, so JoBeth was honest about it when she responded, "None that I can think of, other than having my car back up and running again."

The man laughed as he turned onto Brockton Drive. "Regarding that… I'm afraid you won't be needing your car again…"

"Excuse me?" She cast her big blue eyes at him with alarm.

He chuckled again and kept driving down the desolate road, away from the homes they had passed by earlier, many decorated for Christmas. "I said that your car won't be of much use to you now."

"I don't understand what you mean."

He gave her a menacing look. "You'll know soon enough."

JoBeth's radar suddenly kicked in, alerting her that something was very off about the driver. How had she not noticed it before? "I think you better let me out here," she insisted. Though farther away from assistance than before, she would rather take her chances of freezing to death than remain in the car with someone who was acting too weird for her comfort.

"I think not," he said in a mocking tone of voice. He pressed down on the accelerator.

She tried to open the passenger-side door, but he had used

the master lock to prevent this. "Stop the car and let me out!" she demanded, hoping that would somehow do the trick.

When he brought the vehicle to a halt, while managing to maintain control on the slippery road, the man said, "I did half of what you asked. Unfortunately, the other half won't be possible just yet."

JoBeth yanked on the door handle, desperately trying to force the door open, to no avail. "Let me go!" she snapped, her heart racing.

"No can do," he responded tersely. "Didn't your mother ever teach you to never get into cars with strangers?" He laughed. "If so, you should've listened to her." He reached into the back seat and picked up a string of Christmas lights. "Bet you're wondering what these are for?"

JoBeth didn't even want to imagine what kind of sick games he intended to play with those lights. All she wanted was to some way, somehow, get out of this alive. Was it too late for that? "Please," she begged him. "I just want out. I won't say anything to anyone about this." She wanted to say *kidnapping* or *abduction*, even if it didn't start out that way, seeing that he was now holding her against her will. But she didn't dare antagonize him while he had her at a disadvantage.

"Sorry, but I have to do this and you have no choice but to take it, as you've reached the end of your road, literally," he snorted, and wrapped the string of Christmas lights tightly around her neck.

JoBeth gasped for air as she tried to loosen the copper wire cutting through her neck. She attempted to claw his face, but he somehow managed to keep it just beyond her reach while strangling her forcefully. When she became too weak to fight anymore, her will to live seemed to fade like fog. Before losing consciousness for good, JoBeth was left to wonder how this could have happened to her. And what came next.

HE TWISTED AND tightened the string of Christmas lights around her short neck till she breathed her final breath and her body went limp. How lucky could he have been? He had been searching for the perfect person to kill. And just like that, there she was. Stranded on the side of the road, looking to trust whoever came along to assist in her time of need. Good thing for him that he beat someone else to the punch in offering to drive her to a service station.

Bad thing for her that she accepted his offer and, in the process, signed her own death warrant. He stared at her for a long moment, admiring his almost work of art. In death, she had brought to life his urge to kill. And if he had anything to do with it, she wouldn't be the last. Unless he got stupid and allowed the cops to catch him in the act or afterward. He didn't intend to let that happen.

Unlocking the passenger door, he undid her seat belt, opened the door and shoved the woman's dead body to the side of the road, leaving the Christmas lights around her neck. He closed the door and drove off on his merry way, humming along to the Christmas tune coming from the radio and looking ahead to when he would be able to go down this proverbial road again.

Chapter One

"My daughter's missing!" the woman cried as she stormed into the office of Dabs County Sheriff's Detective Annette Lynley.

Annette had finally gotten comfortable with the small office she was given a year ago, along with a badge and Glock 43 single-stack 9mm pistol, when taking the position within the Sheriff's Department's Detective Bureau, which included three full-time detectives and two reserve deputies. She'd managed to make the office feel more like home on a professional level, having been allowed to replace the age-old furnishings for something more suitable, including a washed-gray L-shaped wooden desk, an ergonomic mesh task chair and upgraded laptop. But there were bigger things on her mind these days. At age thirty-four, apart from feeling the constant need to prove herself as more than capable of handling the job, Annette and her fellow detectives were dealing with some shocking homicides. The crimes were hardly the norm for Dabs County, located in the northern part of Indiana, and the small towns within, including Carol Creek, where the sheriff's department was located on Elm Street. Till recently, drug-related offenses, domestic violence and juvenile delinquency were the main forms of criminality the Detective Bureau or DB was tasked with responding to. Now they had a bona fide serial killer on their hands, with Annette as the lead detective in the investigation. Dubbed by the local press as "The Christmas Lights Killer," thus far the unknown suspect—or unsub— had strangled to death two attractive young women. In each case, the murder weapon was a string of Christmas lights left around the neck of the victim as the perpetrator's chilling calling card. The killings threatened to put a serious damper on the holiday season in the county, with Christmas little more than two weeks away.

As she sat at the desk, Annette's bold brown-and-green eyes sized up the woman, who looked to be in her early forties and was dressed warmly for this time of year. She was on the slender side, around Annette's height of five-seven and a half, with blue eyes and short, blond-brown hair in a feathered cut. Normally, Annette would have expected the office clerk, Patti Gellar, to prevent visitors from getting very far in this section of the department. Someone usually came out to speak with them. But Patti had been given the day off for a doctor's appointment and everyone else was out in the field, leaving only Annette to handle whoever had a problem, for better or worse.

So handle it, Annette told herself. "And you are?" she asked the woman politely.

"Maureen McCade."

"What's your daughter's name?"

"Juliet." Her voice shook. "Juliet McCade."

"How long has she been missing, Mrs. McCade?"

"Please call me Maureen, Detective. There's no husband in the picture." She frowned. "I raised Juliet as a single mom. With the help of my younger brother, Hamilton."

In that moment, Annette couldn't help but reflect on her own upbringing and what might have been. Having been given up for adoption by her unwed mother while still an infant, Annette had been adopted by Oklahomans Taylor and Caroline Lynley, becoming their fourth child behind three birth children, Scott, Madison and Russell. Though they fully embraced her, and Annette couldn't imagine having been a part of any other family, she still wondered sometimes if she and her birth mother might have found a way to get through the difficult times had they stayed together. Perhaps if there had been an uncle around like Maureen's brother Hamilton to help the cause, things may have turned out differently.

"I haven't seen or spoken to Juliet since she went out last night around seven p.m.," Maureen continued, ill at ease, getting Annette's attention again.

Annette glanced at the quartz clock on the wall and saw that it was 11 a.m. Meaning only sixteen hours had passed since Maureen last saw her daughter. Though one was free to report someone missing at any time, the department usually didn't start an investigation for twenty-four hours from the time the person was last seen. Unless they were talking about a minor or a suspected abduction, or had other clear indication that the missing person was in danger. But given the current situation of women turning up dead, no case of a missing female could be taken lightly.

"I know what you're thinking," Maureen said perceptively. "That not enough time has passed for me to be concerned." She sighed. "Well, I know my daughter. Juliet has never stayed out all night without letting me know where she was and who with. Besides, I got a text message from her, in which Juliet thought someone might be following her. I tried texting back, but got no response. Something's wrong. I can feel it."

Annette twisted her lips musingly. "Can I see the text?"

Maureen took the cell phone from the pocket of her quilted jacket and brought up the text message before passing the phone to her. Annette read the text.

Hey, I think I'm being followed by someone. Maybe it's just my imagination.

The message had been sent at seven forty last night. All things considered, it was certainly unnerving to Annette, to say the least. But it wasn't exactly an indication that a crime had taken place. Or who might have committed it. "In most instances of missing persons, they tend to turn up unharmed, sooner or later," she pointed out, knowing full well that this would do little to appease the worried mother. Truthfully, it didn't give Annette much solace, either, as each individual case stood on its own merits.

Maureen rubbed her nose. "I keep trying to tell myself that. But this is so unlike Juliet that I can't help thinking something bad has happened to her."

"Let's not jump to conclusions," Annette cautioned her gingerly, wanting to believe otherwise. "How old is Juliet?"

"Twenty-one."

"And she lives with you?"

"At the moment." Maureen paused and explained, "She's been staying at my house for the last month. Or ever since the lease to her apartment ended and the rent became more than she could afford, in spite of working two part-time jobs."

Annette could relate, having been down that road of

struggling to make ends meet in her early adulthood. During her college years and after graduating from the University of Oklahoma with a Bachelor of Arts in Criminology, she had worked her fair share of part-time jobs and lived in low-income housing off campus. Of course, her financial position was secure now, after she'd landed a job in law enforcement. Her late adopted father and mother had been a police chief and criminal court judge respectively; and two of her siblings were FBI special agents and the other a law enforcement ranger. So it was natural that Annette had followed in their footsteps and gotten into police work herself, first working as a deputy sheriff in different locations before becoming a detective with the Dabs County Sheriff's Office.

"Won't you have a seat, Maureen?" Annette asked her, then watched as the woman sat in one of the two barrel-shaped guest chairs on the other side of the desk. Needing further insight into the missing young woman, Annette inquired, "You said your daughter has two part-time jobs. What are they?"

"During the week, Juliet works as a sales clerk at a boutique in the Carol Creek Shopping Center." Maureen squirmed in the seat. "Recently, she's been working weekends at a Christmas tree lot on Forrester Lane."

Annette didn't see anything unusual about that on the face of it, but made a mental note. "Does Juliet have a boyfriend?" If so, she imagined that the daughter might have gone to his place.

"She recently broke up with her boyfriend, Chad Lawrence," Maureen claimed.

"Is it possible that they got back together?" Annette clasped her hands together.

"No, Juliet dumped him for cheating on her," she insisted, frowning. "Would you go back to a cheater?"

Annette had been put on the spot, uncomfortably. She thought back to the last man she had been involved with— Eric Rodriguez. After dating for nearly a year and believing he could be the one, Annette had discovered that Eric was anything but the one: he'd been having an affair with one of his married colleagues. The experience had left a bitter taste in Annette's mouth and had her wondering if real love and commitment would ever be in the cards for her. "No, I'm pretty sure I wouldn't," she had to admit to Juliet's mother.

"Didn't think so."

Annette gazed at her across the desk. "Maybe Juliet met someone else and decided to spend the night with him," she suggested. "Or otherwise simply lost track of time. Not too uncommon for young adults these days."

Maureen bristled. "I just need to know she's okay."

I'd like to know that, too, Annette thought. "Where was your daughter going when she went out?"

"She was supposed to meet a friend, Rita Getzler, at a local hangout called the Pear Pub. But according to Rita, Juliet never showed up."

"Hmm…" Annette didn't like the sound of that. "Does Juliet have a car?"

"Yes, she bought a Subaru Impreza last summer."

"We'll try and locate it," Annette said. Given the winter conditions, it was entirely possible that Juliet had gotten into an accident and could be hurt—or worse—and unable to communicate. "Have you checked the hospital?" There was only Carol Creek General in town, but one other hospital and some clinics were spread across the county.

"Yes. They don't show a Juliet McCade as having been admitted."

"That's good," Annette told her. At least insofar as no official indication that Juliet had run into harm's way. "It means she isn't necessarily injured." But still cause for concern to be missing at all.

"Not that we know of." Maureen frowned pessimistically. "We need to find her!"

"We will." Annette suspected that this assurance would fall on deaf ears as long as her daughter was still unaccounted for. "Do you have a photo of Juliet?"

Maureen nodded. She pulled it up on her cell phone and showed Annette. "It was taken last week in our living room."

Annette studied the missing young woman. She was biracial, like her, and pretty with brown eyes and long, wavy brunette hair with side-swept bangs. This reminded Annette of her own hairstyle, color and length when not on duty, though hers was usually parted in the middle, with chin-length bangs, and she preferred a looped updo while at work. "We'll need this picture and a general description of your daughter to work with."

"I understand," Maureen said. "Anything I can do to help bring Juliet home."

Just then, Detective Will Hossack lumbered into the office, after having gone to follow up on a suspected burglary. The thirty-eight-year-old full-time detective and ladies' man had been with the sheriff's department for fifteen years and seemed in no hurry to go elsewhere in law enforcement. Six-four and of solid build, he was dark-eyed, clean-shaven, and wore his brown hair in a Caesar cut underneath the Stetson hat atop his head. "Who do we have here?" he asked curiously.

"This is Maureen McCade," Annette told him. "Her daughter, Juliet McCade, has been missing since last night." Annette made eye contact with the detective warily. She could almost read his mind. Both victims of the Christmas Lights Killer had been missing, at least briefly, till their bodies were discovered. Would this case of a missing young woman also end tragically?

INDIANA STATE POLICE Senior Trooper Hamilton McCade cruised down the lightly snow-covered US Route 24 in his white Dodge Charger Pursuit in District 22, located in Fort Wayne, Allen County. He was on the lookout for anyone involved in criminal activity or violating the traffic laws. As standard practice, he was armed with a SIG Sauer P227 pistol as his primary weapon and had a SIG Sauer P365 subcompact pistol as a backup firearm, while wearing a ballistic vest. Though he had been at this for the past ten of his thirty-six years of life, moving from one ISP district to another while gaining some valuable experience and fulfillment, Hamilton thought it was time he moved up the ranks. Toward that end and in line with his recently completed PhD in criminal justice from Indiana University Bloomington, he had applied to join the ISP's Investigations Command Special Investigation Section. Or, more specifically, the Organized Crime and Corruption Unit within, believing this would better serve his goals of going after those who committed investment scams, trafficking offenses, political corruption and related offenses. There was every reason to believe that he would be reassigned accordingly early in the new year.

But for now, Hamilton was more focused on maintaining the status quo and trying to get through the holiday season all by his lonesome. Although dumped six months ago by his girlfriend, Felicity Sheridan, who seemed to believe the pastures were greener with the investment banker she'd met on an online dating app, Hamilton wouldn't exactly say he was ready to swear off women and romance forever. But it had shaken his confidence in that department, in spite of being a guy in pretty good shape at six-three, and certainly able to hold his own in the looks department, with his deep blue eyes and black hair in a short military-style cut. All he could do for the time being was wait and see if someone who struck his fancy came along, and go from there.

Hamilton drove down West Jefferson Boulevard and saw nothing out of the ordinary. He lowered the brim of his campaign hat, mainly out of habit, as his thoughts drifted to his only living family. His sister, Maureen, was six years older and still living in his hometown of Carol Creek in the adjacent Dabs County, where she was a registered nurse. They had drifted apart somewhat once he'd left for greater opportunities in Fort Wayne. But even that didn't stop him from appreciating how Maureen had always been in his corner when their parents, Sherman and Catherine McCade, had more or less left them to fend for themselves. When Maureen had made a mistake with a one-night stand resulting in pregnancy, with no accountability by the father, Hamilton had tried to step in there as much as possible for his sister and the beautiful girl she'd brought into this world. It was hard for him to believe that Juliet was now twenty-one years old and trying to make a life for herself. While reminding Hamilton of Maureen, Juliet resembled their mother more.

Maybe he would return home for Christmas this year

and the three of them could spend it together and even ring in the new year as a family, before it was time for him to get back to the grind of the life he had established in Fort Wayne. When his cell phone rang, Hamilton snapped out of his reverie. He took the phone from the side pocket of the trousers worn with his uniform and glanced at it. *Wouldn't you know it*, he thought, grinning, when he saw that the caller was none other than Maureen.

Placing the phone in the car's cell phone holder, he tapped the speaker icon and said in a pleasant voice, "Hey, sis. I was just thinking about you and Juliet."

"Juliet's missing," Maureen said in a panicky voice.

"What do you mean she's missing?" Hamilton asked equably.

"I haven't seen her since last night. She was supposed to go out with a girlfriend, but never showed up. She texted me around seven forty to say she thought someone was following her, but didn't respond when I texted back. I hate to bother you with this, but I'm freaking out here, wondering if Juliet's in real trouble."

I hope she's okay, Hamilton thought, not wanting to jump the gun on this. "Have you reported her missing to the sheriff's department?" He knew that there was no timetable for filing reports of missing persons, but there was also no obligation to act upon it right away if there were other priorities. Particularly for a small office usually stretched thin.

"Yes, I talked to Detective Annette Lynley," Maureen said. "And later, Detective Will Hossack. They assured me this was being taken seriously, especially with a serial killer on the loose in Carol Creek."

"Let's hope so." Hamilton chewed on his lower lip musingly. He knew Hossack, having worked with him on a case or two over the years. Hadn't had the pleasure of meeting Annette Lynley. Presumably she was up to the job in locating Juliet. The thought that his niece could have become the victim of the so-called Christmas Lights Killer left Hamilton feeling numb. His dissertation had been on serial killers and the dynamics that drove them to commit multiple murders while instilling terror in their chosen communities. He wasn't prepared to go there, though, knowing full well from past experience that twenty-one-year-olds were prone to staying out all night long and well into the next day without regard to clearing it first with parents. Or even considering their feelings when making reckless and risky choices. He wasn't sure how Juliet fit into this equation, not being as tuned into her life as a young adult as perhaps he should have been. He had to believe that somehow this would end on a good note and Juliet would return home to her mother, safe and sound.

Maureen drew a breath. "I'm really worried about Juliet and what could have happened to her and just thought you should know."

"I'm glad you told me," Hamilton said, trying to remain positive. "I'll drop by the sheriff's office and see what the status is on their investigation."

"Would you?"

"Of course. Juliet is my niece and I want to know she's all right," he promised her.

Maureen heaved an audible sigh, obviously ill at ease.

"If she calls or shows up, let me know."

"I will."

After disconnecting, he headed toward the highway that would take him to Carol Creek. It would be about forty-five minutes to get there on snowy roads. Dabs County was one of the counties within the ISP District 22 jurisdiction, giving Hamilton the ability to travel there, in spite of making a detour from the area he normally patrolled.

When he reached the sheriff's department, Hamilton walked to the brick building, ignoring the cold air hitting him in the face like a slap. The moment he stepped inside, he spotted an attractive and slender biracial woman in her thirties, with pretty, brownish green eyes, a dainty nose and a nice, full mouth—all on a high-cheeked, oval face. Her obviously long brunette hair was in a businesslike updo. About five-seven, a perfect height to his own size, she was wearing a dark blue blazer with matching pants, a white shirt and ankle boots, and carried herself with confidence.

She met his eyes squarely and said with a smile, "Hi, I'm Detective Annette Lynley." She gave him and his uniform the once-over. "I'm guessing that you're with the ISP?"

"Indiana State Trooper Hamilton McCade," he confirmed.

Annette reacted to the name. "You wouldn't happen to be related to Juliet McCade?"

"Juliet's my niece." His mouth tightened as he remembered he needed to cut to the chase. "I want to know exactly what you're doing to locate Juliet, who I believe is still missing?"

Chapter Two

Annette studied the Indiana state trooper. Hamilton McCade was a good-looking man with a square face, profoundly blue eyes, aquiline nose, slanted mouth and a slightly jutting chin, clean-shaven. He was tall, she imagined around six-three, and filled out his trooper uniform nicely. She got only a glimpse of his dark hair in what appeared to be a military cut beneath his campaign hat. Suddenly realizing she was staring, Annette averted her eyes briefly before gazing at him again. "Why don't we step into my office, Trooper McCade," she said, fully appreciating his concern for his missing niece.

"Lead the way, Detective," he said stiffly.

Before they could get there, Will Hossack stepped from his own office and the two men eyed each other. "Thought I recognized the voice," Will said amiably. "What's up, Hamilton? Been a minute."

"Hey, Will." He shook the large hand that the slightly taller Will put before him.

Annette raised a brow. "You two know each other?"

"Our paths have crossed on occasion during investigations," Will explained. "And we might have gone out for a drink or two to talk shop," he added mischievously.

"I see." She almost felt like the odd one out, but knew realistically that with both of them both having been in law enforcement in the area longer than she had, it wasn't too surprising that they would be acquainted.

"So, what brings you our way, Trooper McCade?" Will asked curiously in a more formal manner.

"As I was telling Detective Lynley," Hamilton replied, "I'm here to check on your efforts to find my missing niece, Juliet."

"Wait a sec." Will's head snapped back. "Juliet McCade's your niece?"

"Yeah."

"Never made the connection," Will said apologetically.

"Wouldn't have expected you to," Hamilton muttered. "I understand that my sister, Maureen McCade, was here earlier?"

"Right." Will looked down at his water-resistant boots and back at him. "Detective Lynley took your sister's statement and she can bring you up to date on where things stand."

Hamilton faced her and Annette actually felt a tiny quiver from the intensity of his blue eyes. "Why don't we get to it then."

Annette nodded and glanced at Will, who seemed to silently wish her good luck. Before heading back to his own office, Will told Hamilton, "I know the tendency in these instances is to think the worst, but I'm sure your niece will turn up fine."

"I want to believe that," Hamilton said. "Until it happens, though, I need to be able to reassure my sister that this is not being pushed to the back burners."

"It's not," Annette promised him. What she couldn't bring

herself to say, just yet, was that it worried her that Juliet had vanished at a time when a serial killer was on the prowl. And that the longer Hamilton's niece remained unaccounted for, the greater the likelihood that this might not come to a happy conclusion.

HAMILTON SAT IN the barrel chair on the opposite side of the gorgeous detective's desk. He couldn't help but wonder if she was married. Was she dating? Did she have children? Or was she single, childless and available, like him? He wasn't counting on the latter, figuring it was probably a long shot for the thirtysomething detective to have hung around in her life just waiting for him to appear. Even that was being premature, since they weren't exactly meeting for dating purposes, much less getting past that point to things more intimate and interesting. No, right now, he needed to stay focused on finding his niece so his sister could put her worries about Juliet to rest.

As though reading his mind, Annette said in a serious tone, "First, you should know, Trooper McCade, that we're doing everything we can to locate your niece."

He was certainly happy to hear that, for a start, and said, "Why don't you call me Hamilton, Detective Lynley."

"All right," she agreed. "In turn, you can call me Annette."

"Annette it is." He liked the name that somehow suited her. "Tell me more…"

She paused. "Since you're in law enforcement yourself, I'm sure you know that in most instances of missing persons, where there's no evidence of clear and present danger or foul play, we usually wait at least twenty-four hours before launching an investigation in earnest."

Hamilton understood this all too well and for good reason. He had certainly done his fair share of participating in cases involving missing persons. More than half a million persons were reported missing in the United States annually. The vast majority proved to be alive and well, returning home within twenty-four hours. He got that and found the data encouraging. But there was still that elephant in the room—a serial killer in town—which undermined those usually favorable odds for a young woman's safe return. "In this instance, waiting a day is too long," he argued knowingly, sure that she got his meaning. "The sooner you can locate Juliet, the better."

"I agree," Annette said coolly. "Toward that end, we've put out a BOLO alert for Juliet and her Subaru Impreza."

"That's good," he said, fearing the possibility that Juliet could have been in an accident and was therefore unresponsive.

"We're also using cell tower triangulation to see if we can pinpoint where Juliet last used her phone, whether it was the text message sent to Maureen or otherwise."

Hamilton nodded approvingly. "That can help."

Annette leaned forward. "We're also checking with hospitals for anyone fitting her description, if the patient is unnamed."

Hamilton flinched at the thought of Juliet being hospitalized as a Jane Doe, with her identification missing and Maureen not there by her side. "Okay," he muttered.

"If Juliet isn't found inside of twenty-four hours, we're prepared to organize search teams of volunteers to accompany law enforcement's efforts," Annette informed him. "Beyond that, if need be, we'll notify the FBI, its National Center for the Analysis of Violent Behavior and the Violent

Criminal Apprehension Program within, your department officially, the National Missing and Unidentified Persons System, and, of course, the Indiana Clearinghouse for Information on Missing Children and Missing Endangered Adults."

Hamilton was admittedly impressed that the detective seemed to have all the bases covered in giving them their best shot at locating Juliet. He just wondered if it would be enough. "Well, I thank you for your current and future efforts, Annette."

"It's my job, Hamilton," she stressed. "With any luck, your niece simply lost her bearings, as young people tend to do these days, and will be totally embarrassed about it when she gets home and tries to explain."

He grinned, picturing the scenario, while knowing that as an only child, Juliet had perfected over the years the art of getting back into her mother's good graces after having gone off the rails a bit. Were that the case this time around, too, he was sure that Maureen would be completely forgiving again, although having been scared half to death by her daughter, and they would get on with any plans for Christmas.

Though he almost found himself hating to leave the detective's office, Hamilton knew it was time he did just that. "I won't take up any more of your time," he said, getting to his feet.

Annette stood, too, offering him a smile. "I understand how stressful something like this can be, especially at this time of year. If you want to give me your number, I can keep you informed on where this goes."

Hamilton gave her his cell phone number and was given hers in return, which he added to his contacts.

"As soon as we hear anything concrete," she said, "I'll let you know."

"Thanks." He met her eyes and realized that she had extended a hand. Shaking it, Hamilton noticed how soft her skin felt against his. He couldn't help but imagine that this softness was likely present from her face down to her feet and everywhere in between. The thought caused a stir in him. He released her surprisingly firm grip and showed himself out. Even as he walked away, he sensed her watching him.

After getting back in his vehicle, Hamilton called his sister. "Hey. Any word from Juliet?"

"No, not yet," Maureen said dolefully.

"I just left the sheriff's office," he told her. "They're pulling out all the stops to try and find her." He imagined Juliet being held against her will somewhere, unable to communicate. As bad as that was, it was preferable to what happened to those women killed by the serial killer.

"We'll just pray that they succeed," his sister said. "Or that Juliet finds her way home all on her own."

"Yeah." He took a breath. "Look, I have to go back to work. If she comes home or you hear from her..."

"You'll be the first one I call," Maureen promised.

After disconnecting, Hamilton started up the Dodge Charger Pursuit and got on the road. He thought about Annette Lynley. Even after Juliet's case was settled, hopefully with a positive outcome, he felt he wanted to see the detective again. Maybe get to know her better, if she was open to that. If not, it was still a nice thought.

WHEN ANNETTE LEFT the sheriff's office for home, there had still been no sign of Juliet McCade, now nearly twenty-four hours after her disappearance. *Where are you?* Annette asked in her head as she drove her department-issued white Chrysler 300 Touring L down Cherrywood Street. With no sign of the missing woman's car, Annette wondered if Juliet might have driven off somewhere, with or without someone accompanying her. If so, did she do it under force? Or simply to get away from her troubles, if she had any?

Annette's greater fears were that Juliet had run into harm's way, with no getting out of it alive. But until there was confirmation of this, they had to assume that she was still alive. Annette thought about Hamilton McCade. As a state trooper, he had obviously seen his share of misfortunes. But none hurt like those too close to home. Losing her adopted parents in a car accident a few years ago had devastated Annette. She'd never even gotten a chance to say goodbye to them and thank them again for bringing her into their lives. Having her siblings to lean on allowed her to get through it and carry on.

She sensed a strong bond existed between Hamilton and his sister as well. He must be close to his niece, too. Annette wondered if he had any children. A wife? Was he seeing anyone? Or was his whole life wrapped around his work in law enforcement, which sometimes seemed to be the story of her life. *Maybe it's none of my business*, she mused, turning down Wesmire Lane. The fact that the handsome trooper had entered her world unintentionally and with more important things on his mind than romancing a fellow officer of the law hardly meant he was available and interested. She would do well to keep her eye on the ball. Especially after the disaster her last relationship had turned out to be.

Annette pulled into the driveway of her two-story home on a dead-end street. While the other homes nearby were illuminated outside with Christmas lights, she had opted against putting up decorations inside or out this year. Not that she had anything against celebrating Christmas. Just the opposite. It was her favorite time of the year. But maybe not this year, with the uptick in homicides, thanks in large part to a serial murderer at large. Then there was the current case of a missing twenty-one-year-old to dampen the holiday spirit.

Making footprints in the snow, Annette stepped onto the porch and unlocked the door before heading inside the country-style house that was surrounded by mature red maple trees. She turned on the lights near the foyer and took in the place that had been brand-new when she moved in nearly a year ago. It had an open concept with a spacious living-dining area and a gourmet kitchen, triple-pane windows, cathedral ceiling, and prefinished hickory hardwood flooring throughout. She had put in a combination of modern and rustic furniture and liked the way everything was arranged.

Heading into the kitchen, Annette turned on the kettle and got out a packet of instant hot cocoa. Once the drink was ready, she took her steaming ceramic mug and went back into the living room. She wondered if maybe her house should have some decorations for the holiday. Again, she pushed back at the notion. Apart from her workload, it might be too much to go through with only her to appreciate. Then there was the fact that she planned to celebrate Christmas day in Oklahoma this year with her siblings, in the sprawling house their parents had left them. After debating whether or not to sell it when they died, the Lynley siblings had decided that they would keep the property as a place to meet up or a vacation spot for anyone who wished to stay there.

Annette wondered if she would need to change her plans for Christmas, wincing at the thought of the nonrefundable round-trip ticket she'd purchased to Oklahoma City. She loved the opportunity for everyone to gather in one place but, admittedly, she wasn't in the best holiday spirit at the moment. She wasn't sure how appropriate it would be to leave Carol Creek and its citizens if a serial killer was still running amok. But there was still time to make an arrest and end the terror.

She sat on a corner of the leather square-arm sofa and sipped the cocoa before setting it on the coffee table. She then grabbed her laptop for a video chat with her brother Russell. With just a few months between them, she was closest in age to him among her siblings. But she hadn't been able to catch up much with him of late, now that Russell, an FBI special agent, was a married man again, having wed Rosamund Santiago, a Homeland Security Investigations special agent, last summer. Truthfully, Annette couldn't be happier for the newlyweds, both of whom had experienced tragedies in their lives. She only hoped she could be so lucky as to find true love with the right guy someday.

"Hey," she said when Russell's handsome face, bordered by raven locks in a high, tight haircut, appeared on the screen.

He gazed back at her with crinkled, steel gray eyes. "Hey, sis."

"How are things your way?"

"All good," he told her. "Busy at work, enjoying married life and all that."

"Nice to hear." She thought sadly about him losing his first wife and daughter in a home invasion.

"So, what's happening in your neck of the woods?" he asked instinctively.

"It's crazy around here right now," Annette confessed.

His chin jutted. "How crazy?"

"Since you asked, a serial killer is on the loose and a woman is missing."

Russell's brows knitted. "You think the two are connected?"

"I'm hoping that isn't the case, but I'm starting to worry since she's been missing for a day now."

"Let's not assume the worst, Annette," he said delicately. "These things don't always end badly. Often, it's just the opposite."

"I know," she conceded. "Still, the clock's ticking."

"Assuming the Bureau isn't already on the case, if you want, I can make a call to the FBI field office in Indianapolis and see what they can do to assist."

"Thanks, but we're working it as best as possible at the moment while conferring with other local law enforcement agencies to see if they have similar homicide or missing person cases." She wasn't quite ready to say they were overwhelmed as a small sheriff's office, but they appeared to be headed in that direction.

"Okay. But if there's anything I can to do help, just ask."

"I will," she said, feeling better just talking to him. The conversation shifted to the Christmas gathering. "I'll do my best to make it," Annette promised, knowing that fell flat.

"Do better than that," Russell insisted. "As we both know all too well, life is too short to put it off to next year or later. I think we all need this."

"You're right, we do." She flashed her teeth at him. "I'll be there. Wouldn't miss it."

He grinned. "That's what I'm talking about."

"Say hello to Rosamund for me," Annette finished and Russell agreed, before they disconnected.

After dining on leftover lemon chicken and baked beans, Annette took a hot bath and called it an early night, wondering what tomorrow would bring.

She got her answer when she was awakened by the buzzing of her cell phone the next morning. The caller was Detective Will Hossack. "Will…" Annette tried to keep the sleepiness from her voice as she sat up uneasily in the canopy bed surrounded by traditional furnishings.

"We've located Juliet McCade's vehicle," he said tonelessly. "It was halfway in a ditch off Murdon Street, near the DeLuca Christmas Tree Farm."

Annette tensed. "And Juliet…?"

"No sign of her yet." He paused. "But there's a piece of clothing sticking out of the car's trunk."

"I'm on my way," she said succinctly, and ended the conversation. She feared the worst as she got off the bed. She changed out of her notch-collar pink pajamas and got dressed quickly, grabbed a bagel on the way out the door and headed for the location.

Chapter Three

When she arrived at the scene, Annette was greeted by Will, who, beneath his hat, had a dour look. Face reddened from the cold, he said grimly, "There was a body in the trunk. Deceased."

Her heart sank as Annette gazed at the front of the vehicle from her vantage point. She could see that the trunk was open. Eyeing the detective, she asked warily, "Who?"

"Appears to be the missing woman," Will responded. "Juliet McCade."

As the lead detective on the case, Annette knew she needed to see for herself, even if this was one of the most painful parts of the process. Along with notifying the next of kin. She glanced at a squad car with its flashing lights. Two tall and thickly built deputies stood beside it, conferring with each other. Annette headed toward the back of the Subaru Impreza. In the trunk was the fully clothed body of a young biracial female. Her disheveled brunette hair was long and wavy and had side-swept bangs. Wrapped around her neck was a string of Christmas lights. Annette recognized the decedent from the cell phone picture Maureen McCade had sent. Dead in the trunk was her daughter,

Juliet McCade. Who was also the niece of Trooper Hamilton McCade.

"It's Juliet." Annette sucked in a deep breath, knowing her worst fears had been realized. "Just what we didn't need, and at this time," she muttered, wearing leather gloves to keep her hands warm.

"Yeah. You're right." Will wrinkled his nose. "Unfortunately, we got it anyway. Someone saw to that."

"Hmm…" She walked over to the driver's side of the vehicle and looked inside through the window. There was nothing that caught her eye at a glance.

"The car was unlocked," Will pointed out. "The victim's handbag, cell phone and any identification seem to be missing, though it's likely we'll find them strewn about and buried beneath the overnight snowfall."

"That's a good possibility," Annette concurred, knowing this had been the pattern of the unsub, who seemed mostly interested in buying time in having them identify his victims by scattering their identifying documents and cell phone. Perhaps to put greater distance between him and them, figuratively and literally. "Who discovered the car?" she wondered aloud, knowing that they had assembled search teams to comb the wooded and rural areas of the county after twenty-four hours had passed without word from Juliet McCade.

"Deputies Andy Stackhouse and Michael Jorgenson over there spotted the vehicle while on routine patrol and, after running the plates, realized it belonged to the missing woman and called it in."

Annette glanced at the deputies and back. "Did they happen to see anyone coming or going from the scene?"

"No." Will rubbed his gloved hands together. "Judging

by the snow on the car, I'm guessing it's been stuck in this ditch for hours. Whoever left it here had plenty of time to get away."

"I gathered as much." She was not at all surprised, considering the length of time since Juliet had been reported missing.

Annette wondered if the fresh snow covering the ground had all but eliminated any chance to follow up on tire or foot tracks. Still, she was hopeful that evidence might have been left behind here or there to be recovered by crime scene technicians and the medical examiner in an autopsy.

Before Annette could digest the tragedy further, the coroner's van pulled up. Getting out was the Dabs County coroner and medical examiner, Dr. Josephine Washburn. In her late forties, the slim woman had a short bob in a gray ombré color and blue eyes. "Got here as soon as I could," she said, gazing at Annette.

"Sorry you had to come at all," Annette muttered, knowing the bleak nature of any such visit.

Josephine shrugged. "I could say the same for you, Detective. Unfortunately for both of us, it comes with the territory. So, where is she?"

"Right this way," Will told her, leading her to the back of the car.

The ME frowned as she looked in the trunk. "Not a very nice way to have your life ended."

"I was thinking the same thing," Annette said. She wondered how long it took the victim to lose consciousness and end her misery.

Josephine put on latex gloves as she did her preliminary examination of the dead woman. After a few minutes, she said somberly, "My initial assessment is that the cause of death was ligature strangulation. And, as such, the deceased was a victim of homicide."

"We figured as much, given the string lights around her neck," Annette said sadly, glancing at Will and back.

Josephine twisted her lips. "It looks like the Christmas Lights Killer has struck again."

"So it would seem," Annette had to agree, while wondering how to break this devastating news to Hamilton. As well as to his sister. "What's your estimate on the time of death?"

The coroner considered this while regarding the victim. "Based on her appearance and other factors, I estimate that she's been dead for maybe a day and a half or so. If that calculation changes, I'll let you know."

"All right." Annette thought about the time Juliet had sent the text message to Maureen. Seven forty that night. The estimation of when Juliet died would indicate that she was likely killed shortly after indicating to her mom that someone was following her. Had this been why she'd ended up in a ditch? Trying to get away from a stalker who'd been driving, as opposed to one on foot?

When the crime scene technicians arrived, they went about processing the scene and taking photographs, including of the victim, before Juliet was placed in the coroner's van and transported to the Dabs County Morgue.

While Annette was going over what they knew and didn't know, crime scene analyst Loretta Covington approached them. "I think I may have found something…"

Annette eyed the short CSA, who was in her thirties, with brown eyes and brown hair in a cropped pixie. She wore protective clothing. "What is it?" Annette asked.

"A tire track," Loretta replied. "Just down there a bit. We

think it could have come from another vehicle that might have forced the Subaru Impreza off the road."

"Show us," Will told her.

"Sure thing."

They followed her about thirty feet on the same side of the street that Juliet would have been driving on. Annette took a look at the tire track, which was beneath a clump of bushes, preventing it from being covered over by snow. If this had been made by the driver of another vehicle in pursuit of Juliet's car, the unsub might have temporarily lost control of the vehicle before correcting. Or the tire track could be totally unrelated to Juliet's death.

"You may be on to something," she told the CSA hopefully. "It's worth a try."

"Yeah," Will agreed. "Let's see if we can find out who left the track and take it from there."

"Will do," Loretta promised, and assembled other CSAs to make a cast of the tire track.

Annette knew they would need to look for possible witnesses and gather information about Juliet's acquaintances, her two jobs, and comings and goings. But first things first. There needed to be a positive identification of the deceased, something that Annette wasn't particularly looking forward to as Hamilton McCade entered her head.

HAMILTON HAD BARELY gotten a wink of sleep last night, his mind too active in worry about his niece. No matter how she acted at times as if she was invincible, like a typical twenty-one-year-old, or how much she proved to be a handful for a sometimes overprotective mother, this was not like Juliet. She wouldn't simply leave Maureen hanging for over a day now.

At least that's not my impression of her, he thought as he drove down US Route 30. Something had to be very wrong. After leaving the sheriff's office last night, he had driven around for more than an hour searching for Juliet's car, hoping to find her stuck somewhere, but other than that alive and well. If not cold and frustrated. But he hadn't spotted her or the Subaru anywhere. So, where was she? Had Juliet driven away from the immediate area of her own accord? If so, would she contact Maureen today and ease her concerns?

It would make me feel a lot better, too, Hamilton told himself as he continued driving his duty vehicle, looking for any signs of trouble on the streets. Best to look at the glass half-full than half-empty, he believed. Otherwise, this would probably drive him crazy. He had considered taking the day off to join in the official search for Juliet. But he'd decided to let the sheriff's department do their job without his interference. At least for the short-term. Annette Lynley, in particular, certainly seemed more than up to the task of conducting a missing person investigation. And Will Hossack was a good detective who would do his part as well in trying to locate Juliet, whatever it took.

If they haven't made any progress by the time I take my lunch break, I'll swing back over to Carol Creek and look for Juliet again myself, Hamilton told himself. As he drove down the highway, he spotted in front of him a black Dodge Challenger SRT Hellcat Redeye. The first thing that caught his eye was that the temporary license plate was incorrectly located on the back window. Then there was the fact that the male driver seemed overly cautious in being slightly under the speed limit. Hamilton admitted to himself that the latter may have been a defensive move once the driver realized he was tailing him, as was often the case when drivers became aware of ISP troopers in the vicinity. He may have simply let this one slide, but Hamilton sensed that he should check it out, and give himself something else to think about other than his missing niece.

He motioned to the driver to pull over to the side of the road and, after seemingly weighing his options, the driver complied. Hamilton pulled up behind him, hoping this would be routine and not turn into anything serious. He exited his vehicle and approached the driver's side of the Dodge Challenger. The man inside, whom Hamilton judged to be in his early thirties, had already lowered the window.

"Did I do something wrong, Officer?" he asked in a calm voice.

Hamilton perused him quickly. He was slender and triangular-faced, with messy black hair cut short on the sides. He had blue eyes that looked clear and a chinstrap beard, same color as his hair. Hamilton glanced further into the vehicle and saw a brown paper bag on the passenger seat. "What's in the bag?" he asked suspiciously, thinking it might be a firearm. As such, Hamilton kept his guard up and was ready to access his SIG Sauer P227 pistol in a hurry, if need be.

"Just a ham and cheese sandwich," the man answered coolly. "I can show you, if you want?"

"Do it." Hamilton deepened his voice. "If it's a weapon, I promise you I'm quicker than you are." He watched the man like a hawk while sliding a hand on the firearm in his duty holster. When the man pulled the sandwich out of the bag and showed it was empty, Hamilton relaxed, lifting his hand off the weapon. "What's your name, sir?" he asked the driver politely.

"Mack Cardwell," the man answered.

"Mr. Cardwell, the interim license plate of your new vehicle is in the wrong spot on the back window."

"Really?" Cardwell cocked a brow. "Sorry about that. Where is it supposed to be?"

"Actually, the temporary plate should be affixed to the window on the left side while facing the rear of the vehicle," Hamilton informed him.

"No problem, Officer. I can take care of that right away."

"You do that." Hamilton met his gaze and somehow felt uncomfortable with it. Was he hiding something? "Can you show me your driver's license, Mr. Cardwell?"

"Sure," he agreed. "Happy to cooperate." He removed a wallet from the pocket of his jeans, took out the license and handed it over.

Hamilton studied the license. Mack Anthony Cardwell. The date of birth put him at thirty-two years of age, three months shy of thirty-three. He lived in Dabs County in the town of Laraville on Wailby Crest Lane. Homing in on the photograph and back at the driver, Hamilton believed they were one and the same. Still, there was an uneasiness that gnawed at his insides regarding the man. "Are you in any trouble, Mr. Cardwell?"

"No, sir," he insisted with a straight face. "I'm clean."

We'll see about that, Hamilton thought. "Give me a minute to check on that. Stay put."

"I'm not going anywhere," he promised.

Hamilton went back to his vehicle and ran the name for any outstanding arrest warrants or criminal record. Both came back negative. *Looks like Cardwell's good as his word*, Hamilton told himself, and went back to the driver.

"Any problems?" the man asked, as though confident in the answer.

"None." Hamilton handed the driver's license back and issued him a citation for incorrectly placing the interim license plate. "You're free to go."

"Thanks." Cardwell grinned sideways. "I'll be sure to put the temp license plate where it's supposed to be."

"Good." Hamilton softened the hardness of his stare. "Enjoy the rest of your day."

"I'll try," he said. "Thanks."

Once back inside his car, Hamilton waited till Mack Anthony Cardwell drove off, before hitting the road again himself. He'd barely had time to assess whether his instincts were right or way off about the man, when his cell phone rang. He slid it out of the pocket of his uniform's winter jacket and saw that the caller was Detective Annette Lynley.

"Trooper McCade," he answered, as if speaking to a total stranger.

"Trooper... Hamilton," Annette stammered. "Your niece's vehicle has been located."

"Oh...?" That gave him hope. Except that the detective's tone sounded like the news got worse, not better.

"A body was found in the trunk." Annette sighed. "We have reason to believe that it is Juliet McCade. I'm afraid she's dead." Another pause. "She was the victim of a ligature strangulation. I'm so sorry for your loss ..."

Hamilton muttered an expletive to himself. How could this happen? Who was responsible? Obviously, Juliet didn't put herself in the trunk of her own car. Was this the work of a serial killer? Or someone else who had come after her? Hamilton thought about his sister and how worried she must be in not hearing from Juliet. "Have you told Maureen yet?"

"Actually, I'm about to head over to her house right now,"

Annette informed him. "I thought she needed to hear this face-to-face."

"I'd like to be there when you tell her," he said with a jagged edge to his voice. If he couldn't have come to the rescue of his niece, the least Hamilton wanted to do was be there for his sister in her moment of need.

"I understand," Annette said softly. "I can meet you at her place."

When he disconnected, a wave of emotions surged through Hamilton. From shock to sorrow to anger and everything in between. But mostly he wanted justice for Juliet, whose death had come way too soon, all but ensuring that maintaining the holiday spirit would be difficult. If not impossible.

ANNETTE WAITED IN her car outside the midcentury modern two-story home on Mulligan Road. It was decorated with Christmas lights. A silver Honda Odyssey was parked in the driveway. Though she had done this before, it never got any easier to have to tell a mother, father, brother, sister, or even an uncle, that a loved one had passed away. And yet this was how it was done. Unfortunately, it happened all too often in society these days. Worse in this case was, judging by the MO and pending the autopsy report, the likelihood that the victim had been murdered by a serial killer. If so, it could mean that Juliet had been targeted, though she could have been just as easily randomly selected to go after.

Annette watched as Hamilton's Dodge Charger Pursuit pulled up behind her. Hard as it would be, she welcomed his company in having to break the terrible news to his sister. Maureen would need her brother to help her get through this ordeal. Annette got out of her car and met him in front of the house. "I know how difficult this must be for you," she stated sadly.

"Yeah, I'm still processing it," he admitted, touching the brim of his hat. "Just tell me, was the so-called Christmas Lights Killer responsible for this?"

"It looks that way." She paused. "We'll have a better read on that once the autopsy has been completed, along with assessing and processing the crime scene evidence, or lack thereof."

He frowned thoughtfully. "You never expect this to happen to someone in the family."

"I know." Annette considered the violent end to the lives of her brother's first wife and daughter. "But then, it's always someone's family, right?"

"Yeah, so true." Hamilton sucked in a deep breath. "Let's just get this over with."

She nodded, while knowing it would never be over with till the unsub was taken into custody and held accountable for his crimes. She followed Hamilton up the walkway. The front door of the house opened the moment they scaled the three concrete steps to the porch. Maureen stood there, her face anguished, like a mother who was able to read the dire writing on the wall. Her eyes darted from Annette to Hamilton, and back again. "Juliet's dead, isn't she?"

Before Annette could respond, Hamilton put his large hands on his sister's shoulders and said tenderly, "Why don't we go inside?"

Maureen refused to budge, blocking the entryway. "Just tell me!" she demanded. "Have you found my daughter alive and well? Or not?"

Guessing that Hamilton couldn't bring himself to tell her what she needed to hear, Annette did her job. "I'm sorry to have to tell you that your daughter is dead. Her body was found in the trunk of her car."

Maureen seemed to lose it in that moment. Her legs became unsteady and Hamilton stopped her from falling, guiding her into the house. Annette followed, whereupon she immediately laid eyes on a tall, eastern white pine in a corner of the living room, fully decorated for Christmas, with several wrapped gifts beneath it. She took her eyes away and had a cursory glance of other decorations and the contemporary furnishings on plush brown carpeting, before turning back to Maureen, who was being embraced by Hamilton.

"We'll get through this," he said, trying to comfort his sister.

Maureen pulled away from him and glared at Annette. "Do you know who killed her?"

"We're still investigating it," she said, not wanting to jump the gun.

Maureen favored Hamilton with a bleak stare. "My only child is dead. How do I live with that?"

He sighed raggedly. "By staying strong," he said matter-of-factly. "It's what Juliet would have wanted. We both need to come to grips with this and let the authorities get to the bottom of it."

Maureen nodded as she wiped away tears from her eyes. Though hating to further intrude upon her grief, Annette was still duty bound to tell the victim's next of kin what needed to be done now. "You'll have to come to the morgue to identify the body," she said gently.

Hamilton regarded Annette hotly. "I'll do it."

She had expected as much from him, as the decedent's uncle and a state trooper who had likely dealt with death in his line of work. "Okay."

Annette was sympathetic enough to allow them to take the time needed to deal with their emotions before Hamilton positively ID'd the body. She also knew this was her time to leave them alone to commiserate, while wishing there was more to say or do. But there was never enough on either front. All she could do now was ensure that justice was done for Juliet McCade.

HE COULDN'T HAVE asked for a better victim. She was young and pretty. Gullible and afraid. Simple and not so simple. Ready to die. Yet fighting to stay alive till there was no more fight in her. It was the same way with the other victims. He caught them in a vulnerable state and before they could realize what he had in mind, it was much too late to do anything about it. Other than see their lives flash before their eyes in a final moment of reflection before it all faded to black.

Strangling the latest one with the Christmas string lights had given him a rush of adrenaline that zipped throughout his body. Stuffing her dead body in the trunk of her car was a spontaneous move on his part to throw the authorities off balance while he made a clean getaway. With Christmas just two weeks away, there was still work to be done. Others would die and he would exact more vengeance on the one who'd gotten away.

He drove around town, knowing it was a new day and that there was sure to be more investigating by the cops now that the body had been discovered. They would be doing everything they could to stop him. Well, have at it. He was cleverer than them. Not to mention, much more ruthless and determined to carry out the killings in Carol Creek, ensuring that the Christmas season would be soiled by the specter of death and terror, with him leading the way joyously.

He gripped the steering wheel hard while visions of strangling his chosen ones danced in his head. Soon, another would have the life drained out of her and his Christmas wishes would continue to come true, with an imagined big red bow on top of his pretty presents.

Chapter Four

Hamilton needed just one brief look at the decedent to know it was his niece. Juliet was on a shelf in the morgue refrigerator. He saw only her face, which had lost some of its complexion in death, her eyes closed as though she were asleep. It was framed by tangled, long and wavy brunette hair with the bangs swept to the sides. Just to be doubly sure, he asked for the shelf to be pulled out a bit more. The lanky male morgue attendant, a thirtysomething with curly two-tone hair, complied, and Hamilton checked Juliet's right shoulder. There it was, the butterfly tattoo, telling him he was indeed looking at his sister's only child.

"It's her," he confirmed morosely.

He turned away from the corpse and Annette told the attendant, "We're done." Juliet was returned to the cabinet, where Hamilton knew she would remain till the autopsy. The thought of his niece being put through the process was difficult, but he understood it was a necessary procedure for anyone dying under unnatural or suspicious circumstances. That didn't make it any less unsettling for him. "Sorry you had to go through that," Annette said once they were outside.

"So am I, but it had to be done," Hamilton stated. "I'd rather it be me to identify the body than Maureen."

"I understand." Annette took a breath. "I want you to know that the sheriff's office will do everything in its power to find out who killed your niece and make sure the unsub is held accountable."

Hamilton's lips curled at the corner. "Is that what you told the loved ones of the other victims of a serial killer?" he questioned. "Doesn't seem to be working out very well, does it? How many more women will have to die before this creep is arrested?"

"You have every right to be frustrated," she responded in a calm voice. "No one wanted to see any of the women murdered. Least of all me. But as cliché as it sounds, these things do occur sometimes, even in small towns like Carol Creek. Yes, there's a psychopath out there. And he's chosen to kill during the Christmas season. As the lead detective on the case, with Will Hossack working alongside me, I can tell you neither of us has any intention of letting up till we catch this guy. Whatever it takes," Annette indicated sharply.

Hamilton realized he had been wholly unfair to her and the sheriff's department. They were no more at fault than he was that Juliet happened to have gotten into the crosshairs of a killer. Few homicide cases were solved overnight, no matter the culprit. This was obviously truer when the killer was making a conscious and carefully orchestrated effort to avoid capture.

"Sorry for venting," Hamilton apologized to the detective whom he wanted as an ally and not adversary. "I know you're doing your job in every case that comes your way."

"Apology accepted." Annette gazed at him compassionately. "I need to get back to the investigation, but promise to keep you in the loop."

"Okay." He wanted more than to be kept in the loop so long as Juliet's killer remained free. But now was not the time to be confrontational again. "I'd better go check on Maureen." His sister needed him more now than ever, if she was to get past this and come out whole on the other side. And even that was no sure thing.

Annette nodded understandingly. "We'll get the perp, one way or the other."

Hamilton felt her conviction and hoped they would be able to work together toward a common goal. Beyond that, there was the reality of needing to bury his niece and deal with the aftermath.

When he got back to his sister's house, it pained Hamilton to have to confirm what she had already resigned herself to. It still needed to be said. "Juliet is gone," he said in affirmation. "I'm so sorry, Maureen." As she started to weep, he wrapped her in his arms. "We'll get through this," he promised, while wondering just how long that would take. The fact that his niece was never coming back would likely haunt them for the rest of their lives.

"What did Juliet ever do to deserve this?" Maureen cried into his shoulder.

"Not a damned thing." Hamilton took a deep breath. "No one deserves to be murdered. Least of all a twenty-one-year-old with her entire life ahead of her. This wasn't in any way, shape or form Juliet's fault," he stressed. "She simply happened to be in the wrong place at the wrong time." He understood that this did little to take away the blunt reality of losing someone to violence, but hoped it gave some context nonetheless.

Maureen pulled away from him. "You should go back to work."

"I'm not going to leave you," he told her.

"I need to be alone," she insisted. "To process this."

Hamilton wanted to push back against that, feeling that family needed to be together at a time like this. And as they were only left with each other, that made it all the more important. But as everybody needed to grieve in their own way, he had to respect her decision. "All right," he relented. "I'll go. If you need me..."

"I'll be fine," she tried to say with a straight face. "I have to make some calls and arrangements to bury my daughter."

Her words tore through Hamilton as he was also left to have to say goodbye to his niece. Just as important to him was seeing to it that her death did not go unpunished. The sheriff's department would need to step up and solve this case. Which meant they would need to put a stop to a serial killer, one way or the other. Hamilton owed it to his sister and niece to do his part toward that end, whatever that entailed.

ANNETTE WAS AT her desk that afternoon when she was emailed a copy of Juliet McCade's autopsy report. She held her breath as she opened it and read. According to the report, the cause of death was ligature strangulation, with the manner of death listed as homicide. The weapon used to kill the victim was a string of Christmas lights, resulting in cerebral hypoxia, decreasing the brain's oxygen supply by compressing the blood vessels that fed it. Apart from the deep ligature marks found around Juliet's throat, there was some bruising on her arms, face and legs that the medical examiner believed was due to her struggling against her attacker and trying to stay alive.

Annette exhaled as she felt the same pain of loss and indignation that she had with the first two women who'd died this month in the same manner. But this time, she seemed to feel it more somehow, after the connection of sorts she'd made with Juliet's uncle, Hamilton McCade. Annette could only hope that he and his sister could come to terms with the death and find a way to cope. Meanwhile, a cold-blooded murderer was at large in Carol Creek and making a bold statement that he remained free to terrorize the community and there was no stopping him.

One other thing that caught her attention as she read through the rest of the report was the mention of a hair that was removed from Juliet's mouth. It did not match her own hair, indicating that it may have come from her attacker. Annette saw this as a solid lead toward catching the unsub.

When her cell phone rang a few minutes later, she lifted it from her desk and saw that it was the medical examiner, Josephine Washburn. "Hello."

"Just wanted to see if you received the autopsy report and had a chance to take a look at it."

"Yes and yes," Annette told her.

"I also sent it to Detective Hossack and Sheriff Teixeira," Josephine informed her routinely. "Any questions for me?"

"I wondered about the hair you took from the victim's mouth. What else can you tell me about it?"

"It definitely didn't belong to the decedent. The color was either dark brown or black and a different texture than the victim's hair. Can't say whether or not it belonged to the perpetrator. In accordance with potential evidence in a homicide, I have sent the hair to the Indiana State Police crime laboratory for further analysis."

That was standard procedure for local crimes, as the sheriff's office did not have its own crime lab. "Any other DNA collected?" she asked.

The ME indicated that there had been, but none that held the same potential weight of the strand of hair in terms of identifying who it belonged to. Josephine also said Juliet's body would soon be released for funeral arrangements, hoping to spare the victim's family as much pain as possible.

After the conversation, Annette left her office and stopped by Patti Gellar, the office clerk. "How're the twins?" she asked the fortysomething mother of Mia and Nikki.

"They're growing up way too fast," Patti complained, holding a steaming mug of coffee she was about to deliver to the sheriff.

Annette smiled, gazing at the slender, blue-eyed woman with brown hair in an A-line cut. "That's usually the case," she joked.

"Someday you'll get to experience the joy firsthand," Patti promised.

"Hope so." Annette looked forward to such a time in her life, while knowing that any such progeny would have more love than they knew what to do with. She headed to Will's office, a carbon copy of her own, only with contemporary furnishings that seemed to be more worn. He was standing by his desk when she stepped inside. "Did you read the autopsy report?" she asked.

"Yeah, just had a look." His brow furrowed. "Same old, same old. Sickening."

"There was something new," she pointed out. "The hair removed from the victim's mouth."

"True. Gives us something real to work with."

"Along with the tire track that may belong to the unsub's vehicle."

"That, too," he agreed.

"I'm on my way to brief the sheriff," she told him.

"Hold up." Will grabbed the cell phone off his desk. "I'm coming with you."

Sheriff Dillon Teixeira, whose spacious office was located on the other side of the building, was in his second term as sheriff of Dabs County, after previously working there as a sheriff sergeant. He was fifty-five years old, on a second marriage, and actually reminded Annette somewhat of her adoptive father, Taylor Lynley, both in his muscular stature and crusty blue-gray eyes. His silver hair was medium length with a side part.

"I was expecting you two," he said, dressed in his sheriff's uniform and seated at a large oak desk. "Got the autopsy report and scanned through it. Terrible that this case of a missing person had to end this way."

"Yeah, and the fact that her uncle, Trooper Hamilton McCade, has worked with us makes it all the harder," Will said.

"I agree," Annette echoed his sentiments. "I only just met Hamilton, but I feel for him and his sister, Maureen."

Teixeira rubbed his nose. "Same here. McCade's one of us and deserves justice for his sister. As do the families of the other two young women we've lost recently, purportedly to the same killer." He leaned forward in his brown high-back leather chair and asked, "Where do things stand in the investigation on the latest homicide?"

Annette stepped toward the desk and responded candidly, "We're trying to put the pieces together on how Juliet McCade's vehicle ended up in a ditch with her dead inside the trunk. At this point, the best guess is that she was forced off the road and then someone attacked and killed her, leaving her to be found where she was. We have a possible lead on the unsub with the strand of hair removed by the medical examiner from Juliet's mouth." Annette glanced at Will and back. "It's been sent to the ISP crime lab for analysis and DNA, along with some personal items belonging to the victim that were uncovered at the crime scene."

"We also have a tire impression that may have come from the vehicle driven by the killer," Will pitched in. "It too has been handed to the state police crime laboratory to try and identify the tire and, ultimately, the car it belonged to and the driver."

"Sounds like some positive developments," the sheriff said, rubbing his hard jawline. "With any luck, this will give you the solid evidence needed to pinpoint the young woman's killer. Which, in turn, can allow us to nail the Christmas Lights Killer that appears to be one and the same."

"That's the plan," Annette said, smoothing an eyebrow. She realized that it was anything but a done deal as each potential angle could lead to nowhere. The last thing she wanted was to go back to square one in chasing down a serial killer, as that would only be playing right into his hands. And at the expense of Juliet McCade and the two other victims they believed had been targeted by the unsub.

HAMILTON SPENT THE afternoon doing his regular shift in patrolling his district. Of all the things about his job, he probably best liked the solitude, which gave him time to think and then digest his thoughts. In this case, it was all about losing his one and only niece, depriving Juliet of the chance to be a big-sister-like cousin to his own children.

Assuming he was fortunate to one day have some kids with the right partner. Annette entered his mind as someone he found himself attracted to, in spite of knowing little about her. She was definitely his type and could be a good fit if things fell into place. But, for now, he needed to stay strong for Maureen. He had acquiesced to her wishes and returned to work against his better judgment. If nothing else, it gave him something to focus on other than Juliet's murder as he looked for any activity that drew his attention. All seemed quiet and normal.

When he finished his shift, Hamilton drove to the Indiana State Police District 22 Police Department on Ellison Road. There, he met with his commander, Lieutenant Tony Wilson. African American and in his late forties, Wilson had deep sable eyes and was tall, bald beneath his campaign hat, and built like a brick wall inside his uniform. Hamilton informed him about his niece's murder in Carol Creek.

"Sorry to hear that," Wilson remarked as they stood in the building. "If you need some time to deal with it—"

"I don't," Hamilton cut in. At least not where it pertained to sitting around moping. "But I would like to be available to help in the investigation any way I can, as long as the killer remains on the loose."

The lieutenant's brow furrowed. "I understand how you feel, McCade. But getting involved in cases where it's personal is usually not a good idea. Besides that, this investigation is under the jurisdiction of the Dabs County Sheriff's Department. Wouldn't want to step on any toes, unless invited to."

"Juliet was my sister's only child, so, yes, it's definitely personal," he readily admitted. "But I'm enough of a professional to be able to separate the two. As far as stepping on toes, that shouldn't be a problem, either," Hamilton told him straightforwardly. "I'm already acquainted with the lead investigator on the case, Detective Annette Lynley, and her coinvestigator, Detective Will Hossack. With three murders believed to be connected, I'm guessing that they would welcome any assistance that comes their way." Even if not on the sheriff's payroll, he still wanted to work the case to the extent possible in finding Juliet's killer.

Wilson studied him for a moment. "Let me give Sheriff Teixeira a call and see where they're at in the investigation," he said deliberately, "and get back to you on this."

"Okay." Hamilton didn't want to make any waves. It wouldn't serve any purpose in fighting his commander on this. Especially when wanting his support as Hamilton hoped to get into the ISP's Investigations Command Special Investigation Section. He would work around his official duties, if necessary, till Juliet's killer was behind bars.

Hamilton drove his duty vehicle home, still contemplating the multiple things weighing on his mind. He lived in a three-bedroom contemporary house on Hatcher Pass. Attracted to the turn-key modern structure, finished daylight basement and spacious backyard with crabapple and yellowwood trees, he'd purchased it just over a year ago.

He used the remote to open the two-car garage and pulled up next to his personal car, a red GMC Acadia Denali.

Entering the house, where Hamilton had a Christmas wreath on the front door, he stepped onto ceramic tile flooring and took in the spacious and open setting with floor-to-ceiling windows and plantation shutters, wood-burning fireplace and country furniture. A nice-sized concolor white fir tree sat in the living room, decorated for Christmas. He had picked it out at the DeLuca Christmas Tree Farm and roped a fellow trooper, Al Hernandez, into helping him get the tree back to his house. The French country kitchen had quartz countertops and stainless steel appliances, and a den on the floor had been converted into an exercise room. He removed his hat and headed up the quarter-turn staircase. After washing up in the owner's suite, he went back downstairs and heated up yesterday's leftover chili, before downing it with a couple of slices of bread and a beer.

I'd love to have someone to share this space with, Hamilton told himself, sitting at the pine dinner table in an upholstered side chair. Or maybe share her space elsewhere. Eating alone had never been fun. But it had been this way more often than not since his breakup with Felicity. He had gotten used to it. Yet he was in no way content. If Juliet's death showed him anything, it was that tomorrow was not promised to anyone. No matter how much things appeared to be in your favor in life. He would do well to remember that as he went through the motions of his professional life while hoping to kick-start his personal one.

Chapter Five

Should she or shouldn't she? Annette posed this question to herself as she weighed whether or not to call Hamilton to let him know she was en route to the Indiana State Police Fort Wayne Regional Laboratory in his neck of the woods. Yes, she wanted to keep him in the loop. But it would be presumptuous of her to just expect him to drop everything to meet up with her. On the other hand, if it were her and she'd just lost her niece to what was most likely a serial killer, she would definitely want to be kept abreast of every development—in person, if possible. The fact that it meant they got to see each other again was immaterial, if not something she welcomed as a chance to run into the good-looking trooper who'd captured her fancy.

Opting to make the call, Annette put her cell phone on speaker as it sat in the car holder. "Hey, Hamilton," she said evenly, when he answered.

"Hey." He sounded wary. "What's up?"

"I wanted you to know that I'm on my way to the Indiana State Police crime lab to get the results on evidence involving Juliet's death. If you're not too busy, you might want to join me, and we can see if they have anything that might point toward the killer."

"Absolutely," he responded without prelude. "I can swing over to the lab and meet you there."

"Good," she said, hoping he got her drift. She only meant good as it related to his availability for a common cause.

"So, what will we be looking at?"

"DNA from a hair found in Juliet's mouth, for one," Annette said keenly, while hoping DNA other than the victim's might show up as well among her recovered personal effects. "And a tire track that might have come from the unsub's vehicle."

Hamilton waited a beat, then said tonelessly, "Okay. See you soon."

She disconnected the call and continued to drive, pondering what it would take to capture the Christmas Lights Killer and return life to normal in Carol Creek. A good step in the right direction would be the results from the crime lab, she thought, pulling into the parking lot off Ellison Road. She spotted Hamilton's car with him in it. He got out when she did and they met halfway. "Hi," she said meekly, feeling as if he were towering over her, which wasn't necessarily a bad thing.

"Hey." He eyed her beneath the brim of his hat. "Let's see what they have to say."

She nodded and they went inside the building. In the Forensic Biology Section, greeting them was forensic scientist Kelly Okamoto, in her white lab coat. In her early thirties, she was slender and had short, sandy-colored hair with a small ponytail and brown eyes. "Detective Lynley. Trooper McCade," Kelly acknowledged them.

"Hey, Kelly," Annette said, having met her previously during other investigations.

"Kelly," Hamilton spoke from acquaintance.

"Sorry to hear about your niece," she said.

He nodded. "Hopefully, you have something that can identify her killer."

"Yes and no," Kelly uttered vaguely, leading them to her workstation. "We were able to collect DNA from the strand of hair extracted from the victim."

"That's good to know," Annette told her, having anticipated as much.

"The forensic unknown profile was entered into the state database with arrestee and convicted offender profiles," Kelly said, "as well as DNA profiles from crime scenes." She frowned. "Unfortunately, we didn't find a match. The DNA profile has been recorded in the National DNA Index System in the hope that there will be a hit in CODIS. We'll just have to wait and see."

Annette hid her disappointment that the DNA didn't identify a suspect in the death of Juliet McCade. She could see that it didn't set well with Hamilton, either. But now that the DNA profile was in CODIS, it meant they had something to work with should matching results show up later from the unsub. "Were you able to get DNA from Juliet McCade's personal items, such as her cell phone and driver's license?" she asked the forensic analyst.

"Yes, but it was only a match for the victim's DNA," Kelly answered. "We're still running tests, in case something else shows up."

"If it happens, keep us informed," Hamilton advised her. "Of course."

Annette looked at her. "Is there anything else you can tell us about the hair?"

Kelly jutted her chin. "Yeah, we could determine that the hair almost certainly belonged to a white male."

*Which, in and of itself, narrows down the lists of poten-
tial suspects*, Annette thought.

They left that section of the crime lab with more information than when they'd entered, though less than what they
would have wanted ideally, and went inside the Microanalysis Unit, where they analyzed fibers and tire impressions,
among other things.

HAMILTON WOULD HAVE loved it if there had been a hit on
the hair strand pulled from Juliet's mouth. In his gut, he
felt it belonged to the person who'd murdered his niece. But
apparently, the unsub had managed to avoid any arrests or
incarceration in Indiana up to this point. But he'd made a
mistake in providing them with his DNA, which gave Hamilton hope that it was only a matter of time before they knew
precisely who they were dealing with. He sensed that Annette felt the same.

In the Microanalysis Unit, they met with forensic analyst
Bernard Levinson, twentysomething and of medium build,
with short black hair worn in a faux hawk and blue eyes
behind glasses. Annette wasted little time in asking him
about the tire track. "What did it tell you about the tire?"
she asked pointedly.

Levinson touched his glasses. "Well, we analyzed the
cast made of the tire track," he replied matter-of-factly. "The
impression tells me that it definitely comes from a good all-
season, all-terrain tire."

That made sense to Hamilton, given that they were near
wintertime. And had certainly been experiencing some winter weather of late. "Can you be more specific?"

"I believe it may be a Goodyear tire, but can't be any more
specific at this point without further testing." He gazed at

Annette. "I suggest, Detective Lynley, that you go to a tire center. They can probably match the tire tread cast positively to the manufacturer and the exact kind of tire this is."

"I'll do that," she agreed. "Is there a tire center you can recommend?"

"I know one that's nearby," Hamilton told her. "I've done business with them and know the manager."

Annette smiled. "Let's check it out."

"Good luck," Levinson said.

"Thanks, Bernard," she told him. "You've given us a lead on the tire tread evidence. We'll see where it takes us."

Moments later, they took Hamilton's vehicle and headed to the tire center. It gave him an opening to get to know her a little better. "So, how did you end up working for the sheriff's department?" he asked curiously.

"I applied and got the job," she quipped. "As I assume you did in going to work for the Indiana State Police."

"Walked right into that one." He grinned, having no issue with her dry sense of humor. But he still wanted to know more. "Let me rephrase it. How did you end up as a sheriff's department detective?"

"Oh, that's what you wanted to know. Why didn't you just ask?" she teased him.

"I'm asking now," he said levelly.

"Okay. I come from a family steeped in law and law enforcement. My adoptive parents were a police chief and criminal court judge, and two of my three siblings are FBI agents and the other is a law enforcement ranger with the National Park Service." Annette glanced his way. "Oh, and did I forget to mention that I have a first cousin who is an investigator for a correctional institution?"

Hamilton chuckled. "I can see why law enforcement

would be in your blood." He could only imagine the interesting conversations they had during family get-togethers.

"Right." She giggled. "Having a bachelor's in criminology was a bonus as I worked my way through various jobs in policing before landing my current position as a detective."

"I see." It was obvious to him that even with the family pedigree, she had succeeded in her endeavors largely through her own hard work. As had he. "Have you ever thought about trying to contact your birth parents, assuming you haven't already been in touch with?" he wondered out of curiosity.

"I haven't been, but have thought about it," she voiced musingly. "Or at least my birth mother, since from what I was told, my father was never in the picture. Maybe someday, if the need is strong enough to want to go there for answers and clarity. Or maybe she'll reach out to me. For now, I'm happy to have been with those I'll always consider my family."

"Understood." He respected her fortitude and willingness to embrace the hand she had been dealt through no fault of her own.

"Your turn," Annette said, cutting into his train of thought. "How did you end up as a state trooper?"

"No bloodline to point me in the right direction," he answered wryly. "For whatever reason, I've always had an interest in law and order and education in that field. Got my bachelor's, master's, and eventually PhD, all in criminal justice, while working as an officer for the police department before spending the last decade as a trooper." He wondered if that was too much information for her interest.

"Impressive, especially the PhD," Annette said sincerely.

"Not all it's cracked up to be," Hamilton said, downplaying the achievement. "Still trying to decide how to make the most of it." He believed that getting into ISP's Organized Crime and Corruption Unit would be a good step in the right direction.

"I've thought about going back to school for my master's, though maybe in psychology or sociology, but haven't found the time to do so."

"I'm sure if you're serious about that, it will eventually work itself out," he told her.

"We'll see," she said thoughtfully.

Hamilton almost wished they hadn't arrived at their destination on Coldwater Road, as Annette had piqued his interest and he wanted to know more. Maybe they could pick this up later.

As they headed toward the tire center, their shoulders brushed. Hamilton felt something akin to an electrical current zip through his body in that instant. Did she feel it, too? Or was it only him that was being stirred by her mere presence and thoughts of what they could do were they alone, hot and bothered?

They went inside the store and were approached by Pete Lipton, the manager. "Hey, Pete," Hamilton said, eyeing the fortysomething, stocky man with a brown Ivy League haircut and gray eyes, who had serviced both his duty and personal vehicles.

He gave a nod. "How can I help you, Trooper McCade?"

"This is Detective Lynley with the Dabs County Sheriff's Department." Hamilton faced her. "She's working a case in which we're trying to pinpoint the tire tread found near a homicide."

"Hi, Detective," Pete said. "Happy to help, if I can."

"Thanks." Annette smiled at him. She showed Pete the

cast of the tire track. "Can you identify the type of tire this would have come from?"

The tire center manager studied the tread. After a moment or two, he said equably, "I'm pretty sure this is from a Goodyear Wrangler Fortitude HT."

"Really?" She glanced at Hamilton and back. "Take another look."

Pete did and reached the same conclusion. "Just to be on the safe side, let me show it to my top mechanic, Clayton Serricchio."

They watched as Pete disappeared into the shop. "What do you think?" Annette asked Hamilton.

"I trust Pete's knowledge when it comes to cars and tires. No reason to believe he's off base. But a second opinion never hurts."

"True."

Pete returned in a moment and said, "Clayton took a look at the tire tread cast and backs me up. It *is* a Goodyear Wrangler Fortitude HT."

That was good enough for Hamilton. "Thanks for your help," he said.

"Anytime," Pete replied, shaking both their hands.

Outside, Annette said enthusiastically, "With the exact tire identification, we have an important lead to work with in trying to narrow down the vehicle it belonged to as well as the driver."

"I concur," Hamilton said, while tempering his anticipation that one thing would lead to another. "Hopefully, this will allow us to track down my niece's killer and not prove to be just an innocent driver who simply slipped on the road during wintry weather."

"My gut instinct tells me there's more to it than that,"

she insisted. "The timeline seems to fit the belief that the driver of that vehicle was involved with Juliet being forced off the road...and killed."

Hamilton knew all about the importance of gut instinct, as he relied on his own more often than not. Moreover, he sensed that Annette was onto something here. The sooner the driver could be questioned, the sooner Juliet's killer might be arrested and put behind bars.

"I'll take you back to your car," he told her.

The drive was mostly silent as she stared out the window and he mulled over having a greater role in the investigation and what he could do to help Maureen cope with her daughter's unexpected death.

When Annette returned to Carol Creek and the sheriff's office, she had a mixed bag to report on the visit to the ISP Fort Wayne Regional Laboratory. They seemed a little closer to getting some answers as to who may have killed Juliet McCade, but weren't quite there yet. On another front, she was still a bit shaken by the jolt she'd felt when brushing shoulders with Hamilton outside the tire center. By his reaction, she was sure he experienced the sensation, too. There was no denying that she felt a connection with Hamilton that Annette knew needed to be explored, one way or the other, assuming he was single and on the same wavelength. But first, she needed to stay on track to solving his niece's murder and presumably getting the jump on a serial killer at the same time.

She briefed Sheriff Teixeira in his office on the results from the crime lab. "The DNA may eventually yield some results on who the hair came from. But the Goodyear Wrangler Fortitude HT tire track found near the scene of the crime is solid," she told him. "It could be the break we need to get some real answers."

"I think you may be right about that," Teixeira said, leaning against a corner of his desk. "But with three women dead in the same manner in our town and attributable to a lone killer, we have to assume that the unsub is still on the hunt for others. Meaning there's no time to spare in tracking him down. I'll reach out to the ISP for further assistance in dealing with this serious matter. And even the FBI."

I was hoping you'd say that, Annette thought, wishing her brothers with the Bureau were operating out of the Indiana field office instead of their own respective locations. As it was, she knew that every second counted before the perp might strike again. She wondered if Trooper Hamilton McCade would be called upon to assist in the investigation into his niece's killer. Or would it hit too close to home for him to go deeper into the probe?

"In the meantime," Teixeira continued, "I'll pull Detective Robinson from the cold case she's working on and get Reserve Deputy Shelton Kuen to help out."

"I appreciate that," Annette said, happy to have all the aid they could get in bringing this investigation to a close with an arrest of the culprit. She was sure Will would agree and that Detective Charisma Robinson would not object to putting on hold a thirty-year-old homicide case involving a murdered husband and wife in favor of solving a current serial killer case. "The more feet on the ground, the better."

"Right." Teixeira nodded. "Let's make this count, Detective," he said in no uncertain terms.

"Yes, sir," Annette told him respectfully, while knowing that she was under the gun for delivering results as the lead detective and still trying to get her feet wet with the

Detective Bureau. She certainly was not about to throw in the towel on this investigation anytime soon. Not when women were dying and the killer seemed to be daring them to catch him as if he were a chameleon. Annette felt certain it was only a matter of time before they got him. It was the interim period that worried her for the safety of women in Carol Creek.

In her office, Annette closed the door and sat at the desk. She took her cell phone and called her sister, Madison Lynley, for a video chat. Madison was nearly two years her senior and they were not quite as close as Annette was to Russell, but they were the only girls among the siblings. It gave them a special bond, and she was someone Annette knew she could always count on and be herself with.

When Madison appeared on the small screen, her attractive face and bold aquamarine eyes lit up. "Hey, sis," she said cheerfully.

"Hey." Annette could see that she was standing in uniform near the Blue Ridge Parkway in North Carolina, where Madison was stationed as a law enforcement ranger. "Busy?"

"I can spare a few minutes to talk," she said, her long blond hair with bangs worn in a bun. "How are things?"

Annette twisted her lips. "Truthfully, they could be better."

"Russell mentioned to me that you were dealing with a missing woman and a serial killer on the loose," Madison noted. "Is there more, not to say that this isn't enough on your plate?"

"Well, the cases have merged into one," Annette told her sadly. "The missing woman, Juliet McCade, turned up dead and we believe she was a victim of the serial killer."

Madison frowned. "Sorry to hear that. Makes my own workload primarily involving rowdies, substance abusers, car accidents and wounded animals seem not so bad. So, how is the investigation shaping up?"

Annette filled her in on a few details, including the tire track evidence, and then mentioned casually, "Juliet's uncle, a state trooper named Hamilton McCade, has been involved in the investigation somewhat."

"Trooper McCade, huh?" Madison picked up on her hint that there was possibly more to this. "Is he good-looking?"

"Hadn't really noticed," she lied, chuckling at the absurdity of it. "Okay, yes, he's hot. Burning up, in fact," Annette admitted. "But I know nothing about his marital status or availability, so I'm not even going there." Not yet anyway.

"Hmm…" Madison seemed less than convinced. "If you say so. Far be it for me to give any advice in matters of the heart."

Annette knew that, like her, Madison had endured a painful breakup not so long ago, and was still coming to terms with it. But they were both strong Lynley women and would eventually find the right guy to make a life with. "I'll keep you posted on whether anything emerges with the trooper. For now, we're just professional acquaintances."

"Fair enough," her sister said, not pressing the issue.

They spoke briefly about the still-ongoing plans to meet up for Christmas, and then Annette ended the video chat. She mused about Hamilton for a moment and the sense of urgency in finding his niece's killer, before she called Will and brought him up to date on her visit to the crime lab and tire center.

Chapter Six

"How are you doing?" Hamilton hesitated to ask his sister over the speakerphone while on patrol, as the reality settled in about Juliet. But he needed to know that she was okay, even as the investigation into his niece's death continued.

"I'm fine," Maureen responded. He doubted that but took it as a sign that she was trying to cope as best as possible. "I just wish Juliet had been given a chance to reach her full potential in life."

"I know." He winced at the thought that this wouldn't be the case. "She made the most of the time she had," he said, truly believing this, as Juliet had always been more mature than her years and shown a willingness to go the extra mile in trying to achieve her goals.

"I suppose. But that doesn't make losing her to the whims of a killer any easier."

I can't dispute that, Hamilton thought, driving down the highway. "You're right." He paused, debating whether or not to mention the leads the sheriff's office had in tracking down the unsub. The last thing he wanted was to get her hopes up that an arrest was imminent. "I won't rest till her killer is brought to justice," he promised.

"That's good to know," Maureen said. "If it is the same

serial killer on the loose in Carol Creek, he needs to be stopped so other mothers and fathers won't have to go through what I'm experiencing."

If only I could guarantee that no one else would die before the perp was caught, Hamilton mused. But considering he wasn't even part of the official investigation as yet, his options for working the case were limited. That didn't mean he wouldn't give it his all to do whatever he could to get the desirable results in allowing Juliet to rest in peace. "Why don't you come spend a few days at my house," he told his sister, believing it might do her some good to step away from the place where she'd been living with Juliet and the memories associated with it. "This is a time when we should be able to lean on one another in closer proximity."

"I appreciate the offer, Hamilton," she said, "but I need to be here. I have my job, for one, just as you do, and it gives me something else to focus on. Having a longer commute to work wouldn't help. Apart from that, my entire support group, other than you, is in Carol Creek."

It was a bad idea, Hamilton conceded, realizing that trying to shield her from further pain by pulling her away from her comfort zone and work as a registered nurse at Carol Creek General could do more harm than good. "I understand," he said. "Shouldn't have suggested it."

"You had every right to," she insisted. "I know you're just trying to help and you are. Juliet always looked up to you as her uncle. We're both hurting and trying to adapt to this new reality."

"Yeah," he said broodingly. He had forgotten how insightful his sister was. She was also hardened somewhat from everything she'd gone through over her lifetime. Maureen would need that fortitude as she tried to forge ahead for a life without her daughter. Hamilton steeled himself to have the same courage, though his heart ached at the thought of his niece whom he used to tease and offer advice whenever she needed it.

At the end of his shift, he went into the ISP District 22 building, where Hamilton was summoned to his commander's office. Lieutenant Tony Wilson was leaning over a solid wood adjustable standing desk when he walked in. Hamilton glanced around the space with ergonomic office furniture and a picture window. He turned back to the lieutenant, who said, "Just got off the phone with Sheriff Teixeira. His office has requested our assistance in their investigation of the Christmas Lights Killer. I take it you believe he's the one responsible for your niece's murder?"

"The MO suggests as much," Hamilton replied candidly.

"I see." Wilson stepped toward him. "You did your dissertation on serial killers, right?"

"Yeah." He was impressed that the lieutenant remembered after a brief conversation about it.

"Then that should make you an asset to the sheriff's detectives who are investigating the homicides. Go ahead and lend them your expertise and, hopefully, help apprehend a serial killer. Of course, you'll be continuing your official duties for the ISP."

"Will do, on both counts." Hamilton gave a nod and felt an adrenaline rush at the prospect of doing more to help Annette chase down Juliet's killer. Not to mention another opportunity to spend more time with the striking, thought-provoking detective.

ANNETTE GOT A text from Hamilton, informing her that he'd been recruited to work with them on the Christmas Lights

Killer case. She was pleased to hear this, assuming that his primary role would be employing investigative skills as a longtime state trooper to help in the interviewing of suspects and surveying the crime scenes for any clues left behind. If their prior interactions were any indication, she was sure they would get along fine. And actually complement one another for a common cause in going after his niece's killer.

Annette glanced at Hamilton as he entered the Detective Bureau's conference room that afternoon, where the team was gathered. He gave her a nod and seemed all business in his trooper hat and uniform. As lead investigator, she stood before them to provide a briefing on the case. Taking a quiet breath while calming her nerves within, she said, "We're here to bring everyone up to date on where things stand in the Christmas Lights Killer investigation. As of today, three young women have been the victims of ligature strangulation deaths by what we believe to be an adult male serial killer."

She turned on the slide presentation and used a stylus pen to show a facial image of an attractive white female with big blue eyes and long blond hair. "JoBeth Sorenson was a twenty-seven-year-old English teacher at Carol Creek High School," Annette said. "On December first, Sorenson's Honda Insight broke down on Shadow Lane. Someone picked her up, drove her to an out-of-the way area on Brockton Drive, then strangled her with Christmas string lights, which seem to be garden-variety and easily accessible. Hard to pinpoint where they originated from. A witness reported seeing the victim in a dark vehicle with a man shortly before the estimated time of death."

Annette switched to a picture of a man in his late twenties with blue eyes, dark textured wavy hair and a patchy beard.

"Sorenson's ex-boyfriend, Aaron Heathcote, was initially considered a person of interest in her murder, but he had an unshakable alibi, putting us back to square one." She turned to an image of a Hispanic female with big hazel eyes and thick blond hair worn in a pixie bob. "Yancy Machado is a twenty-five-year-old makeup artist. On December fourth, she was strangled to death with string Christmas lights by someone who accosted her in the parking lot of Machado's apartment complex on Winchester Street. A witness reported seeing a man run from the scene, but she didn't get a good look at him, aside from describing him as a tall white male with dark hair."

Annette sighed as she prepared herself to talk about the last known victim, hoping it wouldn't be too hard for Hamilton to listen to the nightmarish details all over again. Putting his niece's picture on the screen, and recognizing again the similarities between herself and Juliet as biracial, gave Annette a chill. Under other circumstances, it just as easily could have been her who fell into the crosshairs of a serial killer. "On December eighth, Juliet McCade, a twenty-one-year-old sales clerk at a boutique, went missing shortly after she texted her mother, Maureen McCade, to say she thought someone was following her. A search ensued for Juliet, to no avail. Two days later, her body was found in the trunk of her Subaru Impreza, which was stuck in a ditch off Murdon Street." Annette paused, averting Hamilton's hard stare. "She had been the victim of ligature strangulation, with Christmas string lights the murder weapon, same as the previous two victims of the so-called Christmas Lights Killer."

Using the stylus, Annette pointed to an image of a strand of hair on the screen. "This hair was pulled out of Juliet McCade's mouth. We believe it belongs to her killer. We were able to extract DNA from the hair. Unfortunately, it doesn't match any profiles in the state or national databases. It's an important lead, nonetheless." She replaced the image with an image of the tire tread cast. "Someone left this track not far from where Juliet's vehicle was found. The Indiana State Police crime lab and a tire center were able to identify the imprint as belonging to a Goodyear Wrangler Fortitude HT. We believe that whoever was driving the vehicle with this tire may well be the unsub. Or, at the very least, a possible witness. Needless to say, we're trying to locate the car and driver."

Annette waited a beat before saying, "It seems probable that the victims have been chosen randomly. As such, the age range and differences in their racial or ethnic persuasion are likely immaterial to the perpetrator, but rather more a reflection of being opportunistic when a target was available to go after at the right time and place."

She faced Hamilton and held his gaze, realizing that he was eyeing her with understanding and resolve rather than vexation or disappointment, where it concerned talking candidly about his niece. When it came time for them to switch places, he indicated as much, whispering in Annette's ear, "Thanks for more than adequately summing up the case for relative newbies like me. Juliet's death and its horrific nature can't be lessened, if we're to get to the bottom of this."

"You're right," she agreed, but was happy to hear him say it nonetheless. "We all have a job to do, even when it hurts sometimes. Thank you for the support."

He flashed her a genuine look. "Anytime."

Annette took that for what it was worth and gave him the floor as she took a seat at the conference table, curious as to what he hoped to bring to the investigation besides devilish good looks and a strong desire to go after the unsub.

HAMILTON WAS HAPPY to be able to contribute in any manner to solving the mystery of his niece's death. He owed this to Juliet and Maureen to do right by them in assisting the sheriff's department with their investigation. Working the case with Annette Lynley was obviously an added benefit to him, as they seemed to click on some level, though he was still sorting out in his mind to what degree. It wasn't lost on him that being biracial, she resembled Juliet in her physical characteristics. He wondered if this was why she appeared to take Juliet's death almost as personally as he did, believing it could have been her own daughter, assuming she had one. Or even herself at a younger age. Either way he sliced it, Annette had gotten his attention and Hamilton felt they had a common cause that he wanted to see through, wherever it might lead.

He surveyed the others in attendance beyond fellow ISP investigators brought on for the serial killer case. Some he knew, and others he hoped to get to know professionally. "I'm Hamilton McCade," he introduced himself. "Juliet McCade's my niece." He let that set in for a moment. "Obviously, it's been a trying time for me and my sister, Juliet's mom, coming to grips with what happened to her. But we're dealing with the tragedy as best as possible, much like the families of the other victims of this killer who are going through the same thing."

Hamilton certainly didn't want this to be a pity party. He was there to work and not linger over his own misfortune. "I've had the privilege of working with a few of you over the years as a state trooper," he said. "What you probably didn't know was that I have a PhD in criminal justice from Indiana University Bloomington and did my dissertation on serial killers and what drives them. I suppose that makes me a serial killer profiler, which is where I hope to provide some insight into what you're up against in going after this monster."

Hamilton eyed Annette, who looked surprised in learning this new dimension of him as a trooper and person. He didn't necessarily hope to impress her, but imagined it didn't hurt matters any to know that he brought more to the table than his investigative skills, though ever present in his line of work. "Let me just start by saying that as it relates to a general profile of the unsub we're dealing with, the vast majority of serial killers tend to be male. Other than that, they run the gamut in terms of age range, mental stability, intellect, educational level, occupation, motivation, etc. In this particular investigation, there is nothing unique about the serial killer known as the Christmas Lights Killer, putting aside his deliberate use of indoor string Christmas lights to strangle his victims. I believe this is more for shock effect, if anything, given that the murders are occurring during the Christmas season in Carol Creek. But the truth is, history is replete with serial killers who, by definition, have killed two or more persons on separate occasions. Even the ligature strangulation killings are quite common, historically speaking. The so-called Boston Strangler, who may have been more than one person, Hillside Stranglers, Green River Killer, Tourniquet Killer, to name a few, murdered many, if not all, their victims by ligature strangulation.

"So, what's the motivation for this madness?" Hamilton posed the question he suspected they were probably wondering. "Well, once you put aside the often random nature of such attacks and the opportunity to commit them, as Detective Lynley alluded to on the current case, for most serial killers it really comes down to a general dislike for the victims or someone they represent, usually as a reflection of feeling wronged by the person or persons. This loathing, and anger by virtue, can manifest itself through psychotic or sadistic behavior, leading to retaliatory or get-even attacks against those who epitomize the object of hatred. When there's a sexual component to the killings, the perpetrators will often resort to sexual assaults or other forms of sexual appeasement as indicative of their holding power over the victims and imposing their will on them."

Hoping his understanding of serial killers would help his audience with nabbing the Christmas Lights Killer, Hamilton continued. "In targeting young women, the unsub we're dealing with here seems to generally conform to everything I've outlined in terms of motivation, MO, opportunity and an escape route. He has also been smart enough to keep the evidence that could identify him to a minimum. Obviously, that's starting to wane, since he's gotten sloppy by purportedly leaving DNA and tire tread evidence that may well prove to be his undoing. Short of that, the unsub is all but certain to go after other victims who fit his criteria for killing."

After answering a few general questions, Hamilton let Will Hossack take over. As they passed one another, Will quipped, "You really know your stuff, McCade. Why have you been hiding that?"

Hamilton smiled ruefully. "It's always been there. Just never been called upon to apply it to a real-life case."

"You couldn't have picked a better time to lay it out there," the detective said. "For your niece and the other victims of the Christmas Lights Killer, we definitely need all hands on deck if we're to crack this before Christmas."

"That would be great," Hamilton said, walking away. Knowing that Juliet would not get to spend Christmas with Maureen or him was motivation enough. Hoping to avert the same sad outcome for other families gave him even more reason to see the killer stopped cold.

"You're full of surprises," Annette caught his attention after the meeting had ended.

He kept an even keel while responding, "Seemed like as good a time as any to say what I needed to."

"I agree. Maybe you could enlighten me even further."

He cocked a brow. "Maybe. What did you have in mind?"

She smiled teasingly. "Can I buy you dinner, if you don't have other plans? And please don't say you'd rather buy me dinner instead. That's so old-school."

Hamilton chuckled. She was right. Women were just as capable of wining and dining men as vice versa. He had absolutely no problem with that. In this case, having dinner with her under any circumstances was something he looked forward to. He told her lightheartedly, "Far be it for me to go old-school on you. I accept. Dinner it is, your treat."

She laughed. "Was hoping you'd say that."

"Your wish is my command," he said, feeling that the cliché was apropos for the moment, while meaning every word.

Chapter Seven

Annette had admittedly acted on impulse when inviting Hamilton to dinner. It had seemed like a good idea at the time, after he had blown her away with his insight on serial killers and what drove them. Applying his knowledge to the Christmas Lights Killer case could help law enforcement do their job that much faster. Apart from that, she wanted to get to know the trooper better and see if there really was anything there that warranted pursuing him. Or, for that matter, being pursued by him. She was happy that he didn't make a fuss over the who-should-pay-for-dinner thing as some guys might have. As it was, she was more than capable of buying someone she invited a meal. If things were to move in the right direction for them, she was even open to cooking him a meal one day.

They drove their separate vehicles to the Steak Train, a popular restaurant not far from the sheriff's office. Once seated at a table by the window, Hamilton removed his hat, fully revealing for the first time his coal-colored hair in a military high and tight hairstyle. Annette imagined running her fingers through and across it, as he picked up his menu and ordered the ribeye with mushroom gravy along with a garden salad and cheese fries, and lemonade to drink.

"Might as well go the distance since you're buying," he said, a crooked grin on his face.

Annette laughed. "Feel free to do so," she responded, owning up to her offer to foot the bill. She ordered the roasted lamb shank, a Caesar salad and coffee. As they waited for the food and drinks, she dove right into the thing foremost on her mind. "So, is there a Mrs. Hamilton McCade? A girlfriend? Any children?"

"That's a mouthful. Fortunately, we're not eating yet." Hamilton chuckled at his own humor. "No Mrs. No girlfriend. No children. Juliet was the closest thing I've had to a daughter, up to this point." He paused just long enough for Annette to feel relieved, if not elated, that he was single. As if to zero in on this, he said reflectively, "I was in a relationship with a woman named Felicity Sheridan six months ago, but it ended when she decided to hedge her bet with an investment banker she met online."

Annette frowned. "Sorry about that," she said, but felt that his ex had given up more than she had gained in dumping the handsome trooper.

Hamilton shrugged. "Don't be. It happens. Better she showed her true colors earlier than later."

"I agree." She was glad he was able to put it behind him and move on. Not everyone could.

They were interrupted when the drinks arrived, after which Hamilton took up the conversation once again. "Now why don't you tell me your relationship status… Any kids, etc.?"

Annette sighed. "Single and never married," she told him, sipping her coffee. "My last boyfriend, Eric Rodriguez, cheated on me with someone he worked with." The memory still stung, even though she'd gotten him out of her system.

"I don't have any children," she added. *Though I would certainly be open to becoming a mother with the right father,* she thought inwardly.

Hamilton sat back with his drink musingly. "Your ex was an idiot."

"I know, right?" She smiled. "There are more than a few idiots out there," she added, alluding to his ex as well.

"Yeah." He chuckled. "Where did you grow up? I'm sensing it wasn't Indiana?"

"Your senses are correct. I grew up and was raised in Oklahoma," Annette said proudly. "My family still has property there."

"I've never been to Oklahoma, but as a big college football fan, I do follow the Oklahoma Sooners."

She flashed her teeth. "Good to know."

"Do you get back there much?"

"Not much," she admitted. "My parents have passed away and my siblings are all living elsewhere."

"I see." He tasted the lemonade. "My parents are gone, too. They weren't around very much even when alive," he muttered. "It was pretty much just me and Maureen, till Juliet came along."

"What about her father?" Annette asked curiously, hoping her question wasn't too intrusive.

"He was never in the picture." Hamilton wrinkled his nose in regret. "Maureen chose to go it alone in raising Juliet. I pitched in to help as much as I could."

Annette suspected that he had been a good uncle, as well as being a good brother. Now he and Maureen must've lost a good part of the bond they had and would need to rely more on one another to fill the void. Just as Annette felt was the case between her and her siblings after the death of their parents. But ultimately, each of them had to rely on their own inner strength to get over the hump. As Hamilton would need to do in the face of his tragedy.

After the food came and they dug in, Annette turned the subject matter back to Hamilton's dissertation. "What made you decide to take up serial killers to study?"

He lowered his chin. "I guess you could say I've always been a little morbidly curious about the subject—why some people kill as many as they can get away with, before being apprehended, killed or committing suicide rather than be made to answer for their crimes. As such, it seemed like worthwhile subject matter to tackle in my dissertation."

"You certainly have a good foundation on this type of criminal," she said, and sliced the knife into her roasted lamb shank.

"At least enough to have some clue as to what pushes their buttons, so to speak," Hamilton said, forking a generous piece of the ribeye steak.

Annette leaned forward. "Do you think this guy we're looking at could be someone acquainted with the victims as opposed to a stranger or random killer?"

"It's always possible," he conceded. "Or at least could know someone who knew the victims and went from there as an opening." Hamilton dabbed a napkin to his mouth. "But if I were a betting man, which I try not to be, based on everything you've told me about this serial killer and his MO, the odds are that he's chosen to go after women outside his own social group but are still susceptible in some way to letting him in." Hamilton winced before uttering forlornly, "Juliet was a bright young woman. Her text to Maureen gave no indication that she knew who was following her. By the time she came to terms with just how dire the situation was, it was too late."

"But maybe not too late to get the unsub responsible for her death." Annette sat back. "We have clues that can lead to his arrest."

Hamilton nodded. "Yeah, that is something to shoot for."

Hopefully with achievable results, Annette told herself. "Did you ever consider joining the FBI?" she asked, lifting up lettuce with her fork. "I'm sure the Bureau would love to have you working for them as a criminal profiler." She imagined him working alongside her brothers in solving crimes on the federal level.

"I thought about it," he replied, sipping lemonade. "But it wasn't for me. I love my current job as a state trooper, being out in the field and making things happen. That being said, wanting to expand my horizons at this stage of my life, I recently applied to get into the Organized Crime and Corruption Unit within the ISP's Investigations Command Special Investigation Section. Still waiting for word on that."

"Good luck," Annette said, believing he would be great in any capacity of law enforcement he chose. But for now, she was glad to have met him as a handsome state trooper, uniform and all.

"Thanks." Hamilton regarded her curiously. "Think you'll ever make the jump to federal law enforcement, given your siblings' jobs with the FBI and National Park Service? Or maybe go after that graduate degree and take a different direction?"

I should've known that was coming, Annette thought. She tasted her coffee musingly and replied vaguely, "Anything's possible. My brothers and sister are always trying to get me to join them. Right now, I'm happy in my own lane with the sheriff's department. Whatever the future holds, I'll go with the flow. That includes furthering my education and seeing if it means changing courses careerwise."

"Sounds like a plan." Hamilton showed his teeth. She was immediately warmed by that, as Annette could tell that he was genuine. That was the type of person she wanted in her life. But was he interested in anything beyond working together to apprehend his niece's killer?

WHEN HAMILTON WALKED Annette back to her car, the only thing he could think of was wanting to kiss her. He had no doubt that her lips were most kissable. But was she willing to go down that road? And even beyond? Only one way to find out. Before he chickened out and lived to regret it, Hamilton gazed down at Annette and asked doubtfully, "Would it be inappropriate if I kissed you goodbye?"

Her lashes fluttered. "No more than if I kissed you goodbye," she teased him. "So, let's go for it."

"Yeah, let's," he concurred wholeheartedly.

Hamilton tilted his face at the perfect angle and brought his mouth down to hers. Their lips fit together like a romantic puzzle and they kissed. It rattled his bones as she opened her lips ever so much, daring him to do the same. He took the challenge and pulled her closer to him in the process, shielding the evening's chill with the heat emanating from their bodies.

Hamilton could feel his heart racing when he broke the lip lock, not wanting to risk ruining a good thing. And from what he could see, everything was good where it concerned Annette Lynley. "That was nice," he stated honestly.

"Yes, very nice," she said, putting a finger to her lips.

"Thanks for the dinner. Next time, it's on me, if that's

okay with you," he added, unless she preferred to foot the bill on every occasion, if there was more wining and dining to come.

Annette giggled. "Yes, that's fine with me. Next time, you buy."

"Deal." Hamilton was just happy to know there would be a next time. And not necessarily as dinner between colleagues.

"See you when I see you," she said, smiled at him and then got into her car.

"Okay." He waited till she had driven off, before heading to his own vehicle, wondering if this could be the start of something special. No matter that they were brought together by the ugliness of his niece being murdered.

WHILE AT HER DESK, Annette was still thinking about kissing Hamilton yesterday after their get-to-know-each-other-better dinner. The kiss had left her tingling from head to toe, and her vivid imagination had kept conjuring up pictures last night and into the morning of what it would be like to make love to him. She dragged herself from the tantalizing thoughts when Will Hossack walked into her office.

"According to cell phone records," Will said, "on the day she died, Juliet McCade made several phone calls to a Chad Lawrence."

Annette checked her notes to correspond with memory and saw that they were a match. "Hmm…" she muttered. "Maureen McCade said that Juliet's ex-boyfriend was Chad Lawrence."

"Wonder what they were talking about and why they were even talking at all that day?"

"I wonder the same thing," Annette said. "Especially

since they supposedly broke up after Juliet found out he was cheating on her."

Will furrowed his brow. "Maybe we need to have a little chat with Lawrence and see what he was up to the night she died. And for that matter, if he happened to know any of the other victims of the Christmas Lights Killer."

"I'm with you," Annette agreed. They needed to cover all bases in trying to track down Juliet's killer. Though there was no evidence to indicate that Juliet was intimately acquainted with her killer and this perspective certainly went against the grain in the belief that the three murders attributed to a serial killer were likely random attacks, it didn't necessarily mean *all* the murders were random.

Annette knew that, generally speaking, most murder victims did know their attackers. According to the Justice Department, only around one in ten victims of homicide was murdered by a stranger. And for female murder victims, in particular, more than ninety percent of those killed by men were victims of someone known to them, with the Centers for Disease Control and Prevention reporting that over half of female murder victims in the country were killed by current or former intimate partners. As such, Annette took seriously any possibility that Juliet could have been murdered by someone she was romantically involved with.

Riding with Will, Annette was still pondering this when he said, "So, what do you make of Hamilton's take on who we might be dealing with here?"

"I think his insight is sound and has to be taken seriously in forming a profile of the Christmas Lights Killer," she replied matter-of-factly. "Given the nature of the attacks, whether random or not, this serial killer does seem to be operating with a definite chip on his shoulder."

"I was thinking the same," Will said, driving through an intersection before the light could change. "The victims may or may not be lulled by a false sense of security, but once the unsub can get the jump on them, his true nature comes out."

"Which is what scares me." Annette pursed her lips. "He's like a ticking time bomb. Every potential victim could trigger his rage at any time." *That's why we have to find him and try to prevent another woman from falling prey to his homicidal rage*, she told herself.

"Yeah, you're right about that." They arrived at the Carol Creek Shopping Center on Mulbrook Avenue and Will parked in the lot. "Let's go see what Lawrence has to say."

They headed inside the mall to the shoe store where Chad Lawrence was the assistant manager. Holiday shoppers were out in full force, reminding Annette that she had yet to buy Christmas gifts that she planned to bring to the family get-together. While she didn't want to go overboard, she would get something that her siblings would appreciate. Annette mused about the bleak Christmas in store for Maureen McCade and how much it would impact Hamilton with his own life.

In the Best Shoes Shop, Annette and Will approached a tall and husky man in his early twenties, with thick dark hair in a taper fade cut and brown eyes. The name tag on his red store shirt identified him as Assistant Manager Chad Lawrence.

"Can I help you?" he asked evenly.

Annette flashed her badge. "I'm Detective Lynley and this is Detective Hossack of the Dabs County Sheriff's Department. Mr. Lawrence, we'd like to ask you some questions about Juliet McCade."

Chad's eyes darted from one detective to the other. "I still can't believe she's dead," he claimed, standing flat-footed in gray-and-white sneakers. "But I'm not sure what you want from me…"

Will stepped up to him and said point-blank, "Juliet called you a number of times on the day she died. The last of those calls was approximately an hour before we believe she was murdered. You want to tell us what the calls were about?"

Chad stiffened. "We were thinking about getting back together," he asserted. "The calls were part of that."

Annette raised a brow with skepticism. "According to Juliet's mother, she dumped you for cheating on her." He didn't deny it. "Now you expect us to believe she was willing to take you back?"

"It's the truth," Chad maintained. "Yeah, I screwed up, okay. But I never stopped caring for her and wanted a second chance. Juliet seemed open to that." His chin drooped. "Someone stopped it from ever happening."

"Where were you on the night of December eighth, between seven thirty and nine thirty?" Will asked him.

"Right here," he responded immediately. "It's our busiest time of year. Worked all day. The manager, Nancy Ramos, can verify that."

Annette saw no wavering on his part to believe he was lying. "We'll need to speak to her," she told him nonetheless, to confirm his alibi.

Chad nodded. "No problem."

After he called the manager on his cell phone to come out from the back room, Annette asked him if he knew JoBeth Sorenson or Yancy Machado. Chad denied having ever met either woman. Once his alibi checked out, he was no longer considered a suspect in Juliet's death. To Annette, the ex-boyfriend of Hamilton's niece was just another victim of her tragedy, which had ended any second chance between them.

Chapter Eight

Hamilton had never felt comfortable attending a funeral, having been to one too many over the years. Not that anyone would welcome the opportunity to go to one, or think of it as something akin to an afternoon picnic. But this one was especially hard to digest, as it was his own niece's service before she was buried in the Carol Creek Cemetery. Maureen had wanted her to be laid to rest next to Hamilton's parents, hoping they would reconnect in the next world. *I'd like that, too,* he told himself, believing it was a time when their differences in life could be put behind for the greater good in eternal rest.

He noted that Annette and Will were in attendance. Hamilton suspected that at least in part their presence was to surveil mourners in the hopes that someone might stand out as the killer. As morbid as it was, it wasn't uncommon for unsubs to show up at funerals to achieve a perverse thrill from the kill while hidden in plain view. Had Juliet's killer decided to show up, rejoicing in his triumph?

The thought was sickening. Hamilton put an arm around Maureen in support as they sat in the front pew of the church. Juliet's casket was closed and ready for burial. The young pastor, Gretchen Chappell, delivered the eulogy and

Hamilton was moved at seeing his niece, who had had her entire future stolen from her, being given Juliet's just due.

When the service ended, Hamilton walked over to Annette and Will, telling them solemnly, "Thanks for coming."

"We wanted to be here for you," Annette said softly.

"Yeah," Will agreed, adding, "and also keep our eyes open for anything or anyone that seemed off."

"I understand." Hamilton welcomed any part of the investigation into Juliet's killer. Even if it meant showing up at the funeral to scope out a potential unsub. Still, he believed the detectives' support was genuine. "After the burial, Maureen's having a few people over at the house. You're both welcome to come, if you like."

"We'll drop by for a bit," Annette told him, and squeezed his hand. Just touching her reminded Hamilton of their kiss two days ago. He wondered when they might give it another try.

"Okay." Hamilton spotted someone he needed to talk to. "Can you excuse me?"

"Of course," she said.

He raced toward the exit just in time to catch Rita Getzler, Juliet's best friend. "Rita," he called, and got her attention.

In her early twenties and African American, she was small with brown eyes and had brown-blond hair in double Dutch box braids. She faced him. "Mr. McCade."

"Hey." He had met her before, when she was hanging out with Juliet during one of his visits to see his sister. "Got a sec?"

Rita nodded and frowned. "I'm so sorry this happened to Juliet."

"We all are," he told her earnestly.

"I never should have asked Juliet to meet me at the Pear

Pub that night," she moaned. "It's my fault that she ended up in a ditch and—"

Hamilton couldn't let her finish, interrupting by saying, "It's no one's fault. Certainly not yours. What happened to Juliet could have happened to anyone, anywhere. The only one responsible for her death is the person who thought he had the right to take her life. The important thing now is to try and figure out what we can do to bring her killer to justice."

"You're right." Rita sniffled and wiped a tear from her cheek. "How can I help?"

Glad you asked, he thought, and responded, "Did Juliet happen to mention in recent times that someone, perhaps from work or elsewhere, may have been following, stalking or harassing her?"

Rita thought about it. "Not really. Ever since she and Chad broke up, guys have been trying to hit on her, but she seemed to take it in stride. I don't recall her feeling threatened by anyone in particular."

Hamilton pondered Annette mentioning to him that Juliet was apparently at least considering getting back together with Chad, whose alibi for the time of her death had held up. "Did you happen to mention to anyone else the night Juliet died that you were planning to meet at the Pear Pub?"

"Just our friend, Samantha Vaugier, who was also supposed to meet us there," Rita told him.

"And did she?" Hamilton asked curiously.

"Yes. She brought along another friend, Alycia Torres. We had a few drinks while waiting for Juliet to show up. I tried texting her several times, but got no response." Rita's brow creased. "If we'd known Juliet was in trouble…"

"I know," he said, not wanting her and their other friends

to feel guilty for something none of them could have anticipated. He gave Rita his card that had his work and cell num-
bers. "If anything else comes to mind that you think might
be helpful in the investigation, don't hesitate to call me."

"Okay," she agreed, before he let her go.

Hamilton went to be by his sister's side as they prepared
to take Juliet to her final resting place, even while knowing he wouldn't be able to rest himself till her killer was
held accountable.

ANNETTE PUT IN an appearance at the post-funeral gathering,
where she conferred briefly with Maureen, assuring her that
they were working night and day to bring Juliet's killer to
justice. "It's only a matter of time before an arrest is made,"
Annette promised her, feeling this in her heart and soul.

"Thank you for your dedication to this," Maureen said.
"I know Hamilton feels the same way."

Annette felt a tingle at the mere mention of his name.
She was happy to be on the same team with him, even if
they belonged to two different law enforcement agencies.
Solving Juliet's murder, along with murders of the other
two victims, was front and center. "I'm only doing the job
I was hired for by the sheriff's office," she said unassum-
ingly. "Juliet deserves no less."

Maureen nodded, and holding back tears, went to join a
tall, gray-haired man who seemed to hold an affection for
her. Watching them as they shared an embrace, Annette
felt as though she were spying, and turned away and went
in search of Hamilton, who had made himself scarce since
she arrived. Was he purposely avoiding her?

She had her answer when she found him in conversation
with Will in the family room, where they were standing be-

side a bookshelf filled with books, amid contemporary furniture. The two were friends beforehand, she had to remind herself. Will was surely updating him on the case and any progress, or lack thereof.

"Hey, you two," she uttered, getting their attention.

Hamilton immediately turned her way, offering a handsome smile. "Annette," he greeted her. "Will was just telling me that you were about to pay a visit to the DeLuca Christmas Tree Farm in relation to the investigation."

"Yes." She wondered how much Will had told him. "We've learned that last year, the owners, Patrick and Paul DeLuca, purchased a set of Goodyear tires like the one corresponding to the tire track found near the crime scene, for their Chevrolet Silverado. Given the close proximity between the farm and where Juliet's vehicle and body were found, we need to see if one or the other DeLuca could be a killer."

"Hmm…" Hamilton cocked a brow musingly. "A couple of weeks ago, I bought a tree from their farm." His nose wrinkled at the thought. "I'd like to accompany you to question the brothers."

"You're welcome to," Annette responded. "But shouldn't you be here with Maureen as guests arrive?"

"It's starting to wind down here," he said. "If there's an arrest to be made, I want to be there to watch the handcuffs being put on the perp."

"Understandable," she had to admit, given his vested interest as both a member of their task force and the uncle of one of the serial killer's victims. By the looks of it, Maureen seemed to be in good hands with the man she seemed to be close to.

"Why don't you two check out the Christmas tree farm,"

Will suggested, pulling a hardcover book off the shelf haphazardly and putting it back. "In case we're barking up the wrong tree, no pun intended, I'll use the time to search for more vehicles locally that have on them the brand of Goodyear tires we're looking for."

"That works for me," Hamilton said quickly.

"Me, too," Annette agreed, believing they could cover more ground this way, along with the efforts currently underway by others involved in the investigation.

"Then it's settled," Will declared.

It wouldn't truly be settled in Annette's mind till there was a firm resolution to the case. In the meantime, partnering with Hamilton did have its advantages, she believed, as the stirring kiss they shared flashed in her head.

HAMILTON HAD EXPECTED Maureen to push back against his premature exit, believing that it was important to show a united front in grieving the death of their only living relative. Not only did his sister not fight him on this, but encouraged him to do his part in going after Juliet's killer. It was almost as if Maureen couldn't get him out of her house fast enough. Or was this only his imagination?

Whatever the case, Hamilton was more than up for investigating the DeLuca brothers in connection with Juliet's death. At the same time, it was disturbing to think that the owners of a farm that he had been going to for the last several years for Christmas trees could be involved in serial murders.

"So, I assume the tree you bought is in place?" Annette broke his daydreaming. He was driving.

"Yep." Hamilton said succinctly, lifting up the brim of his hat slightly.

"Fully decorated?"

"That, too." He hadn't known at the time that the Christmas season would turn into a bleak one with Juliet's death, though he doubted she would want him to attach negative associations to a holiday that she had loved for as long as Hamilton could remember. "How about you?" he asked Annette, imagining that she had a sprawling tree decorated to the hilt at her place.

"I decided not to put up a tree this year," she muttered defensively. "Or other decorations."

"Can I ask why?" He had some idea of what she might say.

"Between work and plans to spend the holidays in Oklahoma with my siblings, I suppose I just got lazy, and have been using those as justification not to decorate this year."

"I see what you mean," he admitted. "It can get to be a bit much at times. On the other hand, Christmas only comes once a year and is meant to be enjoyed at home and away from home. Decorations and all." He paused. "I'd be lying if I said this Christmas won't be quite the same without Juliet around to give her two cents on how I fared with the tree, lights and the rest. But I'd like to think she would have approved. And even volunteered to spruce up my house more."

"Maybe I will get a small tree after all," Annette suggested. "Though not necessarily from the DeLuca Christmas Tree Farm."

He got her point, given the potential implications where it concerned the farm. "If you do decide to put up a tree, I'd love to help you decorate it." Not to mention have a look at the place she called home. Especially the primary bedroom.

"Oh, would you, now?" she said, a teasing quality to her tone of voice.

"Yeah, sure." He chuckled. "I promise to keep my hands where you can see them."

Annette laughed. "We'll see."

Hamilton took that as a sign that she was still open to spending more time together in an intimate way, which he, too, was all for. And beyond that, once the investigation into Juliet's death had run its course.

ANNETTE WONDERED ABOUT putting up a tree. She imagined it might be fun to do so with Hamilton and have some hot chocolate as part of the experience. Beyond that, she would wait and see how things flowed between them, though if their kiss was a good indication, she saw things sizzling even more should they decide to go all the way. She warmed at the notion, but willed herself to keep it in check for the moment.

They pulled up to the DeLuca Christmas Tree Farm on Pinely Lane. Both she and Hamilton were armed, should they encounter trouble from the brothers. Or whichever one might have something deadly to hide. But there was no need to request backup at this point of the investigation. Or unnecessarily alarm customers on the farm. Then there was the element of surprise if they were, in fact, moving in the right direction.

In the parking lot, they noted a white Chevrolet Silverado with plates that corresponded to the vehicle belonging to the DeLuca brothers. A cursory glance inside and out showed nothing out of the ordinary. Annette looked at the tires. No sign of damage. Only the usual wear and tear. "What do you think?" she asked Hamilton.

"Hard to tell," he admitted. "Could've been used in the commission of a crime. Or not."

She agreed. "Let's hear from the DeLucas."

"Hope they're both around."

They soon found themselves moving between groves of concolor white firs, black hill spruce trees, and Scotch pine trees in search of the suspects. Annette suggested, "Maybe we should separate and cover twice as much ground."

"Good idea," Hamilton agreed. "I'll head in that direction." He pointed down a row of concolor white firs. "If you need me for any reason, just holler."

"Will do," she said, adding, "same to you."

He nodded and they went in different directions. She soon came upon a tall, well-built man in his thirties who had just assisted an elderly couple before turning to Annette. "Need help with anything?" he asked in a friendly voice.

She took a moment to size him up further. He had a round face, blue eyes and black locks in a bro flow hairstyle, and wore a dark brown parka coat over his clothing and black cap-toe boots. Showing her identification, Annette said, "Detective Lynley with the sheriff's department. Are you Patrick or Paul DeLuca?"

"Paul." His eyes narrowed. "What's this all about?"

"I'm investigating the murder of Juliet McCade that occurred very close to your Christmas tree farm."

His features softened. "Oh, yeah, I heard about that." He eyed her warily again. "What does this have to do with me?"

Annette met his hard gaze. "A tire imprint was recovered near the crime scene. We have reason to believe that the killer may have been driving a vehicle with Goodyear Wrangler Fortitude HT tires, such as the Chevrolet Silverado you own."

Paul's head snapped back. "You think me or my brother had something to do with that?"

"You tell me," she shot back at him guardedly.

"We're not killers, Detective," he insisted. "You're way off base here."

We'll see about that, Annette thought. "Would you mind submitting to a DNA swab, just to eliminate you as a suspect?" she asked gently.

"Not at all." Paul jutted his chin. "I have nothing to hide. Neither does Patrick. We're just hardworking Christmas tree farmers."

There was something about the sincerity in his voice that made her inclined to believe he was telling the truth. But the proof was in the pudding. "In that case, Mr. DeLuca, you have nothing to worry about," Annette said, while wondering if Hamilton was drawing the same conclusion with his brother.

HAMILTON RECOGNIZED PATRICK DELUCA the moment he laid eyes on him in the row of concolor white fir trees. He had bought his own Christmas tree from the man, who was in his midthirties and brawny, with blue eyes, a salt-and-pepper Verdi beard, and a dark quiff haircut.

When Patrick saw him, he approached with a crooked grin and said, "Hey, Trooper McCade. Don't tell me you're back for another concolor white fir?"

"Not quite," Hamilton said, walking toward him. "I'm investigating the murder of my niece, Juliet McCade."

Patrick lifted a thick brow. "That was your niece?"

"Yeah." Hamilton could tell that he knew which murder they were talking about, given the proximity to the farm.

"Never made the association." Patrick scratched his beard. "Sorry for your loss, man."

That remains to be seen, Hamilton mused. "The killer

was likely driving a vehicle with Goodyear Wrangler Fortitude HTs," he pointed out. "Much like the Silverado out in the lot. Is it yours?" Hamilton played dumb to see how he responded.

"Yeah, it belongs to me and my brother, Paul," Patrick confirmed. "It's used for the business. Definitely not for driving around to kill women."

"Mind telling me where you were the evening of December eighth?"

"Here," Patrick answered without prelude. "So was Paul. All day till closing at eleven p.m. There were plenty of customers coming and going who saw us," he insisted.

In his experience, Hamilton knew that a clever killer could fake an alibi, even with witnesses. "Would you be willing to submit to a DNA test, if only to remove you from consideration as a suspect?"

"Hell yes, I'll take the test," Patrick said flatly. "So will Paul, if that will clear us."

"It will," Hamilton assured him with confidence, believing that the DNA they'd collected belonged to the unsub in Juliet's death. Now Hamilton needed to find Annette, compare notes, and see once and for all if the DeLuca brothers were innocent. Or if one or the other was guilty as sin.

Chapter Nine

With the DNA tests of Paul and Patrick DeLuca sent to the crime lab for analysis, Hamilton thought it was a good time to broach another subject on his mind as he dropped Annette off at the sheriff's office. "About that dinner I owe you…"

"Yes?" She eyed him with anticipation from the passenger seat.

"I'd love to cook you a nice dinner instead of buying you one," he said.

"You can cook?"

He laughed. "Don't look so surprised. I'm a man of many talents."

"Hmm…" Annette chuckled this time with a decided undertone. "I'll bet." She waited a beat before asking, "Are you inviting me to your house in Fort Wayne?"

He had seriously considered this. But with the driving distance and hazardous conditions, along with the current criminal investigation, it made more sense to stay within the parameters of Carol Creek. "Actually, I have a lakefront cabin in town," he told her. "I like to hang out there in the summertime, but it's pretty cozy during the colder months, too. It has a full-size kitchen and plenty of wood for the fireplace to keep warm, over and beyond the heating system. So, what do you say?"

Annette smiled. "I'd be delighted to have dinner at your cabin," she said spiritedly. "I don't get out to the lake very often, especially during wintertime."

"Then it's a date." Hamilton was sure they could call it that. "I can pick you up here or at your house. Whatever you're comfortable with."

"My house is fine." She gave him the address and they agreed he would show up at six thirty so they could proceed from there.

After he drove off, Hamilton found himself curious about her residence. Was there room enough for two? Especially in the primary bedroom? If he played his cards right, maybe he would get to find out firsthand.

But right now, he needed to pick up some groceries, double-check the firewood, and see to it that the cabin was presentable. Even that, though, would have to wait. He wanted to check in on Maureen and make sure she was holding up all right after the ordeal today of putting her only child in a grave.

When he drove back to her house, Hamilton noted that a blue BMW X5 was parked next to Maureen's Honda Odyssey. *Looks like not everyone has cleared out after the post-funeral gathering*, he told himself. He saw that as a good thing, since keeping his sister occupied was a good way to get her out of the funk she'd been in and back to living her life again. *Something I'm trying to do myself*, Hamilton thought, exiting his duty vehicle while thinking about his date with Annette.

He rang the bell and Maureen opened the door. "Hey," he said. "Wanted to make sure you're okay."

"I'm good, considering," she responded nebulously.

"If you've got company, I don't want to intrude." Even in saying that, he had no reason to believe she was romantically involved with anyone right now.

"Actually, I was hoping you would stop by again as I wanted to talk to you." Maureen opened the door wider. "Please come in."

Hamilton stepped inside the door. He was glad to see that she had left up the Christmas tree and other holiday decorations, knowing that Juliet would not have wanted it to be any other way. Out of his peripheral vision, he spotted movement and turned to the L-shaped sectional, where he saw a man sitting.

Maureen's visitor was in his fifties, and slim with short, gray hair in a low skin fade with a side part, gray-blue eyes behind rectangle glasses, and a gray goatee circle beard. Hamilton recognized him from the funeral as one of his sister's colleagues from work, a radiologist. What was his name?

Hamilton stretched his mind, before Maureen said coolly, "You remember Eddie Huston?"

"Yes," he told her. "Hey, Eddie."

"Hamilton." Eddie stood at nearly Hamilton's height and the two shook hands.

Maureen took a breath and asked her brother, "Do you want something to drink?"

Why do I feel you're holding back on me? Hamilton thought, meeting her eyes. "I'm good."

She fiddled with her hands and said gingerly, "Eddie and I have been seeing each other for a while now."

"Really?" Hamilton eyed the other man. "How long is a while?"

"A couple of months," she said.

"Why didn't you mention it before now?" he asked curiously.

"I wanted to see if it was going anywhere first." Maureen made a face. "Apart from that, I didn't want to scare him off by you giving him the third degree, Mr. Trooper."

"Me?" Hamilton laughed uncomfortably. "I would only be looking out for you, not trying to run your life."

"I told her the same thing," Eddie pitched in with a chuckle. "But I guess your sister just didn't want things to be too weird between us."

"They won't be," he tried to assure her, while getting used to the idea that she was seeing someone. "Did Juliet know?" *Or had she also been kept in the dark?* he wondered.

"She knew," Maureen said evenly. "Juliet got along great with Eddie."

Is that so? How great? Hamilton asked himself, studying the radiologist. "Glad to hear," he muttered.

Eddie met his gaze. "Look, I want you to know that I truly care about your sister and I thought that Juliet was a good kid. I would never have wanted anything bad to happen to her." He paused. "And I certainly wouldn't have wanted to hurt Juliet myself in any way."

"I never said—" Hamilton started, even if he'd been thinking about the possibility.

"You didn't have to," Eddie said flatly. "I know that as a law enforcement officer investigating the murder, you'd consider anyone associated in any way with the victim a suspect. Especially the creepy and leering mother's boyfriend, which often seems to be the case. At least on those true crime documentaries I've seen."

"Those are often exaggerated for TV drama," Hamilton

tried to say, suppressing a chuckle over the all-too-common stereotype. "Real suspects run the gamut," he pointed out. "Depending on the circumstances."

"Be that as it may, I have a rock-solid alibi for the time frame when Juliet went missing and afterward," Eddie maintained. "I was working my shift that night at Carol Creek General. My time card, administrator and patients can verify that."

"So can I," Maureen said supportively. "I called Eddie right after I called you that evening. We video-chatted and I could see that he was at the hospital. He would never have done the awful thing that was done to Juliet and those other women," she stressed.

"Okay, okay," Hamilton said, feeling himself on the defensive but convinced nevertheless of the man's innocence. "You're not a suspect, Eddie," he tried to reassure him. "As it is, the investigation is heating up and we're taking a hard look at others who may be guilty." Or not, he realized.

"All right." Eddie's features relaxed. "We all just want this madness to stop."

"It will." Hamilton felt the pressure of that declaration, knowing the residents of Carol Creek expected nothing less. Nor did he. Or Annette, for that matter. He turned to Maureen and noted that she and Eddie were now holding hands.

"Eddie's asked me to go away with him for the holidays," she said. "His family has a cottage in the Green Mountains of Vermont." Maureen seemed to tighten her grasp of Eddie's hand. "I said yes."

"You did?" Hamilton voiced surprise.

"I need to get out of here for a while," she said. "The memories of what happened to Juliet are just too raw."

"I completely understand," he told her sincerely.

Maureen looked at him. "Really?"

"Of course." Hamilton hated seeing the strain she was under in dealing with the loss of a precious child. If this trip with Eddie could alleviate that, how could he possibly find fault in it? "You should take some time away. It will be good for you."

"Thanks for saying that."

"I mean it, Maureen." Hamilton met her eyes. "I'm glad you've found someone to be with." He glanced at Eddie and back. "You deserve to be happy. Juliet would want that."

"So do you," Maureen uttered, allowing her free hand to rest on his shoulder.

"Actually, since you mention it, I have a date tonight."

Her eyes grew wide with curiosity. "Oh, really. With who?"

"Detective Annette Lynley," Hamilton said proudly. "We've gotten to know each other of late. In fact, I'm making her dinner at the cabin."

Maureen's eyes lit up. "That's wonderful. Detective Lynley is a beautiful woman and an asset to the sheriff's department."

"I agree on both fronts," he said.

"Hope things work out for you two."

"Same with you and Eddie."

"I'll take good care of your sister," Eddie told him.

"Counting on that," Hamilton said, trusting Maureen's judgment and his own that told him this was a positive development. He felt the same way about getting involved with Annette, while looking forward to whatever came their way this evening.

ANNETTE HAD JUST walked into her home after work, anticipating being wined and dined by Hamilton and the potential beyond that, when her cell phone rang for a video chat request from her oldest sibling, Scott. She smiled at the thought of speaking with him, and leaned against the wall in the living room before accepting the call. "Hey, you," she said ardently.

"Hey." Scott grinned at her, his handsome features enhanced by solid gray eyes and black hair that was thick and in a comb-over fade style. An FBI special agent in the Bureau's field office at Louisville, Kentucky, he worked cold case investigations and was married, like their brother Russell. Annette envied both in that respect, while wondering if and when she and their sister, Madison, would tie the knot. "Wanted to make sure you're still on for Christmas," Scott said. "Next up for my pressure tactics is Russell."

Annette chuckled. "We'll both be there," she promised, not feeling as though she could back out now. "So will Madison. Even heard through the grapevine that cousin Gavin plans to show up." Gavin Lynley was a special agent for the Corrections Investigation Division's Special Operations Unit of the Mississippi Department of Corrections, and the next closest thing to a Lynley sibling.

"Seriously?" Scott's eyes widened. "That's news to me."

"Better give him a buzz and confirm his attendance," she suggested.

"I will." He furrowed his brow. "So, what's the latest news on your serial killer investigation?"

Annette brought him up to date on the developments. "With the sheriff's department, the state police and even a couple of your colleagues with the Bureau all working together, we're hoping to stop this before anyone else is killed." She only wondered if that was possible. Especially if the DNA test results on the DeLuca brothers came back negative.

"Yeah, that's always the hope," Scott said. "Unfortunately, sometimes the trail runs cold. That's where I come in."

"You're obviously very good at your job, Scott," she told him, "but our unsub is unlikely to stop what he's doing voluntarily, and this is unlikely to turn into a cold case."

Scott angled his face. "Which is a good thing," he stressed. "The sooner the perp can be flushed out, the better for the investigative team and community."

"I couldn't agree more." Annette imagined that he and Hamilton would get along great and have lots to talk about. She hoped the opportunity presented itself someday. "Well, hate to cut this short, but I have a dinner engagement to get ready for."

"Is that so?" Scott teased her. "Are we dating someone again?"

"I'll let you know," she said simply, recalling the show of support from her family after things had gone sour with her last boyfriend. Annette preferred not to get ahead of herself on where things were headed with Hamilton, not wanting to jinx it.

"Good enough," Scott said without further prying.

Annette smiled. "Tell Paula I said hi." Like Scott, Paula, his wife, was also a member of the law enforcement community.

"Will do."

Upon disconnecting, Annette took a quick shower. Afterward, she blow-dried her hair, then left it down and applied a touch of light fragrance behind her ears and on her wrists, before checking out the wardrobe in her walk-in closet for something suitable to wear on what amounted to a second date with Hamilton. But the first in which they would be at his residence or hers for the outing. Was that a sign that the best was yet to occur between them? Not wanting to overdo it, she went with a nice floral midi dress and black pumps.

When Hamilton arrived, Annette threw on her single-breasted, belted wrap coat, grabbed her hobo shoulder bag and met him at the door. She hoped to invite him in another time. "Hey."

"Hey." He grinned cutely and gave her an appraisal. "You look nice."

"Thank you." Annette saw that he had ditched the trooper uniform for the first time in her presence, handsome as he looked in it. He had replaced it with a dark wool blazer over a purple herringbone dress shirt, brown khaki pants and tan Chelsea boots. His hair looked freshly washed and his face was smooth-shaven. "You clean up pretty well your-self," she had to say.

He blushed. "I keep some extra clothes at the cabin in case I need them."

They certainly came in handy tonight, Annette thought admiringly. She was sure he was even more striking with-out the clothing to hide his obviously fit frame. She cut off the light, locked the door and got into his vehicle.

During the drive, Hamilton revealed matter-of-factly, "Maureen and her boyfriend are leaving town for the holi-days."

Annette sensed that this had taken him by surprise. "That's a good thing, right?" She assumed it was moti-vated, at least in part, by Maureen, to escape the pain as-sociated with her daughter's death.

"Yeah, I suppose," he muttered. "I never even knew she was involved with anyone. Much less seriously enough to share a vacation away from home. Guess it was on a need-to-know basis."

"Are you close enough to your sister that she usually tells you everything going on in her personal and social life?" Annette couldn't help but wonder. She doubted this, based on her own relationship with her adult siblings, their closeness as a family notwithstanding.

"Once upon a time. Not so much in recent years," Hamilton confessed.

"I suspected as much. Maybe with other things going on in her life, Maureen simply waited to tell you when she felt the time was right."

"Yeah," he agreed. "I'm actually happy for her and hope this works out with Eddie, the man in her life. She's had enough disappointments in the relationship department. Maybe this time will be different."

Annette wondered if he was talking about his sister or himself. Perhaps both. "Everyone's allowed to make mistakes along the way where it concerns romance," she put forth. "It's how we learn and grow from it."

Hamilton faced her and said, "You're absolutely right about that. Guess it's something I'm still processing with the mistakes I've made in this regard. Maybe it was easier to project that on my sister and her life, though I wish the very best for her, as always."

"I'm sure she knows that."

"Yeah," he muttered.

Annette smiled, glad to see him own up to his insecurities. It was something that she too was always working at. It gave them something else in common. She looked out the window at the Christmas decorations lighting up homes they passed. She had almost forgotten how beautiful the holiday season could be. Even with the unattractive shadow of a serial killer still on the loose spreading ominously over Carol Creek.

"We're here," Hamilton informed her, moments after they had turned onto Mills Road and pulled into the paved driveway of a rustic, two-story cedar-and-stone cabin.

"Wow," Annette gushed. "When you said you had a lakefront cabin, I wasn't expecting this."

He laughed. "Wait till you see the inside."

"I can hardly wait," she said.

The moment she stepped through the door, which had a Christmas pine wreath on it, Annette wasn't at all disappointed as she took in the spacious layout at a glance. It was an open concept with a high ceiling, hickory hardwood flooring and wicker furniture. A wall of windows with vinyl blinds overlooked Lake Kankiki, and in the living room was a two-story fieldstone fireplace with flames crackling from burning logs. In a corner was a lit and decorated mini-Christmas tree.

"It was the best I could do on short notice," Hamilton said with a grin.

Annette smiled back. "Looks lovely."

"I'll just go check on the food and then give you the grand tour."

"Smells delicious," she told him as the aroma hit her nostrils.

He laughed. "Hope it tastes just as good."

Moments later, while sipping red wine, Annette was shown around the custom kitchen, formal dining room and rec room on the main floor, before they ascended the wooden staircase to the second story.

"It's wonderful," Annette remarked. She couldn't believe he owned this place and wasn't living there year-round.

Hamilton grinned. "If I'd known I would get this reaction, I would've brought you here sooner."

She blushed. "I think this was the perfect time to do so." As it was, they happened to be standing in the primary bedroom suite. It had a large window with a lake vista and rustic furniture, including a vintage sleigh bed.

"Oh, really?" His voice dripped with sexiness. "How perfect?"

She met his desirous eyes. "Perfect enough to take my breath away," she admitted. Or was he managing to do that all by himself?

Holding her gaze, he uttered, "You take my breath away, Annette."

"If I didn't know better, I'd think you were trying to get me into bed, rather than feed me," she said in a deliberately seductive tone.

"And what if I were?" Hamilton questioned, putting his hands on her hips.

"Hmm. I'd wonder about the food burning."

"You needn't wonder any longer. I actually turned off the oven and burners," he said. "I figured our appetites might lie elsewhere for the moment and the food could be heated up afterward."

Annette tasted the wine, knowing full well she wanted him as much as he did her, if not more. "Seems as if you've covered all the bases."

"Not quite." Hamilton grinned hungrily. He took her wineglass and sipped, then set it on the rustic gray dresser. He cupped her cheeks gently and said, "There's still your lips to cover with mine."

"Oh…" She opened her mouth just enough in anticipation for the kiss, which came on cue. It was deep, and made her want much more from him.

Hamilton pulled back. "Not to mention crossing home plate."

Annette suddenly felt hot beneath her clothing. "So, let's not wait any longer to hit a home run."

"I couldn't agree with you more," he responded, taking her into his arms.

Chapter Ten

Hamilton found himself salivating at the prospect of making love to Annette. Yes, he had imagined them having sex from probably the first time he laid eyes on her. But the progress made in actually getting to know the real woman behind the detective would make their being together all the more electrifying. After grabbing a condom from the nightstand, he tossed it onto the cotton chenille bedspread. Then Hamilton began to remove his clothes as he watched Annette do the same. That too turned him on as she slid the dress off, then her underwear, revealing a red-hot body that was toned and taut, with the perfect curves and bends. Long hair hung freely across her shoulders instead of in a restricting updo. Her breasts, medium-sized, were flawlessly rounded, with small, dark nipples. He loved the shape of her long legs and sexiness of her feet, with the small toes proportionate to them.

"You're so beautiful," he had to say, as though this had somehow escaped her notice.

"Look who's talking," she shot back, admiring him as Hamilton stood before her in the nude.

He ate that up, as fitness was an important part of who

he was, but was much more in tune with how she turned him on. "I want to make love to you."

"I want that, too," Annette cooed, reaching out to him.

Hamilton scooped her up and they kissed as he carried her to the bed. There, he went to work on making sure she was pleasured from head to toe with his mouth and deft fingers. He wanted to hold back on his own needs till hers had been met, stimulating Annette to her heart's content. Her breath quickened and her body quivered.

"Mmm…" she murmured, clearly giving in to the sensations as a prelude to what would come soon enough. He maintained the intensity of enjoying exploring her till Annette grabbed him and said, "Let's come together—now!"

Hamilton needed no further instructions as his own needs had built up to a frenzy. He quickly ripped open the packet and put on the condom before working his way atop her, where they were a perfect fit for making love. He moved his face down to hers and they kissed passionately as their bodies merged together and their heartbeats synced. *I doubt I ever wanted to be with someone as much as at this moment in time*, Hamilton thought. He willed himself to wait a little longer for Annette to climax, pacing himself with even and sure strokes.

When it happened, she left no doubt that she was ready for him to finish what they started. "I need you to let go, Hamilton," she begged. "I want to go even higher in satisfaction."

"I want that for you, too," he promised. "For both of us."

With that in mind, Hamilton let himself go, plunging into her moist body with a passion that they both craved like nourishment. His own erratic breathing became all but lost with hers as it gave way to the instant in which they reached powerful orgasms simultaneously. Time seemed to stand still with them soaking in the experience while clinging to one another like a second skin.

When it was over and he had rolled off Annette and lay beside her, Hamilton sighed and said as honestly as he could, "That was amazing."

She made a face. "Just amazing?"

"How about incredible and hotter than hot on a cold winter night?"

Annette laughed. "Now, that's more like it."

Hamilton had to laugh himself. "Any way you want to put it, we were great together."

"Yes, we were," she confessed, draping a leg across his.

"It was well worth the wait."

She chuckled. "So, you've been waiting for this to happen, have you?"

His face flushed. "A trooper is allowed to dream, right?"

"Right. And so is a sheriff's detective," she admitted.

He grinned. "Some dreams can actually come true, if you wish hard enough."

"Very true. Speaking of which, I'm dreaming now about being fed by you, having worked up an appetite. Uh, that is why you invited me over, isn't it?"

"Yes. Of course. Food's coming right up." Hamilton stroked her face, having practically forgotten about the mustard-and-brown-sugar-glazed salmon and mashed sweet potatoes he'd prepared, to go with wine. "Sometimes, though, you have to improvise along the way."

Annette giggled. "I'm all for improvising. Maybe later, we can improvise some more."

"Definitely works for me," he responded quickly. "I'm

more than willing to go a second round in getting to know each other better intimately. Then moving forward from there."

AN HOUR LATER, they were sitting before the fireplace in wicker egg chairs. Annette couldn't believe just how relaxed she felt in Hamilton's log cabin, following their lovemaking and a tasty meal he'd cooked for her. Where had someone like him been all her life? Surely not anywhere within her viewfinder, if not reach. But he was here now and seemed to like her, if the way they made love like there was no more tomorrow was any indication. And she definitely liked him, too, even if she had no idea where this was headed. What was clear to her was that Hamilton seemed to be everything her last boyfriend was not. That alone was enough to give her a warm feeling inside.

Breaking the quiet introspection between them, Hamilton asked thoughtfully, "So, what are your interests besides law enforcement, education and staying close to your siblings?"

You mean besides you? Annette thought to herself, gazing at the fire. She faced him and responded, "I love to travel, jog, work out at the gym, do crossword puzzles, and watch action-packed and sci-fi movies."

"Interesting." He grinned. "Where have you traveled?"

"The Bahamas, Australia, Hawaii and most of the lower forty-eight states."

"Impressive. Can't say I can match you there, but I've spent some time in the United Kingdom, Sweden, Virgin Islands, and my fair share of states, mainly in the Midwest and Northeastern part of the country."

"Not bad," she told him with a smile. "What are your

hobbies?" She imagined with a cabin on the lake, some involved the water.

"In the summer, I love to fish, swim, go scuba diving and boating."

"I kind of figured as much. I enjoy swimming and have been on boats, but not so much the other things."

"I would love to teach you sometime, if you're up for it?"

Annette took that as meaning he wanted to continue to hang out together. "Sure, sounds like it could be fun."

He grinned. "It will be, I promise."

"I'll go along with that." She glanced at the fire, which was still going strong after he had thrown on more logs. "Any nonwater interests?"

"When afforded the time, I like to read spy thrillers," he told her. "And I'm also into watching historical documentaries, comedies and some sci-fi stuff."

"What about all the true crime series on the air and streaming?" she wondered. "With your knowledge of serial homicides, I would've thought some of these might interest you."

"Not really." Hamilton sat back. "Seems like we're being inundated with true crime material these days. Including in book form. I'd rather stick to what I deal with professionally, in real life."

"Same here," Annette had to agree. She only wished there was less crime for either of them to have to grapple with. Hopefully, once they apprehended the serial killer currently at large in Carol Creek, things might settle down in the new year.

"How do you feel about children?" Hamilton changed the subject in a big way.

Annette batted her eyes at him. "Are you asking if I'd like to have children someday?"

"Yeah. Have you thought about it, one way or the other?"

"Of course." She was glad he'd brought this up. "I'd love to have children, two or three maybe. Coming from a big and loving family, I know how wonderful it can be to have children around, watch them grow up and establish their own lives as part of the process."

He nodded. "I imagine that type of environment would have lent itself to appreciate the joys of family."

"Would you like to have children?" she asked, regarding him curiously. "I know that your own parents weren't around as much as you would have liked, leaving you and Maureen to fend for yourselves. And you stepping in as a surrogate dad for Juliet. But what about being a father to kids of your own?" Since he'd opened the door to this conversation, Annette hoped she wasn't pushing him too far.

"I'm open to having kids," he told her matter-of-factly. "If I have the right partner, I see no reason why we couldn't start a family and do better at it than my own parents, while learning from the time I spent with Juliet and how I might have done more in being there for her."

"Good." Annette flashed him a brilliant smile, glad that he was trying to turn Juliet's tragedy into a positive for his own life as a potential father. *I feel as though we're on the same page in being open to becoming parents and the steps leading up to that*, Annette thought. Maybe this was a sign that they were on to something in becoming involved with one another. Or was she seeing things through rose-colored glasses?

"How do you feel about heading back upstairs?" Hamilton asked in earnest.

Annette recalled the sexual talk about improvising when in bed before. "I say let's do it," she stated bluntly, the thought of making love to him again causing a tingle inside her.

He grinned. "I was hoping you'd agree."

Hamilton stood and took Annette's hand, helping her to her feet. They began to kiss and cuddle. By the time they made it to his bedroom, Annette was pretty worked up in wanting to be with him. Only this time, she would be the aggressor, wanting to please him and prolong the action.

After engaging in foreplay that left them both panting and purring, Annette climbed atop Hamilton's rock-hard body. While he caressed her breasts, she guided herself onto him and they let themselves enjoy the experience as they made love. When the climaxes came, Annette locked lustful eyes with Hamilton, arched her back and succumbed to the satisfaction they brought to each other. In the waning moments of passion, she fell upon him and brought their mouths together, enjoying his taste and closeness.

When it was over, Annette fell asleep on Hamilton's chest, and they spent the night together.

Startled awake the following morning by a cell phone ringing, Annette realized it was hers. She slid out of Hamilton's arms, naked, and rolled off the bed. Lifting the phone out of her hobo bag, Annette saw that the caller was forensic scientist Kelly Okamoto of the ISP Fort Wayne Regional Lab's Forensic Biology Section.

"Hey, Kelly," she said in an easygoing voice with the phone to her ear, as she saw Hamilton stirring awake.

"Detective Lynley, I just wanted you to know that we took the DNA collected from Patrick and Paul DeLuca and compared it to the unknown profile extracted from the strand of hair removed from Juliet's mouth."

Annette was tense as she watched Hamilton sit up, sleepy-eyed but alert. "And what did you learn?" she asked the forensic analyst, hoping they might be able to break the case wide-open with one brother, if not the other.

"Neither of the DeLuca brothers was a match for the un-identified DNA profile," Kelly answered. "Sorry to have to tell you that the hair strand belongs to someone else."

"Thanks, Kelly," Annette told her disappointedly, and hung up.

"What did you find out?" Hamilton asked interestedly, gazing at her.

Frowning, while ignoring that she was completely ex-posed to him outside the bed, Annette responded bleakly, "We didn't get a match. The unsub is still unknown and remains at large."

HAMILTON WAS ON PATROL, having reconciled himself to the fact that neither Patrick nor Paul DeLuca was the Christ-mas Lights Killer. As it was, he hadn't really expected a match, considering the brothers had voluntarily given up their DNA. Not a likely scenario for anyone guilty of being a serial killer. But it had been worth a try anyway, consid-ering that the DeLucas did own a vehicle with tires that matched the tire tread evidence near the crime scene that also happened to be just outside the Christmas tree farm owned by the DeLuca brothers.

So we keep trying till the unsub is revealed and caught, Hamilton told himself while driving. His thoughts turned to Annette, giving him a sexual tickle. He was still riding high after the earth-shattering sex they'd had twice yesterday. She had managed to keep pace with him every step of the way and beyond. Or was it the other way around? Whatever the case, she was the real deal as far as he was concerned and he wanted to pursue something with her. He believed she wanted this, too, and they could work toward that once the holidays were behind them and her visit with family. His own family, or Maureen, would be in Vermont. Meaning, he was very likely going to have to spend Christmas alone. Hamilton didn't cherish the thought, but would try not to think about it too much while he kept himself occupied with work.

When a call came in informing him that a car driven by a male murder suspect was speeding erratically through his district, Hamilton joined in the chase of the alleged perpetrator. He pressed down on the accelerator, racing through the streets, till he spotted the brown Buick Encore GX Essence. Tailing it was a white Dodge Charger Pursuit. Hamilton recognized the driver as ISP Trooper Al Hernandez. The forty-five-year-old veteran was a friend, married for the second time, and had four children.

As Hamilton attempted to cut off the suspect, he managed to dart off in a different direction. Hernandez stayed close to him, with another trooper vehicle entering the picture in hot pursuit. Hamilton veered right and headed down another street, sure that he could beat the suspect before he could enter a main street that would allow him to blend in more easily with other traffic, complicating efforts to stop him. *You're not going to get away that easily*, Hamilton thought, gripping the steering wheel tightly as he maneuvered past other vehicles and spotted the Buick barreling toward him.

Suddenly, Hamilton heard the sound of gunfire and then felt his car being hit by a bullet. Then another. He quickly realized that the suspect had slid a semiautomatic weapon out of the window, desperately hoping to shoot his way out of the predicament he was in. Fortunately, the shot missed Hamilton, but was close enough to get his attention. He realized that a bulletproof vest would only go so far in staying alive. Which he fully intended to do.

Just as he removed his own firearm and was prepared to fire back, the suspect's vehicle was rammed from behind by Hernandez. The impact and the high speed at which the perp was traveling forced him to lose control of his car. It flipped twice, ending upside down. The trooper vehicles quickly surrounded it. Hamilton exited his car, weapon drawn.

Trooper Al Hernandez also got out of his vehicle. Thickly built and around Hamilton's height, he was brown-eyed and, beneath his campaign hat, had brown hair trimmed in a short, textured cut. "You okay?" he asked.

"Still in one piece," Hamilton told him thankfully. "Good thing he was a bad shot."

"Yeah. That's for sure."

"My car may need some repair work, though."

"That's one way to get an upgrade," Hernandez joked.

They both turned to the suspect, who appeared unconscious and injured. He looked to be in his midtwenties, was on the lean side, and had two-toned hair in a blowout style and a dark gunslinger beard and moustache. Once it was determined that he was no longer a threat, the suspect was removed from the vehicle, at which time he began to stir. A quick check of his vital signs told Hamilton that his injuries were not serious but he still needed medical attention. After the man was placed under arrest, an ambulance arrived to transport him to the hospital.

Later, the suspect was identified as twenty-four-year-old

Richard Kruger, who lived in Fort Wayne and was the registered owner of the Buick Encore. He was charged with the murder of his live-in girlfriend, Mandy Langham, evading police and resisting arrest, reckless endangerment, and possession of drugs.

Hamilton chalked the experience up to all in a day's work as a state trooper. Still, he longed to be able to move into the ISP's Special Investigations Section, where he could better tap into his skills and insight concerning criminal elements. He had just left the auto repair shop where his vehicle was being worked on for two bullet holes, when Hamilton received a text message from Annette. It said disturbingly,

Another woman has gone missing.

Chapter Eleven

When Annette received word that Lucy Beecham, a thirty-one-year-old assistant general manager for an advertising agency, had failed to show up for work that morning, alarm bells went off in her head. She had even texted Hamilton about it because she suspected it could be related to their current investigation. Though it may have been jumping the gun to assume the worst-case scenario, the report that another local woman was missing at all was more than enough to get her attention in the face of a ruthless serial killer at large.

Following up on this, Annette drove to McKinnon Marketing on Fuller Avenue, where she met with Heida McKinnon, the chief executive officer.

"Thanks for taking this seriously, Detective Lynley," Heida said, as they sat in twill fabric chairs in her spacious office. "I'm really worried about Lucy."

"We take all cases of missing persons seriously," Annette asserted, gazing at the slender woman who was in her forties and had crimson hair in uneven layers and green eyes behind browline glasses. *Especially those that fit certain characteristics hard to ignore*, she thought. "Can you tell me what gives you cause for concern in this instance?"

"Mainly it's because Lucy was supposed to be here at eight a.m. for a presentation." Heida took a breath. "Well, she never showed up."

"Perhaps she overslept," Annette suggested. "Or got the time mixed up?"

"If you knew Lucy, you'd know she took her job very seriously," Heida stated. "She wasn't the type to oversleep. Or have a mix-up on the time. The fact that she still isn't here after ten o'clock tells me something must have happened to her."

Annette had no reason not to believe this was unusual behavior for the assistant general manager. But as a detective, she still needed to cover the possibility that Lucy was missing of her own accord. "Have you tried calling her?"

"Of course," Heida snapped. "Several times. Went straight to voice mail."

"Hmm, that is strange," Annette admitted. "Does she have a husband or partner you could check with on her whereabouts?"

"Lucy is married to her work." Heida sat back. "She's been single and unattached for as long as I've known her. I never asked why, but suspect that she had a bad breakup years ago and didn't want to risk going through that again."

I certainty can relate to that, Annette thought, having gone down that road. But Hamilton had given her good reason to believe that not all hope was lost when it came to finding romance again. Could this have been the case for Lucy, too, without her colleagues being privy to it? "Do you know if Ms. Beecham has had any concerns about her safety? Maybe a stalker or—"

"Yes," Heida broke in, "Lucy did express some fears about a custodial worker, Ross Keach, who kept hitting on her and didn't seem to want to take no for an answer. Out of an abundance of caution for any of our employees feeling threatened, we let him go last month."

Annette took note of this. "Did she talk about having any negative experiences with him after that?"

"Not to me. But she could have decided to keep it to herself at that point."

"Do you have a recent picture of Ms. Beecham?"

"Yes. There's one on my cell phone that we took at the firm's Christmas party two weeks ago," Heida answered, and grabbed the phone from the pocket of her blue jacket and pulled up the photograph.

Annette gazed at the image. Lucy was small and attractive with blue eyes on a round face and long, curly blond hair with blunt bangs. "Can you send this to my cell phone?"

"Yes."

Once she received the picture, Annette rose. "I'll need Ms. Beecham's address and the type of car she drives."

Heida gave the address and said, "Lucy has a Lexus LS 500."

Noting this, Annette told her, "We'll check and see if she's home. If not, we'll consider Lucy Beecham officially missing and investigate further."

Heida furrowed her brow. "Hope you find her and she's okay."

"I hope so, too," Annette told her sincerely.

"With what's been going on lately with a serial killer out there, all kinds of horrible things go through your mind," she admitted.

Don't I know it, Annette told herself realistically. But she still wanted to keep an open mind on the disappearance.

"Let's just wait and see," she voiced tonelessly, while decidedly darker thoughts danced in her head.

ANNETTE WENT WITH Will to the home of Lucy Beecham on York Street. The single-story custom dwelling was in a cul-de-sac and had decorations up. A car was in the driveway. "Not exactly a Lexus LS 500," Will commented.

"True," Annette agreed, eyeing the red Kia Rio. "Wonder who it belongs to?" She recalled that Heida implied that Lucy lived alone. If so, could an intruder—or even a killer—be inside the house, perhaps burglarizing it? Would someone be so bold as to commit such a crime in broad daylight with the getaway car in full view of neighbors?

"We'd better find out." They went up to the door and knocked, while Will yelled, "This is the police!"

Annette heard a dog bark and what sounded like footsteps. She kept a hand close to the firearm tucked in her outside-the-waistband holster. The door opened and a slender teenage girl with brown eyes stood there, looking shocked to see them. She ran a hand through long, straight brunette hair with blue highlights and asked nervously, "What's going on?"

"Maybe you could tell us," Annette said cautiously. "I'm Detective Lynley and this is Detective Hossack. What's your name?"

"Peyton Cortese."

"Is there anyone else inside?" Will questioned.

"No, just me." She seemed to think about it and added, "Oh, and Lucy's dog, Jetson."

"Actually, we're here to see Lucy Beecham," Annette told the girl, sensing that she was not a threat. "Is she home?"

"No," Peyton replied casually. "Guess Lucy's at work about now."

Will peered at her. "Who are you, exactly?"

"I'm her neighbor. I live in that house over there."

Annette followed the path of her thin finger, which pointed at another house two over in the cul-de-sac, also decorated for the holidays, with a Nissan Rogue and a Jeep Gladiator Mojave parked in the driveway. She turned back to the teenager and asked suspiciously, "Is that your Kia in the driveway?"

"Yeah," the girl admitted. "My parents gave it to me earlier this year for my sixteenth birthday."

Annette still wasn't quite convinced the girl was on the level and not a thief or whatever and asked wryly, "Do you always drive your car such a short distance between houses?"

Peyton giggled. "I'm going to visit a friend after I'm done here," she explained.

"Why are you at Lucy Beecham's house?" Will demanded.

The girl ran a hand through her hair again. "Because of her busy schedule, Lucy pays me to take Jetson out for a walk when she's not around and I also water her plants when she's out of town. I was about to take Jetson out when you guys showed up." Her eyes narrowed uneasily. "So, why are you looking for Lucy anyway?"

Annette weighed how much she should divulge, then realized they needed to be forthcoming if they wanted her help. "Lucy's been reported missing."

"What?" Peyton's lower lip quivered.

"She never showed up at work this morning," Annette said. "Which was cause for alarm."

"Mind if we take a look around inside?" Will asked the girl. "Might give us a clue as to her whereabouts."

Including the possibility, remote as it seemed, that the missing woman could be inside her own house and unable to communicate, Annette thought.

"Go ahead," Peyton gave her permission to enter. "Hope nothing bad has happened to Lucy."

"So do we," Annette uttered, and they went inside. Almost immediately, an Australian shepherd raced toward them, seemingly curious about the unexpected company, and jumped playfully on Annette. Annette scratched him under the chin, which seemed to agree with Jetson. She was reminded of the pets she had growing up in Oklahoma. Maybe once she had a family of her own, she could get another dog.

After Will played with Jetson a bit, Peyton got the dog to come to her. She put him on a leash and said, "I'm just going to take him out to do his thing now. I suppose it'll be okay to leave you in here alone."

"We won't damage or take anything," Annette promised. Unless it was called for in the course of the investigation into the disappearance of the assistant general manager. "We just need to find her," she said with a sense of urgency. Peyton nodded and went outside with the dog.

"Let's see if Beecham left any clues about where she might be," Will said. "Or who she could be with."

"All right." Annette took a sweeping glance at the layout, which was an airy, open concept, and the art deco furniture. The house looked clean, and she noted that there were no dirty dishes in the kitchen. In fact, nothing seemed out of place, even with a dog, impressing her. "I'll go check out Lucy's bedroom." She headed down a hall, passing two smaller rooms in favor of the primary bedroom. The first thing Annette noticed right off the bat was that the four-poster bed with its crinkle comforter was made up, as though it had not been slept in overnight. *I never make my bed in the morning*, she thought, as it was the last thing on her mind in needing to get ready for work and grab a bite to eat, before heading out the door. This suggested to her that Lucy may not have gone to bed last night, if she made it home at all after work. *I'm guessing, though, that as clearly a neat freak, she would've made the bed before leaving this morning had Lucy been there*, Annette told herself. Instincts made her feel otherwise in believing that the missing woman had either met up with someone voluntarily, or was lured somewhere by someone. Either way Annette sliced it, this was troubling as far as Lucy's prospects for safety were concerned.

After taking a cursory look around the room with the same art deco furnishings as elsewhere, and seeing nothing that caused suspicion, Annette met Will in the living room and asked, "Did you find anything?"

"Yeah." Wearing a latex glove, he held up a notepad. "This was on the desk in her home office. It says that she was meeting a client at eight last night."

"Hmm…" Annette took a closer look at the note. It didn't mention the client by name or gender. Or where this meeting was supposed to take place.

"What do you think?"

"Honestly, I think that it deepens the mystery of her disappearance. Either Lucy's meeting with this client was more personal than professional and time got away from her or she was being led into a trap."

Will's brow furrowed. "We need to find out which way this goes."

Annette was in complete agreement as her cell phone buzzed. She took it out of the pocket of her flare-leg pants and saw that the caller was Reserve Deputy Shelton Kuen. "Lynley," she answered in an even tone.

"Lucy Beecham's car has been located," Shelton said.

"Where?" Annette asked.

"Just off Boers Creek Road. Near the railroad tracks."

That's not far from here, she mused. "Any sign of Lucy?"

"Not yet," he replied. "The car was empty. We're still checking out the area."

"We're on our way," Annette said, and hung up.

"What is it?" Will looked at her.

"Lucy Beecham's vehicle was found, but no sign of her." They exchanged glances and Annette knew both were wondering the same thing. Would the missing woman be found dead in the trunk of her car, similar to Juliet McCade?

"Let's go," Will said.

Annette bobbed her head, having a feeling that this would end badly.

HAMILTON HAD GOTTEN word that the gray Lexus LS 500 driven by the missing woman named Lucy Beecham had been located near Boers Creek Road. He took a shortcut to get there, wanting to see for himself if this latest disappearance was the real deal. Or perfectly explainable without the presence of foul play being involved. The timing of this concerned him. None of them wanted to see another female victim of a demented serial killer. Yet this was obviously what was going through the minds of everyone involved in the investigation.

All we can do is hope that Lucy Beecham is safe and sound, in spite of her apparently abandoned car, Hamilton thought, as he pulled behind a squad car. Further up, Annette and Will emerged from another vehicle and were approaching the Lexus, which was parked just short of the railroad tracks. Hamilton got out of his car and caught up to Annette. "Hey," he spoke routinely, as if they were still merely law enforcement colleagues and not lovers.

"Hey." She met his eyes briefly, then gazed toward the railroad tracks. "There's still no word on Lucy Beecham's whereabouts."

"Have they checked the trunk?" he hated to ask, with fresh memories of Juliet left in the trunk of her car.

"About to do so right now," she responded uneasily, and they walked over to the missing woman's vehicle. Will was conferring with Reserve Deputy Shelton Kuen, who was big-boned, brown-eyed, and had a bald fade haircut, black in color.

Shelton acknowledged them and said, "I was just telling Detective Hossack that it appears as if the car was left here overnight. A passerby named Florence Oshiro spotted the vehicle this morning, thought it looked suspicious, and called 911."

"Let's get the trunk open," Annette ordered, and Hamilton wondered if it could be done the easy way or the hard way.

As if reading his mind, Shelton said, "The car was left unlocked." He put on nitrile gloves and opened the driver's-side door, whereby he found the trunk release lever and pushed it to open the trunk.

Hamilton could feel the hairs stand on the back of his neck while slowly lifting the trunk lid up with a gloved hand, expecting to find a body. But the trunk was empty, giving him a sigh of relief.

"She's not here," Annette said, a ray of hope in her voice that Lucy Beecham might still be alive.

"So, where is she?" Hamilton asked, as reality set in — the missing woman's car left unattended with no communication from her was still a bad sign.

"Maybe she had car trouble and hitched a ride," Shelton suggested.

Will took out his cell phone and held it up. "There's reception, meaning that she would have called for help if there was a problem with her car."

"According to her boss, Lucy wasn't picking up her phone at all this morning," Annette said. "Which tells me she was unable to do so, for one reason or another." She interrupted herself when her cell phone rang.

Hamilton listened as she answered and said a few terse words to the caller. The expression on Annette's face seemed to go from optimistic to downright depressed in one fell swoop, before she hung up. "What?" he almost dreaded to ask.

"A body has been found in a wooded area about a quarter of a mile from here off Lakewood Road," she stated bleakly. "It's believed to be Lucy Beecham."

Chapter Twelve

"I hate that this has turned into another nightmare," Detective Charisma Robinson said morosely as she greeted Annette and the other law enforcement personnel to arrive at the scene.

"You and me both." Annette grimaced, meeting the blue eyes of the thirty-five-year-old expectant mother with platinum blond hair in a short shag. She had hoped against hope that there would be a different outcome, but seeing the victim was believing that, in fact, Lucy Beecham was dead. Annette eyed the advertising professional as she lay on her stomach in a wooded area and sparsely populated section of Carol Creek. It was less than two miles from Lucy's house. Wrapped around her neck and long blond hair like a scarf were Christmas string lights. She was fully clothed in a navy wool crepe blazer, black straight-leg trouser pants and black leather dress booties. Some of her personal belongings were scattered nearby, as if no longer of consequence to the person responsible for her death.

"Looks like she may have been trying to get away from her assailant," Hamilton deduced.

Annette could see from the dirt and snow on her clothing and positioning of the body that Lucy did appear as though she had been dropped and attempted to crawl or stumble away before the unsub caught up to her and finished what he had started. "I think you're right," Annette told him. "Only the killer was not about to let that happen."

"Which fits the pattern of the other poor women who crossed paths with the Christmas Lights Killer," Charisma remarked. Her words led Annette to muse about Juliet. She could see from Hamilton's expression that his niece's murder had resurfaced in his mind, although it probably never stayed away for long.

"Any idea how the victim might have run into the unsub?" he asked and muttered something under his breath.

"It appears as though she was planning to meet an unnamed client last night," Will said. "Whether or not she ever did is anyone's guess. But this would be a definite person of interest."

"There was also a former custodial worker at Lucy's place of employment whom she accused of harassing her, leading to his firing," Annette pointed out. "He could have wanted revenge as part of the serial murders he was perpetrating."

"Those suspects are a good place to start," Hamilton said, glancing at the victim and back. "Whether either pans out remains to be seen."

"We won't know till we know," she told him, wanting to get the unsub so badly she couldn't stand it. She knew Hamilton was of the same mind, if primarily in memory of his niece.

"Very true," he said, giving her an unreadable look that had Annette remembering their night of passion, even as the gravity of the current situation weighed heavily on her.

Annette gathered everyone and said, "Though somewhat

remote, we need to canvass the area for any possible witnesses, surveillance video, etc."

"I'll jump right on that," Charisma said, and others concurred.

When Josephine Washburn, county coroner and medical examiner, arrived, Annette waited to see her take on the latest casualty to rock Carol Creek.

Frowning, Josephine complained, "Looks like the grinch is dead set on ruining everyone's holidays."

"Tell me about it." Annette tsked, glancing at Hamilton and back. "Have you met Trooper Hamilton McCade?"

"We've crossed paths once or twice." Josephine gazed at him. "Trooper McCade."

"Dr. Washburn," he said knowingly.

"I'm sorry about your niece," she acknowledged.

He gave a silent nod.

Annette broke the awkwardness of the moment by shifting the focus to the present death, when she pointed toward the wooded spot where Lucy Beecham lay dead. "She's over there…"

"Let's have a look," the ME uttered, as she slipped on her latex gloves while visually inspecting the decedent. Then she did a preliminary exam before saying tonelessly, "The cause of death was almost certainly ligature strangulation, with the ligature being the string Christmas lights wrapped around the victim's neck. So, yes, we are talking about a homicide here, as if you had any doubts to the contrary."

"We didn't," Annette had to say bleakly. "The MO and manner of death fit the pattern of the serial killer we're searching for."

"Better find him soon," Josephine warned. "Not sure how many more of these strangulation deaths I can take."

"We're on the same page there," Will told her. "What's the estimated time of death?"

Josephine studied the victim further and said, "Based on a few things, I would have to say she has been dead for at least twelve hours. Maybe more. I'll see if I can narrow that down even more after completing the autopsy."

Annette only needed to do some quick arithmetic to estimate that Lucy was probably killed somewhere between eight last night, when she was supposed to meet with a client, and midnight. Could she have been kidnapped and held for a while before being murdered?

"What do we have here?" Josephine lifted one of Lucy's hands and carefully removed from it what appeared to be a strand of hair. "I'm guessing the victim managed to grab ahold of this during the struggle for survival."

Hamilton winced. "When it's compared with the hair strand found with Juliet, I'm sure we'll find that the unsub is one and the same."

Annette had to agree, having no reason to believe they were dealing with a copycat killer. "If so, we'll still need to connect it to someone we can identify by name and place." Meaning that the DNA profile was a key piece of evidence, but was only one step toward piecing the puzzle of serial murder together.

"First things first," Josephine told them, placing the hair in an evidence bag. "This will need to be processed and you can go from there."

"We found something else promising to add to the discussion," Loretta Covington, the crime scene analyst, said as she approached the group. "A tire track was discovered just up the road that looks an awful lot like the Goodyear

Wrangler Fortitude HT track found near the crime scene of Juliet McCade's murder."

"Really?" Hamilton hoisted a brow with interest. "Let's take a look."

Annette walked between him and Will, with Loretta leading the way, before they came to an area where the street merged with a dirt path that had only a dusting of snow. The partial tire track was clear as day as CSIs protected the potential crime scene from being corrupted. All Annette could think of was that a match here would be further proof that they were dealing with the same unsub, bringing them closer to identifying him. "We need a cast of the tire track," she ordered.

"You've got it," Loretta declared, and proceeded accordingly.

A little later, after updating Sheriff Teixeira on the latest homicide and where things currently stood in the investigation, Annette returned to her office. Hamilton was waiting for her, sitting with his long legs stretched out. She fought to ignore the sexual vibes he exuded by his very presence, along with the images that sprang up in her mind from their recent history. "Sorry," she said. "Took a bit longer than I thought with the give-and-take between me and the sheriff."

"No problem," Hamilton told her. "I understand how much pressure you're under with this case. Every other homicide associated with it only makes the situation more intense and frustrating."

"Exactly." Annette was sure he could relate to one degree or another. "Fortunately, Sheriff Teixeira is allowing us to stay the course till we see this through." She sat at her desk, which separated them, even when she wanted only to fall into his arms. "So, how was your day?" she asked him casually.

Hamilton frowned. "Don't ask."

"Now you've got me curious," Annette admitted. "I'm asking."

He sat back. "Well, I started off the day pursuing a murder suspect and getting shot at in the process."

"Seriously?" Her brows knitted with worry. "Are you okay?"

"Yeah, I'm good. He managed to put a couple of holes in my squad car. Other than that, I escaped unscathed."

"Thank goodness." The idea of serious harm coming to Hamilton was something Annette didn't even want to imagine, feeling as close to him as she was starting to. "So, what happened to the suspect?"

"He flipped his car, sustained minor injuries and faces a slew of charges," Hamilton told her. "Not the least of which is the stabbing murder of his girlfriend."

"Wow." Annette wrinkled her nose. "A tough day for you."

"Not as tough as yours," he said matter-of-factly.

"That's debatable," she countered. "Murder is murder, with consequences for those left behind."

"True enough." Hamilton set his jaw. "Hope Lucy Beecham's murder can give us the answers we need to bring the culprit to justice and let the chips fall where they may as far as lingering consequences."

"We'll see what the crime lab comes up with interview suspects, and see where those chips fall," Annette agreed.

Hamilton shifted in the chair. "I need to talk to Maureen before she hears about the latest murder and freaks out again about losing Juliet."

"I think your sister is stronger than you give her credit for, Hamilton. Maybe you need to just trust that Maureen is doing what she can to move on, even if bad things are still happening out there."

He nodded. "I'm sure you're right on both scores. I just need to hear that from her and then I'll leave it alone."

"That sounds fair," Annette said, knowing full well that her siblings had a tendency as well to be overprotective. She was probably just as guilty in reverse. She liked the idea of having someone in her life who would be just as keen in always being there in her times of need. Someone like Hamilton.

COMING ON THE heels of Juliet's murder, the news that another local female had lost her life to the serial killer wasn't something that Hamilton wanted to share with Maureen. But there was no sugarcoating the truth. Or hiding from it. He was sure, as Annette had suggested, that Maureen was thick-skinned enough to be able to deal with such news without falling apart. She understood that they were working overtime to catch the perp, but even that wasn't always enough to stop crafty killers from killing again and again.

Still, she deserved better, Hamilton believed as he headed to Maureen's house. So did the other families left to grieve the crimes committed by the Christmas Lights Killer. And others like him. Justice would prevail ultimately. Of that, he was certain. It usually did in such cases. Yet it couldn't come soon enough.

Hamilton felt solace that Annette had come into his life at seemingly just the right time. She was the type of distraction that any man could warm up to. Only, the sheriff's detective was becoming much more than a distraction to him. He could actually envision a future with her. Was this what she wanted? Would her family approve of him as another person in law enforcement, encroaching on one of their own?

At least Maureen has my back where it concerns seeing Annette, Hamilton told himself, pulling into the driveway. The least he could do was have hers in the same way as his sister tried to give romance another shot with Eddie.

The moment Hamilton walked through the door, Maureen gave him a hug and said, "I know that another woman has been killed."

He frowned. "Doesn't take long for news to travel in Carol Creek."

"Or anywhere, for that matter," she told him. "Especially of this magnitude."

"We have some strong leads on the killer," he said, hoping this would give her a little satisfaction that they were on the right trail.

Maureen stared at him. "Juliet is gone now and nothing will ever bring my daughter back," she emphasized. "The man responsible for her death will get his, one way or another. Don't let it overwhelm you so you lose sight of what's most important."

He held her gaze. "Which is?" What could be more important than family?

"Being happy in life for as long as you can, never knowing what's around the corner. I honestly felt that Mom and Dad wanted that for us, even if they weren't very good at articulating their feelings."

"You really think so?"

"Yes," she replied firmly. "I wanted it for Juliet, too, and she lived up to that for the most part. Now I want it for you. And me as well."

"Same here." He grinned at her, their lives from childhood to now flashing before his eyes. "So, when do you and Eddie leave for the Green Mountains of Vermont?"

"Tomorrow," Maureen told him. "Between workplace stresses and everything else, I'm really looking forward to this time away to relax and get my head straight."

"I want that for you, too, more than you know," Hamilton said. "Even afterward, hopefully you and Eddie will have more getaways in your future."

"I hope so." She tilted her face and smiled. "Maybe some getaways are in your future as well, now that a certain detective has entered the picture."

He couldn't help but smile at the notion. "We'll see how it goes."

In his mind, Hamilton was already thinking in those terms, while contemplating just what it would take to make Annette all his.

ANNETTE CARRIED HER work home with her that night. She pored over what they knew and didn't know at this point pertaining to the Christmas Lights Killer. Yes, there were still leads to follow on the latest murder attributed to the killer. But the fact that this killer was ruthless and handpicking his victims whenever the spirit moved him told her that they needed to step up their efforts even more. So, where was he now? What exactly was making him tick, aside from the thrill of the kill? Had Lucy Beecham simply been in the wrong place at the wrong time? Or had she been set up to die by someone who had a beef against her?

By the time she called it a night, Annette had allowed those disturbing thoughts to settle down. Hamilton suddenly occupied her mind. The idea that he could have been shot that very day frightened her. She didn't want to lose him to senseless violence. But did she actually even have him? Yes, they had made passionate love together and seemed to hit it off in most areas. Yet he still hadn't fully opened up to her. After all, the man hadn't even invited her to his main house. Why not? Was that somehow off-limits?

Annette tossed those thoughts back at herself. She hadn't exactly welcomed Hamilton inside her house with open arms. So, was she any less guilty in being cautious about not wanting to move too quickly in this relationship if they could even call it one? Maybe she would invite him over for dinner tomorrow. After all, it was her turn to do the cooking. She was open to whatever might happen thereafter.

Chapter Thirteen

Hamilton was sent a copy of the autopsy report on Lucy Beecham, believed to be the latest victim of the Christmas Lights Killer. As he suspected, the assistant general manager of an ad agency had died due to ligature strangulation. Or throttling from a string of Christmas lights. The medical examiner had declared the death to be a homicide. This brought back fresh images in Hamilton's head of what it must have been like for Juliet in her final moments before she stopped breathing. He could only hope that she lost consciousness as soon as possible and had been somehow able to conjure up good thoughts to separate from the horror of the moment.

Driving to the ISP Fort Wayne Regional Laboratory, Hamilton wanted to see firsthand if the crime scene evidence collected in the Beecham homicide was a match for that obtained in Juliet's death, confirming that they were dealing with the same unsub. In the Forensic Biology Section, he got right to it with forensic scientist Kelly Okamoto. "What did you make of the latest hair sample collected?" he asked her.

Kelly scratched her cheek and replied calmly, "Well, the DNA analysis makes it clear that the hair definitely came from a white male." She had a magnified image of the hair on her monitor.

Hamilton reacted. "And how does it compare to the previous strand of hair analyzed?"

"The DNA profile was an exact match between the two strands of hair," she answered. She brought up the hair samples, side by side, on the screen. "Or, in other words, both belonged to the same individual."

So the same killer did perpetrate both attacks, Hamilton mused, peering at the hair strands from two different homicides. And likely, because of the common MO, also responsible for the other related murders committed with Christmas lights. "Any chance that the most recent forensic unknown profile collected might somehow magically show up in the database?" he wondered, realizing this was a longshot at best.

"Sorry." Kelly wrinkled her nose. "We put the second DNA profile in the state database and National DNA Index System and got the same result. There was no match to any arrestee or convicted offender."

"Figured as much," Hamilton voiced disappointedly, "but it was worth a try."

"Always," she concurred. "But the good news is we now know for sure that you're dealing with the same unsub here. And if he ever is arrested, we'll be able to collect his DNA and link him to these murders."

"Yeah." Hamilton sighed. "With any luck, though, we'll be able to nab him before he can get to another victim."

"Of course," Kelly said. "At least the unsub has given us something to work with, even if he's trying to conceal his guilt."

"That can only last so long." But it could still be long enough for the unsub to continue his killing ways.

In the Microanalysis Unit, Hamilton found Bernard Levinson, the forensic analyst who had been tasked with comparing the tire tread castings made from tracks left near two crime scenes. "So, what are we looking at with the latest cast of the tire track?" Hamilton asked urgently.

Touching his glasses while sitting at his workstation, Bernard responded, "I'd have to say that the tire tread looks virtually identical to the Goodyear all-season, all-terrain tread from the first cast."

Hamilton chewed on his lower lip. "Hmm... Can you show me on your monitor?"

"Yeah, sure." Bernard pulled both castings up, side by side. "Though there is less of the tire track in the second casting, you can see enough of it to compare with the first one to see the similarities in the tread."

"You're right," Hamilton agreed. They did appear to come from the same type of tire. But he still needed further confirmation.

"You should check with that tire center again to be sure," Bernard said, reading his mind.

"I will," he told him. "But at the moment, I'll assume these tracks probably came from the same vehicle."

"Looks that way."

Hamilton left the crime laboratory and drove over to the tire center, where Pete Lipton, the manager, studied the cast of the partial tire track found near Lucy Beecham's body and asserted, "Like the other tire track you showed me, this is also a tread from a Goodyear Wrangler Fortitude HT."

"Really?" Hamilton believed him, but put just enough doubt in his inflection that, as anticipated, Pete once again double-checked with his top mechanic, Clayton Serricchio, who reached the same conclusion.

"I'm sure you've narrowed down the vehicles in the local area that use these tires," Pete told Hamilton.

"We have," he acknowledged. "Unfortunately, we're still searching for the vehicle in question." And in the process, the unsub driving it while on the hunt for more potential victims.

After getting back on the road, Hamilton headed for Carol Creek, wondering if Annette and Will had made any meaningful breakthroughs on the case. Beyond that, he thought about the progress made between him and Annette on a personal level and just how far it could go, if both were willing.

WHILE DRIVING, Annette pondered the findings from the medical examiner, and the ISP crime lab's Forensic Biology Section and Microanalysis Unit, that linked the deaths of Lucy Beecham and Juliet McCade. It was chilling, to say the least, when put together like a whodunit mystery that was anything but fiction, the fragments of a deadly puzzle.

We're talking about the same unsub strangling to death attractive women, Annette told herself, as though there was any doubt of that in her mind, with the evidence only confirming this, more or less. The Christmas Lights Killer was preying on those he happened upon or were chosen by design and camouflaged as random. Either way, it wasn't good and incumbent upon them to bring the killer's murder and mayhem to a grinding halt.

She was on her way to see Virgil Flynn, a businessman whom Lucy had been scheduled to meet the night she died, according to Lucy's employer, Heida McKinnon. Had this meeting taken place, only with tragic results? Annette parked in the lot of the Flynn Real Estate Agency on Prairie Street and stepped outside. Though the air was chilly, the snow had mostly disappeared from the streets and sidewalks, while still clinging to rooftops and tree limbs.

She went inside and spotted a slender Hispanic woman in her thirties with brown hair in a short bob, sitting at a desk while talking on the phone. Turning in the other direction, Annette was met by a man of medium build in his sixties with blue eyes and a gray horseshoe haircut. "Detective Lynley, I presume?" he asked.

"Yes," she told him, meeting his gaze.

"Virgil Flynn. Heida told me you would be dropping by to talk about Lucy Beecham. Why don't we step over to my desk?"

"All right." Annette followed him to a corner of the large office, where there was a double pedestal executive desk. He offered her a seat on a padded armchair and sat himself behind the desk on a faux leather chair with flip arms.

Virgil interlocked thick fingers and said, "First of all, I feel terrible about what happened to Lucy. But I had nothing to do with her death."

Annette peered at him. "I understand that Ms. Beecham had an appointment to meet you at eight the night before last," she said. "What was the nature of that meeting?"

"We were going to discuss a new ad campaign," he replied evenly. "She was supposed to come to the office here. Only she never showed up."

"Did she call or text to indicate she was having a problem with making the appointment?"

"No," he claimed. "I tried calling her, but she never picked up. I figured maybe she had her dates mixed up—it happens—or something else came up. I just planned to reschedule the meeting." He drew a breath. "I never imagined anything like that would have happened to her."

Annette felt he sounded credible enough, but still pressed ahead. "How long were you in the office that night?"

"Till around nine thirty or so," he answered. "I had some other business to attend to."

"Can anyone vouch for that?"

"Yeah." He looked at the woman on the phone. "My associate, Diane Fernandez, was here as well, the entire time."

Annette calculated the probable time of death, the location of where Lucy Beecham's body was found, miles away, and the likelihood that the real estate agency owner could have pulled this off successfully. Then there was the fact that his gray hair did not line up with the strands of dark hair believed to have come from the perpetrator in the last two murders.

When she left the office, Annette no longer considered Virgil Flynn a viable suspect worth pursuing.

HALF AN HOUR LATER, Annette met up with Hamilton at the Carol Creek Shopping Center where Ross Keach, whom Lucy had accused of sexually harassing her, was employed as a custodial worker. But had he graduated to something far more sinister?

Hamilton wanted to know the answer to that as much as Annette did, if not more. Especially after the forensic evidence had shown that Juliet's killer had also been the culprit in Lucy Beecham's murder and all but certainly was responsible for the ligature strangulation killings of JoBeth Sorenson and Yancy Machado. Now was the time to end this, if possible, by getting the perp off the streets once and for all.

In the mall, they spotted a tall and solidly built male who

looked to be in his early thirties with dark locks in an angular fringe haircut and blue-gray eyes. Dressed in a maintenance uniform, he was pushing around a rolling trash cart, picking up litter along the way.

"You think that's him?" Annette whispered, as they approached.

"One way to find out," Hamilton told her.

Taking the lead, she got the attention of the custodial worker who seemed to be caught up in his own thoughts, saying to him, "Ross Keach?"

He shot her a cold stare. "Yeah. Who's asking?"

Annette flashed her identification. "Detective Lynley with the Dabs County Sheriff's Department," she answered. "State Trooper McCade. We'd like to—"

Before Annette could complete her sentence, Keach surprised them by pushing her hard enough into Hamilton that they both went tumbling down to the floor as Keach took off running. Hamilton's first concern, of course, was Annette, who seemed shaken up. "Are you okay?" he asked, while still beneath her, having taken the brunt of the fall.

"I'm good," she insisted, still clinging to him. "Did he hurt you?"

Under other circumstances, Hamilton would have welcomed this nearness to her. In this case, though, it went against the grain because it had been forced upon them by a serial killer suspect. He admitted, "Got the wind knocked out of me, but I was able to brace for the fall at the last instant. No major damage."

"I'm glad," Annette murmured.

He gently lifted her off him and both got to their feet in time to see the suspect running down the shopping center.

"Let's go get him," Hamilton said, determined to nab Ross Keach, even if the man had gotten a nice head start.

"Right behind you," she shot back as they ran after the suspect.

They were in lockstep as Hamilton and Annette raced across the mall, dodging shoppers, while narrowing the gap between them and Keach. As they drew closer, the suspect began shoving people to the floor and flipping products on display in a desperate effort to slow them down.

Hamilton watched as Keach darted into a crowded department store, suspecting that his intention was to reach the door that led to a parking lot and then vanish. They couldn't allow him to do that. "We'd better split up," Hamilton told Annette, confident that the detective was more than capable of handling herself in this instance.

"I'm already ahead of you. I'll see if I can cut him off that way," she said, indicating another direction.

"And I'll try to get to the exit before he does."

They separated and went after Ross Keach, while Hamilton hoped no one else got hurt in the process. As he took long strides through aisles, past clothing racks, toys, and Christmas displays, Hamilton spotted the suspect, who had managed to create a real mess by tossing things at him and to the floor in his effort to escape. There was no indication that Keach was brandishing a firearm, which was a relief, since that could really turn this chase into a nightmare.

After Keach pushed through the exit to the outside and was about to break into a full stride in getting away, Annette tackled him from behind, seemingly coming out of nowhere and anticipating his moves. Caught completely off guard, Keach went down hard, with Annette on top of him.

She quickly twisted one of his arms behind him and cuffed him, then did the same with the other.

When he caught up to them, Hamilton heard Annette reading Ross Keach his rights. "Good job," Hamilton told her, impressed, as he roughly pulled the huffing and puffing suspect to his feet and made sure there were no further attempts at escape.

Annette bristled. "You do what you have to do."

Hamilton grinned. "And you do it well."

"Let's bring him in," she spat.

"Your car or mine?" Hamilton asked, half-jokingly.

Annette pursed her lips. "You pick."

He was more than happy to toss the suspect in the secure back seat of his patrol car. Then see what he had to say during interrogation as it related to the Christmas Lights Killer and the murder of Hamilton's niece.

In the interview room, Annette sat beside Will, across from Ross Keach, who was handcuffed and had remained stone-faced ever since being brought in for questioning in the murder of Lucy Beecham and presumably three other serial murders. Observing the interrogation through a one-way window was Hamilton, along with Sheriff Dillon Teixeira and Detective Charisma Robinson.

Annette was still a little sore from first being pushed onto Hamilton at the shopping center and then having to use leg muscles that didn't get as much of a workout during the wintertime. Tackling Keach actually felt pretty good after what he had put them through. His efforts to evade them had necessitated an arrest, with the initial charge of assaulting a member of law enforcement. She wondered how many more charges they could tack on.

After a moment or two of collecting her thoughts, Annette regarded the suspect sharply and said, "Let's start by talking about Lucy Beecham."

Keach furrowed his brow. "Who?"

Annette repeated the name and added, "The assistant general manager for McKinnon Marketing who got you fired after you sexually harassed her. Does that ring a bell?"

"Yeah, I remember that bitch," he sneered. "What about her?"

"Two nights ago, she was strangled to death," Will told him toughly. "You immediately became the number one suspect."

Keach's head snapped back. "I didn't kill anyone," he alleged. "I had nothing to do with her death."

Annette gave little credibility to his words of denial, which most murderers were quick to fall on like a sword. "If that's true, why did you run?"

He waited a beat, then responded shakily, "I got into a fight with a neighbor who was making too much noise. I thought he'd pressed charges. When you told me you were cops, guess I just panicked."

Will glared at him dismissively. "You expect us to believe that?"

"Yeah, it's the truth," he maintained. "Neighbor's name is George Schneider. You can ask him."

"We intend to," Annette said tersely. "Right now, we'd like to ask where you were two nights ago, between eight and ten?" She believed it was more likely than not that Lucy would have been killed shortly after she went missing than later.

Keach lifted his cuffed hands and rubbed his jaw. "I went for a drink after work that day," he claimed.

"Where?" she demanded.

"The Penn Street Bar. I was there till at least midnight."

"I assume others can verify this?"

"Yeah, sure," he said. "The bartender, for one. He tried to cut me off, but I kept the drinks coming."

Annette glanced at the one-way mirror, wondering what the sheriff and Hamilton were thinking, and back to the suspect. "Would you be willing to give us a DNA sample?"

Keach wavered. "Why should I?"

"Because it would go a long way in eliminating you as a suspect in as many as four murders of women in town," she told him bluntly. "Otherwise, you'll be spending the night in jail for assaulting two officers of the law, pending verification of your alibi and statements. That's assuming we can't find new evidence linking you to Lucy Beecham's murder before then."

"I'll give you my DNA." Keach jutted his chin. "If that doesn't do the trick, I want a lawyer," he said for the first time.

Annette looked at Will. By his expression, she could tell that, like her, he didn't believe that Ross Keach was their man in Lucy's death. Or the Christmas Lights Killer.

HE HADN'T MEANT for things to end that way for the latest victim. Actually, he had. Just not the manner in which it all played out. He'd been so excited in getting the jump on her that, after forcing her into the back seat of his car, he had failed to use the master lock to keep her from escaping. This had nearly cost him when he'd been forced to stop abruptly to avoid hitting a deer. She'd taken full advantage of this by getting out and making a run for it.

Fortunately for him, she hadn't gotten very far. Before

she could break into a full jaunt in the wooded area, he had managed to trip her, but had himself fallen in the process. But he'd recovered more quickly than her and gotten back on his feet. While she'd made a valiant attempt to crawl away, he would have none of it. Not when her survival would go completely against his own agenda in taking her life.

With the Christmas lights in hand, he'd pounced on her like a leopard and, with lightning speed, wrapped the string around her pretty little neck, twisting, turning, and tightening as she struggled to breathe, till any fight she had left in her faded like fog. Admittedly, the experience had given him a new thrill and reason to celebrate yet another successful kill.

As for those pursuing him, he could only laugh at their ineptness. Going off course in their attempts to apprehend him only worked in his favor. He was enjoying this way too much to let them stand in his way. Or interfere with his plans. No, there needed to be others to die by the power vested in him with help from the Christmas string lights. Carol Creek might never be the same again. Not his problem. This was simply the way it had to be.

He drove nowhere in particular, but everywhere the car could take him. It wasn't exactly a joy ride, but would be when the time was right to strike again. In the meantime, he sat back, took in the sights of Christmastime and found himself singing along with the Christmas classic tune that played in his head.

Chapter Fourteen

After Ross Keach's DNA failed to match that taken from the strands of hair connected to two murders and his alibi held up, he was released. Though Annette was beyond frustrated, she was more concerned with apprehending the real serial killer than putting away an innocent man. She had no doubt that Hamilton was of the same mind, as was Sheriff Teixeira. They were doing the right thing by investigating all leads and, when going nowhere, moving on to other possible evidence and suspects that could crack the case.

What Annette didn't want to do at this point was allow the unsub to ruin her Christmas altogether. That would be giving one person way too much power that was totally undeserving. As such, she decided to put up a small Christmas tree as a prelude to the larger one she could expect for the family gathering. She invited Hamilton to decorate it with her and then make dinner for him, believing they could both use some time together after another long day.

Hamilton was quick to accept the invite and they picked out a tabletop miniature pine Christmas tree that came with ornaments and a small treetop star. Setting it on the vintage country coffee table, they decorated while listening to some Nat King Cole holiday music and sipping wine.

"So, what do you think?" Annette asked when they were done.

Hamilton smiled. "I think it looks great and it's a good enhancement for your place at this time of year."

"You're right. Maybe next year, I'll get a great big one that can really get me into the spirit of Christmas."

"Maybe next year, we'll be able to take on that task together," he suggested boldly.

She eyed him with a tingle inside at the possibilities. "Oh, you think so, huh?"

"Hey, Christmas is all about believing in remarkable things, right?"

You are so right, Annette thought dreamily. "Of course." She wondered if, in a year, things really would have progressed to the point of them living under the same roof. And exactly which roof would that be?

"So, what do you say we make that meal together?" Hamilton suggested, tasting the wine. "I'm starving!"

She raised a brow. "Are you sure you wouldn't prefer to just sit back and relax and leave the cooking up to me this time?"

He made a playful face. "Now, what fun would that be?"

She laughed. "Never really considered cooking fun, per se. But maybe with you, it could be."

"Only one way to put that to the test," he challenged her.

Taking him up on that, Annette happily gave way to his zest for doing this together and welcomed him into her kitchen as an equal. They managed to take what she had in the refrigerator and made macaroni and cheese, tomato basil soup, and barbecue meatballs. After wining and dining, even feeding each other, they went to bed and made love. Annette gave as much as she took, thrilling in the closeness of their bodies and sense of knowing what the other needed and when to act upon those impulses. When their climaxes came, both seized the long moment to relish in complete unison.

Afterward, Hamilton hummed, "I could get used to this."

"Oh, really?" Annette looked at him. "Just here and at your cabin? When do we get to take this show to your house in Fort Wayne?" She hoped she wasn't being too pushy, but needed to know just how strongly committed he was to giving this a go.

"Anytime you like." He kissed her shoulder. "You're always welcome at my house. I'd love for you to see it."

Her lashes fluttered. "You sure about that?"

"Positive. I would've invited you over sooner, but between the distance from Carol Creek and an ongoing investigation, I thought you might turn me down."

"I wouldn't have," she told him, though his rationale made sense.

"Then consider this an invitation to take our show to my humble abode tonight or whenever."

Annette smiled, more than satisfied that this truly did seem to be headed toward something serious. "Invitation accepted," she told him gleefully.

Hamilton grinned back at her and they cuddled, before exhaustion overtook them and they fell asleep.

In the morning, Annette allowed Hamilton to get some extra shut-eye while she dressed and made breakfast, feeling very much like it was a normal thing these days to have a man in her bed. He had made it seem that way. Definitely gave them something to build upon. She hoped he liked waffles with real maple syrup and bacon.

When her cell phone buzzed, Annette lifted it from the

soapstone countertop and saw that the caller was her nonbi-
ological first cousin, Gavin Lynley. She accepted the video
chat request. He appeared and she took in his handsome
rectangular face. Biracial and two years her senior, Gavin
was gray-eyed and had short, jet-black hair in a lineup cut
and a five-o'clock shadow beard.

"Hey, stranger," she said, smiling.

"Hey, Detective," he tossed back at her. "What's up?"

"You tell me." Annette narrowed her eyes teasingly. "Can
we expect you at the family Christmas gathering or not?"

"Yeah," he promised. "Wouldn't miss it."

"Well, good." She grinned. "Lots to catch up on."

"Looking forward to it." Gavin angled his face slightly.
"So, what's the latest on the serial killer investigation I've
been hearing about?"

"I'll need to get back to you on that," Annette told him,
realizing it would take more time than she had right now.
Not to mention, she would rather there was more definitive
info to share later. "And then you can also fill me in on the
latest from a special agent."

"Deal," he said understandingly. "Catch you soon."

They said their goodbyes and she disconnected, just as
Hamilton walked into the kitchen, fully dressed. "Good
morning," she told him with a smile.

"Morning, beautiful." He walked up to her and gave her
a kiss. "Who was on the phone?" he asked curiously.

"My cousin Gavin. The one I told you worked in corrections."

"Ah." Hamilton nodded. "So, guess I'll have to pass mus-
ter with your large family when all is said and done, huh?"

Annette chuckled. "I don't know about all that," she half
joked. "But I'm sure they'll like you and vice versa."

"Good." He grabbed a slice of bacon and bit into it. "I think you've already won over Maureen."

She lifted a brow. "Is that so?"

"Don't seem so surprised." He laughed. "My sister's always had good instincts, for the most part. In this case, she sees you as a really good catch. And I agree."

Annette blushed. "That works both ways. I see the same in you and I'm glad Maureen can appreciate what I bring to the table," she added gratefully.

"Speaking of which, feel free to bring those waffles to the table whenever you're ready," he said jovially.

"Coming right up." She lifted a steaming waffle and put it on a plate. "You can get your own coffee."

He grinned. "Will do."

HAMILTON FELT THAT things were starting to heat up with Annette. Spending the night at her house was certainly a step up the ladder. Now she wanted to see where he lived and he was more than happy to oblige. If things continued to move in the right direction, they might eventually need to decide where to live together and under what circumstances. He felt this was the right time in his life to think in those terms with this person. And even if he had to fight his way through Annette's siblings and other relatives to win her heart, Hamilton was more than ready to duke it out and win.

But right now, both he and Annette were on the case in trying to put this serial killer investigation to rest. With another victim added to the Christmas Lights Killer's list, it was obvious to Hamilton that they were dealing with a monster of the worst kind, one who was seemingly itching to continue targeting women in Carol Creek throughout the holiday season and likely into the new year.

Hamilton was parked along the side of the road, looking for violators of the state's Move Over Slow Down Law, designed to protect emergency and highway workers from harm. He hoped drivers behaved themselves this morning. His thoughts were interrupted by a call from another ISP member on the Christmas Lights Killer task force, Kendre Fitzgerald, who had been studying surveillance videos at retailers across the state in search of buyers of Christmas string lights in the past few months.

"McCade," he said.

"Hey, I found something that you may want to see."

"Okay."

"It's security camera footage from a store in Indianapolis taken in mid-November," she said. "I'm sending it to you now."

Hamilton opened his tablet and received the video footage. It showed a slender, dark-haired man who looked to be in his early thirties, purchasing two or three sets of indoor Christmas string lights. And using cash to pay for it. Nothing suspicious in that, per se. But something about the man rubbed Hamilton the wrong way.

"What do you think?" Kendre asked eagerly.

"I'm thinking that the customer is rather suspicious," he responded honestly. Hamilton zoomed in on the man's face. Though this made the face grainier, there was an air of familiarity about it that he couldn't miss. If this was their unsub, the timeline for purchasing the indoor string lights would fit. This was before the serial killings began. And buying the lights outside of Carol Creek, or Fort Wayne for that matter, would make sense, too. This would make it harder to connect the dots in identifying the perp. "Find out everything you can about this buyer," Hamilton told her.

"And double-check other stores between Indianapolis and Fort Wayne to see if the same customer shows up on sur-veillance video purchasing Christmas string lights. If so, maybe he used a credit card for some buys."

"I'll get right on it," Kendre told him.

"Thanks, and good work," Hamilton commended her before disconnecting. He took a second look at the video footage and again wondered if he could have seen the cus-tomer before somewhere. And if this could actually be their serial killer.

ANNETTE AND WILL went to an address on Cetona Way, whose occupant, a woman named Vera Cardwell, was listed as the registered owner of a black Ford Bronco Sport Big Bend with Goodyear Wrangler Fortitude HT tires. They walked up the path toward the colonial-style home, when Annette noted the white Lincoln Nautilus parked in the driveway. It made her wonder if the Ford Bronco they had come in search of could have been sold or replaced.

She rang the bell and the door opened a crack. A slen-der, elderly woman, wearing square glasses over blue eyes, peeked out and said cautiously, "May I help you?"

Annette held her badge up to where she could see it. "De-tective Lynley, and this is Detective Hossack of the Sher-iff's Department. Are you Vera Cardwell?"

"Yes."

"We need to ask you some questions regarding the Ford Bronco Sport Big Bend registered to you."

Vera considered this for a moment or two before open-ing the door and inviting them inside. Annette took a quick glance around the gray-carpeted living room. It was full of contemporary furnishings and decorated for the holidays, including a northern white cedar Christmas tree. She faced the homeowner, who had an ash-blond layered bob, and was leaning on an aluminum walking cane.

Vera seemed ill at ease. "What about my Bronco?"

"Do you still have it?" Annette inquired.

"Yes, though I rarely use it anymore. Mind telling me what's going on here?"

Will stepped forward. "We're investigating some recent homicides," he spoke candidly. "We have reason to believe that the person responsible was driving a vehicle with the type of Goodyear tires you have. All we're doing here is going down the line of anyone owning such a vehicle for the process of elimination. No big deal," he tried to say as though true.

Annette jumped in again. "You said you rarely drive your Ford Bronco." She assumed this was due to Vera driving the Lincoln instead. "Does anyone else drive it?"

"Only my grandson, on occasion," she replied unevenly.

"Does your grandson live with you?"

"No. I've lived alone since my husband, Henry, died. Mack has his own apartment. Sometimes he'll drive the Bronco when his own car is giving him problems. Or when he's running an errand for me."

"His name is Mack?" Will asked.

"Yes. Mack Cardwell."

"How old is Mack?" Annette asked in a friendly voice.

"Thirty-two," Vera replied.

Annette pondered that for a moment and asked, "Where is the car now?"

"In the garage. It's too cold to keep it out during the winter months."

Will raised a brow. "Mind if we have a look?"

Vera nodded. "The garage is right through that door," she said, pointing to a door in a hallway off the kitchen. "I don't think you'll find what you're looking for, though. Mack's a good boy and wouldn't hurt anyone."

That's what they all say, Annette thought. Until proven otherwise. "Hope you're right about that," she told her sincerely.

Annette and Will stepped into the garage, turning on the light. A vehicle was hidden beneath a black waterproof car cover. Will put on nitrile gloves and lifted the cover, revealing the Ford Bronco Sport Big Bend. "Wonder why he felt the need to cover it in a garage?"

"Hmm…" Annette asked herself the same question, even while knowing there was nothing suspicious about someone wanting to protect a car and keep the dust off even indoors. There was no outer sign of damage to the vehicle. She studied the tires. Though they displayed the typical dirt and grime from driving, there was nothing that drew red flags.

Will, who had opened the passenger-side door, said, "Take a look at this."

Annette looked inside and saw a tiny spot on the front seat that looked like it could be blood. Had a passenger bled? Under what circumstances? "Could be blood," she said what they both were thinking. But they had no grounds at present to have it tested. Other than that, the inside front and back of the car looked pristine, as though it had been cleaned purposely. So, what was the story on the grandson anyway? Should he be considered a suspect? Or were they getting ahead of themselves? "Put the cover back on the vehicle," she told Will. "It'll keep it protected in case we need to come back later for forensic testing."

They went back inside, where Vera was now sitting

tensely on a rocker recliner. Annette asked her, "When was the last time your grandson drove the Bronco?"

"Two or three days ago, I think." Vera squirmed. "Mack's never been in any trouble," she insisted. "Since his girl-friend left him last year, all he's wanted to do was put the past behind him and make a better life for himself with someone else."

Annette knew all about sour relationships and moving on, having done so with Hamilton, and she couldn't be more excited about the prospects for where this could go. But not all people dealt with broken relationships the same way. Could Mack Cardwell have been on some sort of warped, murderous revenge crusade? "We're going to need to speak with your grandson," she told Vera. "Once we've done so, we'll be able to cross your vehicle off the list." Annette hoped that would be enough to alleviate the concerns of the grandmother. At least till they could officially eliminate Cardwell as a suspect.

Twenty minutes later, Annette and Will drove to an apartment complex called Crow's Village on Wailby Crest Lane in the adjacent town of Laraville in Dabs County. They went up to the second-story unit where Mack Cardwell lived.

"Sheriff's Department," Will yelled, knocking on the door.

After a couple of more knocks and hearing no sounds coming from within, Annette surmised, "I don't think he's here."

Will frowned. "Too bad. I'd love to hear what Cardwell has to say. Or not."

"Me, too." She took out a pen and her detective's card and wrote a note to the suspect on the back that he needed to get in touch with her as soon as possible. She stuck the card inside the door and thought, *If you have nothing to hide, I'll hear from you shortly.* "Let's go," she told Will.

He nodded and knocked one more time on Cardwell's door for effect, and muttered, "I have a feeling we may need to come back here."

As she mulled that over, Annette's cell phone rang. She removed it from the pocket of her leather jacket and answered, "Lynley."

It was Detective Charisma Robinson on the other end. "We've had another woman attacked," she said shakily.

"Oh no…" Annette eyed Will, with the worst-case scenario playing on her mind. "Is she—?"

"The victim's still alive," Charisma responded. "She's been taken to Carol Creek General."

"We're on our way." Annette disconnected and faced Will. "It looks like he has struck again." Will muttered an expletive under his breath. "But the victim has survived, though I have no idea what kind of shape she's in."

Still, it gave Annette a glimmer of hope that the woman would pull through and be able to assist them. She phoned Hamilton to update him on the latest news.

Chapter Fifteen

When he got word that another woman had been targeted and had apparently lived to talk about it, Hamilton headed straight for the hospital. The fact that the serial killer seemed to be picking up the pace was troubling, to say the least. He was getting desperate to go after anyone who crossed his path, making him all the more dangerous.

At Carol Creek General on Femmore Avenue, Hamilton raced inside and spotted Annette, Will and Charisma converged in the lobby. Walking up to them, Hamilton said, "Any word on the victim?"

"She's being treated by a doctor, but is expected to pull through with little more than a mild concussion and a few bumps and bruises," Annette said, relief crossing her face. "The mental trauma of going through something like that is another matter altogether."

Hamilton concurred. "What do we know about her?"

"The victim's name is Gemma Jeong," Charisma said. "She's a twenty-nine-year-old graphic artist, married to an estate planning attorney named Remy Jeong, and the mother of two children."

"How did she manage to escape the killer?" Will asked.

"Good question. Haven't had the chance to ask her yet."

"We should know soon enough." Annette sighed. "I think we can all agree that surviving a serial killer, if in fact that's what this was, is a miracle in and of itself."

Hamilton nodded and couldn't help but think about Juliet, who hadn't been able to wrest herself from harm's way. He would give anything to have had that happen, but it wasn't meant to be. But she could rest in peace more comfortably once her killer was put away for good. "I have other news," he told them. "Some surveillance video has been accessed by an ISP investigator that shows a suspect purchasing Christmas string lights at an Indianapolis store."

Annette's eyes widened. "You think he could be the guy?"

"Yes, it's possible, given that he was purchasing more than one set and the date of purchase was just before the murders began." Hamilton shifted his feet. "More than that, I think I recognize the image of the buyer as someone I stopped recently for having a misplaced license plate in his car window."

"We have a possible lead, too," Annette informed him. "Will and I went to talk to the owner of a Ford Bronco Sport Big Bend with Goodyear Wrangler Fortitude HT tires. She said that it's driven mostly by her thirty-two-year-old grandson, including apparently driving the vehicle the night Lucy Beecham was murdered."

Will gritted his teeth. "We dropped by his apartment, but he wasn't there."

"What's his name?" Hamilton asked.

Annette answered, "Mack Cardwell."

"He's the same person—Mack Anthony Cardwell—I stopped recently on the road in Fort Wayne," Hamilton told them. "I'm almost certain he's the one on the video footage at the Indianapolis store."

"What kind of car was he driving when you pulled him over?" Will asked.

Hamilton furrowed his brow. "Actually, it was a Dodge Challenger," he almost hated to say.

Annette wrinkled her nose. "So, not the Ford Bronco?"

"Afraid not." He considered this discrepancy. "Doesn't mean that Cardwell couldn't have still switched from one vehicle to another to suit his purposes or as a cover."

"Anything's possible at this point," Charisma muttered.

"Guess we need to see what Gemma Jeong has to say and if she can identify her assailant," Annette said.

"Yeah." Hamilton prepared himself for disappointment, but his gut instincts told him that there may be something to the belief that Mack Anthony Cardwell was up to no good and could well be the devious serial killer.

WHEN THEY WERE able to speak directly with Gemma Jeong, the doctor only allowed two people in the room at a time, apart from Gemma's husband, Remy. As lead investigator, Annette went in, with Hamilton joining her.

Gemma, a slender, attractive Asian woman, was half sitting up in the bed. She had shoulder-length, wavy brown hair and dark brown eyes. Considering her ordeal, Annette thought that the graphic artist looked pretty good physically. Remy, who was tall, lean, and looked to be thirtysomething, had black hair in a spiky cut. He was holding her hand.

Though Annette wished she didn't have to cut in on the couple's loving moment, now was the time to hear what she could tell them, when the victim's mind was freshest. "Mrs. Jeong, I'm Detective Lynley with the sheriff's office," she said, showing her badge. "This is State Trooper McCade. We'd like to ask you a few questions about what happened."

Remy frowned. "Can't this wait?"

"We wish it could, but someone apparently tried to kill your wife," Hamilton responded brusquely. "No guarantee he won't try again as long as he remains on the loose."

"I'll talk to them," Gemma said. "This needs to be done" she told her husband. "If there's anything I can do to get that creep off the streets, I want to do it."

Remy relented. "Try to keep it brief."

"We will." Annette glanced at Hamilton and turned back to the victim. "Can you tell us what happened?"

Gemma sucked in a deep breath and said, "At just after eleven, I left my shop on Owen Point Drive to go to lunch. I was about to get into my car, when seemingly out of nowhere, this man is standing there. He asked me for directions and as I was trying to give them, he was suddenly holding some Christmas string lights. He told me he was going to strangle me with them and that I shouldn't fight it."

"But you did?" Hamilton prompted her.

"Yes, my first instincts were to scratch his face. I tried, but only managed to scrape my fingers across his neck. It was enough to draw blood." She sighed. "He called me a bitch and seemed enraged, hitting me and shoving me to the ground. He was about to put the string lights around my neck, but when a security guard came into the lot and yelled at the man to stop, he took off and got away. I called 911 and was taken to the hospital."

Annette locked eyes with Hamilton in this remarkable story of survival against the odds. "We need to get the statement of the security guard," she told her.

Gemma nodded. "His name is Nestor Bedelia. He gave

me his cell phone number and is waiting to hear from you."
Her eyes watered. "He saved my life."

As Hamilton got Bedelia's number, Annette asked
Gemma, "Do you happen to know if the attacker got into a
vehicle after running off?"

"I couldn't say. I was too shaken up to notice."

Annette knew that the unsub couldn't have been driving
the Ford Bronco Sport Big Bend that seemed to be tied to at
least two of the earlier attacks, given that the car was still
inside Vera Cardwell's garage when the attack occurred.
Meaning if her grandson was the culprit here, he would
have either been on foot or was driving another vehicle for
his getaway car. "Had you ever seen your attacker before?"

Gemma rubbed her hand and Annette could see what
appeared to be dried blood beneath two of her long fingernails, likely from scratching the unsub. "Not that I can recall." Gemma paused. "It's possible, though, since we get
people in and out of the shop all the time. Or it could have
been elsewhere."

"Can you describe him?" Hamilton asked.

"Yes. He was tall—maybe six feet—and somewhat slight
in build." Gemma mused for a moment. "His hair was dark
and in a messy style, while short on the sides."

Annette gazed at her. "Any hair on his face?"

"Yes, he had a short beard."

Annette looked at Hamilton and this seemed to register
with him. "Do you happen to remember the type of clothing he was wearing?"

"Didn't really focus on that," Gemma admitted. "But
I think he had on a dark jacket, jeans, and maybe tennis
shoes."

"If it's all right with you," Annette told her, "we'd like to get a sketch artist in here to help you flush out a few more details on your attacker that can help us track him down."

She nodded in agreement. "I'll try my best."

"And we'd also like to collect a sample of the DNA beneath your nails that I assume came from the attacker," Annette said. "That could be important in making the case against him."

"Yeah, sure." Gemma winced, as though in sudden discomfort.

Remy narrowed his eyes and said, "That's enough for now."

"Okay." Annette didn't dare press any further. They had what was needed for the time being in furthering the investigation. "Thanks for giving us your statement," she told Gemma. "We'll try to get the man who attacked you."

Gemma wiped away tears. "Hope so."

Once they were out of the room, Annette regarded Hamilton and asked, "What do you think?"

"Her description seems to fit Mack Cardwell's appearance. We'll need to see what the sketch artist can produce."

"And see if the DNA the assailant left is a match for the DNA collected from the strands of hair from two of the other murders," she said thoughtfully.

"I think we need to pay Cardwell another visit," Will said. "See if he'll talk and provide a DNA sample voluntarily."

Charisma rolled her eyes. "Good luck with that. If Cardwell is guilty, he's not likely to be very cooperative."

Annette was inclined to agree. They would need to be prepared to get a search warrant to collect any potential evidence needed against Cardwell. Assuming he remained a viable suspect after the sketch artist's drawing and the forensic evidence from Gemma Jeong was analyzed. Otherwise, the onus would be on them to track down the culprit elsewhere.

They learned that the doctor intended to keep Gemma in the hospital overnight as a precaution. With her assailant still at large, Annette was taking no chances with her safety even at the hospital, given the perp's hunger for killing and winning. "I want a deputy stationed outside this room," she told everyone, "and even at Gemma's house, as long as the suspect is on the loose. As the only living witness who can identify him, apart from possibly the security guard, the perp may stop at nothing to make certain that doesn't happen."

"I'll get the deputy here and notify the staff as well to be on the lookout for anyone suspicious," Will assured her.

"And I'll make sure that forensics gets the unsub's DNA," Charisma said, running a hand through her hair. "I'm pretty sure that we're looking at the same DNA profile in the database. We just need to see if we can line it up with the latest suspect."

It was something very much on Annette's mind, too. If they could tie this to Mack Cardwell, then there would be nowhere he could hide before they brought him in and held him accountable as a serial killer.

LATER, HAMILTON SAT in Annette's office as they reviewed the case and latest turn of events. Both were gratified that whoever attacked Gemma Jeong had failed to kill her and would never be given the chance to do so again. The question remained in Hamilton's mind, who was the unsub and presumed serial killer? He had strong suspicions about the man's identity, but needed solid evidence to back this up.

When Jenn Eugenio walked into the office, Hamilton met

the brown eyes of the thirtysomething forensic artist, who was petite and had black hair with brown highlights in a short and straight style. She was carrying her drawing tablet. Offering him and Annette a smile, Jenn said, "Hey, guys."

"What do you have for us?" Hamilton asked anxiously.

"Well, I'm happy to say that the victim did a pretty good job of describing the man who attacked her, with my prodding for as many details as she could remember. Here's what we came up with."

Annette, who had been sitting at her desk, stood and walked around it so she and Hamilton could view the image at the same time. "What do you think?" she asked him curiously.

He studied the digital image that bore some resemblance to the man he knew as Mack Anthony Cardwell. "It could be Cardwell," he responded, "or someone who fits his general features, as I recall."

"That's enough justification to go on that assumption," Annette said, "when coupled with the video footage you've seen of someone fitting that description and the fact that we're still trying to make contact with Cardwell to question him about the Ford Bronco he's been driving intermittently." She eyed Jenn. "We need to get this out to all the law enforcement in the state, as well as local media. Whether the unsub is Cardwell or someone else, his image needs to be put forth as a person of interest who has to be considered armed and dangerous. Though his weapon of choice has been Christmas string lights, we have to assume he may also have a firearm in his possession."

"I'll get the ball rolling," Jenn promised. "And send you both copies of the sketch as well."

"Good work," Hamilton told her, which she acknowledged before leaving the office.

Annette's cell phone rang with a call from Kelly Okamoto, from the ISP Fort Wayne Regional Laboratory. She had put a rush on analyzing the DNA removed from underneath Gemma Jeong's nails. Annette put Kelly on speakerphone and said, "You're on speaker and I'm with Trooper Hamilton McCade. What did you find out?"

Without prelude, Kelly responded, "The analysis of the genetic material found under the victim's fingernails showed a DNA match with the forensic unknown profile connected to the hair strands collected from Juliet McCade and Lucy Beecham. Or, in other words, all three DNA samples belong to the same unsub."

In Hamilton's way of thinking, this lent itself even more strongly to the notion that Mack Anthony Cardwell was the likely perp, when tying it to the circumstantial evidence pointing in his direction. But the latest info still fell short of proving that conclusively, with nothing in CODIS to support this as Cardwell's DNA.

As though reading his mind, Kelly said flatly, "If you want to attach the DNA findings to a suspect in particular, you need to bring me his actual DNA for comparison and you'll have your answer."

"We hear you," Hamilton told her, before the conversation ended.

Afterward, Annette put her hand on his shoulder and said firmly, "We need to bring Mack Cardwell in for questioning."

"I agree," he stated, resisting the desire to touch her. "First, we have to find him."

"Beyond that, I think we have more than enough to get

a judge to sign off on a search warrant at his apartment."
She folded her arms. "If we can't get Cardwell to voluntarily hand over his DNA, we'll have to legally obtain it,
and gather any other evidence that may pertain to our investigation."

"I'm with you." Hamilton got to his feet. He wanted to
take her into his arms at that moment. But they were in duty
mode and he needed to act accordingly, hard as that was
whenever he was in her presence. "Let's go find that judge."

Chapter Sixteen

After Judge Suzanne Manaois-Seatriz approved the search warrant, Annette, Will and Hamilton went to the apartment of Mack Anthony Cardwell, accompanied by other armed law enforcement and forensic investigators. With no sign of Cardwell's black Dodge Challenger SRT Hellcat Redeye, the assumption was that he was not home, perhaps deliberately avoiding them. They knocked on the door anyhow, while Annette identified herself and others. When there was no reply, the order was given to use a Halligan bar to force the door open.

Inside, Annette held her Glock 43 9mm pistol in front of her as she stood on the laminate flooring and surveyed the two-bedroom, traditionally furnished unit. It was cluttered and reeked of the pungent scent of marijuana. On a coffee table was drug paraphernalia and what looked to be crystal methamphetamine along with a number of fentanyl pills. Strewn across a rust-colored armchair was a set of Christmas string lights resembling those used to strangle four women and also fitting the description of the lights that had been used in the attempt to strangle Gemma Jeong. Were those the very same string lights used in the crimes?

Wonder how Cardwell would care to explain himself, with

*the potentially incriminating Christmas string lights in his
home*, Annette mused with skepticism. The man was also
facing possible charges for felony drug possession.

"Clear!" Will yelled from one of the rooms after going
through the apartment.

Annette lowered her weapon and placed it back in the holster as Hamilton came up behind her and said, "Looks like
Cardwell may have been dealing drugs, at the very least."

"Or it's just the tip of the iceberg in his criminal behavior," she countered, and directed Hamilton's attention to the
chair. "Who has Christmas string lights hanging around
when the apartment is otherwise devoid of any holiday decorations? Unless Cardwell has them with another devious
purpose in mind."

"I was thinking the same thing," Hamilton said. "And
we both know what that is."

Annette nodded. "Could he have anticipated us showing up here and made sure he was nowhere to be found?"

"He may or may not be on to us, but we're definitely on
to him." Hamilton put away his SIG Sauer P227 pistol.

"Something tells me Cardwell's probably already figured
that out," she hated to say, "whether tipped off intentionally
or inadvertently by his grandmother, Vera Cardwell. Or his
own instincts in believing he's smarter than us."

"Not even close." Hamilton's brows lowered. "He's simply been luckier than us. Till now, that is. If Cardwell's
who we believe him to be, his DNA will corroborate this
and we'll have him dead to rights as the Christmas Lights
Killer."

"That would certainly be the best gift any of us could
have," Annette contended. Short of Hamilton giving her

the gift of his love and wanting them to become official as a couple. Or was that asking too much of him? Or herself?

He flashed her a look. "You've got that right."

Loretta Covington approached them, coming out of the bathroom. "I have what we need to get the suspect's DNA," the forensic analyst said. Wearing latex gloves, she was holding a plastic evidence bag. "A toothbrush, razor and some hair samples he left in a filthy sink."

"Good." Annette smiled at her. "If Mack Cardwell has something to hide, this would likely blow that out of the water."

"That's what I'm hoping for." Loretta nodded.

"Let's get it to the crime lab ASAP," Hamilton said with urgency. "We need to know, like yesterday, if Cardwell's DNA matches the blood Gemma Jeong got from her attacker when she scratched him."

Not to mention, the hair removed from Juliet's mouth, Annette told herself, reading Hamilton's mind. As well as a second hair linked to the same unsub. The clock was ticking and they all felt the pressure to wrap up this case with an arrest that could stand up.

HAMILTON INVITED ANNETTE over to his house while they waited for word on the DNA results. Neither was making any predictions, even if both were optimistic that Cardwell's DNA profile would be a match with the unsub's and prove to be the ammunition they needed to bring him in.

In the interim, Hamilton was happy to show Annette that she was more than welcome to spend as much time at his place as she wanted. Hell, if he had his way, she could just move right in with him. Or would he need to go even further in demonstrating how much she meant to him? Did she feel the same level of commitment?

"I love your house," she commented, favoring him with a generous smile.

"Glad you like it," he said sincerely.

"Hope to spend more time here."

"I hope so, too."

She moved up to him. "You sure I wouldn't be cramping your style as a single man?"

"Positive." He grinned, but became serious again. "Besides, who says I'm a single man? On the contrary, I'm pretty much spoken for these days."

"Is that so?" Annette lifted her face toward his tantalizingly. "So, who's the lucky lady?"

Hamilton held her chin. "I think you know the answer to that." But in case she didn't, he gave her a nice kiss, so as to leave no doubt. "It could only be you."

She licked her lips and giggled. "Just checking."

"No problem," he said, keeping his arousal in check.

Their banter was put on hold when Annette's cell phone rang. It was Kelly Okamoto, who asked that they come to the crime lab. "Be right there," she told her.

"This better be good," Hamilton muttered, knowing this was make-or-break point in the investigation.

Annette nodded. "We'll know soon enough."

The short drive brought them to the lab's Forensic Biology Section, where Kelly was waiting.

Impatiently, Hamilton asked her, "Well…?"

After a momentary deadpan look, the forensic scientist broke into a smile and responded, "It's a match! Mack Anthony Cardwell's DNA is an exact match for the other three DNA samples analyzed."

"I knew it!" Annette exclaimed gleefully.

"I strongly suspected as much," Hamilton agreed. "Cardwell is the Christmas Lights Killer."

"His reign of terror is about to end," Annette declared.

"Glad the lab was able to connect the forensic dots," Kelly told them.

"Me, too." Hamilton grinned. "Now we just need to finish this, once and for all."

"Right," Annette concurred, "before Cardwell can turn his deadly attention to someone else."

A BOLO WAS issued for Mack Anthony Cardwell, and the serial killer suspect's black Dodge Challenger SRT Hellcat Redeye, as well as a warrant to impound his grandmother's black Ford Bronco Sport Big Bend for to examine for forensic evidence that it was used to commit criminal activity pertaining to the investigation. Cardwell was considered armed and definitely dangerous. Annette certainly believed this to be the case and wouldn't put anything past the killer at this point. He obviously thought this could go on forever, no matter how many dead bodies he left in his wake. Well, his days of freedom to hunt and kill as he pleased were over.

Annette felt confident that the suspect would be picked up at anytime now. While awaiting word, she headed home from the sheriff's office, having already made plans to spend the night at Hamilton's house. They intended to make dinner together again. Perhaps beef lasagna and a garden salad. Only this time, in his kitchen, where he got to call the shots. Well, maybe they would have to negotiate on that. In her mind, just being with the man was more than enough to give and take a little. That was how it was supposed to be with couples who were in love.

Wait, did I just say I'm in love? Annette asked herself. Or, better yet, that it went both ways? She flushed at the notion and was hopeful at the same time that this was real between them. And that when this serial killer business was behind them, they could work more on each other and give what they had a real go.

That made her think about Christmas and her family reunion. Should she invite Hamilton? Or would that be inappropriate and insensitive due to his recent loss? But Maureen had taken her own holiday away from Carol Creek, as part of moving on with her life. Shouldn't Hamilton be entitled to do the same thing? *I'd love to introduce him to my siblings and cousin*, Annette thought. It was a big step, but worth it for someone she had really fallen for and seemed to be reciprocating her feelings in full measure.

Annette pulled into her driveway. She grabbed her shoulder tote containing some information pertaining to the investigation and headed inside the house. After turning on the lights, she set the tote on a table, pulled off her ankle booties and headed into the kitchen. There, she removed her firearm, laying it on the countertop for now. She would put it back in its holster to take with her to Hamilton's place, just to be on the safe side, after changing clothes.

Taking a bottle of red wine out of the refrigerator, Annette poured herself half a glass and went upstairs, where she took out her cell phone and gave her brother Russell a call. She owed him one, as they had limited themselves to texting of late, with each caught up in their own worlds. "Hey," she said.

"Annette." She could hear his voice perk up. "You better not be calling to say there's a last-minute change of plans for Christmas?"

She laughed. "Not in the way you think."

"Enlighten me."

Now was as good a time as any to mention she was seeing someone, Annette told herself, taking a sip of the wine. "I'm thinking about bringing someone to the family gathering."

"Hmm..." Russell hummed. "It wouldn't happen to be the state trooper Madison said you had the hots for, would it?"

I'm going to kill her, Annette thought playfully, while admiring her sister for interpreting correctly something that she had wisely picked up on. "I was supposed to spread the word when I was ready to," she complained nonetheless.

"Hey, don't blame me for Madison's inability to keep from reading the tea leaves and relating this in her own humorous way."

Annette couldn't help but chuckle at this, knowing her sister was well-intentioned. "Guess the cat's out of the bag."

"Guess it is. Or should I say, he is." Russell laughed. "In any event, I look forward to meeting him and introducing him to Rosamund."

"I want that, too," Annette admitted. But first Hamilton had to agree to it. She heard a faint sound downstairs, but couldn't figure out what it was. Or where it was coming from. A gust of wintry wind perhaps? Could she have forgotten to lock the door? It was probably nothing to concern herself with, but she should check it out anyway. "Let me call you back," she cut through Russell's easygoing chatter.

"Sure." He paused. "Everything okay?"

"Yeah, everything's fine." She saw no reason to worry him unnecessarily. Or herself, for that matter. After disconnecting, Annette headed down the stairs. Feeling tense for some reason, she went toward the front door and saw that it was locked. It hadn't slipped her mind after all. She let down her guard, but then heard another sound. It seemed to be coming from the kitchen area.

Annette stepped into the kitchen and, startled, dropped the glass of wine to the floor when she saw a man standing there. It took only an instant to realize it was the man they had fingered as the Christmas Lights Killer.

Mack Anthony Cardwell.

HAMILTON WAS DRIVING when he received word that Mack Cardwell's Dodge Challenger was found abandoned on Atmore Avenue in Carol Creek, not far from Creekside Park.

"Looks like he ditched the car in a hurry," Will commented through the speakerphone, "by the haphazard way it was parked. We have all available units in the area searching for him."

"Cardwell may try to access his grandmother's Ford Bronco," Hamilton said, assuming it hadn't already been seized as evidence in a homicide investigation. "Or he may be holed up at her place. Wouldn't even put it past Cardwell to hold her hostage, if it came down to using her as a bargaining chip to try to cut a deal to get himself out of this mess."

"I was thinking the same thing. Deputies have been dispatched to her house, even as we speak."

Hamilton wasn't satisfied that this would do the trick against an unpredictable and deadly foe. "I'm heading over there myself," he said. "At the very least, I'd like to talk to the grandmother, see what she knows, if anything. And when she knew it. As long as Cardwell remains on the lam, nothing's out of bounds as to what he might do next."

"That's true," Will said. "I'll contact Annette and let her know where things stand."

"Okay." Hamilton disconnected. He remembered that they had dinner plans at his house for this evening and more. He knew that Annette had also expected Cardwell to be picked up in short order, putting an end to his reign of Christmastime terror in the town. Maybe that would still be the case and they could continue their own agenda accordingly. But if Cardwell was able to somehow elude the dragnet they had out for him, then none of them would be able to rest easily. Much less enjoy the holiday season to the fullest.

I'll fill Annette in on any details I get as soon as I have them, Hamilton told himself. And if he found that Mack Anthony Cardwell was actually at the grandmother's house, Hamilton would make sure that, as the lead investigator on the case, Annette was in on any action that resulted in the murder suspect's apprehension or otherwise being neutralized as a threat.

When he arrived at the home of Vera Cardwell, Hamilton spotted two squad cars from the sheriff's department. He exited his own vehicle and walked up to Deputies Michael Jorgenson and Andy Stackhouse. "Trooper McCade," Hamilton identified himself, flashing his badge at the thirtysomething deputies, both around his own height. "What do we have here?"

"We went through the house and perimeter," Stackhouse informed him. "No sign of the suspect."

"What about the garage?" Hamilton asked keenly.

"Empty," Jorgenson replied. "According to the suspect's grandmother, Vera Cardwell, he took the Ford Bronco less than an hour ago."

Hamilton frowned. He had suspected this was a possibility once Cardwell dumped his own car. They needed to double down on their efforts to locate the Bronco. "Is the grandmother inside?" he asked.

Stackhouse nodded. "Yeah. She's still trying to process what's going on."

"I need to have a word with her." Hamilton glanced at the deputies and down the street in both directions. "Keep an eye out for any possible sighting of Cardwell," he told them. "He might show up here again, if all else fails."

"We're not going anywhere," Jorgenson said, having already been given orders to stay put and safeguard the property that had now become part of a criminal investigation.

Hamilton rang the bell and the door opened. "Vera Cardwell?" he asked of the rather fragile-looking woman who appeared to be in her seventies and was holding a cane. She acknowledged this. "State Trooper McCade. May I come in?" She nodded silently and let him through. He took a glance around before homing in on a sofa. "Why don't we sit down?" he asked, wanting to make her comfortable. She followed his lead and sat beside him on the sofa, leaning the cane against it. Not wanting to beat around the bush, Hamilton said with an edge to his tone, as though she was clueless, "Your grandson, Mack, is in big trouble."

Vera's voice shook as she responded, "I'm not really sure what to say. Or even think, for that matter. This whole thing has been quite overwhelming."

"For everyone." Hamilton touched the brim of his campaign hat. "Do you have any idea why Mack would resort to murdering women?" He was aware that serial homicides were often rooted in something beyond the mere sport of killing. Or outright insanity, which he was pretty sure didn't apply here, given Cardwell's shrewdness and ability to perpetrate the murders successfully in a relatively short period of time by serial killer standards, while evading capture.

"Not at all." Vera frowned thoughtfully. "Truthfully, I'm having a hard time wrapping my mind around the things he's been accused of. This is so unlike Mack."

You clearly have no idea what he's like, Hamilton mused sadly. At least since he'd turned into a killing machine. "Was there anything in his background that might have led to this?"

She sat back, pondering. "Mack had a pretty normal childhood." Vera paused. "His parents divorced when he was still a preteen. That didn't go over very well with him, but he seemed to get over it. Same when his father, my son, Jeremy, died in a boating accident and his mother, Irene, remarried."

"What about relationships?" Hamilton pressed. "Has Mack had any recent breakups that left him bitter toward women, especially related to the Christmas season?" This seemed like something worth asking, as Hamilton understood that some serial killers targeting certain victims at a specific time were triggered by personal experiences that fueled their homicidal tendencies.

Vera wrung her hands. "Mack's girlfriend, Tricia Laborte, left him last Christmas for a man she met online. She moved to Australia and never really gave him an opportunity to win her back or adjust properly to the breakup." Vera's body quavered. "I thought he had overcome his disappointment. Now I wonder…"

I wonder, too, if this sent him over the edge once Christmas came around again and Tricia had moved on to greener pastures, Hamilton told himself. He peered at Vera. "We need to find your grandson before anyone else gets hurt. Including him."

"I know." She sucked in a deep breath. "I don't want anything bad to happen to Mack," she stressed. "I have no idea where he's gone."

Hamilton's mouth became a straight line. "Did he mention anything at all to you that might be a clue?"

Vera's features strained. "He did say that a detective left her card at his apartment, wanting to speak with him."

"What detective?" Warning bells went off in Hamilton's head like sirens as he recalled Annette and Will paying her a visit.

"The one who dropped by earlier to look at my Ford Bronco's tires. Detective Lynley."

Hamilton's shoulders slumped. He sensed that a desperate and cunning Mack Cardwell might actually make a play for Annette. He got to his feet and told Vera sharply, "If Mack contacts you by any means, tell him he needs to turn himself in immediately!"

"I will," she promised him.

Outside, Hamilton updated the deputies and then got on his cell phone to call Annette and warn her about Cardwell. When she didn't pick up, he texted her. Then he called Will and was told that he, too, had been unable to reach Annette. Both agreed that she might be in danger and Hamilton arranged to meet Will at her house, while dispatching other law enforcement there as backup.

Inside his car, Hamilton contacted the Indiana State Police Special Operations Command and requested the use of its Emergency Response Team and Patrol K-9s to assist in the search for Cardwell. Starting with the neighborhood where Annette lived, in case the suspect had yet to go after her by breaking into her house or in case they had a potential hostage situation on their hands. Or worse.

As he raced there himself, all Hamilton could think of was that he had fallen in love with Annette and she needed to know this. He would be damned if he allowed a serial killer to come between them and the bright future Hamilton hoped to build with the detective well beyond the holidays.

Chapter Seventeen

How did you get in here? Annette asked in her head. Had she forgotten to lock the door after all? She eyed her Glock 43 9mm pistol on the countertop. It was closer to him than her, but deciding that the element of surprise might give her the advantage in getting to it before him, she went for the weapon. But Mack Anthony Cardwell seemed to anticipate this and was lightning-quick in grabbing the firearm just before she could. He pointed it at her and said bellicosely, "Back up, Detective Lynley. Otherwise, I'll have to pull the trigger and forever mar that beautiful face of yours."

Realizing that he had her at a huge disadvantage, Annette complied and took a couple of anxious steps backward. Studying the man, she saw that he was taller than her and of slender build. His face was more triangular shaped than the digital sketch and his blue eyes a little wider-spaced and shifty. The black, short-sided hair was messy and the chinstrap beard not her cup of tea. He was dressed in all-dark clothing, from the pullover hoodie to the chino pants to the rugged cap-toe boots. She couldn't help but detect the noticeable scratch on his neck. *Bet I know where that came from*, she thought, recalling the DNA obtained from material Gemma Jeong had managed to gather beneath her fingernails after scratching her attacker.

Annette wondered if Hamilton, who was supposed to be picking her up later, had any idea that the wanted killer was standing in her house at that very moment. Or was this a fight she would be forced to engage in on her own?

"You know, you really should have invested in a good security system," Cardwell said with a sardonic chuckle.

Now you tell me, she mused humorlessly. When coming to Carol Creek, Annette had mistakenly thought she had left behind big-city crime. As such, she hadn't been in a hurry to have a security system installed. Her bad. Regarding her unwanted houseguest intently, Annette asked coolly, playing dumb, "Who are you and what are you doing in my house?"

Cardwell laughed. "I think you know exactly who I am, Detective, and probably have a pretty good idea why I'm here. After all, it's your sheriff's department that has a BOLO out on me and my face plastered everywhere for everyone to see. Thanks, undoubtedly, to that graphic artist bitch who got lucky and survived her date with death."

"All right, you've got me. I know who you are, Mack Anthony Cardwell," Annette came clean, seeing no reason for pretense at this point. "So, what are you doing in my house?" she demanded, as though it wasn't obvious that he intended to shoot her with her own gun. Or did he have something else in mind, considering his preferred method of murdering women was by ligature strangulation?

"I'm here by invitation, sort of." Cardwell grinned with amusement. "If I'm not mistaken, you left me your card, Detective Lynley, and asked me to get in touch. So, here I am, at your service. Don't blame me if I chose to meet on my terms and not yours." He laughed in an irritating way.

Biting her tongue, Annette forced herself to try and remain calm, so as to not provoke him just yet. "All right, you have my attention, Mack," she said, choosing to speak to him as though they were friendly acquaintances. "Are you here to give yourself up peacefully, so no harm comes to you? I can make sure that no one lays a finger on you and that you're given a fair shake while going through the system."

"Oh, really?" He kept the gun aimed squarely at her face. "And why would you do that?"

"Because everyone deserves to be treated fairly, no matter what he or she might have done," Annette replied unperturbedly. "It's no different with you, no matter what you've done." That hardly meant he should be treated with kid gloves. Like any other killer, he needed to spend the rest of his natural life behind bars and face all the discomfort that came with it. That was assuming he was able to avoid the death penalty in the state of Indiana for his capital offenses.

"Thanks, but no thanks." Cardwell snickered. "I didn't come here to turn myself in, Detective. Or maybe I should call you Annette." He laughed. "I'm afraid, it's too late for that." His eyes narrowed menacingly. "I came for you. In the living room," he demanded. "Now! Or I'll shoot you where you stand."

Unwilling to put that threat to the test, Annette had second thoughts about trying to grab the eight-inch chef's knife that she hadn't had time to wash and put away this morning and that now lay on the counter, near the sink. No, she had to be smart about this. As long as he was holding all the cards—or at least a lethal weapon, her own—she needed to play along for now. "Okay, okay, I'm going," she snorted. "Please don't shoot me."

"Good girl." Cardwell directed her toward the beige, round sofa chair. "Sit," he ordered.

Annette complied, as he kept some distance between them. "So, why the Christmas string lights to kill the women?" she asked, hoping to keep him talking. Like so many demented, overconfident killers, he probably liked to jabber on about himself. At this stage, buying time was her best weapon against the creep.

"Good question." He gave a short laugh. "To make a long story short, I'm taking out on other women the fact that my ex-girlfriend dumped me last December for someone from Australia who she met on a dating site. The Christmas string lights somehow seemed fitting, considering they reminded me of the note she left for me to find that was stuck to the string lights on our tree." He snickered. "Some Merry Christmas to me, huh?"

That explains why, warped as it sounds, he's strangling to death women this month, Annette thought. "Not to seem too analytical or heartless, but if you had such a problem with your ex, why not go after her instead of killing innocent women?"

"Well, truth be told, Tricia moved Down Under—too far away to go after," Cardwell responded tartly. "I couldn't leave my grandmother behind to fend for herself. Not the way my father did when he got drunk and stupidly killed himself in a boating accident, giving my mother a good excuse to jump ship, so to speak, in turning her back on me when she remarried. So, yeah, turns out my ex got lucky and others had to pay the price in her place. But don't worry, her day will come."

"Really?" Annette was weighing how to get him to put down the gun so his advantage would fall apart.

"Yeah. Once I'm done here, I think I'll head to Australia and take care of her."

"You really think that's possible?" she questioned. "You're wanted by every law enforcement officer in the state and beyond. There's no escaping to Australia or anywhere else. My advice to you, Mack, is to let me go, give yourself up, and this thing can end peacefully."

Cardwell gave a wicked laugh. "Afraid it's not going to end peacefully for you." He put the gun in one pocket of his hoodie and removed a string of Christmas lights from the other. "You're about to become my going-away present to Carol Creek. Once I claim you as the final and most prized victim of the Christmas Lights Killer, strangling you with the lights in my hand, I'll use your car to make my escape and work my way to Mexico and eventually Sydney, Australia, where Tricia has set up shop and foolishly believes she is beyond my reach."

Annette watched as he approached her. Her brothers had always told her that the element of surprise was her best defense against an arrogant attacker. *Let's see if that's true*, she told herself, realizing it was either now or never.

While pretending she had surrendered to her fate, Annette waited till he was within feet of her, before she lunged at him, putting all her weight into it as she pressed hard against Cardwell. The momentum forced them both onto the floor, with her on top of him. She rammed her forehead against the bridge of his nose, drawing blood. He bellowed from the pain, releasing the Christmas string lights. He was distracted enough that she was able to grab her Glock pistol from his pocket and roll off him in one motion.

It wasn't until she'd gotten to her feet on wobbly legs, with every intention of shooting the serial killer, if necessary, that Annette grasped that he had managed to empty the six-round magazine and remove the round that had been in the chamber. Cardwell had shaken off the fall and nose butt and risen nearly as quickly, and was once again in possession of the string lights.

"Nice try, Detective," he said, wincing while his nose bled. "I anticipated you might try something stupid and planned for it. While you were upstairs, I took the liberty of emptying the gun of its bullets, in case it fell into your hands and left me in a world of trouble." He chuckled and stretched out the string lights, moved quickly toward her, and gloated, "Now it's time for you to die by strangulation, just like the others."

She found herself backed into a corner, quite literally. Her heart pounded rapidly as she contemplated her next move, short of being strangled to death.

It was minutes earlier that Hamilton spotted the Ford Bronco Sport Big Bend that was registered to Vera Cardwell parked down the street from Annette's house. He tensed at the thought that what he'd feared had come true. Mack Anthony Cardwell had targeted Annette to kill. Hamilton tried texting her again and got no response. That told him she was in trouble and needed his help in a hurry.

He got on the phone with Will. "The Ford Bronco is on Annette's street. I think he may be at her house."

"Cardwell's inside," Will confirmed. "So is Annette. I just got here and can see them both in the living room window. The SWAT team will be on scene at any moment."

"So will I," Hamilton informed him and pulled up behind the detective's blue Chrysler 300 sedan. He got out and rendezvoused with Will just outside the house. "What's happening in there?" Hamilton asked anxiously, his own view blocked.

"Cardwell's pointing a weapon at Annette, who's sitting down," Will told him. "They're talking. I'm sure Annette is playing for time while looking to get out of the dire situation."

Hamilton needed to see for himself. He peeked through the window and his heart skipped a beat as he watched his true love at the mercy of the lunatic serial killer. But judging by Cardwell's body language and loose handling of the weapon, which looked like Annette's Glock 43, Hamilton deduced that it wasn't his intent to shoot her to death. Instead, the gun was meant to keep her in fear till he killed her with his weapon of choice. Christmas string lights. *I can't let it get to that point*, he thought, pulse racing rapidly.

Working his way to the front of the house, Hamilton moved onto the porch quietly and tried to open the door. But it was locked. He guessed that Annette may have locked it after Cardwell had already entered the house. Trying to break the door open would only alert the killer, giving him every reason to finish what he'd started. *I have to be smart about his*, Hamilton told himself. Annette's life depended on it.

He rejoined Will and said, "Why don't you check around back and see if there's another entry point. I'll keep an eye on them and stop Cardwell any way I have to."

Will nodded. "Okay."

Hamilton found his way to the window again and peered through the glass. Annette appeared to be calm, in spite of Cardwell having her at a disadvantage. When the serial killer suddenly put away the firearm and took out what looked to be Christmas string lights, it was obvious to Hamilton that the perp was about to make his move. Pulling out his own SIG Sauer P227 pistol, Hamilton took aim squarely at Cardwell, when Annette suddenly charged at Cardwell like a battering ram. Or a woman hell-bent on going on the offensive against her determined assailant. She knocked them both to the floor, falling atop Cardwell, and then gave him a solid headbutt to the nose.

Just like that, Annette had gotten ahold of her Glock and was aiming it at Cardwell. Hamilton knew that she only wanted to hold him at bay till help arrived. Only, it quickly became apparent that the gun was empty. Cardwell had obviously and cleverly removed the bullets and was now back on his feet in a snap, with a bloody nose, the Christmas string lights in hand, and coming after Annette with a fury. *Damned if I let him hurt one pretty hair on her head*, Hamilton thought doggedly. He took steady aim at Cardwell and fired a single shot through the window. It shattered glass, and tore through the assailant's shoulder.

As Cardwell reacted, Will entered the picture, gun aimed at the killer, and demanded that he surrender. Instead, Cardwell removed from inside his hoodie what looked to be a Smith & Wesson .38 Special +P revolver and pointed it at Will, who took him out.

Hamilton raced around to the front door, which Will had opened, and went inside. Once the threat had been neutralized, he put away his weapon and ran into the arms of Annette, embracing her. "Did he hurt you?"

"No," she said, her voice shaking. "But not from lack of trying."

Hamilton eyed the fallen suspect, then Will. "Is he…?"

"Cardwell's dead," Will said. "He won't hurt anyone ever again."

Hamilton gazed at Annette, who was still in his arms. "I should have guessed sooner that Cardwell might make a play for you."

"There was no way any of us could have known that," she responded. "Cardwell was a loose cannon who had some crazy idea that he could strangle me and then fly off to Australia to kill his ex-girlfriend."

"That was certifiably crazy," Hamilton agreed. He remembered what he had been most afraid of: losing Annette before he told her how he truly felt. "I'm in love with you, Annette."

Will lifted a brow. "Say what?"

"We've been seeing each other," Hamilton confessed.

"Like you hadn't already figured that out," Annette quipped.

Will laughed. "Hard to keep many secrets in a small town. Especially when it's been as obvious as the nose on my face that you two had the hots for each other."

"Guilty as charged." Annette chuckled. "And, just to be clear, I've fallen in love with you, too, Hamilton."

He nearly melted, hearing those magical words. "Music to my ears."

"While you two sing sweet lullabies, I'll call this in," Will said.

Hamilton laughed. "You do that. And I'll do this…" He laid a kiss on Annette's lips, soaking in the moment where the future suddenly seemed a lot brighter, with a serial killer no longer able to come between them.

THE NEXT DAY, Annette still felt relief at having escaped from the clutches of Mack Anthony Cardwell with her life. Even better, she was in love with a handsome state trooper who'd finally professed to loving her in kind. It surely had provided them a gateway to the future that she couldn't wait to embark upon. Wherever this journey took them. But right now, she was on her way to Sheriff Teixeira's office, having been summoned for a final wrap-up of the Christmas Lights Killer case.

Will was already there when she walked in. Annette got a wink from him and wondered if he had spilled the beans to the sheriff about her new love interest.

"There you are," Teixeira said, smiling from his desk.

"Sheriff," she said evenly.

"Now that I have you both here, I just wanted to commend you for your work in bringing the Christmas Lights Killer investigation to a close. You two deserve a medal for ending this reign of terror on Carol Creek. And so does Trooper Hamilton McCade."

"Only doing our job, sir," Annette stressed politely.

"That's what I told him," Will said. "We do whatever's needed to accomplish the objectives of the sheriff's department. Stopping Mack Cardwell was just part of the process."

"Be that as it may," Teixeira told them, "we'll all sleep a lot better now with the serial killer no longer a threat."

"Agreed," Annette had to say.

"Have a Merry Christmas and all that," the sheriff said, before dismissing them.

Outside Annette's office, Will commented, "So, you're off to Oklahoma for the holidays, huh?"

"Yes." She was excited to see everyone again.

"And are you bringing Hamilton along for the ride?"

She pondered the question. "We'll see how that goes. Hopefully well." She smiled. "Merry Christmas, Will."

"You, too." He grinned and headed to his office. Annette

knew he had plans to spend the holidays with his latest girl-friend, a flight attendant.

She grabbed her handbag from her office and went home, remembering she had some packing to do.

"JULIET'S KILLER IS DEAD" Hamilton told Maureen in a cell phone video chat, while in his official vehicle.

Her face lit up. "Seriously?"

"Yep. We got him last night, after he tried to kill Annette."

"Wow." Maureen's brow creased. "Is she okay?"

"She is now." Hamilton grinned. "I told Annette I loved her. Turns out, she loves me, too."

"That's great." She beamed. "I'm so happy for you two."

"As you said, we both deserve to be happy. Maybe something good is coming out of Juliet's death for you and me."

"True." Maureen smiled thoughtfully. "She'll always be with us."

"I agree."

"Enjoy your holiday, Hamilton."

"You, too," he said sincerely.

After signing off, Hamilton reflected upon his good fortune in meeting Annette and what came next for them. He was giddy at the possibilities. When his cell phone rang, he put it on speakerphone. "McCade."

Lieutenant Tony Wilson, his district commander, said, "Hey, McCade. I wanted you to hear this from me first…"

"Uh-oh…" Hamilton was half kidding, but also concerned that his job aspirations had hit a roadblock.

"You got the promotion," Wilson said excitedly. "Just came in. You've been promoted to the Special Investigations Section's Organized Crime and Corruption Unit, effective at the start of the new year."

"I don't know what to say," Hamilton said humbly, though he wanted to shout his enthusiasm from the rooftop.

"Your excellent work has spoken volumes for you, McCade. Believe me, I'm going to hate to lose you. But I know you'll thrive with your new assignment. You'll be reporting to Evelyn Guerrero. Good luck."

"Thank you, sir." Hamilton wished him a Merry Christmas and headed for Carol Creek, eager to share the news with Annette.

"THAT'S WONDERFUL!" Annette gave him a toothy grin as they sat in her living room. "Congratulations!" She knew how much Hamilton wanted the promotion.

He smiled generously. "It was a long time coming, but worth the wait."

"Some things are."

"True enough."

She gazed into his eyes, believing this was a good time to bring up the family reunion. "How do you feel about spending Christmas in Oklahoma City?"

Hamilton cocked a brow. "Is that an invitation to crash your party?"

Annette laughed. "I wouldn't call it crashing. But it is definitely an invitation. I'd love to have you there and show off my good-looking trooper to the family."

"As it is, I was going to ask if you wouldn't mind if I tagged along to Oklahoma for the holidays," he said. "Now that I know, the answer is yes, I'd be delighted to come and get to know your siblings, cousins and anyone else near and dear to your heart."

"No one is as near and dear to my heart as you," Annette had to put out there, knowing that he meant the world to her.

Hamilton blushed and put his arm around her shoulders. "I feel the same way. In fact, so much so that I hope to be able to accompany you to Oklahoma City as your fiancé."

"What are you saying?" she asked, holding his gaze.

"I'm saying that I'd like to take our love to the next level by getting married." His voice cracked. "Will you marry me, Annette Lynley, and make me the happiest man in the world? I realize we haven't known each other that long, but some things you just know feel right. So why wait, if you'll have me…"

Annette put her hands to her mouth, not having seen this coming. At least not before the year was through. "Yes, Hamilton McCade," she told him in the sincerest way possible. "No reason for delaying this moment in time. I would be elated to marry you and become your wife. And, whenever you're ready, the mother of your children."

"Then we're now officially engaged. With the ring coming just as soon as I can get it." His teeth shone brightly. "In the interim, this show of affection for my commitment to you will have to suffice."

With that, Hamilton laid a passionate kiss on her that left Annette seeing stars and counting the days till she was Mrs. Annette McCade.

Epilogue

With the infamous Christmas Lights Killer case put to bed and callous serial monster Mack Anthony Cardwell no longer able to target women, Hamilton welcomed the opportunity to spend time with Annette and her family in Oklahoma City for the holidays, prior to becoming an investigator with the Indiana State Police Special Investigations Section's Organized Crime and Corruption Unit. He'd gotten word that his duties would include, among other things, investigating organized crime with financial motives, political corruption and official misconduct by police officers. He would even be called upon to assist task forces in apprehending serial killers and other serial offenders around the state and elsewhere. He was more than ready to embark on this new direction in his ISP career, while leaving his days as a state trooper behind him.

But he was even more excited that Annette had let him into her life and given him the opportunity to find true, lasting love and build a relationship and family with. That included the extended family who came with the territory in linking with the Lynleys. Even if Juliet would never get to experience this kinship and loyalty, Hamilton was sure that her presence would always be felt in the building of bridges and the children he and Annette hoped to bring into this world.

"Go big or go home, right?" Hamilton joked after getting his first look at the massive two-story residence on Plum Hollow Drive that Annette and her siblings co-owned, courtesy of their late parents. Sitting on a couple of acres of prime real estate, it seemed to have all the bells and whistles, including a winding creek and a Roman-style swimming pool. The outside had all the traditional Christmas decorations and more. *They really went all out*, he thought, impressed. "Your family compound is a sight to behold!"

Annette laughed. "Mom and Dad worked hard and invested wisely along the way to be able to afford and spoil us with this house when I was growing up."

"I can see that." He could also see the value of keeping the property for the current and future generations of the family. Hamilton took in more of the place with its natural lighting through floor-to-ceiling windows, chef's kitchen, and a blend of antique and modern furnishings. A giant loblolly pine Christmas tree sat in the formal living room, fully decorated with lights, tinsel and ornaments. Loads of wrapped gifts sat beneath it in a scene that seemed to Hamilton to be straight out of a family holiday movie.

"Let me show you the rest of the place," Annette said eagerly.

Hamilton chuckled. "You mean there's more?" he asked, teasing her.

"We're just getting started," she replied with a cute grin.

"Oh, really?" He allowed her to take him by the hand and they headed across the hardwood flooring, went up the three-quarter-turn staircase, saw more neatly appointed rooms and went back down to the main floor, before Hamilton asked the obvious question, considering the various vehicles he'd seen parked in the circular driveway, "Where is everyone?"

"Good question. You'll see." Annette flashed her teeth mysteriously. "Come with me…"

Still holding hands, they made their way down a long hallway to closed double sliding doors. They opened the doors and stepped into an Edwardian drawing room with elegant antique furniture. Hamilton immediately broke into a grin as he saw a group of smiling people gathered around an enormous blue spruce tree, again completely decorated for Christmas. They had apparently planned to stay put and allow them this grand entrance as the newest couple and last of the family to arrive.

"Hey, everyone!" Annette uttered jubilantly. She was responded to in kind, before she continued, "I'd like to introduce you to my handsome fiancé, Indiana state trooper and very soon-to-be detective, Hamilton McCade."

"Merry Christmas, Hamilton," the group sang in unison as they gathered around the couple, first embracing Annette affectionately.

Hamilton grinned broadly. "Merry Christmas." He shook hands with the handsome and fit Lynley men and was hugged by the lovely, vivacious and equally fit Lynley women. It became abundantly clear to him that he was a welcome addition to the family. And for that, and being able to take the next big steps in his personal life as a devoted husband and father-to-be, Hamilton felt eternally grateful and ready as he'd ever been to fill those shoes.

AFTER THE WHIRLWIND family gathering, in which Annette couldn't have been more pleased at how well Hamilton was able to blend right in and was equally accepted as someone worthy of her love and commitment, they spent New Year's Eve at his cabin. He had thrown logs into the fireplace and built a fire. The blinds were open and they got to see the moon shining brilliantly on Lake Kankiki.

Annette was already thinking of ways to redecorate the cabin and make a retreat that was a reflection of both of their unique styles. *I have some great plans for this place*, she told herself. Hamilton was entirely receptive to the idea, wanting to make her happy. Which she wanted for him in return. They were even considering whether or not to make the wonderful lakefront property their full-time base of operations upon deciding where to live together. Especially once they brought into the picture children who could benefit from all the great water activities that would be available throughout the year. But that would be up for discussion later, once the demands of their respective careers were sorted out.

For now, Annette was more than happy to be engaged to the man beside her, who had his arm looped around her waist, holding her close lovingly. *If you never want to let me go, I'm good with that*, she told herself, feeling just as smitten with him. "I'm so glad we get to ring in the new year together," Annette cooed.

"Me, too," Hamilton told her. "Even better will be ringing in the next year and the one after that and the one after that, and so on and so forth."

"You'll get no argument from me there." She imagined the day when their children would be gathered around them on such merry occasions. And maybe even their siblings and their children. And they could start the new year in different locations each year. How great would that be?

"Good. Because there's still one more thing left to do to make things between us official," Hamilton said, an intriguing catch to his voice.

"What might that be?" Annette looked up at him curiously.

"Oh, just a little something I picked up that I thought you might like to have." He removed his arm from around her and pulled a small box out of the pocket of his pants. He opened it to reveal a ring inside that he held up for her. "This is for you, my darling. I couldn't let the year pass us by without giving you the engagement ring you deserve as a prelude to the wedding ring, in making you my bride for a lifetime."

With hands to her mouth in shock, Annette took the ring from him. She would've been content to wait till he had more time. She gazed at the multi-diamond ring in 10 karat white gold. "This is gorgeous," she marveled.

"It'll look even more gorgeous on your finger, trust me," he told her. "Allow me…"

Hamilton took the ring and slid it on the fourth finger of her left hand. Annette lifted it up and watched as the diamonds sparkled. "You're right, it's beautiful," she gushed.

"So are you." Hamilton took her hand and kissed it sweetly in a continental manner. "I love you, Annette."

"I love you more, Hamilton," she said back to him, knowing that their love was equal in every way and promised a bright tomorrow.

"Shall we seal the deal properly?" he asked in a heartfelt tone.

"Absolutely." Her teeth shone. "Seal the deal as much as you like."

Hamilton angled his face and kissed her, this time solidly

on the lips. Annette kissed him back just as passionately as the new year came in with a real bang and the rest of their lives began to take shape.

* * * * *

BODYGUARD MOST WANTED

KATHERINE GARBERA

This one is for Donna and Scott Scamehorn, who are always living their best lives and helping us to do the same whenever we are with them. Love you!

Chapter One

Nicholas DeVere was used to seeing his name in the head-lines—The Golden Prince Found Dead at Debauched Beach-side Party. Not the most flattering of headlines, and the truth was, Nick wasn't used to being proclaimed dead. "Nice to see something can still surprise me."

"Surprise you?" Finnian Walsh asked under his breath. His assistant had close-cropped, thick brown hair and was always perfectly groomed. "Please tell me you have a plan to deal with this. The cops think it was murder," he said.

"Breathe, Finn. It's not a big deal," Nick said, projecting a calmness he was used to faking. His tie felt too tight as he considered the news story. He thought it was murder as well.

The first attempt on his life had happened when he'd been only six months old. Since then he'd been kidnapped, blackmailed, and had his vehicles tampered with—more than once. He'd kind of become nonplussed by attempts on his life. But even he had to admit that having his body-guard and lookalike Jack Ingram murdered…well, it was giving him pause.

The loss of so many people he'd known in his life was taking a toll. He'd reached his limit. He was going to prove that someone had been trying to kill him and he was going to catch them before someone else died.

Finn threw his hands up and walked out of his office. Only to return a moment later. "I get that you think you can't die, but those of us who love you wish you'd treat your life with more care."

"I know," he said to Finn's back as he paced in front of the desk.

Nick either had to take himself out of the spotlight, re-nounce his place in the DeVere family and disappear...or put an end to this. The cops were, of course, treating this case like it was their top priority. Given the massive for-tune that he was due to inherit when his father died, it made sense. But Nick had never been one to sit and wait. With his resources, he had a better chance of finding the killer before the overworked and understaffed police department. "I'm not as blasé as I seem. The board of DeVere Indus-tries has insisted on a new bodyguard and security team, and I agreed."

"You agreed?" Finn said.

"I thought that would make you happy."

Finn shook his head as he walked over to Nick, putting the back of his hand to Nick's forehead. "You're not run-ning a fever, so we can rule out delusional."

"You know I don't keep you around for your wit," Nick said dryly.

"You wound me," Finn said. "When you get all agree-able, it makes me suspicious. You only tolerated having Jack as your bodyguard because he looked like you and would handle public events you didn't want to attend."

"Which is no longer an option," Nick said. "I intend to find Jack's killer—"

"What are you, Sherlock Holmes now?" Finn asked sardonically.

"Worried you might have to be Watson?"

"No, I'm much more a Mycroft."

To be fair, his assistant was right about Sherlock's older brother, the mastermind. Finn had a way of organizing and manipulating everyone around him to make things happen. Despite the gravity of the day, Nick smiled. "There weren't a lot of people who knew I'd be in Malibu last night. There were even fewer who knew the security code to the mansion. So, the list of possible killers has to be small."

"Aren't the police working the case?" Finn asked, sitting down in the leather guest chair across from him, casually crossing his legs. He'd been with Nick since prep school and balanced him out.

"Yes. But they want to write it off as a drunken accident. It's only the fact that security system had been disarmed and the cameras turned off that are being forced to investigate further. We both know that Jack would never drink too much to stumble and fall off the balcony."

"Indeed. Especially when he had the twins in his bed," Finn said. "So, when are we meeting the new bodyguard?"

"In an hour. I need the conference room set up. The board and I negotiated, and we agreed they'd hire the company who would comprise the new security team, and I'd pick someone from the group to be my new bodyguard."

Finn pulled his smartphone from his pocket. "What's the company name?"

"Price Security," Nick said.

He heard Finn's fingers tapping as he did an internet search. Nick had done his own as soon as he'd been informed. DeVere Industries was much more than his family's legacy. He'd taken an active role in running and expanding the company since his father's cancer had returned and the old man had to stay at home. He knew how much this legacy meant to his father, and as contentious as their relationship could be at times, he was determined to keep the company thriving as his father would have.

The Price Security website gave away very little. Just the logo and a contact form. And the tagline *Security is priceless, and your life is worth the price.*

He had no idea what they were dealing with.

"I'll dig deeper. I think I've heard of this Giovanni Price, the owner. An hour isn't a lot of time. I'll have Hazel set up the conference room while I prepare some information for you," Finn said, already walking out of his office.

"Thanks."

Finn waved and closed the door behind him as he left. Nick got up and looked out his penthouse office window toward downtown Los Angeles. The board wasn't a fan of the fact that he'd refused to move to their tech campus in Northern California, but instead had stayed in his offices above his nightclub, Madness. Nick hadn't been willing to compromise on this. He was preserving his family's legacy, not sacrificing his lifestyle.

But now…

He wasn't sure that Jack would have been safer in Silicon Valley. He felt Jack's death deeply, not just because they'd been friends, but also because Jack had died in his place. How many more deaths could he take?

He put his hand against the glass window and lowered

his head. He wouldn't ever let anyone see this side of himself. Grief swamped him and he mourned his friend for a moment.

He didn't dwell on it. The only way out of grief was motion. He needed to find out who'd killed Jack so he could bring his own form of justice, and then maybe that mark on his soul wouldn't feel as heavy.

But he knew from the past that it would.

He straightened and looked down at the streets, but in his mind, he wondered who he'd pissed off and why they were coming after him. He dealt in favors now; spread his wealth around him to create the illusion that his life had some higher meaning.

Had someone seen behind the façade? Was that why Jack had been attacked and killed?

He didn't have the answer yet, but he wouldn't stop until the killer was found. Nothing was going to stand in his way. Not the DeVere Industries board, his father, or anyone from Price Security.

LUNA URBAN WAS exhausted when she walked out of the international terminal at LAX. She looked for the familiar black Dodge sitting at the curb, blatantly waiting in the no parking zone for her. She would never admit it out loud, but every single time she returned from a trip, she held her breath as she stepped out of the airport. Giovanni—Van— had never let her down, but a part of her…never could quite believe that he'd be there. He was leaning against the passenger's-side door, talking to the airport security guard.

He wore a Dolce & Gabbana suit that had been custom made to fit his large muscly frame. He was bald and had a tattoo on his neck of angel's wings. He took off his sunglasses when he saw her approaching and left the security guard to turn and smile at her.

"Welcome home, Luna. We missed you. I was afraid that Jaz wasn't going to let you come back to us," Van said in his low, gravelly voice as he opened his arms.

Luna stepped closer to hug him. Price Security was more than a business. As Van liked to say, they were family. The group of misfits that no one wanted, but somehow Van had shaped them into a working team.

"Yeah. Me too," she said. She'd been working as the bodyguard to famed teen rap sensation Jaz. His tour in South America had just wrapped up and she'd spent the night partying with him and his entourage before getting on the flight to LA. "It was fun, but the kid knew I'd cramp his style if I stuck around."

"Keeping him alive isn't cramping his style."

She agreed, but Jaz was young and felt like he couldn't die, so he liked to take risks. And now that the tour was over and he was going back home, her contract was up.

"I hate to do this to you, Luna..." Van started. "But we have a new client and I need all hands at his place in less than two hours."

"Even me?"

"Especially you. The contract said everyone on the team, and they are paying us a bonus," he said. "Have you had a chance to catch up on the blast that Lee sent out?"

"No. Don't glare at me. I'm hung over and jet-lagged. Most people wouldn't even be lucid right now. I'll read the blast while you drive. What's the dress code?"

"D&G, like me. The entire team is getting ready at the tower. We'll go over in the Hummer limo."

Who was the new client Van was pulling out the flashy

labels and big guns for? She opened her email. The words were blurry at first and she had to force herself to concentrate just to read them. Billionaire playboy whose bodyguard died after falling off a balcony… and, at first, they'd thought it was the billionaire himself who'd died.

"Okay. So why me? If he doesn't want Kenji, he's an idiot."

"I agree, but he didn't hire us, the board of DeVere Industries did. And he made some deal with them that he could meet all of the staff and choose his bodyguard."

"You agreed to that?" Van made the decisions on all assignments. He might be pretending to play nice with this billionaire, but Luna knew in the end Van wouldn't budge if he felt the guy made the wrong choice.

"They are offering an insane amount of money for something that should be a cakewalk. Which is making the back of my neck itchy."

But it couldn't be a cakewalk if they were offering that much dough. "What gives?"

"It's Nicholas DeVere."

Oh.

Superrich. Like probably more than a billionaire. His family was famed for its wealth and tragedy. His mom had died in a car crash when Nicholas was only six months old. His cousins and uncles had died in a yacht bombing somewhere in Asia; Nicholas had been partying on shore at the time. He was infamous for escaping death.

Looked like he'd done it again.

NICK WASN'T SURE what he was expecting from the brief notes he'd read on each security agent, but walking into the conference room and seeing five people all dressed in black suits standing in a group wasn't it. There was Xander Quentin, tall and menacing, he was a big behemoth of a man and stood at the back. He had thick black hair that curled around his collar. Then there was Kenji Wada the Japanese American bodyguard the board heavily favored. He was tall; not as large as the behemoth, but still big. He was lean and had a thick fall of jet black bangs that dropped over one of his eyes.

Next was the leader—Giovanni Price. Not as tall as the other two, he exuded a strong aura of menace, even with the angel's wings tattoo peeking over the collar of his white dress shirt. He was bald, clean-shaven, and his eyes, when he noticed Nick, seemed to bore straight through him.

None of them would do. He wanted someone whose loyalty would be to him. A bodyguard he could manipulate to go along with whatever he asked. That left Rick Stone, the stoner in the corner, who looked like he was going through withdrawal, and the woman, Luna Urban, the only team member he couldn't see. Where was she?

He finally spotted her in the shadow of the big guy. She wore her brown hair pulled back in a tight ponytail. She had high cheekbones and a pert nose. Her eyes, when she met his stare, were direct, giving nothing away. He let his gaze drift lower, but the suit gave her an air of androgyny. It was well fitted, and as she stood next to the men, she didn't stand out. In fact, it was almost as if she were trying to blend in and not be seen.

"Thank you all for coming," he said. "I'm Nicholas De-Vere, but then you probably recognize me."

"Should we?" the behemoth said in a crisp British accent.

Nick didn't answer, just gestured toward the large conference table. "Have a seat. Can we get you anything to drink?"

They all moved to the big leather chairs that were dotted around table as Hazel entered. His admin assistant was in her sixties but, trim and fit, appeared younger. She had short blond hair that she wore in a pixie cut. She looked at the serious group and then back at him as if she wasn't sure what to do. He nodded slightly toward the beverages and she smiled.

She went around the table, getting drinks for them. Everyone asked for water except the stoner, who wanted a Fanta. Hazel left as Finn joined them.

"I'm Finn Walsh. I believe we spoke on the phone, Mr. Price," Finn said, going over to offer his hand to Giovanni Price.

The man shook it. "We did. Nice to meet in person."

Price's voice was low, with a rough quality to it. Nick had a feeling it was the kind of voice that could be heard through a crowd. But Price knew how to control it. Nick could tell by looking at him that the man could control almost anything if he wanted to.

"Nice to meet you, as well," Finn said, taking a seat next to Nick and setting down his notepad so he could read it.

Rick Stone will be the easiest to manage. The girl seems like trouble.

They were all deadly serious, and Nick had the feeling that it was going to be difficult to manipulate anyone he chose.

Price cracked his knuckles and then put his hands on the table in front of him. "From our perspective, this job would entail twenty-four-seven detail. I think we are looking for four-days-on, three-days-off shifts so we might—"

"No," Nick said. "I want one guard with me all the time. No days off."

Price leaned back in his chair, crossing his massive arms over his chest. "Why don't you tell us a little about yourself?"

"Nicholas DeVere, only son and heir of Emmett DeVere. I own the nightclub Madness and am known for being a generous man."

"If that's the case, then why did someone try to kill you?"

He stopped and looked down the table at the woman. Luna. She met his gaze squarely and didn't blink or move. He had the feeling she was looking for something in his face, but he already knew she'd be disappointed. No one ever found what they wanted with him, other than money.

"Good question. Perhaps I'm not as charming as I like to think I am."

"Fair point," Price said. "Why are we here?"

"The board will force me to go on leave if I don't have a bodyguard," Nick said. "We are at a critical point with the negotiations on some new contracts, and me stepping out of the way would serve certain parties. I'm not interested in that, so I've agreed to their terms. Also, I won't give the bastard who killed Jack the satisfaction of thinking they have driven me into hiding."

Finn pulled his notepad back and, out of the corner of his eye; Nick noticed his assistant was writing. He ignored it. This was the story he was going with. He wasn't interested in debating the kind of bodyguard he'd accept. Either Price and his team would agree to his terms or Nick would go it alone.

And he really wanted to go it alone. He wasn't about to risk any more lives or waste any more time.

Chapter Two

Something wasn't right here, but Luna wasn't sure what. Spoiled rich men didn't usually try to keep her from doing her job. Normally they were all bravado and then cowered as she took control. But Nick wasn't fitting the profile she'd expected. She had to admit she was dog-tired and not as sharp as usual, but something was off. She ran over the information she'd been given in the car on the ride over. Nick DeVere's doppelganger victim—Jack Ingram—had been his bodyguard for almost three years.

That was a long time. And as much as they were supposed to buy into his whole "rich guy with no real cares" persona, she could sense there was more at play here. She stood while Van let Nick sweat under the weight of his stare—but Nick wasn't sweating. He was cool. Like someone who wanted something and had nothing to lose.

It was a dangerous combination. She knew it, and she suspected that Van knew it too. It might help if DeVere knew that Van had known Ingram. But there hadn't been an opportunity to talk.

Luna wanted to shake her head as she realized the problem. There was too much testosterone in this room. Those two were both used to being the alpha, and neither was going to back down.

There was more to DeVere than met the eye. The file she'd read had mentioned his preference for providing favors to everyday people who crossed his path. He was known as Midas or the Golden Prince in the media. But he wasn't greedy. He spread his fortune around wherever he went.

What was she missing?

She walked over to the large plate-glass windows that overlooked the other buildings in this area of downtown LA. There were a few Art Deco buildings and then some newer less distinct ones. The neighborhood wasn't gentrified yet, but she could see it slowly happening.

There was a glint as she scanned the rooftops. She double-checked it and then launched herself across the table at Nick DeVere just as he stood to say something to Van.

A second later, a bullet hit the glass with a loud sound. Kenji responded to her movements and turned into a shooter's stance, pulling his SIG from his coat pocket. Then he noted the bulletproof glass.

Rick was on his feet and out the door in a flash.

Luna knew the glass wouldn't shatter, but with the rush of adrenaline going through her, she barely registered it. Hitting Nick with her full body weight and knocking him to the floor, she used the momentum to roll him underneath her.

He put his arms around her and tried to roll to cover her, which she countered by staying on top of him. She felt the coiled energy; he was going to try again.

"Stay," she said, forcefully pushing his shoulder as he made to move.

"You're exposed."

"That's my job," she reminded him.

His assistant hit the floor and crawled over to where they were as more shots hit the glass. She wondered if the shooter intended to shatter it, but it would take at least fifty rounds to do that. Luna glanced up into DeVere's icy blue eyes. His strong jaw was locked, and he looked angry. She glanced over at his assistant and saw a mélange of emotions moving across the other man's face. Finn was in love, or at least in deep affection, with his boss.

Luna wanted to get back into the mix, to help the team, but she knew she couldn't leave DeVere until the shooting stopped.

"Someone really wants you dead," she said.

"Or maybe they don't like my windows," he retorted.

"Perhaps. But two tries in as many days...who'd you piss off?"

"I told you, people like me."

There was a humph from his assistant and Luna turned to look at the other man. "He's got enemies?"

"Well, there's—"

"Finn."

Finn arched both eyebrows and sort of shrugged his head. "Not everyone is happy. That's all I'm saying."

Luna put her hand in the middle of DeVere's chest, lifting her head so they were more eye to eye. "It's easier if we have a list of suspects. The cops will run it, but they are always understaffed. Any ideas who might be coming for you? You mentioned—"

"There's a firefight going on. Shouldn't you be concerned with that?"

"I'm guarding you," she said. "And gathering intel. Trust me, DeVere. I'm good at my job."

The bullets stopped.

"Get off of me," Nick said, sitting up with her on his chest and setting her aside. He stood and turned to face the room. "What the hell is going on?"

"Someone is trying to kill you," Luna said.

"Well, they aren't very good, are they?" he sneered. She could tell he was rattled, but only because of the sharp way he'd straightened his tie despite being so at ease earlier.

"They missed on purpose. That was just to rattle you," Van said.

"They'll have to try harder."

"That's not the right reaction," Luna said.

"If I cowered every time someone threatened me, I'd have never left my childhood home. Finn, have Hazel get in touch with that detective who's investigating Jack's death. Tell her what happened."

Finn just nodded and left the room, his fingers flying over the screen of his smartphone. Luna started to follow, so she could speak to the cop herself, but Van stopped her.

"Stay here. I want you on DeVere. Xander and Kenji, go check out the rooftop and see if he left any traces. Lee reported that Rick was on foot chasing someone through the garment district."

Lee was their eyes in the sky, she stayed in the office as a rule in the command center and kept in touch with everyone. The woman was more comfortable in front of her bank of computers than she was in the field. Though she had some solid skills there as well. Van always had his earpiece in and he and Lee were always monitoring everything.

The other men left and she turned to DeVere. "You okay?"

He seemed surprised by her question as he pulled at his tie. She couldn't help but remember how solid he'd felt beneath her. "Of course."

"There's no *of course*. Despite what you said, being shot at isn't normal."

"No, it's not," he said. "After Jack's death and the media claiming it was me...well, I did suspect someone might be gunning for me, which is why I agreed to a new security team."

"Good, I'm glad to hear that." At least he had some sense that he wasn't invincible. "I'd also like to know if there are people who might want to kill you," she said.

Luna was still trying to build a profile for this client in her head. He was polished and smooth, and as the time passed from the incident, he was recovering. Actually, pretty quickly, she had to admit. She was still a bit shaken. She felt like her instincts were a little slow but put that down to the lack of sleep. It couldn't have been something she felt when her body was over Nick's.

"Do you have any rooms where you won't be a target?" Van asked, shuffling them into the hallway.

She should have gotten them out of the exposed room. She glanced at Van, but he just shook his head, which she took to mean it was not a big deal.

"I'm not sure what you mean?" Nick asked. "I doubt that the shooter will come back."

"You never know. Do you have any space without windows, and possibly only one door?" she asked. Van knew she was tired from the last gig, but she didn't want him to start coddling her or having to make excuses.

"Yes. I have a panic room up in the penthouse," Nick said.

"Okay, go up there," Van said. "Will she have a phone signal in there?"

"Yes, of course," Nick said.

"I'll ping you when you can come out."

Luna put her hand on Nick's arm and it was surprisingly muscular for a playboy. "Come on."

"Wait a minute. I'm not sure who you think is in charge here—"

"We are. We were hired to keep you alive and that's what I'm going to do. Luna, don't let him out of your sight until I say otherwise."

"No problem, boss. Mr. DeVere, lead on," she said, urging him to move. He resisted for a moment, and she thought he was going to try to go toe-to-toe with Van, but then he shrugged.

"I want to talk to the cop when she arrives. We can wait in Hazel's office. There's only one window and I'll stay back from it. I'm not a damsel who needs to cower."

"That works for me," Van said.

This job was full of twists and turns. More than she'd expected, especially with Nick's reluctance to speak…but there was a glint in DeVere's eyes that made her believe he knew more than he was telling.

FINN AND HAZEL were both standing in the far corner of her office when he walked in. Nick doubted that the shooter was still anywhere around, but he could appreciate the Price Security team's caution. The board had really done a good job in selecting them.

His phone rang and he answered it without a thought. He wasn't under lockdown even though Van seemed to think he was in charge.

"DeVere."

"Nicky! Thank God. I just saw the news," Verity Vaughn said. She was his ex-wife, but they'd always been on friendly terms. "I'm so sorry about Jack."

"Thank you, Verity. I'll let you know when the funeral is."

"Oh, of course, also where to send flowers…actually, do you want me to take care of all of that for you?" she asked.

"Um, why?" he countered. Verity wasn't normally one to volunteer to do anything for anyone else.

"I need a favor," she said, that pouty note in her voice.

Nick could picture her sitting at her writing desk, dressed in white and making a list of possible things she could offer to get him to help her out.

"What kind of favor?"

"Just a teensy one. Have you heard that Hugh is leaving me?"

"No, I heard that you're leaving him," Nick said. Verity was on her third husband, and she did have a hard time sticking with one man. Rumor in their circle was that she'd found a new lover in the Caribbean and was anxious to move down there to be near him. So anything that helped Verity on her way, he was willing to do. "What do you need?"

"Thanks, Nicky, I knew you'd come through. He's insisting that we stick to the prenup and that means I can't take any of the gifts he's given me. I am sure that if you spoke to him, he'd see reason."

"Send me the list of what you want and I'll talk to him," he said. He had no doubt that Hugh wasn't heartbroken, but the man didn't like to lose.

"Thanks, darling, that's all I wanted. I'll get to work on Jack's funeral arrangements. Should I use Finn as my contact? I assume he's still by your side," she said.

"Yes."

"Great. 'Bye."

She hung up and he pocketed his phone. Turned to see

Finn shaking his head. "If you want to know someone who I don't trust...then it's her."

"Her?" Luna asked.

"Verity Vaughn. His ex. She's shady AF," Finn said.

Everyone was looking at him except Van, who was on the landline. Nick was frustrated with Luna. She was already poking into things that went beyond bodyguard duties. For his entire life everyone—from his father, to the board, to investigators he'd hired—had written off the deaths that happened around him as accidents. He'd always sensed there was more to it. Jack's death would be the last one to happen to someone he knew and cared about.

So he didn't have time for Luna Urban and her list of suspects and theories. Nick was taking action and no one, not even his hotter than expected bodyguard was going to get in his way.

He just ignored Luna; he wasn't ready to deal with everything that had been stirred up since the moment she'd launched herself across the table at him. Turning to Finn he said, "Verity will be in touch regarding Jack's funeral. She's not shady."

"Whatever you say, boss."

Finn and Verity had always had a contentious relationship, which had struck Nick as odd since they were both very similar.

He just clapped his hand on Finn's shoulder. "Thank you for dealing with this and with her."

"Of course," Finn said with a smile.

"Does she have access to your Malibu mansion?" Luna asked.

"What? Yes, but she wouldn't try to kill me," Nick said. "I'm worth more to her alive."

Luna just nodded and wrote something on her smart-phone keypad.

Hazel's phone rang and she answered it before glancing at Nick. "Sir, I have security downstairs, there's a Rick Stone and Detective Miller here to see you."

"I'll go and get them," Van said. "Luna is in charge while I'm gone. Give her anything she asks for."

The other man left and Luna pocketed her cell phone. "I'm going to need access to your files and anyone he came in contact within the last month." She directed this toward Hazel.

Hazel didn't move, just looked over at him.

He smiled at his admin assistant. She only took orders from him. "I'll approve it on an as-needed basis."

He turned to Luna and gestured for her to follow him into the hallway, where they could speak privately.

"Yes?"

"Thank you for everything you are doing, and I know you are very good at your job, but you work for me. At the end of the day, I will consider your advice for my safety but never forget that you have been hired and can be fired," Nick said.

Luna crossed her arms under her chest, pulling the expensive fabric of her suit taut against her breasts, distracting him because it contrasted with her toughness.

"Okay. As long as you remember that dead guys can't pay their bills, so I'll do whatever I deem necessary to keep you alive. And if you don't like it, then you can discuss it with E. DeVere, as he's the one who called and personally hired us."

That was something Nick hadn't realized. His father had hired this team personally? Did his dad know more about Jack's death than he'd let on? He was going to have to take a drive out to Malibu and visit the old man, but not until he got the windows replaced and dealt with Price.

"We can discuss that later. Not in front of the detective," Nick said. "That's nonnegotiable."

"Works for me," Luna said just as the elevator arrived on their floor.

Detective Miller, Van and the stoner were chatting. Seeing the other man with the security team chief and the female cop, it suddenly made sense. The stoner, aka Rick Stone, was an ex-cop. They all stopped talking as they approached.

"Mr. DeVere, are you okay?" Detective Miller asked. She was around five-five but held herself in a way that made her seem taller. She had dark curly hair that she'd pulled back into a ponytail, but a tendril had escaped to twist against her cheek. Her eyes were green and there were bags under them, as if she didn't get enough sleep.

"I'm fine. Luna and the Price team had the situation well in hand."

"Is there somewhere we can talk?" she asked.

"All of my offices have plate glass," he said. "We could talk in the nightclub. As you can guess, there're no windows and lots of seating."

"Great. Where is it exactly?" Luna asked.

"Third floor," he said. "I'll take the detective down there while you gather your troops."

Nick led the detective to the elevator. He wasn't about to allow Luna or anyone from Price to be in charge. That wasn't his way, and the further he got from the bullet incident, the angrier he was becoming. It felt like someone was toying with him. He really needed to take the time to figure out who and put an end to it.

LUNA HAD STARTED to follow Nick and Detective Miller, but Van had asked her to stay. So, she was half listening to Stone's report. It was funny how being on a case changed Rick's energy. The edgy, nervousness that had been dominant before had faded away and he radiated a calmness that came from doing what he did best.

It forced her to acknowledge that, honestly, none of them was good in interpersonal relationships as much as they tried to make them work. Each member of Price Security seemed more comfortable protecting others than they did connecting to regular people.

She didn't delve too deeply into it, bringing herself back to the job at hand. Jack Ingram's death was starting to seem to her like the opening move in a very-well-thought-out plan.

"I tailed someone with blond hair who ducked out of the building where I think the shot came from, but lost him once we got into the garment district. Not sure if he was our guy. He was carrying a gym bag and had on a baseball hat. I couldn't get close enough to stop him," Stone said.

"You're saying 'him.' Are you sure it was a man?" Luna asked, thinking of Finn's suspicions of Verity.

"No, I'm not," Rick said.

"Do you think they knew someone in the district? Did they duck into one of the stalls or shops?" Van asked.

"Probably," Stone replied. "The detective said they think this is a fluke, maybe someone who had been following the case about DeVere and wanted some notoriety. She said DeVere is insisting his bodyguard was murdered. She didn't sound like she believed it."

"Why not?" Luna asked.

"I guess there's some history there. He's been close to tragedy a lot. Detective Miller thinks it's his way of coping.

This shooter might just be someone who wants to ride on the coattails of Nick's near-death experiences."

Van shook his head. "I don't like the way Ingram died either. It was too calculated for a minor copycat criminal. Keep on it. Did you work with her beyond that?"

"No," Stone said. "I just speak cop, and they know I'm one of their kind."

Luna smiled. "That's good news for us. What do you think, Van? Is Nick making too much of the death?"

"No clue. I've asked Lee to look into it, but it might help if we had the police report too," Van said.

"I can talk to some buddies, see what I can get for us," Rick said. "Want me to skip the confab and head to the station instead?"

"Yeah. Do that. Report back to the Tower when you're done."

Stone left and Van turned to her. "DeVere is going to be difficult. There's something he's not telling us. I can feel it."

"Me too," she said. "I'm just tired and not making the right connections. Sorry I was slow in the room."

"Your slow is still faster than everyone else. I promise you'll get a solid eight hours' sleep as soon as we get out of here."

"I'll hold you to it," she said. They got on the elevator and went down to the nightclub. "When are you going to tell him you're here because of Ingram?"

"Maybe never," Van said.

She let it lie for now, but she didn't like secrets. They always led to mistrust, and DeVere was edgy as it was. But it wasn't her call. And, right now, she was happy enough to leave it be.

It was a large space with an Art Deco statue over the bar

that looked like some sort of burly imposing figure. There were sconces on the walls and DeVere and his people were all sitting at a high table in the middle of the club. The detective stood next to them, taking notes on her notepad.

Luna had to smile. Rick had mentioned that the department had been going more high tech, but a lot of the detectives preferred pen and paper. Luna did too. Her brain worked better when she had written stuff down.

"My man followed someone who might have been the shooter into the garment district."

"He told me," the detective said. "We'll look into it. We definitely want to catch whoever took the shot at you, Mr. DeVere. I think hiring Price is the right move. Just listen to them and stay quiet for the next few days."

"Quiet?" Nick asked. "I don't live a quiet life. I have a contract I'm in the middle of negotiating in Silicon Valley and a VIP event Friday night here at the club."

"You should try to postpone everything you can. Maybe have the Silicon Valley people come here and cancel the party," she said. "That will give us a chance to find the guy."

"I can move the meeting, but the VIP event is on," he said. "It's a launch party for a friend's new album and I'm hosting, so definitely not. But I'm sure Price and his team can handle it."

"Of course," Van said. "It's here?"

"Yes," Nick said, turning to Xander and Kenji as they returned.

"What did you two find?" Van asked as they approached.

"Nothing. No trace of the shooter," Xander said. "I talked to a woman who thought she saw a guy with a baseball cap go down the fire escape, but she admitted it could have been her neighbor or one of his friends."

"Same. No one saw anything, and the roof was clean on the building I checked," Kenji said.

"Who did you talk to?" Detective Miller asked.

"Just the people out front," Kenji said. "I'm not a cop, ma'am. Didn't go door-to-door or anything like that."

"I guess that's all I need for now," Detective Miller said. "I'll let you know if we find anything and vice versa, Price?"

"Sure thing. Here's my card," he said, handing it to her.

Detective Miller said her goodbyes and left. Van was talking to the team as Nick went over to Finn and Hazel. Luna followed, not liking how independent their new client was.

"Coordinate with them. Let me know if they have any demands that won't work," Nick said to his people.

He headed to the elevator.

"Hey, wait up," Luna said, catching him by the arm.

"I need to see my father; you can come with me."

He didn't wait for her to answer, just started walking toward the elevator in the back, which she realized must be his private one. Xander noticed her and tilted his head to the side in question.

"Let Van know I'm going with Mr. DeVere and I'll have my tracking app turned on so he can find me. I'll check in when we get to the senior DeVere."

"I will," Xander said.

This job was getting more out of control by the minute, and a big part of that was Nick DeVere. It was time for him to learn who was in charge. And, frankly, she was tired of him treating them like his staff. Her original impression that there was more to him than met the eye was clearly deceiving. He was coming across as a spoiled man-child who hadn't ever heard the word no.

Now he was rushing to his daddy, no doubt to complain

about his new bodyguard. She wasn't going to give him a chance to throw another tantrum. As soon as they were alone in the elevator and the car started its descent, she reached around him and pushed the stop button, turning and cornering him.

"Let's talk."

Chapter Three

Being cornered by a woman in an elevator wasn't unusual.
But Luna wasn't putting the moves on him. She held him
where he was with a grip that would be hard even for him
to break.

"What's up?" he asked dryly.

"Enough of acting like I am an inconvenience. Unless
you want to die, it's time to start appreciating why I'm here.
I'm sure it escaped your notice, but everyone on my team is
working damned hard to keep you alive. Start cooperating
or I'm going to make your life very difficult."

For a minute, all the rage and grief he felt boiled to the
surface, and he lifted her off her feet, turning so she was
pinned in the corner. He stepped in close, leaving her no
room to attack him or to force him back out of her way.

Up this close, Nick noticed that her brown eyes were actually hazel and had flecks of gold in them. She had a small
scar over her left eyebrow and her breath smelled like mint.

"I saw what you did," he said carefully. He really needed
to get away on his own. In this mood, he was dangerous,
and the last time he'd felt this way was three damned days
ago when Jack had died.

He wanted to behave in a way that he knew the DeVere

heir couldn't. He wanted to punch someone or something. Drive way too fast and see if his luck held.

He felt trapped by everything that happened in the last few days and it seemed as if the future was going to be more of the same. He had questions. He wanted answers. He had no time for Luna Urban's interrogation.

"I appreciate everything you have done for me, but at the same time, it's useless. I'm not sure if you've heard about me, but I'm bulletproof. I can't die, but that doesn't mean that people around me don't. Excuse me if I don't fall all over you and suddenly decide you and your team are my new best friends, I think we both know I'll be alive long after—"

"Stop. You're not bulletproof. You've been lucky so far. Today wasn't luck, by the way. That was me doing my job, and if I hadn't been distracted, I would have had you out of the room before that bullet hit the glass."

Distracted? He wasn't going to argue with her about his seeming good fortune when it came to dodging death. The facts spoke for themselves. But she'd been *distracted*?

"What distracted you?"

"You," she said as if she were reprimanding him. She put her hand on his chest and shoved.

He held his ground, arching one eyebrow at her. Ignoring the feel of her hand on his chest. "Was it my handsome good looks?"

"I'm being polite, but the next time I won't be."

She ignored his gibe, which he noted. He had to figure this new bodyguard out and then determine how to ditch her.

He almost smiled. Something about her was different from everyone else who had been around him. She didn't brownnose or pretend to be awed by him. She treated him… well, like he was a regular guy.

"I'd love to see that," he said, stepping aside and hitting the button to resume the motion of the elevator car. "We can talk later. I have to go and see my father."

"Why now? Are you thinking of having him fire us?"

"No. He rarely does what I tell him, but he hasn't responded like this to my other near misses... I want to know why. It might be the board footing the bill, but the old man made the call," Nick said.

"That's not odd. He is part of the board and you're his only son and heir."

She grabbed his arm as they stepped into the parking area, pulling him to a stop and positioning herself between him and the darkened garage. She put one hand under her jacket—no doubt on her gun—as she surveyed the space before she nudged him forward.

"Which car is yours?"

"All of them," he said.

"All?"

"You know they call me Midas."

"So? Midas wasn't foolish. Rushing off when someone just shot at you is. And honestly who owns this many cars?"

He almost smiled again, but then reminded himself he wasn't keeping her around. There was a keen intelligence to her that he'd almost missed earlier when she'd been in the conference room. "I like fast cars. Let's take the Bugatti."

He walked to it, and she dropped to the floor to look under the car before standing again.

"What are you doing?"

"Looking for obvious devices," she said. "Someone killed your bodyguard three days ago and just took a shot at you. I'd feel safer if Xander looked over the car before we took it. Would you agree to that?"

"No," he said.

But then the sentiment behind her words echoed in his mind. *Someone killed your bodyguard.* As urgently as he wanted to speak to his father, he wasn't sure he could handle another person dying for him. Not today. "But if it will make you feel safer, sure."

She didn't question him, just pulled out her phone and sent a text. Five minutes later, Xander, the behemoth, walked toward them. He smiled at Luna and nodded at him as Nick tossed the keys.

He caught them one-handed. "This won't take but a minute. If you don't mind, I'll check out the rest of your vehicles after I do this one."

"No problem. I'm sure Price will bill me for it," Nick said.

"He definitely will," Xander said. "No such thing as a free ride, according to the boss."

"Well, everything I touch turns to gold," Nick said.

Luna stood off to the side, watching the big guy work.

Nick wondered at her relationship with all the men on the team. They seemed to be a close-knit group, but she didn't exactly look like she belonged. "How'd you end up in this business?" he asked while they waited.

"I was making a living doing some mixed martial arts fighting and Van saw me one night. He needed a woman to guard a client. Someone who was good at hand-to-hand combat. I turned him down flat. But he offered me a lot of money, promised to train me, and I gave it a go. Turned out I was good at it," she said with a slight shrug.

She was downplaying it. Making it seem like Price's training would have worked with anyone, but he knew it wouldn't have. He also got a clear picture that her loyalty would always be to Price.

"How long ago was that?" he asked. She looked like she was in her late twenties, but something in her eyes almost made her seem older.

"Ten years," she said.

"You don't look old enough to have done this for ten years," he said, trying flattery to see if that had any effect on her.

"Thanks," she said, kind of looking down and away. "But I am plenty old."

He wanted to ask more questions but cautioned himself. He didn't want to get to know this bodyguard. He hadn't even meant to let Jack get as close as he had. He should have stuck to his routine of rotating bodyguards, of changing his habits, but he'd started to feel like the curse had been lifted. It had been almost three years since the last similar incident.

Three years, and he'd thought that maybe he was on the other side of the bad karma that had been following him around since his birth. But he knew that had been a misjudgment and one he wouldn't allow himself to make again.

"You're good," Xander said, tossing the keys back to Nick.

He caught them in one hand and then walked to the car. He heard the sound of Luna's heels on the concrete as she walked beside him. He didn't look at her. She was his bodyguard. Not someone he was getting to know, and he was determined to remember that.

LUNA WASN'T ENTIRELY sure why Nick thought he was bulletproof, but she watched him carefully as he drove through the LA traffic. It wasn't too heavy, and he hit the community lane and didn't look back. He drove over the speed limit, but she felt safe. He had the music blaring and she could tell that conversation was the last thing he was interested in, which suited her. But she had to keep herself busy, otherwise she was going to drift off to sleep.

She reached over, turning the volume down. "About those enemies…"

"I don't have any," he reminded her.

"Finn mentioned Verity Vaughn," she prompted him. Luna didn't know much about his ex-wife. In fact, she pulled out her phone and sent an info request to Lee.

"Finn and Verity don't get along, that was just him acting out."

"You said you're worth more to her alive," Luna continued. She wasn't going to just write this off. Former partners often turned killers.

"She's got her own money," he said. "Verity can be very demanding, and she usually turns to me to smooth things out for her."

"Why do you do that?"

"It's easier to give in than to try to fight with her," he said. "She's difficult, but she's not a killer."

"We'll see. Anyone else like that?"

"No."

"You've only had one lover?" she asked because he was being a pain. He wanted to ignore the fact that someone had shot at him.

"Not quite."

"Anyone else who's *demanding*?" she asked.

"I'm sure *you* are," he said. "Most people I know just want to make their own life easier."

"And you help them with that?"

"When I can," he said.

"Do you say no sometimes?"

"On occasion."

"Recently?"

"I see where you are going with this—" he started.

"Listen," she said, cutting him off. "You don't want to believe that someone you know, someone you've talked to, would try to kill you, but honestly, that's probably who it is."

Luna had read the articles and knew his reputation as a tragic wealthy figure. The public knowledge of the incidents that he'd been close to had been written off as accidents and from what she'd read that seemed to truly be the case. But Nick believed there was something more.

"Nothing is ever that simple. And there are only a handful of people who have been in my life for all of the...incidents."

"I thought the only times you were intentionally targeted were in the recent death of your bodyguard and today's attempted shooting." Van had mentioned that Nick thought he was bulletproof, but the other near-death experiences had all been ruled as accidental. Did Nick know something more he wasn't sharing?

"Yeah, never mind," he said, turning the radio back up and driving a bit faster.

She watched the cars around them, looking for anyone who might be following them. She kept herself alert, going over everything he'd said and she'd seen while they'd been at his office. The impression she'd had of a shallow playboy was gone.

Their conversation in the garage had revealed more than he'd probably expected it to. But he wasn't a frivolous man, and unless she missed her guess, he felt more about his bodyguard being killed than he wanted the world to see.

They arrived at his father's mansion in Santa Barbara before she knew it. She watched for any vehicles that might be tailing them but didn't see any. It was odd in her book that someone would have tried to shoot him and then disappear, but she knew Van would figure that part out. She pinged Lee with her location to make sure the team knew where she was.

"This place looks nice," she said wryly as they were waved through the guard gates.

"Understated isn't something that we DeVeres do," he said.

"Yeah, I got that. What are you hoping to find here?" she asked.

"Answers," he said. "You'll have to wait while I go and speak to him."

"I'm not doing that."

The place had enough guards and active and passive security, but she wasn't leaving her client. His life was in her hands. She'd never known her father or, for that matter, her mother, but she imagined that Nick might need his father after everything that had happened today.

"I'm not budging on this. My father is ill and I don't know you."

"Sure, I'll give you privacy while you talk to him. But I'm not staying out here with the car," she warned him.

"I wouldn't expect you to since it's hot today," he said, a hint of unease in his eyes. "The agreement that your agency signed has an NDA attached to it."

"Yes. The moment I left with you, I was on the clock. I won't be discussing anything that happens in your life with anyone but the team."

"Good," he said, getting out of the car.

As they walked up the steps, the front door to the mansion opened to reveal an older man with thin, close-cropped gray hair. He wore a suit and stood tall and easy in it. He nodded at Nick as they got closer.

"Your father will be pleased to see you again, Nicholas."

"I'm sure. Aldo, this is Ms. Urban, she's my new bodyguard. This is Aldo Barsotti, my father's butler."

"A pleasure to meet you, Ms. Urban, please call me Aldo. As we weren't expecting you, I'll need a moment to make sure your father is ready."

"Don't bother. I'm not bringing Ms. Urban in with me," Nick said, striding past the butler and up the large spiral staircase.

Luna sighed, moving quickly to stay on his heels. Nick acted like he wasn't in danger here.

The butler closed the door behind her and Luna started up the stairs after Nick. She called back over her shoulder, "I need to be outside of the room he's in."

"Of course, Mr. Nicholas has always just done what he wanted," Aldo said, keeping pace with her.

"I've noticed. Have you worked for Mr. DeVere for long?" she asked. Remembering what Nick had said about only a handful of people being around for all of the "incidents."

"Almost forty-five years," Aldo said. "Follow me. Can I offer you a drink?"

"I'm good," she said, following the butler up the stairs and down another wide hallway. As they got closer to the closed door at the end, she heard Nick's voice on the other side. "Is there another entrance to the room?"

"Only a balcony," Aldo said.

"Can I see the balcony?" she asked.

"You can through that large window," he said gesturing to the one at the end of the hall. She walked to the window. For a large house, it was quiet, and it was clear to her that there weren't many people here. She opened the window, looked out at the balcony, and then down at the landscaped garden below.

She was going to need to speak to Nick about his impulsiveness. This was the kind of behavior she wouldn't tolerate. Even Jaz, the teenaged rap star, had heeded her warnings and allowed her to secure locations for him. She should have been able to secure the area before Nick had gone in to speak to his father. That was something she would put in place after they left.

She soon found the best position to keep an eye on both exits from the room.

Aldo stood outside the door to the bedroom. Luna would have liked to talk to him further to try to get more information on Nick. The fatigue she'd carried with her since she'd landed was still there, but she had found her second wind. Things were starting to make more sense now.

Putting the pieces together, she had the feeling that Nick thought his bodyguard had been killed because of him, which was odd if it truly was a freak accident. But Van suspected there was more to Ingram's death than just an accident too. Also why was Nick so determined to take the blame for it? Was there something else she was missing? Before she could make more sense of it, there was a loud crash from Nick's father's room.

She ran for the door, which was now open because Aldo had rushed in at the sound. She found a lamp smashed on the floor and an older version of Nick standing over it. She scanned the room, looking for her client, found him not too far from his father, but in the shadows.

"See. I told you I had a bodyguard. And she's very good at her job."

She went to Nick's side, pocketing her gun. "What's going on?"

"Just seeing how good you are, my dear," the older man said.

"How *good* I am?"

"At keeping my son safe. After all, you weren't by his side," he said.

"I agree, sir. That was an error in judgment. We still haven't hammered out all the details of my employment yet," she said.

"She had the balcony and this door covered," Aldo added.

"For pete's sake," Nick said. "She's great. I want to know why you didn't tell me about that the threat you received."

"What threat?" she asked.

Chapter Four

Nick wasn't pleased at all with his father. The old man was being cagey about some letters he'd been receiving for thirty-two years. The exact amount of time that Nick had been alive, in fact. His father was supposed to be taking it easy after his latest chemo treatment, but instead he was hurling lamps to the floor to check the reaction time of his bodyguard.

Though why his father hadn't mentioned it before, Nick wasn't about to get into. Their family kept secrets close and didn't share them, and Nick could even understand that his father might have been reluctant to worry Nick when he was younger. But now, when his father was terminal and Nick's life was on the line, he'd finally had no choice but to come clean.

"It's nothing for you to worry about. Nicholas, we can discuss it—"

"No, Father, we can't. She signed a NDA, you're good to talk in front of her. Aldo, I need a drink."

"Of course, Mr. Nicholas," Aldo said. "Emmett?"

"I'll have one too. Bring it to my study if you don't mind," he said.

"Father." His dad was acting like they were going to

have a social visit. After he'd dropped the bomb of receiving the letters every year, he seemed to want to move on. But there was no moving on from that. Nick deserved to know the details.

"Son, you asked for a drink. And I have kept all of the letters in a file in my study," his father said, following Aldo out of the room.

"Where are we going? I would like to secure the room and the area before you two go inside," Luna said, walking between him and his father.

"Just down the hall there. The next door on the right," Nick said, gesturing to it.

"Wait here," she said, walking into his father's study.

Nick turned to the old man. "You're being a little bit dicey with the information, and that's not like you. And you slipped up by hiring Price yourself instead of going through the board. Just level with me."

His father sighed and then reached over to touch the side of Nick's face. Something he hadn't done since Nick had been a little boy. "When your mother died, I promised myself I wouldn't allow that to happen to you."

"And you haven't. But was there a chance it could have?" he asked. The police thought he had survivor guilt in the extreme, but Nick had always sensed that the incidents in his life were connected. He just hadn't wanted to admit it.

"Yes. There was. It will make more sense when you see the letters," he said and then sighed. "There's no easy way to put this. Before I met your mom, I played the field."

He rolled his eyes. "Dad, I didn't think you were saint. Is there really a reason for me to hear this now?"

"When you were born, I got the first letter saying that

I had another son and that he should be my heir," Emmett said.

"Do you? Dad, do I have a half brother?"

"No," he said. "Aldo and I have researched every lead and gone back to every woman I slept with. There is no child of mine out there. I thought it was just a blackmail attempt and ignored it," his father said.

"But the letters kept coming?"

"Yes. Right after your mother died in that horrible crash, I got another one. It was vaguely threatening. Stating that if I didn't want to lose you in the same way, I'd recognize my true heir."

Nick's heart beat faster as he listened to his father's words. What was the old man saying? "Was Mom murdered?"

"I don't know. The police never found any evidence of vehicle tampering and there were skid marks as if the car skidded on the road and slid off the edge of the cliff."

But his father hadn't been sure. Aldo came up the stairs at the same time as Luna called all-clear. He put his hand on his father's arm to steady the old man as they walked to the study.

This changed everything. Who was this heir that someone was speaking of? He would have Finn start looking into it. He couldn't help but wonder how his father had kept this a secret all these years and why. Why not just tell him, so they could work together?

Entering his father's study, Luna stayed by his side. And it was odd, but for a moment, he felt like he knew her—knew this stranger—better than he knew his father or Aldo.

What else about his father's life was he hiding?

Aldo handed him his drink and Nick downed the whiskey

and soda in one long swallow. His father opened a drawer in his desk with a key and then leaned down for a retinal scan. Nick set his empty glass on the side table and walked over to his father's desk just as the old man took out a large file and set it on the surface.

"This is everything. The last letter came the day that Jack was killed. It said specifically that they were tired of waiting and they were going to kill you and then come for me," his father said, pushing the file toward him.

"Sir, we need to let Detective Miller know about this," Luna said.

Nick glared at her. "I will."

He opened the file and looked down at the letter, which had been printed. He'd have Finn run diagnostics on the paper and ink and start narrowing things down. But Luna was right, the police should have been notified from the beginning about this.

"Why didn't you go to the cops?"

"I wasn't sure the threat was real. Jack's death is the first time any of these letters has been tied to us," his father said.

"But you knew they were threatening me?" he asked.

EMMETT DIDN'T ANSWER. Nick just moved away to look out the window. Luna followed him wanting to offer comfort but that wasn't why she was here. She forced herself instead to scan the yard to make sure it was clear. She noticed that Aldo moved next to the older man, urging him back from the exposed position.

She turned to Nick, who just shook his head, walking over to the desktop where all the letters were. His expression wasn't readable. But she didn't have to be Nancy Drew to figure out he was pissed and, she suspected, hurt.

She walked over to him.

"What do you want to do?" Luna asked.

"Take these letters home," he said. "But I suspect Detective Miller will want copies too."

"I can take photos of them and send copies to you and Miller. Sound good?"

"Yeah. Make it quick."

She could tell he wanted to leave; he paced the room like a caged lion. He wanted to attack, she could see that clearly, but he didn't have a good target for his rage. His father, though strong and lucid, was a weak man.

Aldo was supporting Emmett and urging him to the desk and the tall leather chair. Luna stopped scanning the documents with an encoded app on her phone and pushed the leather chair closer to Aldo and Emmett.

Aldo smiled his thanks. Luna just went back to what she'd been doing. The early letters had been printed on a dot matrix printer. Wow. Emmett really had been receiving these threats since Nick's birth.

When she finished, she emailed a copy to Lee back at Price Tower, asking her to inform Detective Miller about them and to see if she wanted to talk to Emmett DeVere.

"I'm good here," she said to Nick.

He looked…well, gorgeous and moody, as he always did, but something had changed in her client the moment his father had revealed he'd been keeping the threat to himself all these years.

Aldo was watching Nick and Emmett both, his gaze flickering, and Luna felt the tension between the two of them and realized their complicated relationship might have something to do with her current assignment. Emmett seemed to make Nick even more arrogant and impulsive and risky.

Why? She'd read the cursory file about the DeVere family and knew that father and son had seemingly had a strained relationship for years, but this was something else. This was different.

"My boss has informed Detective Miller. She'll be in touch with you."

"I'm not sure I want to discuss these with her," Emmett said.

"As it's evidence in an ongoing case, I don't think you have a choice. You can do it when she comes or she'll get a warrant, and if that happens, there's a chance the press will pick up on it," Luna said.

The old man had had her sympathy when she'd first seen him. He was old and frail-looking, but his eyes revealed a wily intelligence. She'd always hoped for a better parent-child dynamic than life had showed her and was usually disappointed.

"Yeah, Dad," Nick said, coming back over. "You might not get your own way with this. Don't think of it as doing something for me, but instead doing something for Jack. You always liked him."

"Of course, your father will cooperate with the police. This matter has gotten too serious not to," Aldo said. "When do you think they will be contacting us?"

"I'm not sure," Luna said.

"Thank you. Do you need anything else?" Aldo asked.

Luna glanced over at Nick. He'd rushed here to make sure his father was okay. Somehow, she had a feeling that the fact that his father had kept this a secret for all these years was something he hadn't been prepared for.

"No," Nick said. "Luna, will someone from Price be with the detective?"

"Yes," she said, knowing that Lee would have Rick make contact with Detective Miller. He was really good at this type of thing since he'd spent all those years as a DEA agent. "We can leave whenever you are ready."

His father turned away to face the large bay window. Nick didn't even look over at his father, instead he spun on his heel and left.

She moved to follow him, but Aldo stopped her with a hand on her arm. "Thank you for everything you've done this afternoon. It's never easy with these two."

She smiled at the older man. "You're very welcome."

She found that Nick was waiting for her at the top of the stairs. "Didn't want to give you any more reason to grump at me."

"I don't grump, I protect," she said, hiding a smile. He wasn't as blasé about the attempt on his life now. The letters had changed something for him.

She'd glanced at them herself and couldn't shake the feeling that something was off. The letters weren't concrete and didn't really seem to relate to any events—no incriminating details or information that tied the letters to specific crimes or attempts on Nick's life. They were just vaguely threatening.

"It feels like badgering," he said of her commands.

"Great, if that makes you listen. I plan to keep you alive… and now we know that I've seen the letters, I think this might be even more serious than we thought," she said.

"The shooter didn't have you convinced?" he asked with a teasing grin on his face.

He was practically flirting with her. Odd, but not unexpected. She was pretty sure this was his defense mechanism, his way of making sure he still had the upper hand. She'd seen a chink in the façade he liked to project to the world. It made sense that he'd want to steer her back to her first image of him. But it wasn't going to work. She finally felt like she was glimpsing the real man behind Nick DeVere.

She'd wanted to make Nick into the spoiled playboy. But she'd seen his real fear for his father, and then his true disappointment in him. She'd never forget that. He was starting to be more man than client. These little pieces of the person that made him seem more real to her. And that was dangerous for her and for him. The threat to Nick was real. She had to stay sharp.

No matter how much she might long for something else.

"I mean he could have been aiming at someone else," she said. "It's not always all about you."

He threw his head back and laughed. "Darling, it's always about me, which you will learn quickly. Let's go. I have to get out of this place."

"Did you grow up here?" she asked, because he seemed restless like he wanted to talk. Glancing over at Nick she noticed how comfortable he was in this place. He walked thorugh the rooms as if he knew them well.

"Until I was eight, and then it was boarding school," he said. "But Father traveled a lot back then. So, it was usually me and a nanny."

"A nanny?"

"We didn't keep them for long. Usually six months," he said.

That felt odd to her, but given that Emmett had been receiving threatening letters about his son, maybe not so odd. She followed Nick down the stairs, carefully watching the interior for any signs she might have missed on the way in, but saw nothing untoward.

She snapped a photo of a portrait she hadn't really had time to study. It was of Emmet, a woman and a child. She supposed it must be Nick and mother, but she wanted to verify it before making an assumption.

Nick noticed she had the camera app on her smartphone open and then shook his head. "My mother. I don't have any memories of her, so this image is what I usually see when I think of her."

Luna nodded. "I didn't know my mom either. I always think of the mom from *Boy Meets World* when I picture mine."

He looked at her. "I don't know what that is."

"It was a TV show in the '90s. One of the group homes I lived in had a poster on the bedroom wall of the family," she said, remembering the clean but old, tired room she'd been put in. She'd shared it with Mazie.

"I didn't take you for an orphan," he said.

"What did you take me as?" she asked as they walked outside. She did a quick visual check of the Bugatti, but since they'd parked in a gated driveway, she felt like the car was probably safe to drive.

"Tomboy with a close relationship with your dad. Maybe someone who was trying to be the son he never had," Nick said.

"Nope."

Interesting. She'd noticed most men clients she'd had over the years often thought that. Or they'd thought she'd been victimized as an orphan. Her background wasn't sad or extraordinary. Just a girl who'd had to raise herself, and figure out what she wanted to do, when fate stepped in. Or rather, Van stepped in.

When they were both in the car, he looked over at her.

The setting sun cast a shadow on his cheekbones, making her very aware of how good-looking he was.

"Am I what you expected?" he asked.

"Hmm." A nice noncommittal sound so she didn't have to risk letting him know that she was intrigued by the man, not just her client.

NICK SHOOK OFF the vestiges of disappointment the further they drove away from his father's house. He didn't know why he'd been surprised that his father had kept something so important a secret for so many years. That was sort of the old man's MO. He tried to control every detail of Nick's life while staying aloof and distant.

When he'd been younger, Nick had allowed himself to believe that had been for his own protection. The letters that they'd seen today...those went back to the time of his birth.

Well, hell.

"So?"

"I'm not sure what I expected. As you know, this was sort of a last-minute assignment for me. I didn't have time to really do as much research on you as I would have liked."

"First impressions then," he said.

"Asshole."

He looked over at her, arching one eyebrow. She didn't give much away, which wasn't surprising. Most of the bodyguards he'd hired had kept to themselves. They didn't get involved because once a relationship become personal, mistakes could happen. Had Luna made one in her past?

"Sorry. Rich asshole," she said.

He hid a smile as he turned his attention back to the road. They were getting closer to downtown and his club, so he needed to be alert as the traffic was heavier here.

"Fair enough. It's kind of my vibe."

"Ha. That's a lie. Your vibe is someone who is very spoiled but also very generous. For as much as you want me to believe it's all about you, I don't think it always is."

He didn't like that. "It is about me. Sometimes I have to make it about someone else to get what I want, but in the end, it's all me."

"Good to know. I won't be flattered if you do something nice for me."

"Oh, you should be flattered," he said.

He liked her. But that was all it could ever be. He'd linked the tragedies that always seemed to happen around him to something else a long time ago. He thought he'd just been lucky, sort of like Midas. Everything he touched worked out for him. But sometimes the tradeoff was that other people got hurt.

He'd tried to limit his close relationships because of that. Finn had said he was paranoid because of the way the events unfolded and that it was probably survivor's guilt. But Nick had always thought it odd the way the incidents had been staged.

He intended to get to the bottom of it, and now with his father's letters, which he'd had Luna send him a copy of.

He'd have to be careful with Luna and the rest of the Price Security team. He wasn't about to put another person's life in danger. He'd always been the invincible one. His last nanny had said that, like Harry Potter, his mom's death had given him a sort of magical protection. And he knew that she'd meant it to soothe a small boy who'd lost his mother,

But her words had always been oddly true. He felt untouchable.

Luna wasn't.

And as clever and funny as she was, he knew that she could be killed just like Jack, his cousins and his mom had been.

"For the party, I'll need you in evening wear."

"Great. I look really good in a black suit and tie, as I'm sure you've already noticed," she quipped.

"That won't do. You'll have to dress like a woman who I'd be dating. I don't want anyone to know I have a new bodyguard."

"The shooter will know. Rick chased someone through the garment district," Luna pointed out.

"The world doesn't know."

Luna drew in a breath, like she was going to argue with him.

"Don't bother. This is a nonnegotiable for me. You either wear a dress and act like you're my latest fling or I get rid of the team altogether."

"You know you can't do that. But, fine, I don't really mind a dress. What else?" she said.

"No weapons. I don't want my guests to feel anything other than a good time," he said.

"How am I supposed to protect you without my weapon?" she asked.

"You said that Van hired you because you were good at hand-to-hand combat. I think the biggest threat at the party will be men hitting on you."

"I doubt that. The risk is yours, not mine," she said. "Why won't you take this seriously?"

"You saw the letters," he said. "Someone has been threatening me for decades and I'm still alive."

"By chance," she said.

"Not chance. Fate," he retorted.

"Fate? Isn't that the same thing?"

He shrugged. He wasn't going to get into his complex relationship with karma and fate. But he knew that he was untouchable. Luna Urban, who grew up in a group home and worked as a bodyguard for the rich and famous...well, not so much.

"Trust me on this," he said as he hit the button to open the armored doors of the underground garage at his club and penthouse. He parked the Bugatti and then turned off the engine, turning to face her.

"You can go home and get your stuff. I'll have a room ready for you in the penthouse when you get back," he said.

"Again, I can't leave you alone."

"You can. I'm going to be upstairs. Leave the behemoth to watch over me. You said you needed sleep. I want you alert and ready," he said.

"We can check with Van. Normally, I'd work—"

"This isn't normal, Luna. None of it."

"As I said, we'll check with Van."

He got out of the car and she followed him, close by his side, always scanning the area around them for threats. She was very good at her job and he liked that. But it also made it more important that he find a way to get her and all of Price Security off the case.

He knew that Jack's killer was going to come for him again and this time he wanted the murderer to get close. Close enough for Nick to confront him and then kill him. It was time for Nick to stop letting fate decide.

Chapter Five

Van agreed with Nick. Luna arrived at Price Tower and knew she should sleep, but she'd caught a second wind. Lee was waiting for her with a no-nonsense look on her face. The older woman was the communications hub for their team and their unofficial mother. She made sure that everyone stayed in line.

"Hey, girl. Good to have you back in Cali," Lee said, hugging her. "The boss wants you to sleep, and we'll catch you up later on everything. The letters you sent are interesting. But I haven't had a chance to really dig into it. Rick and Detective Miller are with the older DeVere. I want a full rundown on that house. Was it like the Rich Wives shows that we watch?"

"It was. Why are you telling me all this?"

"Because you won't sleep if I don't. And this case looks like it's going to be a quick one. You need to grab all the rest you can right now," Lee said.

"I agree. Did Xander stay with Nick?"

"Yeah. He's safe for now. I'm surprised you guys didn't have any trouble at the father's house," Lee said.

"I was, too, but I think whoever is behind this knows that Nick and his dad have a strained relationship."

"You think it's an insider?"

"That's my gut. What about yours?"

"Not sure yet. I want to finish analyzing the letters, and Rick mentioned that Nick told the detective that there had been other incidents before Jack's death. I'm cross-referencing them," Lee said. "You get some rest and I'll have it ready for you when you wake up."

Lee left her at the door to her apartment. She was tired but also, as she'd said, wired. She wanted to be doing something, not sleeping, and as much as she knew that later she might regret it; she just couldn't force herself to nap. She packed her stuff for the job, including the one evening dress she had. She got out her laptop and started doing some research. Just putting Nick's name into the internet search engine pulled up pages and pages of stories.

She rolled her shoulders and took out a regular spiral notebook and Bic pen. She started at the beginning with the car crash that had killed his mother and left him unscathed.

There had been five other accidents that had been close to Nick, but he'd survived. Always someone close to him had been killed. Yet the accidents weren't similar and, she had to admit, looked like accidents on the surface.

She heard footsteps outside her apartment door and then someone knocked. She closed her laptop quickly and glanced at the perfectly made bed, tempted to ruffle the sheets, but she wasn't good at petty deceit. Seemed pointless to her.

She went to open the door, unsurprised to see Van there.

"No sleep?"

"Couldn't," she said. "I did some internet searching."

"Me too. I'm not sure about this case," he said. "At first,

I thought that DeVere might have set up Jack, but I don't think that's the case."

"Me either. It's odd," she admitted. "Nick is definitely in some kind of danger."

"Is he? Or is he just trying to stir up something?" Van said.

"What did you see that makes you think that?" she asked. "I didn't get that vibe. He seemed shocked when his father showed him the letters."

"I'll trust your gut. His assistant is guarded. Plays his cards close the chest. Not sure what's going on there. Lee's running him through the databases to find out everything she can."

"I will watch him and the woman—Hazel too."

"Good. Grab your notes and let's have a debrief in ten minutes."

She and Van met up with Lee and the others in the communications room, which was really just a big room that sort of resembled the family room in one of the group homes she'd lived in—except everything was new and clean, and everyone had their own space. Luna's spot was a large chair big enough for two people to sit in. She liked to curl her legs up under her while in the team meetings.

Lee had some sort of massive recliner and Van sat on a leather armchair. Kenji was slouched on the long couch, playing a game on his phone. When they'd walked in, he'd sat up and put it away.

"Lee, give us the rundown," Van said.

Lee ran through all the information they'd collected so far. Nothing new from what she'd told Luna earlier, at first. Then she mentioned that she'd found out the last three accidents had been at events where Nick's inner circle were participants.

"Who?"

"The ex—Verity Vaughn, some heiress. His assistant—Finn. And then another name kept popping up—Thom Newton. They will all be at the event on Friday. I think that we should divide up and try to speak to them. Who wants who?"

"I'll take the heiress," Kenji said.

"I can try to do Finn," Lee said. "Since you already rubbed him the wrong way, Van."

"Good that leaves me with Newton," Van said.

"I'll have Xander on the door and, of course, Luna will be with Nick. The cops had pretty much written off his theory that Jack was killed in his place until the letters were found."

"What do you think?" Kenji asked.

"He's definitely been close to a lot of tragedy. But Luna doesn't think he's the kind of man who'd set this all up for attention, and she's spent the most time with him. But the accidents are too far apart to make sense. I mean why try at random times over years only to stop, and then why do it again now? Has something happened to change it?" Van asked.

She knew that Van was just putting these things out there so they'd all keep looking for the connection. She planned to get to the bottom of it. Tonight, she'd have a chance to start finding out about the other accidents from Nick. She was very good at getting information out of their clients, and she had a feeling that on this job, it was what she'd need to do to protect him.

PROCESSING EVERYTHING THAT had happened to him today wasn't that hard. He shoved it down and then poured himself a Jack and Coke. He set it on his desk next to the printout of the letters his father had received. The behemoth—Xander—sat in one of the guest chairs facing both the door and the windows. Though why he was watching the window was beyond Nick.

They'd moved his desk into the small alcove where his dressing area was. The walls were closing in around him; he hated this feeling. It reminded him of the time he'd been kidnapped. They'd left him in a locked closet in an abandoned house while negotiating with his father.

He did a deep breathing technique and then forced his attention on the letters. The sooner he figured this out, the sooner he could get back to living his life. At least he had something solid to look at.

The door to his office opened. Xander was on his feet and at the door before it cracked more than a few inches. He looked at whomever was on the other side and then nodded and stepped back.

Hazel stepped in after giving Xander a stern look. "I've just got the mail."

"Of course," Xander said. "Apologies."

She ignored Xander as he moved back to his chair and turned to Nick. "I've had a few inquiries about Friday's event and directed them to Finn. Also, the DeVere board agreed to come here for the contract discussions. Mr. Price is insisting on metal detectors at the doors and a screening process."

"I'll discuss it with him," Nick said.

"I thought so. I told him we'd have to wait for your approval," she said.

"I'll speak to Price and then let you know. Anything else?"

"Ms. Vaughn called again. I tried to put her through to Finn, but she hung up. She will probably try your cell."

She had tried his cell about eighteen times, and he'd kept hitting Ignore. He'd spoke to her once today and he wasn't up for another chat. "Thanks. Is that all?"

"Um, no there is one more thing. My son is back from his latest tour overseas and I'd like to take a few weeks off," she said. "I know my timing isn't—"

"It's fine. Take as much leave as you need," he said. Hazel had never taken a sick day and had rolled her vacation over for the last three years. "I think it's safe to say it won't be business as usual for the next few weeks. Do you have a temp lined up?"

"Yes. The agency is sending her over tomorrow. I'll go over everything then and have the security team give her a background check."

"Great. Thank you, Hazel," he said.

She just smiled and nodded at him as she turned to go.

"Did you know your boss was trying to install metal detectors?" Nick asked Xander.

"Your life is being—"

"Stop. You guys can't use that justification for everything. My invited guests aren't going to be screened like criminals."

"It's as much for their safety as it is for yours," Xander said. "You're the one who claims to be bulletproof."

Nick squared his shoulders. He was a man used to having the final say and these people from Price Security were wearing on him. "What are the other alternatives?"

"I'd say metal detectors are the easiest and everyone is familiar with them. We could do infrared scans, but Van thought you'd balk at that," Xander said.

He was right. "Does it have to be an obvious scanner or is there a way to have it be more subtle, like mounted in the foyer but not a small walkway?"

"It's not as effective," Xander said. "Let me see what I can work up. We'll need to get someone else in here to watch you if you want me to work with the security installation team."

"Have them come up here to you," Nick said, turning his attention back to the letters.

The event might not be the best idea right now. He'd cancel it, except the detective and Price had both told him to. Nick felt it would be like a signal to whoever had shot at him this afternoon that he was running scared. And he did not like being told what to do.

Xander had been right. He wasn't about to put his guests in danger. He needed the venue as safe as it could be. He messaged Finn to hire some extra bouncers for Friday's event. He then messaged Price to tell him he'd have some extra bouncers under his command during the evening.

Nick didn't like living his life like this. But if it meant getting to the bottom of these incidents, then he'd do it. He pulled the letters back over to him. He could have read them on the screen, but his brain found patterns better when he was looking at paper instead of a computer monitor.

The most astounding thing was how ordinary the notes all looked. Just typed up on a word processing program and printed out in the generic font that loaded with the program. Some had been printed in the late '80s, so they were from a dot matrix printer. Glancing down at the single-spaced printouts, he realized he would have dismissed them at first glance.

It was only when he started to read them that the menace came through. Something so small. Just words on the page. They couldn't hurt him. They weren't meant to hurt him. They were meant to steal his father's peace of mind and to make him afraid.

And as much as Nick wanted to pretend that his father had kept this from him to protect him, that wasn't the reason. His father had kept silent because he had a deeper secret.

Nick wasn't sure what that secret was, but a part of him had always wondered if his father had been having an affair when his mother had died. Aldo had made a comment when Verity and he had gotten married, about fidelity and the DeVere men. Was the real reason for his father's silence that he *knew* he had another son? Possibly another heir?

Nick wasn't going to let this go until he got to the bottom of it. The door opened and, once again, Xander was there before the door swung fully open.

"Wasn't expecting to you this early," the behemoth said, stepping back as Luna walked in.

LUNA HADN'T WANTED to be back this early, either, but the job *was* Nick DeVere. And he was here, not at Price Tower, so she needed to be here too. There were questions she wanted to ask, and she needed to see his reactions. Van asking her if she trusted Nick had made her realize that she needed to be doubly sure.

She wasn't going to pretend she hadn't been shaken when she'd been pressed on top of him after he'd been shot at. But it would take a colossal ego for him to set up a hit and then act like he was surprised. She wasn't ruling it out. Not yet.

The family dynamic she'd observed between him and his father had set off warning bells. Those two men were playing a dangerous game with each other. It seemed to her that they both had hidden agendas. That was fine in normal family dynamics, but people were getting killed.

"I was ready early and thought I'd come and give you a break."

"Perfect," he said then turned to Nick. "Later."

Xander left, closing the door behind him, and Luna turned to face Nick. He looked massive behind his desk, which had been wedged into a corner with only the smallest amount of space left on one side for him to walk around it.

"Missed me?" he asked drolly.

"You know it," she said. "I had a feeling you'd be going over those letters. I've always found two brains are better than one."

"Depends on the brain," he said.

"Fair enough." Something was different about him from the time she'd left. She couldn't put her finger on it just yet, but he'd changed in some way. "Anything new?"

"Nope," he said. "It always surprises me how dark the soul can be."

She moved closer to see which letter he was reading. Glancing down, she read, and realize it was the one sent after his mother's death.

Guess forever wasn't as long as she hoped. Better luck next time.

That was harsh. Who sent a letter like that? There was no threat in it per se, just malice. "Yeah. I think love can do that to people."

"Whoa, what?" he asked. "Love? Love is supposed to be hearts and flowers."

"Has it ever been that way for you?"

"No," he said, shaking his head. "But..."

"But?"

He just shrugged, but she didn't let it go. "I'm a girl. That's what you were going to say, wasn't it?"

"Maybe. I would have said woman, it's not correct to call you a girl."

She shook her head. "Love isn't bound by gender, you know."

"I do know," he said. "Still, love? These letters seem..."

"Like obsession. I think love is so tightly linked to dark fascination, and that always leads to the shadiest places." She'd seen it so many times. Like her latest client who had been threatened by a fan turned stalker turned obsessive if-I-can't-have-you-no-one-will.

"I am obsessed with cold-brewed coffee, but I've never felt the need to threaten someone for it," he said.

"Nick."

"I know. I'm being glib. But only because that's easier than having to admit that someone out there might have been trying to kill me my entire charmed life."

She got it. She'd worked around enough high-profile clients to know that the whole silver-spoon lifestyle came at a cost. "At least you're not alone."

He didn't respond, just pushed his chair back and stood. "I'm always alone. No matter how close you might be to me, you're paid to be here."

Wow. She understood the sentiment, but surely he had friends who weren't paid to be around him. "I wasn't talking about me."

"Who then? Finn? Hazel?" he asked. "I just don't form those kinds of attachments."

But he did, she thought. She'd seen the brief glimpse of

guilt and loss in him when he'd spoke of his previous body-guard. And no matter how they'd left his father's house, on the way there, Nick DeVere—Mr. I Don't Form Attach-ments—had been worried. But he had somehow shoved all of that aside.

"It's not a bad thing to form attachments."

"Says you. I'm reading a letter that proves otherwise. My father must have had an affair, it's right here. And even if his lover didn't kill my mother…well, she certainly took a mor-bid pleasure in rubbing the fact that he'd lost her in his face."

She agreed. "I noticed a later letter that was similar. The one from when your yacht was blown up."

Nick didn't say anything. Just riffled through the papers on his desk until he found it.

"'Goodbye to your heir. Guess it's time to do the right thing by your bastard,'" Nick read aloud. He dropped the paper onto his desktop and moved around his desk toward the main part of the room.

She stopped him.

"I need to pace. I can't just stand here in the corner," he said.

"You can't. It's not safe."

"I'm not safe for you, either," he said, using his body to try to overwhelm her and push her into the corner. The wall was at her back and she could feel the rage coming off him. But it wasn't directed at her.

He needed an outlet for that anger, and she was the only one available at this moment. She had two choices here. Let him think he had the upper hand and let this play out, or take control and force him to calm down.

Luna wasn't sure that either of those was a good option. "Do you have a gym here?"

"Why?"

"Sparring might help you, and it will be a lot safer than if you insist on forcing me into a corner. Which I thought you'd have learned by now."

"What makes you think I didn't let you overpower me?"

She just quirked her head to the side, trying to see the truth in him. But it was hard. Trying to sleep hadn't helped her. There was something about Nick DeVere that was shrouded in mystery. What was he hiding?

"Let's take this to the mat."

"Yes, let's do that," he said. "It's in my penthouse."

"Let me guess, all glass windows?"

"No. It's a closed room. I think you'll like it," he said, reaching for the door and opening it. "I'll show you your room too."

She pushed in front of him. "You have to learn to let me take the lead."

"I've never been a follower."

Chapter Six

Nick's first martial arts teacher had been Risa Young, when he was fourteen. He'd been kidnapped a month earlier and his father had sent in some highly paid ex-military types to rescue him. He'd been saved, but there had been a lot of blood shed on the way out. Nick hadn't been able to sleep for a few months afterward.

He'd gone to Aldo and asked for self-defense lessons. And Aldo had hired Risa. Her lessons had been succinct and to the point. In combat, there was no place for gender roles or for pulled punches. Spar and fight to win—otherwise what was the point.

Over the years, he'd had more bodyguards than many realized. He'd lost a few of them to "accidents" and each of their faces was deeply embedded in his mind. Just another name on a list of those he was responsible for and had lost. He wouldn't let Luna or anyone from Price be added to it.

That was pretty much the ethos by which Nick had lived his life since that moment. But as he'd changed into his Gi and put on his black belt, he wondered how well-trained Luna was. She had said she was more of a street fighter, and while Nick knew he needed to work out his rage in a constructive way, he'd never liked beating up on someone who wasn't his equal.

When he came out of the changing area, Luna was waiting for him. She'd changed into a pair of black high-waisted leggings and a matching black sports bra.

"Do you have any formal martial arts training?"

"Some. I did judo for a while and kick boxing," she said.

Of course, she had. "So, mostly all kicking?"

"I can punch too. I mean mixed martial arts is my specialty," she said.

He rolled his neck. "That works for me. I don't know how intense we want this to get."

"As intense as you need it to be," she said. "You had the look of a man about to do something stupid earlier."

"Some would say that's my usual look," he said.

Luna shook her head as she took up a position across from him. "I know better than that. It's been a while for me, so give me a chance to warm up before you go too hard."

He just bowed to her and then fell into a ready stance. She did the same. He hadn't sparred with anyone in a long time. He preferred to come down here and do forms, and try to keep his center when Finn and Hazel were coming at him with the demands of running a multinational corporation along with his nightclub and social events.

He liked his life, staying busy for him equaled staying sane, but there were times when the noise he used to drone out the emptiness was too much, and he had to come down here and find center again.

As they danced around one another, each making feints and moves, Nick realized that he wasn't going to find peace while she was here. Luna Urban...she was the focus for him.

He groaned inwardly. He knew the feeling that was swelling him. Sex was always a nice distraction, but she was bodyguard. His bodyguard. He knew that if he made a move on her, she'd have to rebuke him. Maybe that was what he wanted. Some fake reason to fire her. To get her away from him. But as he watched her ponytail swing with each move she made, he knew that wasn't it.

Her neck was long and slender, but there was power behind her forward punches when she connected with him. He moved in closer, watching the way she moved. She was feminine, there was no missing that, but there was a strength that intrigued him.

Nick had no doubt he was physically stronger than she was, but the way she moved and cannily watched him made it clear that overpowering her wasn't the way to win. It was the combo of that knockout body and the keen intelligence in her eyes that was making it impossible for him to stop thinking about tackling her and pinning her to the ground.

His body stirred as he remembered the feel of her pressed against him when she'd tackled him in the conference room earlier. It had been there in the back of his mind all day. He wanted to know if it was just adrenaline turning him on or the woman. And did it matter?

Not really. He wasn't going to pursue her. He slept with women who were one and done. It was safer and neater that way. But at the same time…she was more than a distraction; she was the kind of puzzle that he wanted to solve.

"You're not really into this," she said after a minute, stopping and dropping her arms to her sides. "Did you think of something about your father's letters?"

He should say yes. Instead, he shook his head.

"You have had a tough day," she said. "Getting shot at

and learning that someone has been threatening you all of your life. That would be enough to rattle me."

Her voice was melodic and soothing. She was being reasonable, giving all these logical things to blame his distraction on. And he was being a man. Just a full-on masculine, chest-thumping guy, staring at her mouth as she spoke and wondering what she would taste like, what her kiss would be like. She was used to being in control, yet she was cautious. Would she be different in intimacy?

"Nick?"

"Hmm?"

"Is that it? What can I do to help?"

He looked at her for a long moment, sizing up the desire in him, just to take what he wanted—the way he always did. Kiss her. And to somewhat see if she wanted him too.

"Something that I don't think you'll agree to," he said.

She put her hand on her hip, thrusting her chest out and making him very aware of all of the curves of her body, which he'd been trying to ignore. He groaned out loud this time.

"Try me."

Chapter Seven

Try me.

She could tell from the tension coming off him that what he had in mind wasn't a no-holds-barred sparring session but something more intimate. It had happened before, an attraction when she was protecting someone, but usually it took more than a few hours. And it was never this powerful.

Then again, nothing about Nick DeVere was normal.

He watched her with that intense gaze. There was something so acute in the way he examined her. His eyes moving over the length of her neck and then down to the scooped neck of her sports bra. That awareness that she'd first felt when she'd been on top of him in the boardroom was back. This time it felt more like a slow, low throbbing that originated from deep inside her body. She felt her breath starting to quicken.

He hadn't moved. Hadn't done anything but stand there in his Gi and observed her with that space between them. He was waiting. He wasn't pushing, and he certainly wasn't a man who was going to try to take anything from her.

Luna knew that. Had seen his careful control in every situation they'd been in. Even when someone had tried to shoot him. This need for control was part of the puzzle she was trying to solve when it came to who Nick DeVere really was.

And this was important, but her heart was beating faster and, really, all she could do was look at his mouth and wonder how it would feel against hers.

Not smart.

And she always had to be smart.

A girl on her own was vulnerable in ways that many wouldn't realize. She always looked out for herself, and taking a kiss from Nick, a kiss that she wasn't about to deny she wanted, would be dumb.

It could compromise her on the job. That would compromise her place at Price Security, and that would cost her the only family she'd ever known.

That was a price she wasn't willing to pay, but one kiss…

Surely she could have one kiss without losing control.

"I want to do more than try you," Nick said. "But I'll settle for one taste of your lips. I know—" He put his hands up by his shoulders. "I'm your client and I shouldn't be asking, but you did ask what I needed."

"I did," she said. Hearing him say that he wanted her wasn't a shock, but what did surprise her was how those words had seemed to intensify the feelings slowly building inside her. She usually thought of herself as one of the guys, as a bodyguard. But suddenly, with Nick in this workout room, she felt like a woman.

She was aware of every part of her body. Her breasts felt fuller and she was standing taller, shoulders back, watching his gaze move further down her chest, lingering over her average-sized breasts. Luna didn't lack confidence in her body, she knew that she was enough for Nick. That he was seeing a woman he wanted.

"This can't happen," she said, vaguely aware that her voice had dropped to a huskier timbre. Her body didn't seem to understand the assignment. One kiss was what he'd asked for, but she was moist and her breasts were full…and she wanted more than a kiss.

A hot coupling against the wall would be a nice starter. Luna shook her head. It had been a long time since she'd had a lover, but the truth was sex was complicated for her. Why was she suddenly look at tall, dark, and arrogant over there and wanting him?

That wasn't her.

"Why not? Are you afraid to kiss me?" he asked.

"I'm not afraid of anything," she said.

Another lie.

She'd been afraid of a lot of things, but most of them weren't physical. Afraid of being alone. Afraid to lose the family she'd found and cherished. Afraid to let Van down.

But for the first time in a very long one, she was afraid to touch someone. She wasn't sure what it was about Nick DeVere that was causing this sensation, but it was definitely there. And she'd be an idiot to ignore it.

She'd never been one to throw caution to the wind. The only time she had was when she'd joined Van and Price Security. So…

What did that mean?

"Luna."

Just her name from his lips in that deep resonant tone of his voice and she knew that, no matter how many arguments her mind might throw up, she was going to kiss Nick.

So she exhaled, stepping forward, closing the gap between the two of them. She put her hand on his chest, feeling the heat of him through the fabric of his Gi. Spreading her fingers, she reached the naked skin at the open in the vee of the uniform and looked up at him from under her eyelashes.

"Nick."

Their eyes met and, for a moment, she saw something… maybe it was the only real emotion she'd seen from him since they'd met. It was naked and vulnerable. It was raw and sensual. Then he put his hand lightly on her waist, pulling her into the curve of his body and bringing his mouth down on hers.

For all that she'd wanted him, for as intense as those feelings were, the first brush of his lips against hers was soft.

But the impact…

She felt it all the way to her core, and everything feminine and sensual inside her sprung to life, demanding that she deepen the kiss. She put her hand on the back of his neck, tipped her head to the side and thrust her tongue into his mouth.

He tasted so good. There was no awkwardness to the deepening of their embrace. He tasted good as she sucked his tongue deeper into his mouth. Sending shivers of sensual heat through her body. This was what she'd been craving since the moment she'd held him underneath her even though she hadn't wanted to admit it.

This wasn't going to be just one kiss.

And this risk might not yield the results she'd wanted because, honestly, she had no idea what was going to happen next. Something she hadn't felt since she'd left that MMA ring with Van all those years ago.

This.

This was exactly what he'd needed. It was odd that the woman providing it wasn't blonde and busty. Or maybe not. Blonde and busty wasn't really his type. It was what he knew that certain audiences expected of him.

She tasted better than he'd hoped, and those curves, which had been on display in the leggings and sports bra, felt even better pressed against him. Well, almost pressed against him. He kept his hand on her waist and his mouth moved over hers with a surety that came from practice. But with Luna, it felt more like instinct. His mind wasn't working, and he wasn't doing this to have some leverage later, as much as he might have wished that were the case.

He kissed her because she was providing the distraction that he needed from the bombshell his father had dropped.

He heard the door open a split second after Luna did, and she had already stepped away from him and moved into a fighting stance as he realized they weren't alone.

"Xander, what's up?"

"Boss is here. He wants to talk to DeVere about Thom Newton."

Nick was used to jumping from one thing to the next, but his body wasn't done with Luna and there was a part of him that wanted to ignore Xander and get Luna back in his arms. Except the behemoth was going to take more effort to avoid, and Nick was pretty sure Luna had compartmentalized him back into the client category.

"What about Newton?" Nick asked as he walked toward the door. Thom was always coming up with ideas that were going to be the next big thing and asking Nick to invest in them. The only trouble was the ideas rarely panned out and often ended up being not all that well thought out. But the man had gone to prep school with Nick and Finn before his family had lost their fortune in the dot com bust…so Nick kept taking meetings with him and inviting him to parties.

"Just a few things that Van thinks Luna should be aware of," Xander said. "I can spar with you if you want while she's gone."

"Thanks, Xander," Luna said.

She gave Nick a long glance before she turned toward the dressing room. Again, he felt very much like he had as a child being passed between his father, Aldo and a nanny.

He wasn't a child. "She can spar with you, Xander, and I'll go talk to Price. We need to get some ground rules in place."

"I'm not staying here," Luna said. "And going up against Van with that kind of—"

"You. Work. For. Me."

"I know," she said. "But the truth is, this is personal."

Xander quietly left, which Nick was only aware of on a peripheral level.

"I get how it's personal for me. How's it personal for you?"

"Damn. I knew the lack of sleep was going to catch up with me at the wrong time," she said.

Interesting. What was she hiding? It hadn't occurred to him that the threat could come from someone who had manipulated the board into hiring them. Was there someone on the board who wanted control of DeVere enough to threaten his father and try to kill him?

He used his leg to kick Luna's out from under her and brought her down beneath him. His body pressed to hers in an unbreakable hold. Unlike in the boardroom earlier, he was ready for her counter moves and kept her pinned down.

He was turned on, but the threat to his life took precedence and he shoved his lust away. "Talk."

"About?"

"Don't be clever. This isn't the time for that. Why is it personal?"

She licked her lips and groaned as his cock jumped and he knew she could feel it pressed between their bodies.

"It's been a very long time since my dick overruled my brain. Now, I'm not saying you're not tempting me, but I need answers."

She shook her head, her cheek brushing against his shoulder. "I wasn't trying to distract you. I'm just…damn. Van knew Jack Ingram."

"The hell you say."

Nick rolled to his back, next to Luna. That wasn't what he'd been expecting. "Does he think I set Jack up?"

"I'm not sure. But I know he wants to find whoever killed Jack, and he's not sure what you are hiding."

"Hiding? I'm the one who's life is being threatened," he reminded her.

"You're also the one who said you were untouchable and that others die around you," she said in a low, quiet tone that made him question if he'd actually held her underneath him or if she'd simply let him.

She rolled to her side, putting her hand under her cheek and looking down at him. Now that he didn't feel the threat from her, lust was making a play for control. It would be a distraction, but he wasn't sure he wanted one just now.

"I didn't kill Jack. He was a friend," Nick said quietly. "If I'd thought that there was any chance of him being in harm's way, I wouldn't have…"

"Wouldn't have what?"

"Let him go in my place," Nick said.

He remembered all the good times with Jack. The close calls where Jack had been his bodyguard and saved his life, and the fun times when they'd partied through more than one forgotten weekend. Now the man was gone.

And no matter that Nick hadn't intended for Jack to die in his place, there was no question it was exactly what had happened.

Maybe talking to Van would help him see things, form another angle, and finally figure out who wanted him dead.

LUNA HAD NEVER felt this deep a longing to say screw it and just give in to her own desires, but the cost was way too high for her to indulge herself. Nick watched her with that level gaze, and her mind was trying to run calculations and figure out the risks, but her body was wanting a kiss. A real kiss. One that wouldn't stop until they were both naked and he was buried deep inside her.

But the risks.

She would be compromised, and that meant she wouldn't be able to continue acting as his bodyguard. Let's face it, she thought, that was the only reason she had to be by Nick's side.

And there was another risk. She'd compromise herself on the job and let down the only family she'd ever had or known.

She had to get up, but seeing Nick this vulnerable, seeing him for what might likely be the first time since they'd met, just letting her in and being totally honest with her, was another kind of aphrodisiac.

He made her want to take the risk; except she knew it would have to be this one time. That was it.

She'd never be this close to him again.

She didn't make sense in his world, she had to remember that.

Luna forced down the need coursing through her body and tried to get her brain back in the game.

"What do you mean—go in your place?" she asked.

He sighed, a deep heavy one that she'd never heard from him before. Putting the heels of his hands on his eyes, he stayed still for a minute. Luna did the same.

"I threw a private party at the beach house. At the last minute, I had an email from the DeVere board that needed to be dealt with. I thought about canceling. Jack and I look very similar, and more than once he's enabled me to 'be' in two places at once. This time, while I was dealing with the board, he went to the party."

"So you feel responsible for sending him in your place? You know you didn't make him go," she said, her mind going to the rational place that his guilt-ridden one couldn't allow.

"I didn't stop him."

"Did either of you see a threat coming? Did you deliberately stay safe, knowing he'd die?" she continued.

"No. What kind of asshole do you think I am?" he asked, getting to his feet.

Luna stood. "I don't. You do."

He looked at her for a second and then nodded. "I get your point. But if you've ever had anyone die in your place, you'd understand that being logical isn't easy."

She reached out to squeeze his shoulder in a gesture of comfort, but the electric tingle that went up her hand and arm and straight through her body wasn't comforting. She was still turned on, still wanted his naked body against hers, still in a place that was very dangerous.

She dropped her hand. "I get it. To be honest, that's why I can't just let my guard down with you."

"Are you tempted to?" he asked.

She could almost see him changing gears. She noticed he still had an erection and his body was tense. He stood close to her, and it seemed as if he were poised and ready to pounce if she gave him the least bit of encouragement.

"More than you know," she admitted.

"Do it. I'm not going to rat you out to Price."

"I can't."

"Why not?" he asked.

"I wouldn't be effective as your bodyguard. I might screw up and get you killed," she said.

"You are too highly trained for that to happen," he said.

She shook her head, feeling her ponytail slap against her neck and wishing it would help her snap out of this mood she was in. For the first time in her adult life, she wanted something that she knew—*knew*—she couldn't have. Nicholas DeVere. The charming, billionaire playboy who she made no sense with.

"I'd be compromised. I'd make a mistake. And that's not why I was hired. So, as much as I want to know how you feel moving inside me, I'm going to keep my distance from now on. And I'm going to ask you to do the same," she said. "I like you, Nick. I want you to find out who is threatening you and your father, and keep you alive."

"You can't say things like that to me and expect me to keep my distance."

"You have to," she said. "I won't say it again."

"Can you really just decide to stop wanting me?" he asked. "You don't seem that emotionally cold to me."

She wasn't, but sensibly stopped herself from admitting it to him. She needed to stop letting him push her buttons and she had to go back to being his bodyguard. Sparring with him might have been the dumbest idea she'd ever had.

"I have to. I'm not willing to take the risk."

"To my life?"

Luna nodded.

"I think there's more to it than that," he said, moving closer to her.

It took all of her willpower to stay where she was and not lean in to him. Not touch him and, conversely, also not run away. She was in that fight-or-flight mode, but the fighting had channeled into something different. She noticed his Gi was mussed and she could see his chest underneath it, she remembered each time her body had brushed his.

"What else could there be?" she asked, distracted.

"Price and the boys. You don't want to let them down, do you?"

She tightened her lips and chided herself for being so transparent. "No."

"I thought so. I'm pretty sure you're denying yourself and making having sex with me into some kind of hair shirt so you can prove your worth to your boss," he said.

"You're wrong. Yes, Van and everyone at Price Security mean a lot to me. But you do, too, Nick, and keeping you alive is the only reason I'm in your life. There aren't a lot of places in the world where I make sense, but Price Security is one of them. Being your bodyguard is another."

He looked as if he were going to argue further. But she wasn't ready to go another round with his probing questions that made her face uncomfortable emotions and facts about herself.

"We should get down to Van. I'll meet you in the hallway after you shower," she said.

"Not coming in with me?"

"Definitely not."

"Are you sure that's wise? What if I'm threatened in there?" he asked.

"Xander is outside waiting for us," she said. "He'll be in the change room with you."

"The hell he will," Nick said. "How do you know he's there?"

"He saw us together…"

She knew Xander wouldn't say anything to the others, but she had to get herself under control. She wasn't about to ruin this job just because she wanted Nick.

He opened his mouth as if to say more but simply closed it and shook his head before heading for the changing room he'd used earlier. She went and notified Xander before going to shower and change herself.

Chapter Eight

Nick walked into his penthouse not really in the mood to be nice or charming. He had masturbated in the shower to get rid of his hard-on. But his emotions—the ones Luna had stirred in him—were harder to assuage, although somehow easier to focus on than the fact that his father had spent all of his life hiding this mess from him.

The behemoth followed quietly behind him, and Nick was surprised at how silent the other man was.

Nick stopped at the bar, looking at the bottle of Maker's Mark, more tempted than he wanted to admit to get drunk so he'd have an excuse for doing whatever the hell he wanted. But the truth was that had never been his style.

"You good?" Xander asked.

"Why wouldn't I be?"

"I can think of several reasons," Xander said. "The boss will be up in a minute. You mentioned you had a room without windows."

Nick gestured to a large room he used for parties when his guests needed more privacy than an open area could afford. He stepped into the room, remembering the debauched, three-day drunken orgy that he'd hosted for Jack's last birthday. It had been a weekend to remember. But the place had been cleaned and long couches and chairs had been brought in to make it resemble nothing more than a sitting room. And Jack was gone.

Losing Jack had been the catalyst to finally getting his father to level with him. But Nick couldn't help feeling that if his father had been honest earlier, maybe his bodyguard would still be alive.

"Nice room," Xander said.

The door opened and Nick didn't have to turn his head to know that Luna had entered. His body seemed to have some kind of radar that sensed her presence. His blood felt heavier in his veins and, even though he'd just jacked off, he felt his cock stirring again.

That somehow almost made him smile.

Sure, someone had been threatening him since his birth, the very thing that Nick had always suspected, but he still wanted Luna. He knew he wasn't going to be able to rest until he had her. It wasn't that he couldn't have sex with someone else. He could find a partner easily. It was that he wanted *her*. He needed Luna Urban.

He didn't know why or how she'd become this throbbing need in his soul, but she was.

"Should we bring a table in here?" Luna asked. "Lee likes to have one for her laptop."

"I'll get it. Why don't you catch Nick up on the latest?" Xander said as he turned to go.

Finally, Nick turned to Luna and noticed that she had the buttons on her jacket done up and that her hair, which had been in a ponytail since he'd met her, was down, curling around her shoulders and framing her face. The change in hairstyle should have made her look softer but, if anything, it seemed to emphasize the steel core that was so much a part of her.

Was that why he wanted Luna and not just sex? He'd always been drawn to strength, but had rarely indulged himself there. He'd always chosen the role of someone who indulged others.

"What update?" he asked, trying to match her professionalism, determined to have her but to not let her know how badly he wanted her.

"A name keeps coming up in your schedule. Thom Newton."

"Thom is harmless."

"Finn thought so, too, but once we started comparing the dates on the letters that were sent to your father and the timing of Newton coming into your life, a pattern is emerging."

Nick rubbed the back of his neck. He'd known Thom from boarding school and, though his family's fortunes ebbed and flowed, Nick didn't really think the other man could be the killer. Most of the time Thom came to him with get-rich-quick schemes. Some of them seemed to have potential while others…were a ridiculous waste of time. Nick had lent Thom money more than once over the course of their acquaintance.

"Honestly, I'm worth more to Thom alive than dead. He doesn't know my father or anyone on the board. Or does he?"

Luna pulled out her smartphone and scrolled through her notes. "There is one vague connection to one of the board member's daughters. But otherwise, no."

"Sheree Caster? He hooked up with her once. I don't think he's a threat," Nick reiterated.

"Why not?"

"He doesn't have the personality to kill anyone. And he certainly wasn't sending threatening notes when I was a baby."

"True, but his mother might have," Luna said. "The notes all mention him as an heir. Did you father have an affair with Newton's mom?"

"Aldo will know," Nick said, glad to have a reason to walk away from Luna. Up close, he was having a hard time keeping his eyes off her lips and mouth.

He called Aldo.

"Nicholas?" Aldo asked as he answered the phone.

"Yes. Aldo, we need a list of all the women my father had affairs with. I think we should start from before I was born," Nick said.

"I'm not sure your father will agree to that."

"I'm not asking out of morbid curiosity. Someone thinks their child is the DeVere heir, remember?" he asked. "We both want to keep him safe. We need to rule out suspects."

Aldo cleared his throat. "Indeed, sir."

"He trusts you and so do I," Nick said, knowing that Aldo would do anything for his father.

"Of course. I'll get the list over to you shortly."

"Thank you, Aldo."

Nick hung up the phone and turned back to Luna. "Aldo will send it."

She simply nodded at him but looked as if she wanted to say something more. He walked over to her, ignoring the fact that even though she wasn't wearing any perfume, she smelled so damned good.

"Do you need anything else from me?" he asked.

For a second, her gaze flickered to his mouth and then she licked her bottom lip and he knew what she wanted. He wanted it too. That kiss that wasn't going to let them escape. The one that had whetted their appetites and made being near her a form of torture he wasn't sure he could endure.

But the door opened before she answered, and he found himself surrounded by the Price Security team. When he glanced at Luna, she was still watching him.

IT TOOK ALL of Luna's control to stay focused on the meeting Van conducted and not on Nick. As soon as it was over, she was going to have to talk to her boss and let him know... she wasn't the right woman for this job. She still wasn't sure why, but she was struggling to be objective about Nick.

It was one thing to say that maybe it had been too long since she'd had sex, but it was more than that. She normally wasn't that sexual, and ignoring her desires had never been this hard before. But as she'd sat across the room from Nick, watching him, she'd seen how the pressure of every moment of his life being analyzed was affecting him.

Though he had always lived his life in the spotlight, this was different. They were delving into a very private part of his existence, and as much as he was willing to discuss it to possibly find the person trying to kill him, he definitely didn't like it.

The team filed out and Luna glanced at Xander, who had to have observed the fact that she'd been feeling more than protective toward their client. He just nodded as she got to her feet and followed Van out the door.

"Van, got a second?"

She watched as the rest of the team trailed Lee to the elevator and, when they were alone, Van turned to her. She almost told him to never mind, but the truth was that this man had saved her and put her on a path she was meant to be on. A path she'd almost compromised in Nick's workout dojo earlier today. A path that, she suddenly realized, had a fork in the road.

"I do. What's up?" he asked, his voice that low rumble she knew could go from comforting to threatening in a nanosecond.

"I told Nick you knew Jack. He is eaten up with guilt over the fact that Jack died in his place. I think you should come clean with him. Nick had nothing to do with Jack's death other than the fact that someone wants him dead."

Van gave her that slow head nod he did when he processed information. "What else?"

"I want him. I haven't given in to it, but there's a chance I will. Maybe you should reassign me."

Van raised both eyebrows at her and then gave her that slow smile of his. "You would never compromise his safety."

Van's faith in her was reassuring, but Luna wasn't as sure as he was. It only took one distraction to lose a client.

"What if—"

"Don't go down that route. The fact that you are even talking to me about your feelings tells me I can trust you to do the right thing," Van said. "If things change, let me know."

"Change?"

"If it becomes more than want," he said.

"I...won't let that happen."

Van reached over and squeezed her shoulder. "You're human, kid. This is the first time in all the years you've worked for me that this has come up. I have to think there is a reason for that."

"What's the reason?" she asked because, like Van, she

knew Nick was different, or sensed that he could be. But she hadn't been able to figure out why.

"Only you will be able to figure that out. But I'm not going to blame you for catching feels for the man. The heart wants what it wants."

"I'm not sure it's my heart doing the wanting," she admitted.

That surprised a chuckle out of Van. "Whatever it is. For now, we're good. I'll talk to DeVere about Jack. Might be good to compare notes and see if anything shakes out."

"Okay," she said. What else was there to say? Van trusted her to do the right thing, not only on the job and for the company but for herself. Luna knew her past made her complicated when it came to commitment, and it was hard to ignore the fact that she craved a man who wouldn't be in her life after the job was over.

Was that why she was into him? Even though these feelings were strong and something she'd never expected to experience, maybe they were temporary. Temporary had always been where she felt the most at home. She couldn't deny that about herself.

Luna wondered if it was the same for Nick as she followed Van back into the room. Nick and Xander were talking quietly. Nick's eyes flicked over to her and, for a moment, she couldn't look away. She just stared across the room at him, her pulse racing and her mind indulging in what it had felt like to have him under her on the sparring mat.

He raised one eyebrow at her and she shook her head before looking away. She noticed that Finn stood off to the side, watching the two men. The emotions on his face were hard to read, but she could see that they were complicated.

Of all of his entourage, Finn was the one who was closest to Nick. Maybe there was more to be learned from him.

Luna knew he'd been talking to the team, but it was time for her to have a one-on-one. She might not be able to control her emotions for Nick, but she could protect him, and that meant talking to everyone, ruling out every possible person who could do him harm, and keeping him alive until the person trying to kill him was caught.

PRICE AND THE rest of his team left, with Finn following them out, and Nick was alone again with Luna. Hearing the Price Security team and Finn discussing his life hadn't been his favorite thing. He hated dissecting every traumatic moment down to the last detail. Though a part of him was relieved he had concrete proof after all these years that it wasn't some ego-driven mania that had made him think someone had been trying to kill him.

"Now what?" he asked Luna.

"I'd like you to reconsider my wearing a gun at the VIP party on Friday," she said.

"No."

He didn't care how many times she asked, he wasn't backing down on that. They'd come to arrangement about the metal detectors for his guests and the list was being vetted by Price Security. Luna had been quiet during the meeting.

"Fine. What do you usually do during the afternoon?" she asked.

"Work, take calls, that sort of thing. Why?"

"It's probably for the best that you pretend to be back to 'normal' so whomever is after you thinks you've relaxed your guard."

He wasn't sure anyone was going to believe that given

the way Price Security was all over his building and his life. But at the moment he was ready to do something that felt normal.

"I'll have to be in my office with all the windows," he said dryly.

"That's fine. They are bulletproof and I'll be in there with you. What did Jack do usually?"

"Stayed in the office, went over security footage, vetted my schedule," he said.

"Great. I'll do that. Did he have a desk in your office or just sit at that little table?" she asked.

"Just sat at the table," Nick said as he gestured for her to lead the way out of the sitting room.

"Why are you being so cooperative?"

"I did hire you and, as you pointed out, it would be foolish to ignore your advice. Plus… I need something that I feel like I'm in control of and work is the one area this hasn't touched," he said.

She stopped and turned to him. "Control is an illusion."

"No one knows that better than I."

"Are you sure about that? It still feels like you are playing a game with me."

"Maybe that's because you are," he said.

"What game?"

He shook his head. "Seriously?"

She breathed in deeply through her nose and then licked her lips again. "It's not a game, Nick. I don't get the feelings you stir up in me. They don't make sense. I don't like it. My world is normally very neatly ordered and you are…not."

He almost smiled because hearing that she was as confused by their attraction as he was reassured him. Also, it gave him an excuse to not think about the fact that there were too many moving pieces in his life right now.

His father wasn't who Nick had believed him to be. He was now suspicious of people he'd known for most of his life. And his new bodyguard had him tied in knots.

"Glad to hear that."

"Well, I'm not. I can't do this. You weren't wrong when you said I don't want to let down Van. And yet…"

He took a step closer to her. She was the one thing he wanted that he couldn't have. He knew it. Rationally, it made no sense to place either of them in jeopardy, and sleeping with her would do that. But at the same time, he couldn't resist her.

"Yet?"

"Please. Just let me pretend that I'm in control of this," she said quietly. "I've always been very good at not wanting what I can't have."

"But not this time?"

"No."

He saw the struggle on her face, knew that he was making it harder for her, and there was a part of him that wanted to keep it going, but he couldn't. "What did you want that you couldn't have?"

Her arms came up, wrapping around her waist. She tipped her head to the side, seeming to study him, and he had the feeling she was trying to decide if she could trust him with the truth. "You know everything about me, Luna. You can trust me."

"Just normal orphan kid things," she said.

He had almost forgotten she'd been raised in the foster care system because of the way she held herself and moved.

He had filed the information away. That was his habit.

Tucking little bits of things people told him away so he could use them later. He never knew what would be of the most value, but everything a person said had some weight to it.

"Like wanting a family?"

"Sometimes, or just siblings, or a new car, or someone to worry about me," she said. "But I had somehow gotten used to telling myself that I was better alone. And I think I believe it most of the time."

"But not now?" he asked.

She didn't answer him for a long moment and then dropped her arms to her sides. "I have Price, so I know that I'm not alone, but part of me always believes that it's only temporary. That one day soon, he will leave or I will let him down. That's why I'm trying so hard to resist you, Nick."

"Because of Price?"

"No, because I know that anything that happens between us would be temporary, and I'm not sure I would be able to believe myself if I had to pretend like that was enough."

Temporary.

His entire life had been that—of course, on a grander scale than Luna's had been. Her words resonated, and he knew that, deep inside he feared the same thing. That he collected information about people so he could use it as leverage to keep them in his life.

Luna protected those she cared about for the same reason.

Chapter Nine

Luna didn't spend too much time dwelling on the past. If she'd learned anything in her life, it was that regret had no place in it.

Instead of regretting her lapse of judgment from the day before, she woke early and worked out in her room, feeling restless despite the fact she'd finally slept. She'd been given the room next to Nick's and entered the main living area of the penthouse, finding a woman sitting on his couch, holding a to-go cup of coffee and looking a bit put out when she realized that Luna wasn't Nick.

"How did you get in here?"

"I have a key. Who are you?"

"Who are *you*?" Luna countered.

"Verity Vaughn."

The ex. The one who was supposedly planning Jack's funeral, and not a threat.

"Luna Urban, Price Security."

Verity got to her feet, tossing her long blond hair as she did so. She passed the to-go cup of coffee back and forth between her hands. Luna suspected the other woman was nervous. Because her energy made it seem that way.

"The bodyguard? Seriously, Nicky needs someone big

and tough like the dude who was downstairs. You look like I could take you."

"You can't. Why are you here?"

"To talk to Nicky," Verity said slowly. "I'm planning his last bodyguard's funeral. And just so you know, he was way tougher than you."

"Are you threatening me?"

"No," Verity said, walking closer to Luna, her high heels clicking on the tiled floors. "Warning you."

"Verity, leave her alone," Nick said, coming into the room.

Luna glanced over her shoulder, noting that Nick hadn't gotten less attractive overnight. He adjusted his tie as he walked toward his ex-wife. He bent to give her a kiss on the cheek and then turned away.

Luna wasn't jealous of Verity Vaughn. Not in the least. But there was something fierce and elemental that went through her as she watched Nick kiss the other woman. As if her body and soul had claimed Nick for herself. But he wasn't hers. He was only hers to protect. Hers to guard. Hers to keep safe.

She repeated it to herself, trying to make herself remember it.

"Why are you here?"

"Jack's funeral, which I almost have totally planned. I would be done, but I'm still dealing with Hugh."

Nick glanced over at Luna for the first time that morning. Their eyes met and held for a moment. As much as he was charming and affable, and seeming to indulge Verity, Nick was clearly annoyed with the other woman. Luna gave him a slight smile before turning away from the two ex-lovers and doing a perimeter sweep of the room.

The sun had risen and the streets below the Art Deco

penthouse were busy with cars and pedestrians. Luna wasn't worried about Verity's presence in the penthouse, knowing that Xander would have cleared her to come up. But she was determined not to walk into any more surprises until they caught the person threatening Jack.

She texted Xander, who just thumbs-upped her message. She wanted to ignore the conversation, which involved a favor that Nick owed Verity, but Luna's mind was busy putting together the puzzle pieces. What kind of favor did Verity have in mind, and why did Nick's ex-wife think he owed her anything?

Finn had said that she might be a threat, but Nick had dismissed her as harmless.

As Luna watched them interact, she leaned heavily into the body language training she'd had last year. There was palpable tension between the two of them when they thought the other wasn't watching. But when they looked at each other, it was all big, toothy grins and easy conversation.

There was definitely more there than met the eye. But what? Murder? Why would the woman responsible for killing Jack then plan his funeral? Though, from what Rick had said, killers were complex and needed attention despite not wanting to get caught.

This was the first time Luna had been this close to a murder. Normally, she spotted threats and kept her clients safe. She had been part of routine team investigations because, as Van always said, they each brought unique skills and viewpoints, so he liked having everyone's perspective.

This was different. Luna was on the front lines of danger. The right information could crack the case and save Nick.

But no matter how professional she felt this morning, she couldn't forget yesterday in his workout dojo. She was trying to be the person she always was. A sexless, bionic woman who did her job. But reality was more complex. She wasn't sexless or bionic. She was just a woman who was more jealous of the ease that Verity had in Nick's house than she wanted to admit.

Nick glanced over at her and she realized that she wasn't even close to knowing how to stop feeling turned on when he did that. Like, right now, she was struggling to keep her pulse steady and to control the need in every fiber of her being to touch him. That, she wasn't going to do.

"Luna, I'm going to text you an address I need to visit this morning. Will you clear it for me?"

"I will," she said. "Where are we going?"

"Is she going, too, Nicky? I thought we'd do it together," Verity said.

"I'm definitely going," Luna said. "I am his bodyguard."

Verity just tossed her hair and took a sip of her coffee. Luna had to admit she really didn't like the other woman. But Nick ignored his ex and came over to her.

"We are going to Verity's current husband's house to see if I can get some of her stuff back," he said. "I owe her a favor. It shouldn't take long, and when we get back, the dresses I ordered for you should be here."

"Dresses?"

"That one you have won't do. We want the world to think that I've let my guard down. That means showing up with a date on my arm, not a soldier," he said.

"I don't think that's what we want," she said pointedly.

"It's what I want," he said.

Damn. The word *want* echoed in her mind. She definitely didn't need to be thinking about what he'd wanted yesterday or how his mouth would feel against hers if she finally gave in.

NICK HADN'T SLEPT WELL. He hadn't been able to stop thinking about Luna, and what she had said, all night. She only made sense in his world if he was in danger. That was a hard truth to face, and he knew that he should man up and shove his feelings down as he always did. But seeing her and Verity together made that so much harder.

Verity was beautiful and always had been, but next to Luna, all he could see was the artificial layers his ex used to protect herself from the world. They were a barrier she wore to manipulate the people around her, like her volunteering to plan Jack's funeral just to get Nick to go and negotiate with her husband.

Luna didn't need any of that. She was real and honest, and there was nothing artificial about her. And as much as he knew that she really had no place in his life, that wasn't enough to stop him from thinking about her. To try to create a spot for her.

He was looking forward to seeing her in the dresses he'd picked out for the upcoming VIP event. He could tell she wasn't pleased with the fact he had done that, but he didn't care. He wasn't a man who lived his life by anyone else's rules, and now that everything in his life had been upended, he felt even more determined to do what he wanted.

The door to his penthouse opened and Van walked in. "Great, you're both awake. We need to talk. I just found something in one of the letters."

Nick felt a tingle go down his spine. The letters. He'd been over them himself several times and nothing had stood out.

"Which one?" Nick asked.

"What letters?" Verity asked at the same time.

"Verity Vaughn, right?" Van asked her.

"Yes," she said in that haughty tone she reserved for staff.

"You need to leave."

"I'm not—"

The piercing sound of an alarm rang out. Luna was next to Nick in a flash, one hand on his arm, the other pulling her weapon from her shoulder holster.

"Fire alarm," Van said. "I'll take Ms. Vaughn. You get Nick out of the building."

"Wait a minute—"

"You don't have a minute," Luna said, urging him with her as she moved through the penthouse. She stopped as she opened the door, using her body as a shield as she scanned the hallway for threats before she reached back to take his arm again. He shrugged free of her.

He appreciated she was trying to keep him safe, but he wasn't about to watch her be attacked—or worse, take a bullet for him. "I'll go first."

"You'll do what you're told," she said. "Stay to my right and just slightly behind me while I check the stairwell."

"I've got him covered," Van said.

"What about me?" Verity asked.

"You're fine," Van said.

Nick didn't like this at all. But he'd been wanting someone to believe him for years when he'd said he thought someone was trying to kill him. He just hadn't envisioned it going down like this. Everything was slipping out of his control.

"Clear…but I'm not sure we should use the stairs," Luna said. "It's too quiet. I don't like it."

Van came up next to her and together they formed a protective area around Nick and Verity. He was the damned damsel in distress as far as Price Security was concerned.

"I agree. If the alarm was tripped, then it's a trap," Van said, turning to Nick. "Is there another way down?"

"There are two sets of stairs," Nick said.

"I'll take Verity and go to the right. You take Nick and go left," Van instructed Luna.

"I'd feel safer with Nicky," Verity said.

"You don't get a vote. Get him downstairs and out of the building," Van said.

Luna nodded and her face tightened. Nick saw a stillness in her that he'd seen when she'd launched herself across the boardroom a split second before the bullet had hit the glass.

In this split second, Van and Verity had left and Luna had turned to him. "This isn't the time to be the boss. I need you to follow my every instruction," she said.

"I will."

He wanted the person threatening him caught. He wanted Luna safe. So, for just this once, he was willing to take orders.

They entered the stairwell she'd quickly glanced into and cleared. He followed her closely, watching for directions. She motioned for him to stand in the corner while she partially descended the first flight of stairs, glancing both above and below as she did so.

She'd looked over her shoulder and started to motion him forward when a gunshot rang out. A bullet hit the wall just next to Luna's head and she returned fire. Motioning for him to get down, a second bullet set debris ricocheting off the wall, cutting Luna's face. He saw the blood dripping down her cheek.

Fear and anger gripped him and, though he knew he'd hired her to keep him safe, he couldn't stand by while she got injured. He let out a primal yell of anger and rage, and stormed the stairs in the direction of the shooter. He heard footsteps pounding in front of him as the assailant ran down the stairs.

Nick pushed harder, using the handrail and skipping several steps, trying to catch the person fleeing. He was vaguely aware that Luna was behind him, keeping pace with him, but he didn't slow his steps. He didn't stop.

It was time to put an end to this. He was ready to get his life back and to protect Luna. As he'd told her yesterday, he wasn't prepared to let another person die in his place. Not even the woman who'd been hired to protect him.

LUNA WAS PISSED. She followed Nick down the stairs as bullets flew by. Now that Nick was exposed, she knew she wasn't in any danger. He was. Making ground catching up to him, when she was close enough, she tensed her body and launched herself at him. She caught him by the waist and used the force of her body to push him to the ground.

He struggled underneath her, but she used all of her strength to hold him down and was tempted to pinch the nerve in his neck to knock him out. She was so mad at him right now. She knew that she needed to be clearheaded, but he kept putting his life in jeopardy. Kept acting like his life didn't matter and that he didn't respect her skills. She looked down into his blue eyes and the barely contained anger within them.

She was so angry, she couldn't speak. On the verge of losing control, which she couldn't allow to happen, she got off of Nick's body and stayed in a shooter's pose until she heard the outer door at the bottom of the stairs open and someone escape out of it. She grabbed her phone, alerting her team that the suspect was in the alley, and then turned back to Nick. He had moved to sit, his back against the wall, watching her.

"What the hell were you thinking?" she demanded.

"That I'm not letting you get injured to protect me," he said.

"That's literally my job, Nick. You aren't going to do that again," she said.

"I'll do whatever I have to," he said through his teeth. "I can't sit still and watch you get injured."

Before she could respond, he pulled a handkerchief from his pocket and pressed it gently to her face. Her cheek had burned when the debris had first hit her, but she'd ignored the rest of the pain. Pain was easy to ignore. His touch on her face wasn't.

"You could have been killed," he said as he moved to his knees so that they were facing each other. His body heat wrapped around her and she felt the exhalation of his breath on her uninjured cheek.

"So you thought it would be better if *you* were?" she whispered. She reached up to touch his face, knowing that no matter what she'd said yesterday, she was already compromised.

Luna closed her eyes. She was going to have to quit. There was no way she could be objective where Nick was concerned.

She felt the brush of his lips against hers and her eyes opened, their gazes met, and she let go. He was alive and safe, despite the fact that he hadn't listened to her, and for just this one moment she wanted to celebrate that. She moved her mouth against his, her tongue thrusting deep into his as she leaned forward until his chest was against her breasts. His free arm wrapped around her waist, pulling her against him as he ravaged her mouth, kissing her deeply and with more passion than she expected.

She shouldn't have been surprised. Whatever else she thought about the attraction between them, it was mutual. She'd realized that yesterday in the dojo and today on the stairwell as they'd both been trying to save each other. But she knew this had to end.

Except, right now that didn't matter. All that mattered was the way his mouth felt on hers. The sensations and feelings spurred by his heat flowed through her body, turning the adrenaline from the chase into something more sexual.

Her center was moist and aching. She craved him. Wanted him right here in the stairwell, even though her smartwatch was vibrating—she was pretty sure Van the rest of the team were waiting for her to check in.

Luna put her hand on his face as she sucked his tongue deeper into her mouth and then reluctantly broke the kiss.

His mouth was wet and swollen from their kiss and she licked her own lips as she got to her feet and then offered him a hand to help him stand. He got up and looked as if he wanted to say something, but she shook her head. She wasn't going to talk about any of this.

She glanced at her watch. The latest message told her to meet in the club in Nick's building. That area had been secured.

She put her hand on the small of Nick's back and felt an electric tingle go up her arm as she directed him through the building to the club. He stopped her before they could enter.

"I want to talk to you alone," he said.

"Boss. Oh, my freakin' God, Nick. Are you okay?" Finn asked, coming toward them before Nick could continue. The other man looked pale and scared. He noticed the blood from Luna's face that had splattered onto Nick's collar.

And went even paler.

"I'm fine," Nick said. "Luna is the only one who was injured."

"Are you okay?" Finn asked.

"I'm good."

"Well, okay. The board is here in the conference room. Kenji wouldn't let any of them leave during the alarm, which freaked them out. So you're going to have to get up there and calm them down."

"Not yet," Luna said. "We need to go into the club and talk to Van."

"Why?" Nick asked.

"The alarm wasn't triggered by smoke or a fire, it was deliberately set. The building is being locked down until we can talk to everyone."

"I thought the shooter got away," Nick said.

"We don't know that they were working alone," Luna said.

"You could still be in danger," Nick said, looking directly into her eyes.

She felt the heat in his gaze and it did little to cool her down. It was only her fear that he could have been shot and killed that tempered her desire. His wanting her made it harder for her to ignore her own feelings. But her wanting him could cost him his life. She had to stop this now.

"No. You could. Finn, come with us. I want to know the

names of each of the board members and when they arrived," Luna said, directing both men into the club area where Van waited.

Chapter Ten

Nick felt edgy and not really in the mood to listen to interviews conducted by the Price Security team. But Luna wouldn't let him out of her sight and also wasn't up to talking to him alone, so he went to the grand piano he kept in the VIP section of the club and sat down.

Finn followed him over, bringing rocks glasses with whiskey for both of them and sitting next to him.

"So far, this whole 'find who killed Jack' thing is wearing my nerves down," Finn said as he took a healthy swallow of his drink.

Nick straightened his tie before doing the same with his own whiskey. "It is. I could do with a lot less being shot at."

"Me too. So who do you think it is? Price said he has a lead based on one of the letters, but wouldn't share any more information. That man plays his cards very close to the chest," Finn said.

Nick cracked his knuckles and then ran his fingers over the keys, finding solace in the familiar. His mind was whirring with possibilities, fears, and a little bit of anger toward Luna for endangering herself. He soon found himself playing the classicized version of "Dancing On My Own" made popular by a TV show. Finn stayed close to him as he played. His friend was worried about him.

But he had no words to reassure Finn. That was probably why he was playing the piano instead of talking to the board of directors, several of them people he'd known most of his life.

Luna had advanced the theory that maybe someone on the board was colluding with Thom Newton to threaten him. Was that possible? Nick started to go over every interaction he'd had with the different board members. But he knew he had to go further back than the last ten years, when he'd been running DeVere Industries.

He had to go all the way back to when he was a child.

There were five board members who had been there then. There were three more who were children of previous board members, so they would have a connection to his family. His father had handpicked most of them. DeVere wasn't publicly held; it was a shared investment group with Nick and his father holding the lion's share of the power.

He heard the low irascible rumble of Mitch Dumfries voice, a big bear of a man who his father had met after the Mitch had left the army. He'd been instrumental in bringing in government contracts when DeVere had started out.

Nick found himself switching to a Chopin étude, which helped him to think better. Mitch had apparently known Nick's mom. Had Mitch had a crush on his mom? Or maybe they'd dated before she met his dad? Something that Nick had never really thought about until now. Until he'd read the letter that had gloated about Nick's mother's death.

But if Mitch had known her and had wanted her for himself, killing her would have made no sense.

"Enough with études. I can't deal with this angsty music right now. Play something upbeat," Finn said.

Nick lifted his hands and stopped playing, turning to the other man. "Like what? I'm not sure of the right music for post-someone-tried-to-kill-me."

Finn put his arm around Nick and hugged him tight, whispering, "Stop scaring me."

Nick hugged Finn back. "I'll try."

"Should we try to get back to normal?" Finn asked after he finished his glass of whiskey.

"Yes, but I'm not sure what normal is anymore. It's only been, like—what?—three days since Jack's death. But it feels like a lifetime."

"Nicky! Tell them to let me leave," Verity called from across the room.

Nick sighed. He had forgotten that Verity was there and still needed him to go and talk to her soon-to-be ex-husband.

"I'll deal with her if you want," Finn said, turning and standing up from the piano bench.

"You're just looking for a fight," Nick pointed out. Those two would never get along.

"I am. I suspect she is too. As much as I'm not Verity's biggest fan, we do both love you, and seeing you shot at isn't the easiest thing to deal with."

"For me either. I've always felt unbreakable…" he trailed off. What was he going to say? That he knew those around him weren't? Was he being selfish by keeping Price on the job and by letting Finn, Hazel and Verity stay close to him?

"Don't stop feeling that way. I suspect that's part of what's kept you safe all these years. I'll take care of Verity. You do what you need to. The board is here for the negotiations, and Loni Peters has some new business. She wouldn't elaborate."

"Thanks," Nick said as Finn walked away. He looked down at the keys and thought of how everything made sense when he had a focus. Sometimes it was music. Others, business. Or a woman.

Luna danced through his mind.

What was he going to do about her? That kiss. Hell, if they hadn't been interupted, he wouldn't have stopped kissing and touching her until he'd buried himself inside her body, taking her until they both screamed.

Another distraction, but part of him believed it was more than that.

He should be coming up with a strategy for the board meeting and whatever new business Loni was going to spring on him. It was something he could control. In the boardroom, no one second-guessed him for long.

But he knew that control was an illusion. If he'd had any doubts, that alarm had put them to rest. Price had been bringing the board members down one at a time for questioning. Nick ignored them while he sat at the piano.

In the background, he heard Price questioning the board. Some of them sounded bored and annoyed, others sounded worried.

Nick wasn't sure what to make of that.

"We are almost done with the questioning," Luna said, coming over to him. "Xander swept the boardroom, so you are cleared to go up there when you are ready."

He looked over his shoulder at her. "Thanks. I want to talk about what happened in the stairwell."

"I don't."

"Well, we don't always get what we want, do we?"

"No."

She stood there, holding his gaze in that steady unflappable way she had, and then she exhaled and moved to sit next to him on the bench in the same spot that Finn had vacated.

"Okay. Talk."

LUNA HAD TRIED to stay away. But her job was to protect him. They were interviewing everyone who had access to the building and the codes needed to bypass security. Price and the rest of the team had that handled. Being close to Nick seemed the smartest place for her to be.

She was still edgy. She should have anticipated he'd run after the assailant. He was too determined in his belief that he couldn't be killed. But she knew that he could be. That, more than likely, someone he knew was the culprit. She had pretty much ruled out Verity as the killer; she'd been in the room with them when the alarm had gone off.

But that didn't mean Verity wasn't working with someone else.

"I could have caught the gunman if you hadn't brought me down," he said.

"What? No, you couldn't have. He had a gun, and if we hadn't been giving pursuit, he probably would have stopped and aimed and hit you," she said.

"Or you," he said.

"We've been over this already, but it's my job to keep you safe. And I wanted to wait until later to have this discussion. But you need to stay behind me. Let me do what I'm good at."

His fingers moved over the piano keys. The music wasn't familiar to her but it stirred her, fanning the flames of restlessness in her soul.

"Who else have you protected?" he asked. "Tell me more about you so maybe I can stop from trying to interfere."

She smiled to herself, he wasn't looking at her, just moving his fingers over the keys, and she couldn't help but keep watching as he did so. His fingers were long and nimble, and he played with the same expertise that he seemed to bring to everything he did. She wasn't surprised by that.

"Well, I just came off tour with Jaz, a pop star. He was being threatened by a major fan," she said, remembering the six months she'd spent in South America with Jaz. "Unlike you, Jaz listened to me. I didn't get in the way of his concerts or parties, but I still kept him alive."

Nick stopped playing. He didn't turn to face her, but as she looked at his profile, that strong jaw and the sharp blade of his nose, she knew he wanted to. He was good at controlling his impulses. That meant that he hadn't dashed around her without thinking. He'd deliberately put himself between her and the gunman.

"You're not bulletproof," she said. "I need you to understand that."

He did turn then, and she saw passion on his face. It was dark and angry, fueled no doubt by the shooting and being trapped in this room. This place where he'd always been the demigod in charge of his world. But the power had shifted with the threat to his life and it didn't take a genius to realize that Nick would rather risk his life than accept it.

"I understand more than you. Those letters only confirmed what I already knew. Someone has been trying to kill me since I was born. I'm still here, but my mother, cousins, friends, bodyguards aren't. What exactly do you think I'm missing?"

He had a point. She saw the events from his perspective, but at the same time she knew his impulses could be a death sentence. "You're getting reckless. That is changing things. Also, these attempts aren't even trying to look like accidents, as they did in the past. There is a new urgency in the attacks that wasn't there before."

Nick reached for his whiskey and took a swallow of it. "So where does that leave me?"

"Under my protection," Luna said. Trapped in her throat were the words she longed to say to him. Promises that she knew better than to make. That no one else would die. That she believed she could keep Nick safe. But he had to want to be safe. "Putting yourself in danger won't bring those you lost back."

He turned to her then, looking down his nose at her, and she shivered at the expression on his face. It was fierce and determined. "I realize that. But watching others get hurt… you're still bleeding, Luna. You won't let me help you, you won't let me try to keep you safe, you won't—"

"You're right. I won't. You hired me for this reason."

"I hired you because I thought you'd provide cover while I investigated Jack's death. But that's not working," he said.

Slightly shocked that he'd thought of conducting his own investigation and that he'd thought she would be malleable. "I can't provide cover if you duck around me."

She just kept hammering away at his lack of self-pres-ervation. She had a thick skin when it came to men who thought she wasn't up to the job of protecting them. It did hurt a bit, though, to think Nick had viewed her that way.

"Going to ignore the personal part?" he asked.

"I am. We're not doing personal."

"I want to," he said. "I need the distraction from all of this."

"That's not my job."

"And you're all about the job, right? Is that why you kissed me in the stairwell?" he asked.

She heard the taunting note in his voice. She suspected he had the same chaotic energy coursing through him that she did at this moment. A fight or a kiss...something physical was the only way to channel it.

"Perhaps. Is that why you're playing the piano?"

He rubbed his jaw and then nodded. "It is. Shall we go up to the boardroom?"

She knew he was frustrated that she wouldn't discuss kissing him, but she still didn't know why she had. She'd been scared for him and angry and scared for herself. And it had been too long since she'd felt anything like that for one person. She'd given into her desires, and while she didn't exactly regret it, she knew it couldn't happen again.

Nick was glad to have DeVere business to concentrate on. He conducted the meeting and ignored Luna sitting in the corner taking notes. Remembering what Finn had said, it was hard not to look at the board with different eyes. Was there someone who wanted to be the chairman enough to kill him?

Honestly, he thought it would be easier to try to get the other members on that person's side and vote him out. Killing went beyond a need for power and to a certain malice that he wasn't sure anyone on the board harbored toward him and his father. That didn't mean he was right, but as he looked around the table, he determined that most of those in the room didn't have the time to hatch a plot to hurt him.

For a good third of the board, this was one of many companies in which they had a large share. He knew that most of them were more concerned with making money, and as long as the bottom line stayed in the black, they were happy.

"So the latest employee contracts were negotiated almost fifteen years ago and the workplace has changed," Nick said. "Some of the benefits and working conditions that we are being asked to accommodate are pretty much standard in other companies. We've been doing the expanded family leave unofficially, but I think it's time we get it into the contract."

Mitch raised his hand. "That's fine. But this work-from-home thing, I'm not sure it will work."

"What are your concerns with it? Finn will share the study we conducted that showed worker efficiency is up when they are at home."

Nick heard Finn's fingers tapping on his tablet and knew his assistant was sending the study to the board as he spoke.

"My main concern is infrastructure," Mitch said. "A lot of our remote workers are in rural areas without the capability of high-speed internet connection."

Nick nodded and smiled at Mitch. "I want to shift the office costs in the budget to providing that to our remote workers. We can reduce the size of the office space we are currently using. I have two proposals to finish evaluating that were put together by the workers group, but they are suggesting taking the unused office space and renting it out and using those funds to upgrade remote workers' internet and home offices."

"That might work," Mitch said.

"I don't think it will," Loni piped up. "I mean how do we know they will use the upgraded equipment and services for work only. I'm not sure we want to be providing all of that to our workers' homes."

"We should trust them," Nick said.

"Well, yeah, but that doesn't mean they will be honest," Loni said. "We've seen that they can't be with that entire coffee bar service we provided. The security footage showed more than one worker taking snacks and coffee home."

"We dealt with that six months ago, and there have been no incidents since then. I think this is the time for us to show that we value our workers. They can easily find work that pays close to what we do that will allow them to work from home. I'm putting this forward for a vote."

Nick wanted to make DeVere a place where people wanted to come and work. More than just a job. Something the older board members tended to resist so he kept pushing them.

They voted and everyone but Loni agreed, and it passed. Loni then raised her hand to discuss new business.

"I'm sorry to have to be the one to bring this up, but with Everett's health declining, we need to talk about a succession plan. I know that Nick is next in line, but given that someone is trying to kill him, we might need to have someone else standing by."

Nick leaned back in his chair and crossed his arms over his chest. She had a point. "We need someone who knows the business inside and out."

"I agree," Loni said.

"Do you have a name?"

"I do. Finn Walsh. He's been by your side since you took over from your father and, frankly, his availability is better than yours. I think he's a solid choice to succeed you."

Nick glanced over at Finn and saw his assistant looked flushed and seemed unnerved by Loni's comments.

"I agree. Finn would make a good chairman," Nick said. "He already knows our systems. Any other names?"

Mitch, David and Rochelle all had other suggestions but agreed Finn was their first choice.

Nick conducted the rest of the meeting and asked the succession team to get the paperwork ready for Finn should something happen to himself. Nick then closed the meeting and the board all trickled out. Finn stayed and, for one of the few times since Nick had known him, seemed at a loss for words.

"So…"

"So?"

"This is just so unexpected. I mean I had no idea that anyone saw me as anything other than your assistant."

"Finn, you're my right-hand man and they all know how intelligent and capable you are. I'm glad Loni suggested it. I've been so focused on other things, I didn't even think of putting a plan in place for you."

"Are you okay with that?"

He was. There was no one he trusted more than Finn to run DeVere Industries if he wasn't around. He knew his friend would stick to their code of ethics and continue growing the business for decades. "I am."

"Great. Well, then, I guess I better get back to my desk," Finn said.

Luna came over to him when the boardroom was empty. She'd been taking notes the entire time and put her notepad on the table next to him.

"What did you think?"

"That you're more than just a pretty face," she said. "I had no idea you could be that…"

"Smart?"

"Ha. No, not that. You always carry yourself with arrogance, and I guess I expected you to rule over the board, but you listen and put your employees first. Not exactly what I expected from a self-proclaimed playboy."

Her words touched him and he shook it off. He had more money and luck than one person should be gifted with and he'd always tried to put it to good use. But there was something about knowing Luna saw the good him that made him...well, not think about her as only his bodyguard.

"Glad to hear that."

Chapter Eleven

The boardroom seemed to suit him as much as being in the club or sitting at the piano. Each facet of this man was more intriguing than the one she'd seen before. She'd already decided to keep things professional between them, so Luna tucked this new revelation deep inside and knew she'd pull it out years later when this job was over, and Nick had moved on and forgotten about her.

She didn't dwell on the memories tucked in there. He'd asked her about the meeting and her impression of him, but she'd seen on his face that he'd wanted to take things personal. There was even a part of her that understood his motivation. They'd both been shot at. One of them could have died. And they were bonded now by that. She was the only person other than Nick who understood what it had been like in the stairwell.

"What now?" he asked. "I know Price has some theories on one of the letters. Is he still here?"

"I'm not sure. I've sent a message to him, but Xander was the only one to see it. And he's not leaving his post downstairs. I suspect that Van is going over the security footage and analyzing it," Luna said, sensing that her coworker felt guilty that the alarm had been triggered while he was on watch.

Heck, she still felt slightly guilty about kissing Nick. There was a part of her that wanted to be the perfect bodyguard, which she knew she could never be because she was human. She couldn't take her emotions out of the equation. But seeking perfection was part of her makeup. Perfection meant that she could work for Price forever, that they could never abandon her.

She had to remind herself that none of them was perfect. The same went for Xander. He'd been downstairs watching the door and screening all entrants to the building. She knew he'd add watching the security footage as well.

"So it's just you and me for now?"

She hesitated to say yes because "you and me" had conjured up an image of him in her arms. "We are."

"You're so wary now. Why?"

"Being alone with you… I know you want to talk about the kiss."

"And you don't," he pointed out dryly. "Do I seem like the type of man who forces a woman to do something she doesn't want to?"

"Definitely not. You're the type of man who seduces her into thinking it was her idea," she said.

He winked at her. "You do see me."

"I do," she said. If only he was the man he tried so hard to convince the world he was. Instead she saw the complexities that went beyond the billionaire CEO playboy. And *that* man…he was harder to resist. She saw the similarities between them despite the disparity in their backgrounds. He understood her.

"So if we can't get physical—"

"We definitely cannot."

"Tell me about yourself, Luna Urban. You grew up in a group home and had an image of your parents from a 1990's TV show," he said. "What else?"

"I'm a kickass woman who doesn't let emotions get in the way of doing my job," she said. As if saying the words out loud would make them true. But in a sense, it did. She had cared for all of her clients. Most of the people she'd been hired to guard were decent, and scared, and going through a tough time in their lives. And Luna had to admit that helping someone when they were vulnerable was important to her.

It was as if she sometimes thought she was protecting the vulnerable girl she'd been. She knew that what was in the past couldn't be changed, but by taking care of someone else, she comforted that girl who'd had no one.

"You are pretty kickass," he said then straightened his tie, something she realized he did when he was… *Nervous* wasn't the right word, but it had to do with an emotion he didn't want to express.

"You're not too bad either."

He gave her a distracted nod. "I'm sorry. I shouldn't have run after the shooter."

She smiled over at him. "It's okay. Just don't do it again."

"I can't promise that," he said. "My mind knows you're capable and that I hired you to keep me safe, but when bullets are flying, I can't cower. I need to do something."

That made perfect sense to her. He was a man of action. Even conducting the board meeting, she'd noticed that he'd had a hard time being still. He moved always.

"I can see that. You really aren't someone who can wait, are you?"

He tipped his head to the side. "Are you seeing me?"

"It's kind of my job to read people," she admitted.

"Am I that easy?"

"Not at all. I'm guessing, based on twenty-four hours of knowing you. I think that you're very used to adapting and changing yourself to be whatever someone needs you to be."

"How do you mean?" he asked.

She might be a little too real for him right now. But this was who she was. She couldn't just pretend. Not with Nick after that kiss. Since she was definitely going to be lying to him and herself about how deeply it affected her, she had to balance that with the truth.

"Well, when you're with Finn, you're his boss and his bro, and then with Verity, you're all charm and generosity. With the board, you were forceful but fair, listening to everyone's point, even the ones you didn't agree with, before making a decision."

He turned so that they faced each other, barely an inch between the two of them.

"What about with you?"

Luna thought about it but had no easy answer. Because she was his shadow, she was seeing parts of Nick that she was pretty sure he hadn't meant for her to. He wanted her to see him as a man who didn't need her protection, yet at the same time, he needed her to stay alive.

She shrugged as he lifted one eyebrow at her as if to say, *I'm waiting.*

"With me, you are cocky and arrogant, and then a flash of vulnerability comes through," she said. "That's when you are most like yourself."

NORMALLY, NICK ALWAYS had a planned outcome for every conversation or interaction he started, but with Luna, he didn't. He hated that, because with everyone else, he always got a read that let him know who they expected him to be. If he could anticipate that, he stayed in control. Luna was shattering all of it.

"Cocky and arrogant, I'll own, but vulnerable? I told you. I'm unbreakable."

Raising both eyebrows, she just matched him with that level stare. And he wondered what it was she was looking for in his face. Part of him knew that it was only the juggling act and the different façades that kept him ahead of everyone else. Yet, somehow, she was trying to see past it.

"I scare you," he said as the realization dawned.

That was the only thing that made sense to him. She had thrown him off kilter, and he'd done the same to her. It was why she had put that barrier of her job between them. Why she was busy picking him apart. That was exactly what he did when he was unsure. He looked to the other person and found their weakness.

"You do," she admitted. She brought one arm around her waist and then seemed to realize what she'd done and dropped it. She turned and walked to the plate-glass windows, looking down at the street.

He remembered yesterday when she'd done that and seen the glint of a scope. Was he reading her wrong? Was she just doing what she had to, to protect him? Was she determined to not let her control break again because he'd been shot at?

She took her job very seriously.

"I'm sorry," he said again. He wasn't one of those guys who had a problem apologizing. He screwed up from time to time, owning it wasn't an issue for him.

"For what?"

"Making this harder for you than it should be," he said. "Maybe I should text Jaz and get some tips."

She gave an ironic laugh. "Uh, don't do that. I'm not sure late-night parties are what you need."

"You partied with him?"

"That's what he does to wind down after a concert," she said.

"Then why the objection to my party on Friday?"

"Jaz wasn't being threatened by an unknown assailant. We knew who the stalker was, I was just there to make sure that Jaz was safe."

"Was that easier?" Nick asked.

"For me? Sure. For Jaz? I don't think so. It's never comfortable to think someone wants to kill you."

She had a point. "Has anyone ever tried to kill you?"

She shrugged. "Not like you mean."

"Then how?"

She shook her head. Why? Why had she said that? She could have just said no and he'd have let it go.

"When I aged out of the care system, I was on the streets for a few months. I had to fight for food one time."

And that fight had changed her life. She'd lost and been left bleeding on the street. She still didn't know how she'd gotten to the emergency room, but when she'd woke up in the recovery room, one of the nurses, Jean, had offered her a place to stay while she recovered. Jean's kindness had changed Luna's life.

Jean had let her stay until Luna had a job and money for an apartment. That one fight, that brush with death, had changed her. It had made her stronger, but it was very different from Nick's brush with death. Someone had been stalking him his entire life and, instead of making him afraid or forcing him into hiding, Nick had lived his life in the spotlight, taking chances and risks that others might not.

Because he thought he was unbreakable.

And, honestly, she could see why. He had survived things that many others wouldn't have.

"What happened?" he asked.

She shook her head. "I fought, I lost, and then someone was kind to me. It changed me. As I imagine your survival after all the 'accidents' in your past did to you."

He nodded at her. "They did. My father wanted me to be protected all the time, but the truth is that no one can protect me. Not even you, Luna. At first, I thought it was fate or the universe, but now that we've seen those letters, I have to accept it's a real person."

"Does that make it easier?" she asked.

"Easier to find them. I mean fate is kind of a nebulous concept. I've never met a person who I couldn't figure out."

"Me either."

Their eyes met and they both smiled at the same time. There was so much to like about Nick DeVere. So much to tempt her into believing he saw her and understood her. But her old fears stirred reminding her that she no one ever really saw her.

Her phone vibrated and she looked down at the screen. "That's Van. He's on his way up with some footage for you to review."

"Great. The sooner we find out who's trying to kill me, the better," he said.

Then she'd be out of his life. The thought came quickly and with a twinge of sadness. She knew it was for the best. She had no place in Nick's Art Deco tower or his life. Not really. But that moment on the stairs, that kiss, made her want a place.

She'd always been so careful to not lust after things that were out of her reach, so why was he different? Why was he calling to her on a soul-deep level? And why was she having such a hard time ignoring it?

"Luna?"

"Yes?"

"Why are you so determined not to admit there is something between us?" he asked. "I could get it if you thought I was a jackass, but you don't, do you?"

She chewed her lower lip between her teeth. Then took a deep breath. "This job is all I have—"

"You've said that."

"I mean that, in my life, everyone leaves. So if I let you in, compromise your security for a few hours in your arms, I'll lose not only my job but everything."

HER HONESTY TURNED him on and at the same time made him realize there was still so much to her he didn't know. There was a truth to her Nick both admired and really hated. Now, he couldn't try to tempt her and seduce her into his bed as if she were just another hookup.

Everyone leaves.

She'd put into words a feeling that he'd had all of his life but had never been able to vocalize. Except, for him, everyone didn't leave. He kept people around him with favors and money. Something he'd never really taken the time to acknowledge before.

"I won't let that happen."

"It's not up to you. I don't know why I'm so attracted to you," she admitted.

He quirked an eyebrow. "Thanks for that."

She made and offhand gesture. "Your ego is big enough not to have taken a hit from that. You know what I meant. There is no reason for us to have this attraction."

"Chemistry would be a neat explanation but except it feels like something more."

"Except that," she said.

Luna rubbed her inner wrist in a comforting motion and he knew that he couldn't push any further with her. He'd just exist on cold showers until the person threatening him was found and Luna moved on to her next job.

Because a lot of her objections were based in fact. They weren't going to bump into each other after this job was over. She'd go on to her next client and he'd be back to his life of parties, favors, and board negotiations. The attraction between them would fade as new people came into their lives.

He should just let that be the end of it.

But he couldn't. He didn't want to. He wasn't sure if it was that ego she'd mentioned or something deeper. Yet he didn't want to just walk away from the feelings Luna aroused in him.

"Sometimes I feel the same as you do. That everyone leaves."

"You are literally surrounded with people," she pointed out.

"I know. But they are here because they need something from me," he said.

"I don't need anything from you," she said.

"I'm paying you to be here," he said. "But that doesn't matter. If you live your life from that place of fear, you aren't really living."

"Is that why you aren't canceling the party on Friday?" she asked.

"Partially. I'm not a man to cower or back down. I hear what you're saying, Luna, but the truth is, whatever this is between us is bigger than the both of us. It is strong. You're not really my type, yet all I can think about is how you felt underneath me in the dojo. I know someone is trying to kill me and, in the stairwell, when I would have stayed back and let Jack when he was alive protect me... I jumped in front of you."

She stared at him with those wide brown eyes and he wondered if she was really getting what he was saying.

"It makes no sense for me to do that. But I did it because it was you," he admitted.

"Me? Please don't do this. I'm like the worst person to have a relationship with. I've been left alone for so long; I suck at making anything last...except this job. This job and this sort of family I've cobbled together for myself is all I have."

You could have me.

The thought was in his mind before he could censor it, but he didn't say it out loud. When had he ever been enough for anyone? Even Verity, who'd married him for his contacts and money, had moved on to someone else. He knew what Luna wanted. Secretly, he had always wanted that too. A real family. The kind that TV shows and movies always portrayed but that Nick had never experienced in real life.

Even Finn's and Hazel's families weren't like that.

"I'm not sure what you're searching for exists," he said.

"You're right about that. But I like what I have," Luna said softly. "I think I would like being with you, but the truth is we don't know if you're attracted me because of who I am or if you're attracted to me because we're in danger. And I'm not you, Nick. I have confidence when I'm on the job because I know I'm good at it. But in life… I don't know who I am away from Price Security."

Her words were painfully honest and made him wish he could tell her that she was what he wanted. But she was right. There was no real way of knowing what was true and what was due to the situation. But his gut made him want to believe that what he felt for her was real.

Except, his track record wasn't the best. He couldn't remember a single person he'd felt something this strongly for after they'd left him, and wasn't that the proof he needed that she was right.

"I won't make promises that can't be kept. The only way to know if what is between us is real is to test it out and see if it lasts."

"That's a risk I won't take," she said.

"I will. But only when you're ready," he said.

"What makes you think I will be?" she asked.

They'd had enough soul bearing for this afternoon. "No one can resist me."

She rolled her eyes and shook her head. "We will see."

"We will. So after we meet with Price, it will be time for you to pick out a dress for the VIP event, and I need to go and see Verity's soon-to-be ex."

"What's his address? I want to send someone to check it out before we go over there," she said, switching back into bodyguard mode.

He gave it. He didn't know what his next move with her

would be, and that excited him. The unknown had always appealed to him more than following a set path. And with Luna, nothing was as he expected it to be.

Chapter Twelve

Luna was glad to be around Price, Lee and Kenji. She needed to be in a place where she wasn't alone with Nick and where her expertise was needed. Lee had tied one of the letters Nick's father had received when he was fourteen to one of the deadly incidents, and had uncovered its police report. Though it had been written off as an accident, the officer who'd penned the report had claimed that some of the coincidental facts didn't add up.

"Is Officer Peters still with the force?" Luna asked. "It'd be nice to talk to him."

"He's retired and moved to Arizona. Lee is trying to track him down," Van said. "Nick, what do you remember about the accident? It happened while you were home for the summer?"

Nick leaned back in his chair, straightening his tie as he did so. As much as he might have wanted to track down the person responsible for all of his near misses, it must have been painful to be delving back into his past.

"Yes, I was. My nanny was injured in the accident," he said.

"That's Constance Jones?" Kenji asked as he made notes on the pad in front of him.

Luna listened to the questions they were asking Nick, but she was also comparing the letter to the incident report and two newspaper articles that had run at the same time. A few of the online gossip sites also had some write-ups.

So, she pulled them up on her tablet. She was looking for someone or something that matched the description of the shadowy figure on the security tapes who'd pulled the fire alarm this afternoon. She wasn't sure it could be the same person. The attacker today had been about Nick's age, maybe a few years older. So back when Nick was fourteen, they wouldn't have been old enough...or would they?

What was she missing?

Constance had been driving Nick home from Marina del Rey after he and friends had taken his father's yacht to Catalina Island. Constance had been on the yacht with Nick, and her car had been left in an unsecured parking lot.

Further down on one of the gossip sites, Luna read a statement from a surfer who'd seen someone near Constance's car, and as that area was ripe with thieves looking for wallets in unlocked vehicles left by swimmers and surfers, he hadn't really thought much of it. When he'd gotten closer, the person had walked away and the surfer had forgotten about it until he'd seen the accident on the news.

Not really much to go there. The surfer hadn't been able to identify the person he'd seen; he wasn't even sure of their height or gender.

Luna made a note of it, but that wasn't much. It was weak.

This entire case was weak. The person she'd seen in the stairwell, who Rick had chased, didn't seem old enough to have been stalking him for Nick's entire life.

"Constance could tell you more, but as I remember it, we'd turned off the freeway and onto a curvy road that was also a bit downhill. She pumped the brakes and I know I heard something pop, not sure what, and then she said she couldn't steer almost at the same moment that the car careered off the side of the road," Nick said.

His voice was rougher than she'd heard it before, and, maybe for the first time, Luna truly understood what he'd meant when he'd said he didn't want anyone else to get hurt. These letters were solid proof that Nick's theory about someone trying to kill him was indeed true. But the reality of the people he'd known, the ones who had mattered in his life, being killed or injured, had been with him for a long time.

"The accident report says the car flipped three times before landing on the roof. Were you injured?" she asked.

Constance had suffered multiple injuries—including a spinal fracture that had left her paralyzed from the waist down. She'd been transported to the hospital and treated, according to the police report, but Nick wasn't mentioned.

Possibly because he was a DeVere and police reports were public. Maybe his father had suppressed it.

"Not a scratch. Constance couldn't walk…and I walked away," Nick said bitterly. "Where is the connection here, Price?"

Van pushed a piece of paper toward Nick and Luna leaned forward to see; it was a copy of the letter Everett had received after the accident.

There's only one woman who is raising your true heir. Too bad the spoiled brat survived. There's always next time…

There was anger and true malice in that letter. How on earth had Everett not thought to share it?

"So?" Nick asked.

Luna remembered something she'd read on the gossip site in the comments section. She started scrolling to find it again as Van mentioned that this "accident" had been specific in targeting not only Nick but his nanny.

Luna found what she was looking for,

"There's also this comment. Might be nothing but… 'The DeVeres have always used their staff and discarded them. Not surprised that the boy was fine but his nanny was paralyzed. Bet they let her go without any compensation.'"

Nick cursed under his breath, shoved his chair back from the table, stood and walked a few feet away. Luna pushed the tablet toward Van so he could look at the comment. The person had posted anonymously but she knew that Lee, with all of her mad computer skills, might be able to trace it.

Luna walked over to Nick and stood there next to him. She wanted to comfort him. That wasn't her job but that didn't stop her from reaching for his shoulder and gently squeezing it.

"We took care of Constance," he said.

"I never thought you wouldn't."

"But others would have. What is the point of this?" he asked. "I don't want to relive every one of these traumas."

"The point is that now that we've confirmed her accident was connected to the letters, there is a chance the attacker left clues that no one was looking for. The point is these clues could leads us to finding Jack's killer and your stalker ."

NICK NEEDED TO get away. The letters had put a new spin on his entire life. And, as much as he appreciated the validation of what he'd always suspected in the back of his mind, he honestly hadn't been prepared to deal with it becoming fact.

He wanted to punch something, or someone. He needed to get in his car and drive as fast as he could, and maybe, just maybe, he could outrun the thoughts in his head. How was it that he was always unscathed? He hated that somehow he'd been lucky enough to emerge from all of the attempts without a single injury. Constance hadn't let the loss of her mobility slow her down, but there were times when he'd seen the effect on her.

His father had taken care of Constance. She'd been given a home, and staff to take care of her, and received a generous settlement that assured she'd want for nothing. Nick visited her twice a year, but he knew he did that partially out of guilt. The fun-loving woman Constance had been was still there, but Nick's own feelings overshadowed it. She was fine with who she was now, but part of him always wished that he had been injured instead.

"Can we leave?"

"Not yet," Luna said. "I think we need to still go over the arrangements for the VIP event. Today's incident—"

"Finn can handle that."

She looked as if she was going to argue with him, but then gave him a nod. "Where do you want to go?"

Hell.

He couldn't just leave. He had to make sure Luna and her team checked out any location so that they'd all be safe. Somehow, before Jack's death, it had been easier to just think of himself as really lucky and leave it at that. Sure, there were times when things were uncomfortable, but the truth was, he hadn't really dwelt on any of it and now he had no choice.

"Verity's ex. Can we go see him?" he asked.

Luna glanced over at the table. While the Price team and Finn were all pretending to not be listening to their conversation, he knew they'd heard it all.

Kenji caught Luna's eye and nodded.

"Is my car ready?" he asked the team.

"It will be in a few minutes. I had to get Rick up to Xander's post," Van said, standing and coming over to them.

Nick looked at the other man. There was a toughness to Van that Nick respected, but he saw empathy in the man's eyes and wasn't sure how to deal with that.

"We're going to find the person behind this. Once they're caught, I think… It won't make the past easier, but it might help you to finally move on," Van said.

"What makes you think that?"

"Experience," Van said. "I'd like to go over all of the incidents with you at some point."

"I'll do that," Luna said. "You and the team focus on tracking down the person who posted the comment I found on the website. I'm willing to bet that's not the only accident people were commenting on. Maybe there's a pattern to be found."

"I'm sure there is. Kenji is also looking into Reddit and other online forums where the DeVere family is discussed."

"People do that?" Nick asked. He knew that there were some online gossip sites that covered his parties and activities, and he used them to monitor what events got the most attention, but he hadn't been aware that there was anything else about his family.

"All the time," Finn added from his seat. "I can send some links. I monitor most of them for unflattering photos and comments. I never thought to look for anything tied to Jack's death."

"I wouldn't have expected you to," Van said to Finn. "Until Everett shared these letters, there was no reason for you to think that the incidents in Nick's past were anything other than freak accidents."

Nick knew he should be angrier with his father but a part of him—the man who'd just had to relive the accident with Constance—almost understood why Everett had kept them hidden. It was easier to just chalk it up to coincidence than to admit that someone had been stalking Nick for his entire life.

"Thanks, Finn. Actually, thank you all for everything you've done today. I'm sorry that you are in this situation."

"That's not really in your control," Luna said. "I'll check in when we are at the location."

Van nodded at her and turned back to the table as Nick led the way out of the room, but not toward the garage. Instead he took the elevator back up to his penthouse.

Without looking at her he went to the bar, pouring himself a large glass of whiskey.

LUNA STOOD AT the side of the room and looked around for danger. But the penthouse was Nick's sanctuary, the one place that he let his guard down. The marble floor with the thick Persian rugs spoke of opulence and the kind of breeding he had. The grand piano, right in the center of the room, was set so that whoever was playing would be seen from every angle.

"Why do you have two grand pianos?" she asked. Remembering the one down in the bar and talking about this one up in his penthouse now. She had meant to the first time she'd seen it.

"Because I can," he countered.

Nick was in a mood and she didn't really blame him. He was ticked off that they'd been shot at in the stairwell. She was too. She wanted to go seven rounds with him in a boxing ring and use all of her skills to lay him low and remind him that she was in charge.

But that wasn't an option. No matter how ticked off he made her, she was on the job, and that was the one place she'd always been able to keep her cool. None of her other clients had rattled her the way that Nick did.

And she *was* rattled. He'd been reckless and she wanted to yell at him but couldn't. He was the boss, as he'd succinctly put it. But if he died, no one was going to pay their bills.

"Yeah, you do. You're just arrogant enough to buy two high-price luxury items." She'd said it just to irritate him, but mainly because she knew it wasn't a fight she wanted with him. It was something primal, physical.

Even if he was still doing favors for Verity. A woman Luna admitted she was jealous of and didn't trust.

Even her mind was reluctant to say she wanted sex. But she did. Dirty, late-night-in-a-club sex. The kind that didn't matter or come with emotions. The kind that was just a way of letting off steam.

Except she couldn't do that with Nick. Her feelings for him were already too intense.

And she was stuck in this penthouse with him. Only him and this sexual need that was growing because she'd put him firmly off limits. Why was she so contradictory? She couldn't look to her parents and blame one of them because she had no clue who she came from. She had to only look at herself and own the fact that once she decided not to do something, she had the overwhelming urge to just do it anyway.

Do *him*.

He slammed his whiskey glass down on the counter of the bar and, on his way to the piano bench, threw his suit jacket toward the large sofa that dominated the conversation area. He lifted the black thing that protected the keys—she had no clue what that was called—and sat down. He linked his hands and stretched his arms forward before he started playing. "Toxic" by Britney Spears.

The music suited her mood and the way he played it was slower than the Top 40 radio play version. It was moody and dark, angry and sensual.

It had been a mistake to challenge him. She'd known that but had gone ahead and done it anyway.

She felt like the walls of his gorgeous Art Deco building were closing in on her. She'd always had the freedom to have a few hours off, a few hours away from a client, but Nick didn't work that way. And this was an important contract, so she wasn't going to mess it up by asking for time away.

If there was one person she'd hold her tongue and do something this restricting for, it was Van. Only him. He wanted this job; he needed to find out what had happened to his friend Jack Ingram.

But Luna knew there was going to come a time when she snapped and either dragged Nick into the boxing ring or the bed. It was a toss-up right now which one she'd enjoy more…well, that was the lie she was going with.

NICK WAS IN a destructive mood. Hell, hadn't he been in one for his entire damned life? It felt that way. It felt like fate was keeping him alive as some sort of cosmic joke that he wasn't in on. Or maybe it was karmic payback for a former life? He didn't believe in that kind of stuff, but that explanation was all he had.

Luna was needling him. She was ticked that he hadn't let her run after the madman shooting at them. And maybe he should have. Then she'd either have caught him or maybe be dead. He got to the tricky fingering in "Toxic" and concentrated for a moment as he played, then he stopped and looked over at her.

"You are the most frustrating woman I've ever met."

"Ditto."

He shook his head, wishing he'd brought his whiskey over with him. Instead, he started playing Rachmaninov's Concerto No. 2. He had to concentrate to remember it and play the notes correctly. It was one of the first pieces he'd mastered. The one he used when he needed to get back to his Zen.

But he wasn't finding it. Jack dead. His father hiding letters from someone who'd been gloating after an incident that had almost killed him. Luna with her damned kissable mouth standing behind him, glaring at him. Making him want to take her. Right here in the middle of the penthouse on that thick Persian rug.

She was justified in being upset with him. He got that he'd hired her to keep him safe. But there weren't words, or he didn't know how to say them out loud, to tell her what it felt like when he watched someone else be shot instead of him.

He was weary. Like, soul-deep fatigued with this life. This was something that had started with his mother's death. His entire life had been in the shadow of someone who hated him and his father. And, at this moment, there was no way out. No way for him to move past this.

"Nick, stop. That song…it's sad."

He stopped abruptly and turned around to face her, swinging his entire body. "You don't like sad."

"Who does?" she asked.

"I don't know. Everyone should. That's life, isn't it?"

"It can be," she said. "But then sometimes, in the middle of something huge like this, you can find peace."

"Yeah, right," he said. "Did you find peace in foster care?"

"I did," she said. "It took me a while because everyone was always talking about finding a permanent family, and one day I decided I didn't need one. I stopped looking at each house as anything but an opportunity to learn."

He crossed his arms over his chest. How had this beautiful, complex woman never been wanted by a family? "That brought you peace?"

"It did. Find the thing that will bring you peace now," she said.

Her words hung in the air between them.

"Let's go see Verity's ex. If nothing else, it will distract both of us," he said.

He was aware of her following him down to the garage. When they were alone for a split second, where he knew that the security cameras in his building had a blind spot, he was tempted to pull her into his arms. To take what she'd already said she didn't want to give him. But he held himself in check.

In his entire life, this was the first time where he could see that it wasn't fate but an actual person who was forcing his life onto this path. He might have always survived the incidents without a physical injury but his soul had taken multiple hits and he wasn't sure that he could take many more.

He was angry and more determined than ever to find the person responsible and make them pay. Pay for his mother, Constance, his cousins, Jack and...for Luna. Not just the cut on her face, but also the fact that she'd been brought into his life and he couldn't keep her.

NICK WAS QUIET as he drove through the streets of Los Angeles. It just made Luna realize how much of the public man he kept hidden. "Want to talk about it?"

"No."

Watching his profile and sitting close to him in the car, the scent of his cologne was starting to become familiar. That was something that happened with each of her clients, but with Nick it was different. His scent made her pulse race and brought with it the remembered feel of his mouth on hers.

She turned her attention to the mirrors, watching their back as they drove. The house had been cleared and Rick had let Miller know about the shooting. The detective had sent a patrol car to drive by the neighborhood before they arrived. Even she didn't feel great about letting Nick leave his penthouse, but they knew that they couldn't make him stay.

"Tell me about Verity. How'd you two hook up?"

He glanced over at her and sardonically lifted one eyebrow. "Are you sure you want to know about us hooking up?"

She didn't, but she could tell that Nick needed to talk or to do something that would help him mellow out a bit. And, for whatever reason, his ex seemed like something that would be safe to discuss. "Actually, was she ever targeted?"

Nick tipped his head to the side and then shook his head. "We were only married for three months. There wasn't anything at our wedding or on the honeymoon. Jack was my bodyguard then. I'm not sure if he kept any records, but I don't think that anything was going on. Is that weird?"

"Not sure," she said, but took out her notepad and jotted that down. "How old is Verity?"

"Twenty-eight," he said shortly. "She's too young to have rigged Constance's car."

"What about her parents?"

He swerved through traffic and onto the shoulder, bringing the car to a halt as he turned toward her. "East Coast money who don't really care about the DeVere fortune. In fact, they liked me with Verity because I wasn't after her for her money. But please look into them. I'm sure they'd love to know that they are suspects in this."

She knew he was lashing out because he felt so powerless at the moment. She got it. She'd probably have kicked a bunch of dents into the walls of her bedroom if she'd been in his place. "We're more discreet than that. Was her fortune a factor for you in marrying her?"

"No. I like her. She's fun at times."

That wasn't really a reason to marry someone. "Did you love her?"

"Love her? No," he said.

"Then why marriage? It's not as if either of you had to get married," Luna pointed out.

"Dad had his first diagnosis of kidney cancer. So I thought it might be time to think about the future," Nick said.

That made sense. "And then he got better, and you decided you didn't have to?"

He shook his head, resting both wrists on the steering wheel and looking ahead of them, not at her. "Not exactly. Verity is difficult to live with. I know the same could be said of me. We were both too much to be a couple. So we divorced. Dad continued chemo. That's it."

That's it. But it wasn't it. Another relationship where he'd been left alone. She saw the pattern in his life because it so closely mirrored her own. She knew he was being blasé about it, but he must have gotten married for more than the idea of the future. "Did she ask for the divorce?"

"I did. I just wanted— Why does this matter?" he asked her. "This has nothing to do with keeping me safe."

"It does and it doesn't. I think you need to talk, and this is helping. I'm not sure what else to do."

"We could have sex. Right here in the car. That would help," he said.

"I already told you no. I'm not a casual sex person," she said.

Nick rubbed the back of his neck as he turned to look at her. The expression in his eyes filled with heat and questions. "I am."

"I know. It's how you protect yourself."

"And not having sex is how you do it?"

"Sometimes. Mostly, I work and don't have time for a personal life," she said carefully. She hadn't had a relationship in a while. Her job just wasn't one that left time for that, and she liked it that way. Relationships scared her. Sex was complicated for her. The first time she'd done it, it hadn't been great, and she'd realized that sex wasn't really satisfying for her, so she'd stopped seeking it out.

Luna thought it might be different with Nick given that the kisses they'd shared had made her hotter and had been more pleasurable than anything she'd experienced before. But if her past had taught her anything, it was that real life seldom lived up to her expectations.

"And then there's us."

Us.

That was a complication neither of them needed. She wished she could be like Nick said he was. Just have sex and let it mean nothing. But in her heart, she wanted it to mean something. If she was going to get naked, it had to be with someone she trusted. Not someone she was with just to get through something.

"Yeah, I thought we decided there wasn't an us."

"You did," he said, putting the car back into gear and easing back onto the highway.

Nick was quiet for the rest of the drive and this time she left him to his thoughts. She watched their back and kept herself alert to any threat outside the vehicle, ignoring the one that was sitting right next to her.

But then, that threat wasn't on Nick. It was only she herself who was in danger. Because, no matter what Luna had said or wanted to believe, she was becoming more and more compromised when it came to Nick.

Chapter Thirteen

The next two days started to feel almost routine for Luna. She was rested. She'd drawn a line in her mind and put Nick on the other side of it and it seemed, for now, he was he was staying there.

The visit to Verity's ex's house hadn't netted them any more information and a background check on both him and Verity's family had cleared them of any connection to Nick or the threat to his life. In fact all she'd learned was that Nick put on a different persona depending on who he was dealing with. It made her leery of giving into her feelings for him.

Was he only acting like someone she could undertand to woo her into his bed?

Which as soon as she had the thought she immediately dismissed. Nick didn't have to work that hard to land a woman in his bed.

She'd also learned more about Nick's life and habits. He started his day early with a workout; she always joined him on the treadmills in another of the rooms in his penthouse. Then he had a quick breakfast smoothie before going on calls all morning. During that time, she observed and listened to his conversations. Thom Newton's name came up several times, and though Nick didn't want to consider him a suspect, Luna did.

She'd discovered that on the day the fire alarm had been pulled and they'd been shot at in the stairwell, Thom had signed in on the building visitor's log, but he hadn't signed out. And he hadn't been in the group of employees and other visitors held outside by the Price team.

She tracked him online and noticed that most of his feed was filled with photos of him with Nick or at events that Nick attended. He seemed to be a low-level influencer with invites to a lot of LA-based events and deals to promote fitness-oriented products like the smoothie Nick had drank that morning.

Nick leaned back in his chair after he hung up the phone and rose. Luna was on her feet and by his side, knowing he liked to pace midmorning and still didn't seem to get that pacing near a window was dangerous.

"I think we can agree that whoever was shooting at me is taking a break," Nick said.

"I don't think we can," she said.

"What were you working on over there?" he asked.

"More digging into your friend Thom Newton."

He shook his head, turning but moving so he wasn't in view or range of the window. "Are you still going on about Thom?"

"Yes. I want to go and talk to him," she said.

"Why? I told you he's harmless."

She scanned the horizon and rooftops then took a quick glance below to make sure that traffic, both vehicular and foot, was moving along. "Really? Then why was he on the visitor's log two days ago when you were shot at and yet he wasn't in the group of people we questioned?"

Nick furrowed his brow and his jaw tightened. "I don't know."

The quiet way he controlled his face reinforced that he wasn't happy with this latest part of the investigation. He considered Thom a friend. He'd known the man most of his life, and though Finn had mentioned that Thom was someone always trying to make it seem that he and Nick were besties, the relationship wasn't that close.

"Let's go talk to him."

"I can't. I have a meeting, and the party is tonight. He'll be there," Nick said. "We can question him then."

"'We'? I think it would be better if it was just me."

"Luckily, I'm in charge," he said, moving back to his desk and clicking something on his computer.

She knew he was trying to definitively end the conversation. But she wasn't done yet. Now that she'd had sleep and a few days to go over everything, patterns were emerging. While Nick thought he was unbreakable and couldn't be harmed, he'd come very close several times and there were only a handful of people who'd been near him for most of those incidents.

Thom Newton was one of them.

"You can either cooperate or I'll go to Van, who will go to Everett—"

"Are you seriously threatening me with my father?"

She hid a smile at the exasperation in his voice. "I didn't want to, but you're kind of pushing me into a corner. I was hired because I'm good at my job. Let me do it."

He rubbed the back of neck and she saw the stress of the last week in him. He did a good job of hiding it most of the time. He was acting as if nothing had changed, and going about his daily routines and life as if someone hadn't killed his lookalike bodyguard and then tried to kill him twice in two days. She appreciated that he was probably nearing his tolerance level.

"Once you meet Thom, you will realize you are barking up the wrong tree."

"Why do you say that?" she asked, moving over to the table she'd used while he was at his desk. She picked up her pen, ready to jot down anything useful Nick said.

"He's weak. He's not the kind of person who could plot this out."

"Okay then, is he someone who could be used?" she asked. Because, as the evidence seemed to suggest, there might be more than one person involved. Or not all of the incidents in Nick's life were connected.

The kidnapping when he was fourteen seemed isolated and traced to a group with a vendetta against Everett De-Vere. Also, there hadn't been a letter tied to that event.

"Yes, but would he try to help someone kill me or Jack? I don't think so. He wants to be in my inner circle," Nick said.

"Finn mentioned that as well. What's so special about your inner circle?" she asked.

"I'm in the center of it," he said.

Luna smiled at him. She knew he was deflecting. "I'll ask Finn."

"It's ridiculous, really, but those who are close to me get offered a lot of luxury perks and deals from big-name brands. I know Thom wants those introductions."

"So why haven't you given them to him?" she asked.

Nick shrugged and looked back down at his computer monitor. "There's something not quite right about him."

That was precisely why Luna needed to talk to him. "I'm questioning him tonight. I'm not asking you, Nick."

"I'll do it with you. If he is in any way responsible for Jack's death, he's going to pay."

THE DRESSES NICK had liked weren't exactly the kinds of dresses that she could move in. They'd compromised, and she'd ended up with a sequined formfitting number made of stretchy material. It had a slit up the side that ended midthigh, and Luna had done several laps around the room to make sure it didn't hamper her movements.

She wasn't entirely certain Nick wanted her to be able to move. He kept trying to protect her even though sometimes that meant putting himself at risk. And this dress... well, it was definitely one that Nick had picked out so she couldn't wear a gun. Reading the incident reports had only sharpened her desire to protect him and find the stalker. Nick had been alone for too long.

Everyone on the Price team, and even Finn, thought that Nick should cancel the VIP event. But Nick wasn't a DeVere for nothing and, of course, had refused. He had surprised her when he'd invited Thom Newton to come early to the reception for a rapper and his entourage Nick was promoting.

But first, they had the red carpet to get through and the screening of all of his guests. Kenji was to be on the red carpet with Rick. Lee was on the metal detector monitors with Van. Xander was at the door, having trained the extra security and bouncers hired for the event.

The Price team was in place and the Art Deco building was as secure as they could make it. She would be by Nick's side all night and, along with questioning Thom, wanted to see who else came out of the woodwork. Since the men of the Price Security team appeared to the public to be the bodyguards, Nick wanted her to be low-key, hence the figure-hugging dress and no gun. He thought, and Van had agreed, that his apparent lack of protection might force the hand of whomever was behind the attacks.

Luna wasn't as sure since her gut was telling her this was an inside job. Someone in Nick's close circle. Finn was nervous, too, and had been in to speak to Nick three times. Finally, he'd left to go downstairs after telling her she looked great.

"You do, by the way," Nick mentioned after Finn closed the door.

She glanced over her shoulder at him. Nick looked delicious in the bespoke tux. Some men were born to wear formal wear and Nick was definitely one of them. The custom-made tux jacket extenuated his muscled shoulders. God, he made Daniel Craig as James Bond look like some dude. Her pulse sped up and her throat felt tight as she fought the urge to drag him back up to the penthouse.

He didn't fiddle with his bow tie or the button on his jacket. He stood there with the same ease as most men did when they were in gym clothes.

"You, too," she said. She'd done a good job of keeping her emotions in check. The investigation was demanding, which had provided the distraction she'd needed, but late at night, when she was alone in her bed, her thoughts always drifted to that kiss in the stairwell.

Seeing him now, dressed to the nines and ready to walk the red carpet and pretend he was chill when someone was trying to kill him…that turned her on. She liked his guts. Liked the way that, even though the facts were telling them someone he knew was trying to kill him, he still wouldn't hide.

It might have made her job easier if Nick had a little bit of natural self-preservation, but Luna admitted to herself she liked that he was willing to face danger head-on. There was so much more to Nick DeVere than even he would admit.

"Thanks," he said with a wink. "So, for tonight, I want you on my right side. We'll be meeting everyone who comes up the red carpet. The photographers that your team vetted and Getty Images will be there. Once we've greeted everyone and gone inside, I'll say a few words and we will have a toast. Then the general invitees will start to trickle in."

"We've been over this," she said. "I'll be on your left and you will stay slightly behind me so I can protect you at all times."

He looked as if he was going to argue but she simply held up her hand to stop him. "It's that or I change into my suit and carry my weapon."

"Fine," he said. "I don't want Lil' M to know you're my bodyguard. He likes his women, so be on your guard."

"He won't know I'm your bodyguard unless he gets handsy, and then he'll definitely suspect something's up," she said, a clear edge in her voice.

"He's not handsy with someone else's woman."

"It's hard to believe you live in the twenty-first century," she said sarcastically.

"I didn't make this world, I just live in it," he said.

"Fair point," she said, putting her mind back to Thom, whom they were both interested in talking to. "I guess we'll know if Thom was the one shooting at you by how he reacts to me."

"We will. I've asked him to come early, but he was vague if he could. Which… I hate to admit it, but that's odd. He's always trying to get into the VIP room here," Nick said.

"That's good. Means we are on the right track. I'll talk to him. I'm really good at finding out things that people want to hide," she said. She thought it was her face; she looked like someone everyone knew, and they trusted her.

"Great. Hope someone I've known half my life is trying to kill me," he quipped.

"I just want to put an end to this so you can have your life back."

He moved closer. She wondered if he was doing it deliberately; she'd done so well at keeping him physically at bay. But he was right there. She could see his individual eyelashes, so thick and black around that intense gaze of his, and smell the mint of his breath.

"Ready to leave me?"

She wasn't. He was making her question parts of herself she'd never really thought about, and it wasn't comfortable.

"I just want you safe."

That was the truth. She did want him safe. She wanted herself to be protected, also, because Nick had a world of people around him to fall back on and she just had a small circle that she didn't want to let down. She'd forced herself back into her bodyguard role these last two days to maintain that distance.

But standing this close to Nick proved to her that it was all an illusion. She hadn't stopped wanting him. She hadn't stopped reacting to him. She hadn't somehow lost her lust for him.

And even though she knew it put them both in danger,

it took all of her willpower not to touch him and tell him that leaving him when the job was over would be one of the hardest things she'd ever do.

NICK HAD SPENT the afternoon dwelling on what Luna had said about Thom. Then he'd gone into his meetings before again looking at the letters his father had received. He wondered if there was any way that Thom could be his father's bastard. When Nick dug deeper into Thom's past and his family, the murkier things became.

For the most part, Nick hadn't paid much attention to Thom. He had said he was from a prominent East Coast family, but today's digging had revealed he wasn't. What else had Thom lied about? Thom's mother seemed to have no connection to DeVere Industries or anything that would have brought her into Everett's circle. And, most important, Thom was two months younger than Nick.

Did that mean he wasn't his father's bastard? Nick wasn't sure. But he intended to get some answers tonight. But he had to distract Luna, who also wanted to question Thom.

The cut on her face had started to heal and had been covered with makeup for tonight's event, but Nick knew it was there. Knew she'd sustained it by protecting him. And it was all good and well that she was his bodyguard, but he didn't like seeing the reminder of his failure to protect her. Didn't want to see anyone hurt in his place, especially not Luna.

Over the last few days as she'd quietly shadowed him everywhere he'd gone, he had started to see beyond the lust that had first attracted him to her to the woman she was. She was intelligent and really good about reading people. She knew when to leave him alone and when he needed to talk. He'd watched her handle Finn and the temporary secretary/assistant Hazel had hired with ease.

Luna was good with people. Something that he guessed she'd had to learn to be when she'd found her peace in not wanting a family. Ironic because he knew that everyone wanted one in some capacity. Hell, he wanted his to be closer even after learning his dad had been lying to him for most of his life.

Nick was good with people in a different way, and her quiet manner had showed him that people responded to her in a way they didn't to him. He thought she might be able to get answers from Thom. Hell, he knew she could. But if Thom was behind the attacks, then there was a pretty good chance that once he realized Luna was on to him, he'd snap. And Nick wasn't going to stand by while she was shot at again.

All of that wasn't doing much to distract him from how good she looked in the red dress he'd selected for her tonight. She'd dug in her heels and had insisted on a slit in the side of the skirt of the formfitting dress so she could move in it. That, he'd easily given in on. The slit revealed her long shapely leg.

The bodice hugged her curves, emphasizing her breasts and the long arc of her neck. He was glad he'd insisted she leave her gun in her room because there was no way she could have hidden it under that dress. And there was no way anyone would look at her and see a bodyguard.

Much like Jack, his doppelganger, had seemed like a friend, Luna looked like she belonged at his side. Like a girlfriend. A partner in crime.

She'd let her hair down only the second time since he'd met her and it curled around her shoulders. Though he'd thought it was dark brown, he realized there were warm rich strands of red running through it.

It looked soft and bouncy, and he wanted to bury his hands in it and kiss her. Kiss her and maybe convince her to stay up here. To stay safe until he talked to Thom, which, logically he knew made no sense.

She'd proved to him time and again that she was great at her job. So he had no excuse for wanting to lock her away, except that, deep inside his soul, he needed her safe.

If Luna were hurt, it was one scar that might not ever heal. And that was a risk he didn't want her to take, but one that he couldn't keep her from. So he was doing everything in his power to keep her out of harm's way.

"Van mentioned earpieces," Nick said. Realizing that he wasn't sure if he was getting one or not.

"I have one that I'll put in. Do you want one?" she asked.

"I think it couldn't hurt for me to have one," he said.

"Okay. Come on, lets go to the security room and get you set up. You know everything you say will be recorded, right?"

"I do," he said. "Maybe you'll be able to pick up on something I miss."

She stopped him with her hand on his arm as he was about to step into the hallway and he moved aside for her to go first. "You don't miss much."

"I try, but I'm not you, Luna."

She flushed and he noticed it because he saw the color spread up her chest to her neck and then her cheeks. Interesting. "I'm very aware of that."

"Good."

They were both fitted with earpieces and it was odd to hear the private communication going on between all of the people on the Price Security team. But he was glad to be a part of it. He knew that they were watching not only for Thom but for anyone else who was suspicious, and this way Nick would be part of his own security and maintain a thread of control.

Something he'd thought he'd wanted from the beginning. He'd had a vague idea of how this would play out, but nothing so far had been what he'd expected. As he scanned the crowds as people arrived and paparazzi took photos, he realized that he was more nervous at this event than he'd been at any other. Ever.

It was easy to say it was either because he planned to confront Thom or because he knew that the chances were strong his attacker would strike again.

But he knew it was because Luna was at his side. And he had no idea how to handle that.

Chapter Fourteen

The deejay in the booth was playing tracks off Lil' M's new album mixed in with classic club tracks from all decades. He was doing a good job of keeping people mingling and dancing, which made certain aspects of security slightly easier. Rick was in the booth with the monitors and, since most of the attendees were dancing, Luna was able to watch the crowd around Nick.

He was approached a lot and she was always tense until Xander came on the comms and verified the person had been cleared. Nick was jovial and charming, as always, but that tension she'd sensed on the red carpet remained.

Nick was good at playing the part of the playboy with no cares. Slipped into the role like he did his Hugo Boss suits each morning when he went to his office.

When they were alone for a minute, she noticed he was scanning the crowd. "Who are you looking for?"

"No one," he said. "Just making sure my guests are happy. By the way, you haven't had a drink all evening."

She knew he was lying and suspected he was watching for Thom Newton who, so far, hadn't showed. "I've noticed you have had a few."

"Yeah, but it's not big deal. I'm a heavy drinker," he said.

"Why?"

"Why do you think?" he asked.

"To be numb?"

"Sometimes. Mostly it's social and this crowd likes to party, so over the years... I started out drinking to be numb, then eventually I was drinking so much that it was normal and I wasn't getting drunk or numb. But things have changed. I know my limits, and tonight we're working."

"I am. You're the host. If you get sloshed, I've got you," she said.

"I don't want to be numb around you, Luna," he said.

Before she could respond, Finn came up to them, looking dashing in a dark navy suit with a white shirt and tie. "So, Verity is here with some hot, young thing and looking a little too pleased with herself."

Nick twisted his head and Luna did the same, spotting his ex standing on the other side of the room on the fringes of the dance floor. She had her blond hair pulled back into a low bun at the nap of her neck. She wore a strapless, white sheath dress that hugged her curves. She was breathtaking, looking like a young Grace Kelly. But the way she smiled told Luna that Verity was aware that every eye in the room was on her. And she liked it.

"That's fine. Have you seen Thom?"

"No. Want me to text him? I'm surprised he's not here. You know he's got a new business proposal for a music streaming service. Figured he'd want to work the room and use you to help him get investors."

Nick's mouth tightened and he nodded. "Like the world needs another streaming service."

"You're preaching to the choir but Thom...he's always looking for a get-rich-quick idea," Finn said.

Verity and her date headed toward him and Finn grabbed cocktail from the tray held by a passing waiter. "I'm out of here. I'll let you know if I see Thom."

"Thanks," Nick said.

Luna turned so that she faced Nick. "I thought we agreed I would question Thom."

Nick put his hand on the small of her waist, it was big and warm even through the fabric of her dress. "Just because I didn't object doesn't mean I agreed with you."

"I'm not going to let you—"

"Not now. Verity is close enough to hear," Nick said under his breath, brushing a kiss against her cheek.

"Nicky! I didn't realize that...what was your name again?" Verity asked Luna.

"This is Luna," Nick said. "And your date is?"

"Lorenzo Palmieri. Ren, this is Nick and his...date?"

Nick pulled Luna into the curve of his body and a shiver went through her. For a moment, the music seemed muted and the crowd and even Verity disappeared as their eyes met. Her lips parted and he quirked one eyebrow at her. He knew she still wanted him. Hell, it wasn't like she'd been pretending she didn't.

Luna took a deep breath and pulled her training and professionalism around her like a big, cold coat, forcing the heat that Nick generated into her away.

"We are dating," Nick said. "Ren, how do you know Verity?"

"Oh, Nicky, this is the man I'm going to marry once I get free of my horrible husband," Verity said.

Lorenzo put his arm around Verity, seeming to comfort her when the music changed to a Latin beat and Mr. World-wide came on. "Excuse us, I told Luna we'd dance if this song came on."

"I'm not sure dancing is such a good idea," she said as he led her to the dance floor. "I can't really see the crowd."

"Trust your team," Nick said. "Plus, I need a moment where everyone will leave me alone. Van, can you keep watch?"

"I'm on it," Van said in their earpieces.

It was no surprise to her that Nick used his entire body to dance. His hips easily found the rhythm and Luna, who was pretty much a sway-back-and-forth dancer, wasn't sure how to move with him.

Nick put his hands on her hips. "I've got you."

That was all he said. His words were low and whispered into her ear, the one without the earpiece. And that cold coat she'd mentally donned a few minutes ago melted away. The heat of the music, the passion in Nick's eyes and the way his body brushed hers repeatedly as they moved on the dance floor wiped it all away.

She took a deep breath. Wondering if it was okay to let her guard down for a moment. To take this one dance with the man she wanted almost more than she needed her next breath. But as she did, as she put her hand on his hip, followed his easy steps, swaying her hips along with his, she knew it wasn't okay. That this one dance was going to make it almost impossible for her to stop wanting more of him.

And what she really needed was some kind of alarm to go off, or for Nick to be threatened so her professional armor could return, but that didn't happen, and she was helpless to tear her gaze away from him or to stop the mental images of his naked body moving over hers.

NICK NEEDED THE DISTRACTION. The one time he wanted Thom at an event, the man hadn't showed up. As much as it hurt to think that the other man might be playing a part in threatening him and killing Jack, he was beginning to believe that had to be the case. Thom would do anything for money and a place in the world. Possibly, this was how he thought he was going to achieve it.

Luna's body under his hands, having a legitimate reason to touch her, knowing they were as safe as they could be in this moment, allowed him to let his guard down.

He couldn't ignore that Verity was up to something. But Nick wasn't really in the mood to deal with her. He wanted Luna.

And he knew she wanted him too. The only time he felt like he had an advantage over her was when he touched her. It was clear that she wasn't sure what to do with him. She'd done a good job the last few days of acting as if she didn't want him, but her quickened breath when he'd pulled her into the curve of his body and the way her eyes kept dropping to his mouth told another story.

He'd always been good at seeing what a person wanted from him. Seeing the way that he could manipulate them into doing what he needed them to do.

For just this once, he didn't want to use those skills to take advantage of Luna. Yet he knew he was going to. He wanted to distract her so that she'd stay out of his way when it came to questioning Thom.

Nick wasn't feeling at all civil—in fact, he was pissed and could end up beating the truth out of Thom if necessary.

"What are you up to?" she asked, leaning into him, her breasts brushing against his chest as she whispered in his ear without the communication device.

"Dancing," he said.

"I'm not going to let you put yourself at risk," she said then bit the lobe of his ear.

A pulse of desire shot down his body and he hardened. He stopped moving for a split second, using his hands on her hips to pull her into direct contact with his erection. "I want you."

Just those words were torn from him. For this moment, in the middle of the chaos that was his life, their eyes met and, for the first time, he was telling her the absolute truth.

She wouldn't be here if Jack hadn't pretended to be him and been killed in his place. She wouldn't be here if he hadn't been shot at in the stairwell and their investigation had led them to Thom Newton as a suspect. She wouldn't be here if he hadn't manipulated her onto the dance floor.

So that didn't feel *exactly* like truth.

But for Nick and his world and his life, this was the most honest he'd allowed himself to be for a long time. Maybe ever.

"I want you, too, but we already decided that wasn't going to happen."

"We did," he said, turning and leaving the dance floor. Maybe the time for games was over.

He heard Luna behind him.

"Nick."

He glanced back at her.

"You can't just leave me like that," she said.

He nodded. He knew he was putting them both in danger. He wanted to punch someone, start a brawl. But instead he noticed Finn up in the roped-off VIP section, talking to Thom Newton.

"Let's go. That's Thom," Nick said, turning on his heel and heading for the stairs that led up to the balcony area.

Luna was hot on his heels, keeping pace with him and trying to get in front of him. But Nick wasn't worried about Finn or Thom. He knew he could physically take the other man and intended to use that to force a confession from Thom.

"How rude," he heard someone say. As he turned, he saw a masked man heading quickly toward him.

He moved to face the man as Luna shoved him hard to the side and stepped in front of him. She let out a low groan and folded in on herself for a second as the man turned and ran.

Luna kicked off her heels and started after him. Nick heard Luna's voice in his earpiece. "Suspect moving toward the southeast corner of the room. Lock it down."

Nick righted himself and followed her. He heard the rest of the Price team giving commands, but was only focused on Luna and the man who'd tried to approach him. He caught up to them as the man disappeared into the crowd.

"Where did he go?" Luna asked.

"I'm not sure, possibly that way," he said, gesturing to the stairs on the other side of the club that led to the dessert buffet.

"I'll go up," she said.

"I'm coming with you."

She shook her head. "Stay behind me. He has a knife."

He followed her up the stairs, spying a pattern on the side of her dress that he hadn't seen earlier. It was like a drip of…

Luna had been stabbed.

And she was still going after the man.

His heart raced, and not with fear for himself but fear for her. This had gone on long enough. After tonight, he was getting rid of Luna and Price Security. He had made a promise to himself that no one else would be hurt in his place and it was time to deliver on that.

THE PAIN FROM the knife wound in her side was numbed by adrenaline as she moved through the crowd. She heard Nick behind her and was thankful the Price Security team was watching out for him. She wasn't going to let the attacker get away. But the crowd at the top of the stairs was thick and Luna was struggling to keep her eye on the blue-suited man.

Nick brushed past her. "I'll go to the left."

She wanted to stop him, but he was gone too quickly. She turned to follow him as the masked man emerged from the crowd, running straight toward Nick. The man raised his knife and Luna ran as hard as she could, trying to get between them, but the attacker brought his arm down, slashing Nick as Nick punched him hard in the stomach.

Nick balled his fists and punched the attacker again as he spun for the stairs. Luna raced after him, her heart practically beating out of her chest.

Catching the bottom of his jacket, she felt a piece of paper under her fingers. As the attacker pivoted his body and turned, the jacket tore free of her, leaving her holding the paper, which she gripped tightly as she sprinted after him. But he was down the stairs in two leaps and into the crowd.

"He's on the dance floor," Luna said.

"House lights on now," Van said in her earpiece.

Nick was behind her as the house lights came up and the music stopped, Kenji taking over the deejay station. "Everyone stay where you are. We've had an emergency. Remain calm."

Everyone looked around and Luna heard a cry of shock

as someone looked at Nick and saw the gash on his left arm. The fabric of his suit had been cut and a nasty knife wound was visible. Some of the partygoers close to them were looking panicked and then Van's words came over the loudspeaker.

"Be calm. Everything is under control." His voice was loud and calming while still putting the fear of God into everyone to make them obey him.

"I just said that," Kenji complained in their earpieces.

"Yeah, but you didn't say it like the boss," Rick said. "I've found the mask near the side door."

"Which side door?" Luna asked, putting her hand on Nick's uninjured arm and propelling him off the dance floor and into a corner where she could keep him protected.

"The one behind the stage. Xander, did anyone leave that way?"

"That camera…the image is static. Damn, I didn't realize it. That's on me," Xander said.

"We'll regroup after we've searched all the people still in the club."

"My guests aren't criminals," Nick said. "Please treat them with respect."

"We will," Van said, coming over to them. "I'm going to ask everyone to leave in an orderly fashion. Kenji and Rick, you watch them. Luna, you keep Nick out of the way."

"It's my—"

"Enough," Luna interrupted him. "Enough of this. You've been injured and the guy got away. We need to patch you up and then regroup. Sorry if your circle of pampered party-goers doesn't get a goody bag on the way out, but the night is over and you're staying put."

Nick looked at her like he was going to argue.

But she was done with him pushing her boundaries and doing things his way. Now that the threat had passed, she couldn't stop reliving the moment when the assailant had rushed Nick with that knife in his hand. Nick was lucky that he'd turned and had taken the blow on his arm.

Luna knew the knife had a thick hunting blade. She had to examine his wound and make sure he didn't need to be transported to the hospital.

"I still want to talk to Thom," Nick said.

"We'll bring him to you. Finn isn't leaving, either," Van said.

"That's fine," Nick said.

"We need a first-aid kit. I'm not sure how deep the cut on Nick's arm is," Luna said.

"On my way," Xander said. "Lee's checking the static feed from the camera."

"Luna's injured, too," Nick said.

"Are you good, Luna?" Van asked.

"I'm okay. We'll take care of Nick first," she said.

Nick moved around in front of her as the last of the partygoers left. "No, we won't. Your dress is soaked around the wound…are you okay?"

"I'm fine. It burned at first," she said, trying to get at Nick's wound. As she lifted her hand, she realized she still had that paper in it. She looked down at it.

"What's that?" Nick asked as he shrugged out of his jacket.

She read it. "Dry-cleaning tag. I ripped it from the attacker's jacket."

"Good. We'll track it down," Van said, as Xander, Finn and Thom arrived.

Nick turned to Thom. The man was visibly white as a

sheet, and Finn looked like he was about to have a panic attack, but was holding it together focusing on Nick's injuries. Finn took the first-aid kit from Van and went over to Nick.

"Take your shirt off," Finn said.

Nick unbuttoned quickly and shrugged out of it.

Luna couldn't help herself. Her eyes widened at seeing his naked chest for the first time. He was in shape, no shock there, but his muscles weren't overly developed. She had to turn away, seeing him half naked with an open wound nearly put her in emotional overload.

She wanted him, so lust was coursing through her like oxygen through her lungs, but she had let him down. He'd been hurt on her watch. He'd almost died.

"Thom, we have some questions for you," Luna said, turning her attention to the job.

Van stepped in front of her. "The questions can wait. Go upstairs and clean your wound and come back."

"I'm fine," she said.

She knew she wasn't at her best. It was nerves and determination keeping her on her feet at this moment. Her side ached and her soul felt battered and weary, but she wasn't leaving Nick alone. She wouldn't leave him vulnerable again.

Chapter Fifteen

Luna went into the club bathroom already cleared by the Price team and took off the sequined dress. The wound on her side was worse than she'd thought. She reached for the antiseptic wipes in the first-aid kit when the door opened partially.

"Okay to come in?" Lee called.

"Yes, I could use a hand."

Lee wasn't a fancy person by nature and Luna smiled to see her friend dressed in a cocktail dress. Her short salt-and-pepper hair had been styled into a fancy updo. Lee's eyes went straight to Luna's wound.

"That's pretty bad. I have a compression bandage. Is your tetanus up to date?" Lee asked.

"Yes. Is Nick's?"

"Finn said it was," Lee said, coming closer and taking over attending to Luna's wound, which wasn't deep enough to need stitches.

The bandages Lee used to close the wound seemed to do the job and Luna turned toward the full-length mirror to check it out when her friend was done.

"What happened out there?" Lee asked. "I mean I heard

it in my earpiece, but I couldn't get a clear shot of you or the attacker on the monitors."

"I'm not sure. We spotted Thom and were heading that way when the attacker came out of the crowd with the knife," Luna said, replaying the incident in her mind. She couldn't figure out how he'd gotten past the metal detectors with that hunting knife. In fact, Xander would have made sure they'd been installed in a way that no one could sneak anything in.

"The knife had to already be here," she said.

"That's my thought, too," Lee said.

"Enough discussing this without the entire group," Van said through their earpieces. "Luna, you good?"

"Yeah, Lee patched me up. We're on our way back to you," Luna said after she put her dress back on, she led the way out of the bathroom, but Lee stopped her.

Lee took her earpiece out and Luna did the same.

"Nick's reckless. You didn't do anything wrong."

"He is, but I should have anticipated it," she said. She knew what Nick was like. He'd been ready for a fight all evening and despite all of that, she'd gone out on the dance floor and had that moment where she—

"Stop beating yourself up. Nothing went perfect tonight," Lee said. "Nothing ever does. Xander and I double-checked every feed on the security cameras before the first guest arrived. So how did that one go static?"

"Someone knew what we were planning?" Luna asked.

The bathroom door opened and Van walked in. "Ladies, I want to do this as a team. I'm going to assume you took your earpieces out to have girl chat."

"What's girl chat?" Lee asked. "Just so we know if that's what we were doing."

Van came as close to looking chagrined as he ever did. "Two of my favorite girls. Chatting."

"Nice save, boss," Luna said. She couldn't help but feel a little better about the evening even though the blood on her dress was crusting over her irritated side and her feet ached from wearing heels. "Shall we go join everyone else?"

"I told them if I didn't come out in two minutes to come and join us," Van said in that gravelly voice of his before winking at them.

Luna followed Van and Lee out of the bathroom and saw that some chairs had been drawn into a circle where she'd left Nick. She avoided looking at him, save for one glance where she noticed he'd put his dress shirt back on but hadn't buttoned it. Finn was right next to him, biting his nails and watching Nick with a closed expression.

Thom Newton had been slightly drunk when they'd stopped him and was slumped in his chair next to Rick, who was trying to convince the man to drink a Fanta Orange drink.

"Okay, now that we are all here, let's get started," Van said as they all took their seats.

Nick reached behind him for his jacket and handed it to Luna. "You look cold."

She was, but had a feeling it was the combination of shock and exhaustion. She slipped her arms into the jacket, briefly inhaling the smell of Nick and his aftershave. But then she turned her attention back to the group.

"Thom, we have a few questions about the night of Jack's murder. You were at the party, right?" Van asked.

"I was. I go to most of Nick's events," Thom said.

"Even those you aren't invited to," Nick said. "What were you doing there?"

"It was your birthday... I always crash, you know that."

Nick nodded. "Why is that?"

"Why are you questioning me?"

"Until I got stabbed tonight, I thought you might have been the one to kill Jack," Nick said.

"What the f—"

"Don't get offended. We both know you've always been loose with the truth," Nick said.

"And we would like to know what you saw the night of the party," Van said, taking over the questioning.

Luna sat back, observing the dynamics between everyone in the circle. Not her team—she knew them, trusted them—but more Finn, Thom and Nick. Nick was in the center of the two men and it was clear that he was important to both of them. Finn's response was more emotional. He wasn't trying to maneuver himself into seeming to have a closer relationship with Nick, the way that Thom was.

"Thom, do you know anyone who hates Nick?" Luna asked.

"A few people don't love him. But hate? I don't think so," Thom answered.

He looked around the room before turning to Nick. "I know it seems like all I'm after is your connections and investment in my business deals, but I always thought we were friends. I'd never do anything to hurt you, Nick. And if I heard someone else wanted to, I'd let you know."

Nick reached over with his uninjured arm and clapped Thom on the shoulder. "Thanks, Thom."

"Rick, take Thom home. The rest of us will debrief the evening," Van said.

As they got up to leave, Luna remembered the dry-cleaning paper she'd torn from the attacker's coat. She found it on the small table where the mask was still laying and brought it back. "Do we know where this cleaner is?"

Thom glanced over. "Is that Gold Cleaners? They are just up the street from this building. I use them."

Van looked at Rick, who put his hand on Thom's shoulder and had him sit back down. They'd almost cleared Thom, but that had put him right back in the center of their investigation.

NICK DIDN'T BELIEVE in coincidence. Fate, he'd always believed in. But it seemed to him that someone was trying awfully hard to paint Thom as the mastermind behind the attacks. It probably would have been more believable if Thom hadn't been drunk and crying and telling Nick how much he loved him before turning and throwing up all over the floor.

Even Van seemed to come to a similar conclusion and once more ordered Rick to take the other man home. Nick glanced at Finn, and his assistant rolled his eyes before getting to his feet. "I'll go with you."

Thom slung his arm around Finn's shoulders and as Nick watched two of his boarding school friends head out the door, he realized he might never be able to figure out who was threatening him. This thing with Thom had felt wrong from the first time Van and Luna had brought him up. Boarding school had been a different world, and no matter that most of the boys who'd been sent there came from a privileged background, they'd all been dealing with a lot of stuff.

Their own stuff. Too much of their own life to try to ruin his.

"Okay, so the dry cleaner seems a bit too obvious," Nick said. "So who else knew we were looking at Thom?"

Nick was tired. He wanted nothing more than a hot shower, and to be alone with Luna. He needed to make sure she was okay. To make sure they were okay. She hadn't met his eyes once since she'd reentered the room. And seeing her over there, her hair mussed, wearing his jacket, which made her look smaller than she actually was, made it damned hard for him to remember she was his bodyguard.

"I'm not sure," Luna said. "The board was questioned and we had a few discussions around them. Someone could have overheard."

"That's true. The board all seemed to check out," Van said. "Lee—"

"I'll go over them again," she said. "Also their assistants or people in their offices. There is a chance they talked once they got back."

"Good call. Xander, what about the construction staff and bouncers?" Van asked.

"Most of them were out of earshot when you were interrogating the board, but that doesn't mean someone didn't overhear Newton's name," he said. "My gut doesn't think it was the construction crew, but I'll run their names past Lee."

Nick listened to them all trying to find connections. What about his father? He hadn't spoken to Everett since he'd turned over the letters. Nick pulled his phone out and texted his father and Aldo to see if another letter had arrived.

Nothing new, Aldo texted back.

"Is there something you want to share with the group?" Van asked him.

"My father hasn't received any more letters," Nick said. "Do you think that means the attacker knows that he turned them over to me? That I know there is one person who is behind all my accidents?"

Van leaned back in his chair, crossing his massive arms over his chest as he took a moment to digest what Nick had said.

"It's probably a good theory and points us back to this building. All of the information has been discussed here. The letters, Thom as a suspect, the setup for the party..."

Xander and Lee both got to their feet. Xander looked at Lee, who nodded to him. Nick had no idea how, but it seemed the two of them were communicating. "Xander will sweep for listening devices. I'll go over the video footage from when we were hired and look for a pattern. Okay to leave?" Lee asked Van.

"Yes," he said. "Kenji?"

"I don't like the hunting knife after the high-powered sniper rifle. This attacker is trained in a lot of different disciplines...and the change from cutting the brake wire on his nanny's car to this type of attack makes me think that it's two different people."

"Related?" Luna asked. She pulled her phone out and started taping on the keyboard. Nick knew she liked to take notes.

"Based on the letters, I'd have to say yes," Kenji said. "How was the previous bodyguard killed?"

"Pushed off the balcony. Made to look like he stumbled and fell," Nick said. "So, more similar to my nanny and the yacht accident where my cousins died. There was a gas leak on the yacht."

"So sometime between Jack's death and now, something changed," Van said.

"What?" Nick asked.

"That's the million-dollar question," Van said.

"I've got the money," Nick responded. "I need answers."

"We all do. Let us work on this. Kenji is good with puzzles and this is just a new part of the one we've been trying to solve since you hired us."

Kenji nodded. "I'll get it."

"Is that all for tonight?" Nick asked. "I need a shower."

"Yes. That's it. We will regroup in the morning, hopefully with some answers," Van said.

Nick stood; Luna was on her feet at the same time. She moved next to him as they walked to the elevator and, though the room had been cleared, she was still alert. And as he'd seen tonight, there was no way to order her to stay safe. She was always going to put herself between him and danger.

Luna hadn't felt this tired since she'd landed in LA. But her mind was clearer tonight than it had been then. She wanted to get out of this evening dress and have a shower herself, but a part of her didn't feel safe yet letting Nick out of her sight.

When they got to the penthouse, she didn't head for her room after making a sweep of the apartment, though Rick had cleared it after the club had been emptied and before they'd all had their confab. Mentally, she knew Nick was safe here. But emotionally she was still reliving the moment when he'd stepped around her to put himself between her and the attacker.

There were two things warring in her mind. Two thoughts that kept circling around. The first scared her more than she was ever going to admit. And it was that, in her entire life, Nick was the first person outside of the security team to try to protect her. She couldn't allow herself to follow that thought any further. It stirred up feelings she didn't know how to process or handle.

The second was that he had been injured on her watch. That she should have anticipated he'd dart around her because his anger at the person who'd kept threatening him drove him. He'd already done it once before.

Her second thought was so much easier to handle.

Nick was pacing in the center of his penthouse, circling past the large sofas set up to form a conversation area around the grand piano on a pedestal in the middle of the room. He had energy that she wasn't sure how to handle and it seemed to be sparking bolts of lightning.

"You can go shower. I'm sure you're ready to get out of that dress," he said curtly, nodding his head toward her room.

He was mad at her? Maybe he thought the same thing she did. That she'd screwed up tonight. "I don't want to leave you alone," she admitted.

"I'm safe here," he said tightly, gesturing to the entire penthouse. "Your team went over it more than once."

"I know." She wondered if he felt safer knowing that someone other than her had his back. And that made her angry. Anger was so much easier to deal with at this moment than the fear and the other thoughts in her head.

"Luna."

"Nick." She wasn't going to let him push her out of the room. Whatever was on his mind, they needed to clear the air. She remembered the first backstage party with Jaz, when he'd wanted her out because he was doing illegal drugs and sleeping with two groupies, but she had held fast. She had never stood in judgment. She'd been hired to keep her client safe.

That brought her back to Nick.

He breathed in deeply through his nose. It was the first time, she realized, that he was barely holding on to his temper. The tendons in his neck stood out strongly. Clearly visible as he still hadn't buttoned his shirt. Not that she was looking.

"You're mad," she said.

"I am," he said. "I hate that you got hurt tonight. I heard what Lee said. That knife wound was deep."

It had been, but she'd had worse injuries in the line of duty. Somehow, she sensed telling him that wasn't going to diffuse his temper. "The one on your arm isn't anything to laugh at. We both weren't at our best tonight," she said. "I think…the truth is, I've been telling myself if you hadn't tried to get in front of me, I would have been prepared."

He stopped pacing and walked over to her, his open shirt flapping around his strong body. He came so close that she could see the pulse ticking at the base of his neck.

"That's bull," he said, his jaw clenched. "I already told you I'm not letting anyone else get hurt instead of me."

Luna was having a hard time keeping her eyes on his face and not letting it drift lower. Part of her, the most primal female warrior part, needed to strip him naked, examine his wounds and then make love to him so she knew he was safe.

She was already dealing with too much emotional junk involving Nick. She couldn't add something else to the mix. But her body yearned for him. She wasn't sure she was going to survive the battle warring inside her.

"I know what you said, but you hired me to protect you."

"Then maybe I'll think about firing you," he said.

That pissed her off, and she leaned closer until her nose was almost touching his. "I'm not going anywhere until we find the person or persons responsible for this," she said.

He sighed and touched her then, his hand coming to her waist on the uninjured side of her body. His fingers were light when he touched her, and he pulled her ever so slightly toward him. "I don't want you hurt again."

She put her hand on his naked chest. Felt the heat of him and the rapid beating of his heart under her palm. "Me either."

He cleared his throat and seemed to be going to speak again, but Luna knew there were no words that would bring either of them the solace they wanted. She shifted slightly and brushed her lips against his.

He didn't hesitate to pull her into the curve of his body, angling his mouth over hers and deepening the kiss. She stopped thinking, just shut off anything that didn't directly relate to his fiery body under her mouth and her hands.

She needed to affirm they'd both survived and tomorrow would be soon enough to return to her safety zone. For tonight, she was going to celebrate the fact that he was here with her.

Chapter Sixteen

Luna tasted of champagne and something that was unique to her. He deepened the kiss, pulling her more fully into him. Running one hand down the side of her torso until he reached the slit at the top of her thigh. When his fingers touched her bare skin, a tingle went up his arm. He wasn't stopping until she was completely underneath him.

He lifted his head, as much as he didn't want to, realizing he had to make sure she wasn't just kissing him. Did she want this too?

"I need you tonight. I don't know if you are on the same page," he said.

"I am. I don't want to think beyond this moment. I'm afraid if I do, I'll have to walk away."

"Just one more thing. Birth control? Do you want me to use a condom?" he asked.

She chewed her bottom lip between her teeth for a second and then bobbed her head up and down. "I'm on birth control, so the condom is up to you."

Nick was pretty sure in that moment she'd committed to this. But perhaps she'd made that decision before she'd kissed him. He wasn't going to overanalyze the one good thing that he'd found in his life since Jack had been killed.

He started to feel the panic again that he'd felt when he'd seen her push her way around him to put herself between him and a knife-wielding assailant. Damn.

He wasn't going to be able to breathe properly until he had her naked and made sure that every remaining inch of her was okay. Her hands were on his chest, running over him, the tips of her fingers lingering on his nipples. He stood there for a moment, letting the white-hot heat of lust rule him. He could easily just stay there, but being passive wasn't what he needed.

Nick wanted to prove to himself, at least, that he still had some control over something. And sex was the one place where he always got what he wanted and made sure his partner did too. It was a relief to turn his mind off and let his body take control.

He undid the zipper of her dress and the fabric, which had been skintight a moment earlier, gaped away from her body. With a delicate shrug of her muscled shoulders, the sequined cloth fell to her feet. She stepped out of it and then kicked off the heels she'd put back on when they'd met with the entire group.

He groaned as his cock hardened.

She made a move toward him, but he stopped her. "Not yet."

She tipped her head to the side. "Do you think you're in control here?"

"Aren't I?" he asked, walking slowly around her body. Admiring the feminine strength of it. The muscles of her upper body contained more strength than even he could guess. The curve of her waist and the flare of her hips emphasized the power she held.

The bra she wore was sheer and lacy, so delicate, compared the tough woman who wore it. He used one hand to flick open the fastening. Then stepped up closer behind her, his mouth on the nape of her neck as he slowly drew the straps of the bra down each of her arms and tossed it aside.

Goose bumps spread down her back and arms. Nick cupped her breasts as he pulled her back against him. She was naked except for her panties, and he loved the feel of her like this. He looked over her head down her body, holding both of her breasts in his hands. His thumbs stroking her nipples.

Luna moaned and her hips moved until his cock was nestled between her butt cheeks. She tipped her head back and to the side and he moved his mouth up her neck before leaning forward and taking her mouth in his. She sucked his bottom lip between her teeth and bit him gently.

His erection throbbed with need. It felt good to be alive. He'd had sex before, when it was just something to do. A need that had to be scratched. But after this evening, having Luna in his arms was anything but ordinary.

It was a moment when he realized that all of his near misses had been nothing compared to the one today. Because, for the first time in a long while, he had someone he cared about.

Nick ripped his mouth from hers for a minute to shove that thought down. He wasn't going to allow himself to care for her that way. People he loved died.

He took one hand from her breast and moved it lower along the center of her body as she shivered in his arms. He traced his fingers around her belly button and felt something…

His fingers were running over a small stud piercing. He toyed with it and felt her hips swiveling against his.

He brought his mouth back to the side of her neck as he trailed his way to her panties. He cupped her through them. Felt the heat of her on his fingers as she rocked her hips into his hand.

His erection was hard, pressed against her back, her pussy hot against his fingers. Nick knew that the moment he took her panties off, he wasn't going to be able to resist tasting her, getting inside her and taking her until they were both exhausted.

He wanted this to last.

Needed something with Luna to feel like it wasn't just happening in the moment.

He continued to finger her through her underwear until she turned in his arms. Her hands went to his neck and she went up on her tiptoes to kiss him full and hard.

He felt her hard nipples brush against his chest as she lifted one thigh so that his cock was rubbing right at her center. The illusion that he'd been trying to build, that he was in control of Luna, their love making, or anything, was shattered.

But as her mouth moved down his chest and her fingers undid his belt, he couldn't really be that upset.

LUNA WAS ON fire for Nick. She usually kept herself under tight control when she was working, and she'd been on duty for…well, she couldn't remember the last time she'd had a moment to herself. Coming off tour with Jaz and straight onto working with Nick hadn't been easy.

She knew that there would be repercussions for this night, but she'd already shoved that thought aside and left it buried in the back of her mind. Nick's touch had awakened parts of her that she tried to ignore, had to when she was working because the job came first.

As she bent lower to undo his pants and pushed her hands under the fabric of his underwear, shoving it down his legs, she felt his fingers against her shoulder. She bent to bring his briefs all the way to the floor and, from her stooped position, looked at his cock. It was hard and thick, jutting out from his body.

She slowly ran her fingers up his legs. Taking her time as she watched his cock jump slightly as she got closer to it. But she just drew her fingers across his abdomen while cupping his balls with her other hand.

He groaned and his hand moved down her shoulder to her wrist, took it and placed it on his erection. She wrapped both of her hands around his shaft and stroked it up and down, tightening her grip each time, feeling him getting harder as his hips moved against her motions.

She squeezed his balls and then dropped to her knees and took him in her mouth. He groaned this time. The sound was guttural, almost as if it had been ripped from some place deep inside him. She sucked him until she felt him at the back of her throat, her fingers still moving on his balls. She tasted something salty and delicious.

He pulled his hips back and her mouth away from his cock. He lifted her into his arms, carried her to the sofa across the room and set her down on it. Ripping off her panties, he slid down between her legs. She felt the warmth of his breath against her pussy and then the touch of his tongue.

Luna reached for his cock, needing to touch him while he was touching her. She tried to move so she could take him in her mouth again and he shifted so that she could get his cock in her mouth. She sucked hard on him as she felt his tongue on her clit, just teasing strokes at first and then the edge of his teeth as he nibbled at her most delicate flesh.

Her body clenched and she felt the first fingers of her climax. Her hips were moving frantically as she tried to get his mouth where it felt the best. She tasted more of his cum, swallowing it. Then she felt his finger in her pussy, shoving up and into her deeply.

Everything in her body screamed out as she came hard on his finger and finished sucking him dry. He collapsed against her thighs and she rested her head on his thigh. She looked up his body and their eyes met.

"That wasn't what I'd planned."

"I'm not usually one for breaking a plan, but that worked," she said.

He smiled at her. "I want to be inside you, but I need some time. And I think we could both use a shower."

"Together?" she asked. Still not ready to let him out of her sight.

"Yes. How's your wound?" he asked as he got to his feet and offered her his hand.

She stood next to him, realizing he still wore his shirt. She looked at her side and saw some blood seeping from her bandage. "Fine. Might need to change the bandage. How's yours?"

He took his shirt off, looking down at his arm. The bandage was still clean and nothing seemed to be leaking out of it. She ran her fingers over it and the leaned into kiss it. "I'm sorry you got hurt."

He put his hand under her chin and lifted her face to his, bringing his mouth down on hers in the gentlest kiss she had ever received. "I'm sorry you did."

He didn't say anything else and neither did she. She felt

her mind trying to take control and ignored it. She simply slipped her hand into his and walked with him to his bedroom. He took a deep breath as soon as they were in there.

"The bathroom is through there," he said, catching her shoulder and looking closely at her shoulder blade. "I need to shave—you have some beard burn on your back."

"I don't mind," she said, looking over her shoulder at him.

"You don't?" he asked. There was a note in his voice she couldn't place.

"No one will see it but you and I... I guess I like that we have something private," she said, knowing those words were the truth and probably not the wisest thing for her to admit.

He pulled her into his arms and hugged her close. She held him, too, breathing in the scent of sex and Nick. He didn't say anything, but really, what could he say? She was guessing he was aware they were in a bubble that would only last until morning and then reality was going to be back.

But, for tonight, there was only Nick and, for the first time in her life, Luna thought this person was hers.

Only for tonight.

NICK SHAVED WHILE Luna showered and then he joined her. He saw that the wound on her side was slightly bloody, but when he checked the bandage, he thought it might be just dried blood that was being washed off the wound.

He caressed her as he washed her and then took her standing up in the shower. She dug her nails into his back as she came and he used his hand on the wall to support himself after he did. They washed off and got dry, and he saw Luna's expression shift back into bodyguard mode and shook his head.

"I get Luna the Lover until morning. Then you can be my bodyguard again," he said as he took one of his monogrammed bathrobes and wrapped her in.

In the back of his mind, he knew he wasn't sure he could let her continue to be his bodyguard. It would be smarter if he switched to Kenji. He was the one who everyone had thought Nick should have chosen from the beginning.

But another part of Nick wasn't ready to give up any part of Luna. Maybe because he knew it was inevitable. To save her, to keep her safe, he was going to have to step away from her.

There was no way he could have her and keep her alive. And the irony of that wasn't lost on him. He'd hired her to keep him safe, but tonight had drawn a line under his belief that he was unbreakable.

She wasn't either.

"I'm not—"

He put his fingers over her mouth. Whatever well-thought-out argument she was going to make, he didn't want to hear it. "It's been a shit day. Let's just have a moment where I can hold you and pretend that I'm not Nick DeVere."

She put her hand on the side of his face and gave him the most tender look he'd ever seen. "I want to be with Nick DeVere."

He hugged her close for this moment, holding her in his arms in his steamy bathroom and knowing that it couldn't last.

He lifted her off her feet and she twisted out of his arms. "You shouldn't be carrying me."

"Why not?"

"Your arm is injured," she said, moving to check it.

Emotions that he didn't want tangled in his throat. Even

now, when it was just the two of them, she was still looking out for him. And, yes, it was a little thing, but for him it didn't feel that way.

In a life that had been filled with paid staff and yesmen, he'd found Luna. And her memory would linger long after she was gone. She was changing him, and though he had no way of knowing if that was a good or bad thing, he couldn't deny it.

"I'll be fine," he said, picking her up again.

She didn't argue, just wrapped her arms around his shoulders and rested her head against him. He set her down on his bed and then got in next to her, pulling her to his side.

She nestled close and he heard her sigh.

"What?"

"I can't stay here all night."

"Why not?"

She looked up at him. "Someone will come check on us in the morning. I need to be back in my bed."

"Stay with me."

"I can't, unless you don't want me to be your bodyguard anymore," she said.

"I don't."

"Oh." She pulled away from him, sitting up. "Okay, then. I don't blame you."

She didn't?

"Great. I'm thinking you need to get some place safe. Seems like Xander should be in the field and you should be in a room with Lee, monitoring things, so you'll be protected," he said.

That had been easier than he'd anticipated.

"What are you talking about? If I'm off the job, then I'll

go. I probably will need to have my actions here reviewed as well."

He shook his head. "No, I just want you somewhere safe, where you can't get hurt."

"Wait, do you want a new bodyguard because I screwed up tonight?"

"No. You did the best in that situation. Even Price said that no one could have handled it better," Nick said. "You're a damned good bodyguard, Luna."

She smiled over at him. "Thanks. But I'm not stepping aside because you think I might get hurt again. I'm not going to pretend that sleeping with you was my best idea, but the truth is, I needed to feel you and touch you after tonight. Had to make sure you were okay."

He wasn't ready to stop talking about replacing her, but he could see she was done with it. Her confession had struck a chord inside him, reminding him of how lonely they'd both always been. How they'd both carved lives that kept them from making contact with too many people.

But now that he'd had her this close, he didn't know if he was going to be able to easily let her go.

Maybe it was the fact that, at this moment, they were completely safe. His attacker had been chased off and, though he hadn't been caught, for this one night he wasn't an immediate threat.

"I needed that, too," he said.

"I know," she admitted, coming closer to him again as he pulled her back into his arms.

"I like holding you."

"I like being held by you," she said. "I don't want to get used to it."

He didn't have to ask why that was. The truth was that

they both knew this wasn't going to be something they could sustain while she was working for him. And, once she wasn't, he had no idea what the outcome of this would be.

For tonight, he simply wanted to enjoy holding Luna and not worry about the future. He'd never felt like he had much control over what fate had in store for him and that hadn't changed. But he had.

Chapter Seventeen

Luna was gone when Nick woke the next morning, as he'd expected her to be. He looked at the empty pillow next to his, struggling with emotions he wasn't really sure he wanted to acknowledge. But they were there nonetheless. He liked her.

He headed to the gym for his treadmill run and found Luna waiting for him. It was almost as if the night before hadn't happened. Was she going to pretend like it meant nothing?

He didn't ask her, just ignored how hot she looked in her sports bra and running shorts as she got on the treadmill next to his. Then he noticed the bandage on her side. It had been changed and looked fresh. Nick hadn't changed his bandage this morning as it appeared clean. She must have replaced hers after she'd left his bedroom. For some reason, that pained him.

That reminder of the threat they were facing, and how real the attacker was, made him decide to stay silent. He turned to the panel on the treadmill and picked a punishing run, hoping it would distract him. To a certain extent, it did, but he wasn't going to be able to let this be.

Nick hit the stop button after a long run. Luna did the

same. Sweat was dripping down the side of her neck and his eyes traced that moisture before he felt himself stir. Then he lifted his eyes to hers.

"Are you going to act like last night didn't happen?" he asked. His frustration was evident in his voice. He knew he had to get his emotions under control before he started his day. He was always cool and calm. After last night, he'd noticed that there were a lot of appointments showing up on his calendar today, including a couple of on-air interviews to discuss the events of the night before.

"No. We're both adults, that would be silly," she said, resting her arms on the handles of the treadmill. "There's a lot going on today. Van handled the detective last night, but they want you downtown to fill out a statement this morning. I have a feeling a lot of the partygoers are being asked to do the same…it's for the best that I go back to being your bodyguard and not your lover."

Lover.

What did that mean to her? He'd had more than a few lovers and, of course, an ex-wife. But no one had made him feel the way that Luna did. "Sure. I'm your boss again, right?"

"Sure," she said back to him. "We need to talk about you not following my direction when we are in a dangerous situation."

"Sure," he said again.

"Really? Are we going to do it this way?" she asked.

"I am," he said, keenly aware that he was pushing to see if she cracked; instead, it seemed as if he were the one in danger of crumbling. He cursed and turned his treadmill back on. As usual, talking to Luna was making him more frustrated.

He heard her treadmill start up as well. Listening to the

pounding of both of their feet distracted him for a few moments but he kept going through possibilities in his mind of who was threatening him. That gave him a focus. He knew the detective was going to have a lot of questions for them.

Once his run was finished, he stepped off the treadmill and Luna did the same. He took a gym towel to wipe his face and neck and tossed one to her.

He was going to shower, but she stopped him with her hand on his arm. She'd meant her touch to be professional, and it was, but his body reacted as if she were caressing him. "I'm trying to keep you safe. Seeing that wound on your arm, knowing you were hurt last night... I can't let that happen again."

He understood because he felt the same way. "We need to figure out who is attacking me and set a trap."

"Yes to finding out who, but traps don't always work. Let's talk to the detective and then run down to the dry cleaner's and see if we can find someone. Also, I think we should try talking to Thom again today."

He liked the plan she had laid out. They were working together as a team, which suited him right now. Once they had another suspect, he'd be tempted to leave and confront them on his own despite their agreement. He didn't want to let Luna get hurt again.

"Why do you want to talk to Thom again?" he asked as they headed back toward their respective rooms.

"He was drunk last night. Sober, he might remember a detail that he left out last night," she said. "Also, he was at the party the night Jack died, maybe he saw something that he didn't realize was important."

"I hadn't thought of that. Are you just going to question him?" Nick asked, seeing a different side to Luna than the physical one he was familiar with. She was very good at her job as a bodyguard but now he saw her analytical mind.

"I imagine that Rick will be the one to do it. He's really good at interrogation…that word always sounds sort of negative to me, but he just talks and get them thinking and leads them back through events. I've never seen anyone as good as he is at getting someone to open up," Luna said.

"When I first saw him, I thought he was a stoner."

Luna gave Nick a half smile. "He does give off that vibe sometimes. You caught him on a bad day."

"I don't think so. I saw him move, and once he went after the shooter, it was like a different man. You're not like that," he said suddenly. Luna was the same all the time. She didn't switch on when she was guarding him and switch off.

"I'm not," she admitted. "I think it's because I define myself as kickass woman all the time."

He smiled at that. "As you should. What does Rick do?"

"If I had to guess, he switches into cop mode when he's working. His job was tough. He was undercover for a lot of years, so, for him, personal and work are two very different modes."

Nick tucked that piece of knowledge away. It made him realize how grateful he was to have Price Security working for him. It seemed to Nick they had all bases covered.

Luna had to talk to Van and let him know about last night. But a part of her wanted to keep that for herself a little bit longer. Van wasn't an idiot, and he had probably already put two and two together. But she wanted to tell him so he could take whatever action was needed, so she didn't lose his respect or trust.

For this morning, as she stood next to Nick, waiting to

be called in to talk to Detective Miller, she was good. She noticed a few people from the night before and knew from Finn, who'd been leaving as they arrived, that Verity was in with the detective now.

Finn and Nick were going over his schedule and Luna just kept alert, watching the surroundings and running over everything in her head. She was fairly certain Nick wasn't going to be attacked at the police station. That left her free to go back to the beginning. Her team had started taking over security for Nick's event from the first day they'd been hired.

There had been a lot of outside vendors hired for the event and Price Security had talked to and vetted all of them. Van and Kenji were interviewing them again today. So the vendors, like the caterers, bartenders and the outside bouncers Nick had hired, were all covered.

Who else had known any details of the event beforehand?

Finn. Luna looked over at him and Nick as they talked. The bond between the two of them was strong and more than employer and employee. Her gut really thought Finn was harmless. Last night, watching his face after Nick had been stabbed, had been telling.

Unless Finn was a really good actor.

Both men glanced over at her and she smiled at them. "What?"

"I want to go to see my dad later today. Can you let Price know? I don't want to take a chance of bringing last night's intruder to his house."

Luna nodded and texted Lee to let her know.

"As if this didn't start with him," Finn said.

"Letters, yes. But a guy with a knife or gun? He's old and frail."

Finn snorted.

"You know what I mean. He wouldn't stand a chance against that guy from last night."

"He won't have to," Luna said. "Aldo would protect him."

Nick looked over at her. "You're right, he would. But if we can take steps to keep that from happening, all the better."

"I agree," Luna said.

Finn left a few minutes later. Nick gestured to the free seat next to him, but she shook her head. Standing, she had a better view of the hall and the room. Nick just shrugged and went back to his phone before pocketing it.

She loved the easy way his body moved and it was hard to keep from remembering the touch of his hands on her body the night before.

"How much longer do you think they'll be? I have to be at the TV station KTLA at one."

"I'm not sure," she said. "I'll text Van, so he knows your schedule."

She sent the message.

"How will that help?"

"Van's in there with the detective," Luna said.

"I hadn't realized they were working together," Nick said.

"She agreed to it this time, and sometimes it's better to have more than one set of eyes on a person as they talk and give their statement," Luna explained.

"Are you good at reading people?" he asked her.

"Sometimes. Most of the time. You are too."

He shrugged again. She noticed he was doing that a lot today. At first, she'd thought he was just chill because the danger from the night before had passed, but now she wondered if he wasn't trying to project that image to her.

"What do you see in me?" she asked him, trying to get

him talking so she could figure out what, if anything, he was hiding.

Luna remembered his anger this morning and it would take a lot of self-control to hide that. If she'd learned anything during her time as Nick's bodyguard, it was that he didn't give anything away when it came to his feelings. He only let everyone see what he wanted them to.

"That your job means everything to you," he said. "I know that I threaten that, so you're not sure what to do with me."

Fair point. But then, she'd pretty much told him that. "Nothing beyond the stuff I told you."

"You like blending into the background, you're always watching and anticipating, and even when something doesn't turn into a threat, you stay tense and alert," he said. "I see it in your eyes. Even when you were dancing with me last night and I was turning you on, you still had an eye on the crowd."

He was spot-on with his read of her and, as he talked, that chill vibe ebbed—but then it was back. Maybe he was just trying to be… That was it. He was *trying* to get to a place where he could just go with the flow, and not succeeding. Just like her.

"What about me?" he asked her.

"You like to stand out and want all eyes on you. You do genuinely care about people and listen to them when they talk to you. You seem to cultivate relationships, and though you told me you deal in favors, I notice that you rarely ask anyone in your circle for a favor in return."

"You're right. I seldom need anything from them," he admitted. "But that doesn't mean I wouldn't."

"I know. You're tougher than you want anyone to see you

are," she said, remembering last night when he'd tried to protect her against that hunting blade.

"I've had to be," he said.

That was something he kept from the world. So, if his attacker knew him, knew that he'd lay down his life for the right person against his playboy persona, then that might give them an advantage.

LUNA WAITED OUTSIDE while Nick went in to give his statement. Verity watched him leave the waiting area and then turned to Luna. Today, his ex had bloodshot eyes. She was still slightly tearing up as she watched Nick enter the conference room where the interviews were being conducted.

"Nicky's the best," she said to Luna.

"He is," Luna agreed. "You two seem to have a close relationship."

Though everyone had told her that Verity was harmless, Luna hadn't really had a chance to spend time with her the way she had with Finn. While Finn's loyalty to Nick seemed clear, Verity's was still foggy.

"We do. I shouldn't have ever divorced him," she said, dropping down onto one of the chairs.

Luna followed her. "Why did you?"

"Well...the truth is, despite all of his upbringing, Nicky is a bit much sometimes. I thought we would be jetting around the world all the time, but he just works and hangs out here in LA."

"And you wanted more?"

"I did. But now...well, of course, I have Lorenzo, and it's probably better that Nick and I are friends, but there are times when I miss him," Verity said.

Jealousy stirred inside Luna, and though she'd drawn a

line between the night she'd spent in Nick's arms and today, she couldn't help that. How could Nick be attracted to both her and to Verity? she wondered. The woman was nothing like her. Maybe, she worried, Verity was truly the kind of woman he needed by his side. Verity understood Nick's lifestyle in a way Luna never could.

That didn't matter because she had only been in his bed one night, and she was going to do her damnedest to stay out of it.

"You seem to spend a lot of time around him. Is there anyone you noticed who might be trying to kill him?" Luna asked. She'd observed that Verity liked to talk about herself and just making a statement like that might lead her to saying something they could use in the investigation.

"Well, I mean…on the surface, I would have to say no. But there are people who try to get close to me to get to him."

"Why would they do that? He seems pretty open," Luna said.

"To certain people, he totally is, but there are others who'd used those of us close to him to get access to Nick before. Finn, Thom, Hazel and me have all had people come at us for that connection," Verity said, putting her tissue into the big designer bag she was carrying. "I guess I'm the biggest target for that."

Luna hadn't realized that Thom and Hazel were part of Nick's inner circle. In fact, she was pretty sure this was just Verity's impression since Thom didn't feel a part of it and Nick didn't consider him a close friend. And Hazel was his admin assistant, not someone he socialized with.

"Why are you the biggest target?"

"I mean everyone knows I'm the most social, and that

Nicky trusts me. That's why I'm his beneficiary. I guess he could have changed it to Finn when we got divorced, but he didn't. I know that pisses Finn off."

That was news. "What do you mean by that?"

"What do you think I mean? If Nicky dies, I get everything. But, honestly, I never think about it. I don't know what the world would be like without him."

"How did you meet him?" Luna asked, her mind trying to process everything that this could mean. Verity had seemed too self-absorbed and, frankly, too wealthy to be concerned about Nick's fortune, but maybe Luna had written her off too easily. She had seemed to be around whenever these recent attempts on Nick had been made.

"I skied into him in Switzerland. We had a laugh after he saved me, and more. We just connected."

Interesting.

The door opened before she could ask Verity another question and the other woman rushed to Nick's side. Luna followed, watching the woman's hands, but his ex just threw her arms around Nick and hung on to him as she kissed his cheek. She noticed that Nick didn't pull Verity close but loosely hugged her back.

"Sorry about that. I'm just so happy you're okay," Verity said. "I was rushed out last night and only heard from the detective you were hurt."

"I'm fine," Nick said. "I have a very busy day, so I have to go now. But we'll catch up soon."

"That sounds fab. I've sent Finn all the arrangements for Jack's funeral. The viewing and services start tomorrow night."

"He's informed me," Nick said, looking at Luna. "I think they are ready for you to give your statement."

"Okay. I'm just waiting for Kenji."

"I'm here," he said, stepping up behind her. "Sorry, parking is a bitch and I couldn't find a spot. Go on, I've got your boy."

"Thanks," she said.

Luna walked into the conference room and pulled out her notebook before she sat down. She had already gone over the previous night a few times on her own, but hoped that maybe when she added her observations, it would reveal something that they were all missing.

"Before we start, I just learned that Verity stands to inherit everything if Nick dies," she said. "Not sure that's important, but I think we should look into it."

"We will," Van said.

"We've investigated her already," Detective Miller said. "So far, she seems clean."

"We'll just double check," Van said.

"Fine. Keep me in the loop. Now, Luna, take me through the night from the time you stepped on the red carpet."

Luna pulled her notepad closer to her and started walking through the previous night. She hoped that the detective and the Price team found something helpful in her account. Luna couldn't help feeling like everything was happening more and more quickly.

Chapter Eighteen

Nick seemed more tense than he'd been the last time they'd gone to see his father, which felt like a lifetime ago but had only been a few days. His hands were glued to the steering wheel and he drove fast, expertly weaving in and out of traffic as he hurried toward Malibu.

Luna kept an eye on their back, but no one was following them. "Do you want to talk about it?"

"Which 'it' are you referring to?" he asked sarcastically. "There's so much messed up in my life right now."

"I meant…what do you want to talk about?" she asked, sensing there was something on his mind.

"Nothing. I don't want to discuss anything that will simply lead us to more questions," he said.

She kept her gaze to the mirrors but turned briefly to look at him. Her breath caught in her chest at the heated feelings he stirred in her. She wished she were more comfortable in her own skin so she could admit to herself, and maybe to him, how much she liked him. But she couldn't do that. So, the bodyguard in her leaned deeper into the seat and started doing what she did best. "Questions are what lead us to the big discoveries."

"Like what? That someone I know is trying to kill me?

That someone who's been in my building really doesn't like me?"

"Nick."

"Sorry. I'm in a nasty mood. It doesn't help that Jack's viewing is tonight. I haven't spoken to his mother since Finn and I called to let her know he'd been killed... I'm not ready to deal with relatives."

She reached over, putting her hand on his thigh and squeezing to give him some comfort. He put his hand over hers, rubbing his thumb against her knuckles. "Surely you've done it before."

He gave a harsh laugh. "That doesn't make it easier. His mom...she was heartbroken, but didn't blame me. I had a huge life insurance policy on Jack just in case, so she was compensated, but I know it's not money she wants."

It wouldn't be, Luna thought. "Why is Verity still the beneficiary of your policy?"

"I just never got around to changing it. I have more than one policy, by the way. Finn has one, Aldo has another. I just want to take care of the people around me."

"What about Hazel, your assistant? Does she have one?"

"No. She's only part of my work life. The others are more like family," he said.

And family mattered. She got that. It was interesting that he said he wasn't close to anyone but did so much for those three alone. Verity now seemed an unlikely prospect. "We haven't really looked into Aldo. He's been with your father all along."

"Aldo? Are you kidding me? Do you think that old man was the one with the knife?" Nick asked as he took the exit from the freeway leading toward his father's Malibu estate.

"I'm not ruling it out. I think we should just ask where

he was last night," she said. If she'd known about the life insurance policy that Nick had just mentioned, she would have put him on her list earlier.

"Are you kidding me? Aldo is my father's closest—I don't know what to call him—friend, I guess. He was the one to take and pick me up from boarding school. I just can't believe it would be him," Nick said.

"Did he hire the nanny who was injured?" she asked.

Nick clenched his jaw but didn't answer, which meant that Aldo had. She really didn't want to believe that the man who'd been watching over Everett and keeping him alive and safe all these years had been secretly plotting against Nick.

"Logically, I understand what you're trying to do. But Aldo? I don't buy it. Also, the letters specifically mention Dad's true heir. Aldo still isn't able to give birth," Nick said.

She smiled at the last sardonic statement. That was a wrinkle. "Does he have a lover perhaps?"

"No. The guy is always with my father. When I was younger, he'd come to fetch me and then take me to my dad and stay with him. I have never really seen him with someone romantically. I think we can rule him out."

"Possibly," Luna said. She wasn't crossing anyone off her mental list until she had solid proof they weren't involved with the attacks. She was still considering how a criminal partnership would work for any of their suspects. Even so, Nick had valid points about Aldo.

The older man didn't appear to have a child who could be thought of as Everett's secret heir. He also seemed very loyal to, and genuinely cared for, Everett. It made no sense that he'd try to kill Nick now. Was there any reason he'd be working with someone?

"Luna, I don't want you grilling Aldo when we get there.

I'll bring up last night and find out where he was. If he was with my father, we drop this," Nick said. "I know you are trying to conduct your investigation, but I am drawing a line here. Agree?"

She could see that this was important to him. Learning that someone close to him was probably behind the attacks was a difficult thing for Nick. Hearing it might be the man who was his father's companion was too much. She got that. Nick was on a knife's edge, waiting to see when the next attack would come.

She was running possibilities and trying to rule out as many people as she could so they could figure this out. But telling Nick that very thing wasn't going to make him less tense or get them closer to the truth.

NICK WAITED FOR Luna this time before walking up to the front door of his father's mansion. He wasn't sure what he expected from this visit, but he needed more information about his father's past. He wasn't going to allow himself to entertain the possibility that Aldo might have anything to do with the attacks. That would be a betrayal he might never recover from.

Of the two older men in his life, it was Aldo who'd been the one to comfort him and to spoil him when his father had been distant and cold. To lose the man he'd always, deep inside, thought of as his father, would hurt almost as much as losing Jack had.

He knew Luna was just doing her job. And it felt like they were running out of time. The attacks had come closer together for a reason. Did someone know more about his father's condition?

Actually, wait a minute.

He stopped before he knocked on the door, turning to Luna, who was scanning the yard and driveway.

"It can't be someone who would benefit from my death."

"What? Why not?" she asked.

"The urgency has been coming from my father. He's the one who only has a few months to live. It's his will that the letters are demanding be altered. So, my death wouldn't get them anything. It only serves to force my father's hand," Nick said.

Luna nodded, her face grim. "You're right. We need to know if anyone other than you benefits from his death."

"Great. So Aldo will still be on the list," Nick said.

"Are you sure?"

"Yes. Dad wouldn't stiff him after all those years of service," Nick said as he raised his hand to knock on the door. "But it does widen the search."

"We want to narrow it. Maybe there will be a connection we haven't seen before," Luna said. "I'll have Lee run a search once we speak to your father. You know I have to come in this time."

"After last night and all the safety measures I thought we had in place, I'm not going to argue with you on that," he said.

The door was opened not by Aldo but by his father's housekeeper, Mrs. Prentice. That wasn't all that surprising. Aldo was really his father's butler and valet and mostly needed at Everett's side.

"Hello, Nicholas. Lovely to see you. Was your father expecting you today?" Mrs. Prentice asked, stepping back to let them enter.

"No, he wasn't. But I need to speak to him," Nick said. It was an old habit left over from childhood, trying to justify coming to talk to his father. He knew that Mrs. Prentice wasn't gatekeeping him alone. Her job was to keep everyone from Everett.

"I'm sure he'll be glad to see you," she said. "He's in the solarium, and I'll be serving lunch soon. Will you and your guest be joining him?"

"We might be," Nick said. "Let me talk to him first."

"Very well. You have about fifteen minutes until he has to eat. I'll leave you alone for twelve minutes," she said. "It takes some time to set his spot and get him ready to eat."

"That should be good," Nick said.

"What's her name?" Luna asked as they left the foyer and Nick led the way to the sunroom.

"Ramona Prentice," Nick said. "Adding her to your list of suspects?"

"I am. She's a woman and she's very protective of your father and his schedule. Also, she looks old enough to have a child your age or slightly older."

She wasn't wrong, except that he'd met her family on numerous occasions and she and his father…well, he couldn't rule out that they'd never been lovers. "Fine. We'll ask my father about her too."

He entered the solarium, which was a large glass-enclosed room with Spanish tiles on the floor. There was a round table that seated six in the middle, and a love seat and arm chairs off to one side in a conversation area. His father, seated in one of the armchairs, looked up when they entered.

"Nicholas, I wasn't expecting you today, was I?"

"No, sir. Did you see the news from last night?" he asked his father, going over to the love seat to sit close to him.

He was aware of Luna's frown as she took in all of the

open space around them. She started to speak and Nick raised his hand to stop her.

"We're safe here. There's a cliff drop at the end of the garden to the beach below and two, high, security fences on either side. You have a clear view of the yard," he said.

She just shook her head and found a position to watch the entire backyard, scanning constantly by turning her head from side to side.

If someone were to fire at them, Luna would use her body to protect him. He'd talk fast so they could get out of there.

"I didn't. Aldo left a note that there was an incident at your club," his father said.

Nick quickly brought his father up to date on the attack and Emmett reached over and took Nick's hand. "You were stabbed?"

"Just a scratch. Luna's wound was deeper," Nick reassured his father. "Where is Aldo, by the way?"

"He asked for the day off to go and meet a woman," Everett said.

"Was he home last night?"

"He was. We played cribbage until eleven, when I take my last dose of medicine, and then he helped me to bed," his father said. "Why?"

"Just covering all the bases. I'm afraid I have to ask you something that I really don't want to." Just the thought of asking about his father's love life and possible partners who would want him dead wasn't something he'd ever thought he'd do.

"I think you better stay for lunch, if that's the case. Luna, will you join us?"

"Only if you are eating in a room that's not as exposed as this one is."

"We can eat in the formal dining room," Everett said.

Nick helped his father up and led them to the room with only one window that Luna could easily see from the table.

LUNA WISHED SHE'D brought someone else from the team with her. Watching the dynamic between Everett, Nick and Mrs. Prentice was interesting, and she observed as much as she could in between scanning the surroundings. The window here overlooked the backyard that led to the cliff and the ocean. So, she felt better about protecting Nick in this room. She knew he'd probably try to shelter his father in the event of another attack and factored that into her own preparations.

Mrs. Prentice was friendly but not overly so toward Everett, and when Nick saw her watching the older woman, he all but rolled his eyes.

"How's James doing?" he asked the housekeeper as she set a plate down in front of him.

"Oh, very well. He's out on the boat today with Mr. P and our grandkids. I'm so happy he's back on the West Coast."

Nick asked a few more questions about her husband and family, and Luna acknowledged that she could probably rule Mrs. Prentice out as a suspect. She would still have Lee run a check on her, but it seemed less likely that she would think her son was Everett's given how she talked about him and her husband.

After the housekeeper left, Everett turned to Nick. "What was that about?"

"Luna and I are trying to rule out possible women who work with you, or know you, who might be behind the letters," Nick said. "Mrs. P is the right age."

"She is. But she's never been interested in me that way," Everett said.

"We're going to need to know who was," Luna said when it seemed that Nick wasn't going to.

"Who was what?"

"Your romantic partner," Nick said succinctly.

"Ah, Aldo and I have been tracking them down. I thought he sent you the information. None of them had a child that was mine," Everett said.

"He did send the dates you had…affairs. We need the names, so we can check into the individuals. One of the avenues we are investigating is whether someone has a life insurance policy on you. We know they want you to change your will, but perhaps there are other areas that you and Aldo didn't consider," Luna said.

Everett didn't say anything, just continued eating his meal, and with the dose of medicine he was on, she understood he had to eat. But she also had a feeling he was stalling.

Nick sighed and put his cutlery down. "Father, I need this information. The attack last night… I can't keep living like this. Luna and Price Security are the best in the business. You know that, you were the one who hired them. They think this is a good way to find something that we might be overlooking."

"I know, son. I will give you a list. It's just that I don't want to believe someone who I was close to would have been scheming to kill you."

"No one wants to believe that," Luna said. "The person behind these attacks on Nick and the letters you received seems to be someone who has a lot of knowledge of the two of you."

Nick pushed his plate away, rubbing the back of his neck again. "You're right. When my cousins and uncle were killed on the yacht, I became Dad's sole heir. Only a handful of people could have known we'd all be there together."

"That's right. I'll have Aldo go back through my calendar and find out who was working for me then. I wonder if there's a connection we missed," Everett said.

"Possibly. We also need to find out more about the car crash with the nanny," Luna mentioned. "Would it be possibly for me to have Lee Oscar from Price Security get in touch with you? She's an expert at doing a deep dive on people."

Everett took the last bite of his lunch and pushed his plate away. She could tell he didn't want to talk to anyone about this, other than perhaps Nick, but they didn't have much time left. They needed answers and the sooner, the better.

"Of course," he said at last.

"Thanks, Dad," Nick said.

A look was exchanged between the two of them but Luna couldn't read it. It was clear their relationship was complex and more nuanced that she'd suspected the last time. She'd seen the distance between the two of them, but there was also a closeness, perhaps brought on by tragedy or personality, that she suspected wasn't comfortable for either for them. They were both very strong, dominate men used to getting their way.

They kept secrets from each other and, for the first time in Nick's life, there couldn't be any. It seemed that they were both trying to figure out how to deal with it. She messaged Lee to get in touch with Everett about staff and people he'd dated. Lee texted back that she was on it.

Lee also mentioned that they'd checked out the dry

cleaner. The suit the tag had come from had been delivered to Nick's building four days earlier.

Nick said goodbye to his father and, when they were in the car, Luna mentioned the dry cleaner.

"Was that your suit?"

He shrugged. "I don't think so. But it might have been Jack's. I can try to get in touch with Hazel when we get back. I think she probably received the suits. We know it wasn't Finn's."

"I don't think it was Finn who attacked you. The other man was three inches taller than he was."

"Yeah, the other guy was my height and build," Nick said.

Her mind was adding more possibilities to the suspects list. Could it have been someone from Jack's past?

They'd already ruled that out, but Luna felt like they had too much information and hadn't found the right connections. Tonight, while Nick and Van were at Jack's funeral, she was going to put the pieces of this puzzle together before anyone could hurt Nick again.

Chapter Nineteen

Funerals weren't ever going to be his favorite thing. Nick had been to so many that he'd developed a routine. Finn was circulating around the room and Kenji had taken over watching him tonight. Fearing another possible attack, Nick hadn't argued. He knew the time had come to get Luna as far away from him as he could.

This afternoon at his father's, they'd operated as a team again, and he couldn't deny that he liked it. Maybe a little too much. There was something about having someone who got him and wasn't always deferring to him. But there was more to his feelings than simple teamwork. He and Finn were also a good team, and while he loved the man like a brother, there was something very different when he was with Luna.

Nick was afraid to name it as love. But it was the only thing that made sense.

"I've checked out the room where the viewing will be. If you want to have a few moments alone with the deceased, I can offer you some privacy by staying at the back of the room," Kenji said.

Tonight the Japanese American wore a black suit, white shirt and slim tie. He had his thick black hair swept back with a fall of bangs over his left brow. Nick knew he was carrying a gun because Kenji had point-blank told Nick that he never went on the job without one.

And though Nick had been throwing out stipulations left and right at the beginning of this security detail not more than a week earlier, now…he was tired. Constantly being on guard and never knowing when an attack would come had worn him down.

"I'd appreciate that," Nick said, going into the room where the coffin waited at the end. There were chairs and love seats set up around the room to give those who came to grieve a place to sit and talk if they wanted.

Nick also knew there'd be a buffet and drinks, Verity had texted him all the details. But he hadn't wanted to look at them. He hated that Jack was gone, and as he leaned over the casket and looked down at his friend and bodyguard, his heart ached.

Jack had been hired at first because of his likeness to Nick, but over time the two men had become good friends. Jack was nothing like him. He was quiet and introspective, sort of like Luna, always watching everyone and every thing. But, eventually, he'd loosened up, and when they'd gone out he'd been a good wingman and a lot of fun.

For a while, Finn and Jack had had an affair, which had made Nick feel like a third wheel. But that had ended over a year ago. Finn had only said they'd wanted different things. Nick hadn't pushed for more details. But he knew now, more than ever, that loving someone who was a bodyguard was hard.

He'd experienced that with Luna. And they'd only made love once. What would it be like once he was out of this? Could they continue their relationship? How would he feel knowing she was guarding someone else, putting her life in danger for another person?

Nick wasn't sure he could do it.

But he was also very certain that the moment he tried to tell Luna what to do, it would be the end of anything between them. He looked down at Jack, realizing that he'd let his mind drift to get away from grief.

He leaned over and touched Jack's shoulder. He knew his spirit had left Jack's body, but he needed that connection one last time. "I'm sorry. I never meant for you to die for me."

Jack's eyes, of course, stayed peacefully closed, but Nick couldn't help the flash image of the body he'd identified in the morgue. He took a deep breath and blinked so that he didn't cry. One tear seeped out of his right eye, and he reached up to brush it away.

He straightened and fiddled with his tie before turning to find Kenji where he'd said he'd be, at the back of the room, watching the door.

"I'm done."

"Okay. Before we let those in who have come to pay their respects, we need to establish your movements. I think it might be best if you stay in one place and let people come to you," Kenji said.

"I'll try. I'm restless. It's not easy to sit and dwell on what happened."

"Yeah, death sucks. We can move, if you need to, but it will mean that I'll have to position myself close to you. Your conversations won't be private," Kenji said.

"I'm not hiding anything," Nick said.

"Good, then I guess we're fine. If you want me to interrupt, put your hand in your left pocket," Kenji said before he took another circuit around the room and then spoke into his earpiece to let Price Security know it was okay to let other people in.

Nick hadn't been offered an earpiece tonight, and given that he was holding a viewing for his last bodyguard...he wasn't sure how he felt. Tonight his emotions were all over the place.

As much as he was sure that Luna was safer away from him, he still missed her. He wished she were here, by his side, keeping that silent watch of hers, using her acerbic wit to make him feel lighter than he should. The guilt weighing on him was deserved.

Knowing what he did now, he should have pushed his father harder a long time ago. Should have made sure his theories weren't brushed aside by everyone as the paranoia of a young man with too much money.

He should have...what? He'd told everyone, yet they hadn't listened.

His father's dismissal wasn't surprising. But Aldo should have defended him. He'd known what was going on yet had kept silent.

Nick had always known that Aldo was loyal to his family, but he'd thought that loyalty had extended to him as well. With this investigation, he'd come to accept that nothing was like it had seemed.

LUNA SAT ON the floor of her room in the penthouse with all of her notes spread out around her and her tablet next to her on the floor. Lee sat across from Luna, leaning against the wall, her laptop on a tray on her legs. She was monitoring the comms at the funeral and watching the security cameras here at Nick's building while also helping Luna analyze the information that had been collected so far.

"Kenji says Nick seems edgy and that he doesn't seem to like many of his friends," Lee mentioned.

Luna had declined an earpiece, needing to focus on the information at hand. She felt like she was missing something. She didn't want to believe that sleeping with Nick had taken her edge away, but she knew she was too invested in finding the person behind the attacks on him to be neutral.

Instead of just doing her job, this had become personal. He'd been stabbed—hell, she'd been stabbed, and the wound was a dull ache in her side. That made her even more determined to solve this.

"I don't think they are his friends mostly. I mean Finn is, but otherwise, Nick keeps most people at arm's length. He's just so charming, no one seems to realize what he's doing," Luna said.

Only because she'd been inside his arms could she see now how artificial most of his interactions with other people were. Even with Verity. Nick had treated her the way he had treated Thom and the rapper he'd hosted the event for. She had no doubt most of them thought they were closer to Nick than they actually were.

"Is there anyone on Everett's list who has a connection to this building or to Nick?" Luna asked.

"There is one person on the board who has a very tenuous link to them both," Lee said. " Ben Kovacs."

Luna shifted the papers around on the floor and found the profiles of the board members from DeVere Industries. Kovacs didn't look familiar to her, which meant that she'd never seen him in person. Odd, because most of the board had been here the day she and Nick had been shot at in the stairwell. "He wasn't at the board meeting the other day, was he?"

"Nope. His aunt had an affair with Everett in the eighties," Lee said. "She's on the list that they sent over this afternoon."

This sounded promising. "Is he close to the aunt?"

"I'm not sure," Lee said, her fingers moving over her keyboard quickly.

Luna kept digging through her notes, pulling her tablet close and doing her own search on Ben Kovacs. He was the same age as Nick and had joined the board five years earlier, after the yachting accident that had taken the lives of Nick's cousins and uncle. He'd taken one of the seats vacated by their deaths.

Luna felt like she was on the right track with him. He wasn't married but lived with his girlfriend and her kid.

"Kovacs might be a good lead," Luna said.

"Ah, well, the aunt doesn't have any kids. So she's out as the letter writer. Unless Kovacs is actually her kid," Lee said.

Lee's fingers were still moving and Luna continued her search, ending up on Facebook where Ben's mom had shared a picture of herself pregnant with him in a birthday post.

Ugh.

Every time she got close to something, it slipped away.

"Nope," Luna said, air dropping the link to Lee, who cursed under her breath.

"What am I missing?" she asked her friend and coworker.

"What are we all missing? I think we need a break," Lee said. "We're focusing too hard."

"You think so?"

"I know so. I'm sort of the expert on these things, even Van says so." Lee tipped her head to the side and then smiled.

"What else did he say?" Luna asked, realizing that Van must have responded in Lee's earpiece.

"That I'm wise beyond my years."

"You are," Luna agreed. "Could you mute for a minute?"

Lee tapped her ear so that their conversation would be isolated. Van and the team would have heard her ask for privacy.

"What's up?" Lee asked.

"I slept with Nick," she said. Just blurted it out.

The worst part wasn't the sex. If it had just been sex, then she wouldn't be feeling like she had to alert the team. But it wasn't *just* sex. It had been more than that. From the moment she'd tackled him to the ground, she'd known he was different.

"He's hot, so I get it, but I'm guessing this isn't a girl-talk thing," Lee said. "What's the problem? You know that these situations can elevate that need to copulate."

"I'd love it if you never used the word *copulate* again," Luna said.

"You're diverting. What's up?"

Luna tried to find a way to put it into words. She had a circle of people she cared for in the Price Security team. There had never been a lover in the past for whom she'd felt anything more than strong affection. Normal feelings. Normal to her.

This was unnerving. Was it deep affection? Could it be love? She had no idea what love felt like.

It was just that she knew she wasn't herself. She wasn't functioning on the job the way she wanted to. She was worried about Nick tonight, and not just his physical safety. It would be hard for him to be at Jack's viewing and essentially be alone.

Finn was there, but he'd be busy making sure Nick was protected socially from those who'd take the viewing as an opportunity to network.

"I think I care for him," Luna said at last. And then immediately wanted to punch something.

She'd tried so hard to define herself in a way that had nothing to do with her past growing up in the foster care system. But this…suppressing her emotions always reminded her she hadn't. She'd never learned how to let her guard down and care for others. That's really where she was right now, and it wasn't a great place.

"I think you do, too," Lee said. "You know, it's okay to fall in love with him."

"No, it's not! I think it's making me sloppy."

"You're not sloppy. If anything, you're more diligent than ever. You just have to give yourself permission to care about him and let him care about you in return," Lee said.

Luna knew that was the truth, but she wasn't sure she was ever going to be able to do that.

"The team is heading back. You good?"

Luna nodded. She wasn't good, but Lee had given her something else to think about. And for now that was enough.

NICK WALKED INTO his building knowing the place that had once been his sanctuary was now another goldfish bowl, but that didn't bother him as much when he saw Luna waiting for him in the living room of his penthouse. She wore a pair of faded jeans and a T-shirt. Her hair was up in its customary ponytail and he felt a mix of lust and affection when he saw her.

Everyone had theories that they wanted to discuss, but he just wanted to take Luna in his arms and into his bed. He needed to just be with her after the long night he'd had. He knew this would be the last time he held her. He'd made the decision to have her removed from guarding him. Seeing Jack's body in the coffin, and talking to those in his circle who were now aware that he was in danger. It had made his vision clear for the first time.

He had to get Luna away from him so she would be safe. Then he needed to go through the people who were close to him again and get justice for everyone in his life who had been hurt. That was his plan.

"Did you two find anything useful?" Van asked from behind Nick.

Nick had almost forgotten the entire team and Finn had come up to the penthouse. Almost.

"We've eliminated another person as a suspect," Luna said.

"Who?"

"Ben Kovacs."

"Why did you suspect him?" Nick asked. Ben was a good guy and had brought a lot of new ideas to the board table.

"Your dad had an affair with his aunt and he got the spot on the board after the yacht incident," Lee said. "Seemed a bit coincidental."

More than a bit if he was looking through the lens that the Price Security team was using. "But he's not a suspect?"

"Well, it seems a bit of a long shot," Luna said. "He's on the maybe-but-not-likely list."

"Who else is on there?" Finn asked.

"You, Verity, Aldo, Hazel," Luna said.

"I guess I'll take comfort in the not-likely bit," Finn said. "I'm not trying to kill him, you know."

"We do," Van said. "That's why Luna said 'not likely.' We can't just decide we like you and cross you off."

"Ah, you like me?" Finn asked, flirting.

Van just gave him a small smile and Nick realized that he hadn't been paying attention to anything but Luna and staying alive. Was there something going on between Finn and Van?

He looked at Finn, who just raised both eyebrows and smiled back at Nick. That was a possible bright spot in all of this.

"So, ruling them out. Who's left?" Nick asked. He didn't think any of those four could possibly be the attacker.

"Staff here. Some of them are temporary or were outsourced for an event. That makes it harder to track," Lee said. "I'm working on it, but it's taking me some time."

"So where do we stand?" Nick asked. "How much longer until we know what's going on?"

"That's hard to say. We won't know until the attacker gets clumsy," Van said.

"That's not encouraging," Nick said.

"We know. Lee and I have a solid list and, now with the names of your dad's former lovers and partners, we should get something soon," Luna said. "For tonight, that's as far as we've progressed."

"I guess that's our cue to leave," Van said, coming over to clap his hand on Nick's shoulder. "Rest assured we'll catch this son of a bitch."

"Thanks," Nick said.

Everyone left the penthouse and he turned to Luna, who watched him with that look in her eyes he'd only seen the night they'd made love.

He shrugged out of his jacket and took off his tie, tossing them on a nearby chair. "I need a drink."

She followed him to the bar area and then, when he went to the piano and sat on the bench, putting his whiskey glass on the top of it, she sat next to him.

She smelled of spring flowers and he took a deep breath, needing to clear out the stench from the funeral home.

"You okay?" she asked.

"No," he said, putting his hands on the keys and starting to play Elton John's "Someone Saved My Life Tonight."

She leaned her head on his shoulder and put her hand on his thigh. His cock hardened, but right now his heart needed *this*. Needed the piano and the music and Luna. Just her body next to his on the bench while he poured out the emotions that he hated feeling.

The senseless loss of Jack's life, the disappointment in his father and Aldo, the affection for Luna that he wasn't sure would last. He played until his hands were almost numb and he had reached a null state. He finished his whiskey and then took Luna's hand and led her to his bedroom.

Chapter Twenty

Lee hadn't really given her any peace of mind when Luna had told her about sleeping with Nick. This was more than sex to her. And the type of man that Nick was, she knew he cared for her, but this wasn't going anywhere. There was no time, when she looked into her future, to make a traditional home with anyone.

And a man like Nick…

As much as the secret place in her heart wanted it to happen, she had to be realistic.

"It doesn't seem like you're thinking about sex," he said dryly as they entered his bedroom.

"I was thinking about you, does that count?"

"It would if you were ripping my clothes off," he replied.

"I was worried about you tonight," she said, slipping into his arms and hugging him close to her.

This had to be the last time she slept with him. Even being apart and working on the investigation, Nick had still been on her mind.

"Were you? Don't trust Kenji?"

"Oh, I trust him. He's really the best of us. And that's saying something."

"Then what was it?" he asked, tipping her head back

with his finger under her chin. Her lips parted as he did that, wanting his kiss.

"I know you. Tonight was going to be a war between what you want the world to see and the grief and sadness you feel at losing one of the few people you genuinely cared about," she said.

"How do you see me so well?" he asked.

She shrugged. She didn't want to tell him that, for her entire life, her survival had meant watching the people around her and being able to read what they were going to do next. It wasn't a skill born from happy memories. That was why she was so frustrated at not being able to figure out who was threatening him. When she successfully completed a mission, it gave someone else the security she'd never had.

"You can trust me," he said.

"I know."

"So?"

"I've always had to be observant."

"Foster care stuff?"

"Yeah," she said, not wanting to delve back into memories that weren't pleasant. "I just learned to watch how people were when they didn't think they were being observed. I could anticipate their behaviors and protect myself."

His hands slid down her back to cup her butt; she felt the ridge of his erection against her belly.

"So what do you see in me?" he asked.

Too much that she liked. But she wasn't going to say that out loud. "Well, I know that you play the piano when you are trying not to admit you're sad and hurt. I know you like seeing Finn happy and flirting with Van."

"How do you know that?"

"You had the tiniest smile on your face, your lips quirked

right here when you watched the two of them," she said, touching his mouth.

He leaned down until his forehead rested against hers. She felt the warmth of his breath against her lips and hers tingled. She would much rather be getting naked than talking to him right now. Saying this stuff out loud only made her want to find a way they could be together.

No matter that every other relationship in her life had proved to her that it probably wouldn't. For just once, she wanted to dream about a future with Nick. Just once, she wanted to think to herself that she could find a relationship that would last. Just once...she wanted to love someone and be worthy of them loving her in return.

Luna didn't have the heart to pretend she wasn't in love with Nick. She might have experienced love before, but she knew what these feelings were this time. She'd kept them hidden inside herself the way she'd tucked away a raggedy old bear in her first foster home.

She turned her head, kissing him, sliding her tongue over his teeth, rubbing against his tongue as he sucked hers deeper into his mouth. His hands cupped her butt and lifted her up onto her toes. She moved her arms, twining them around his shoulders. She sighed and a wave of what felt like sunshine went through her as he pulled her even closer to him.

There was something exciting about being back in his arms. A feeling of coming home. She raised one of her legs and drew it up high, wrapping it around his hip, and felt the ridge of his cock slide against her center. She rubbed her hips against it, enjoying the feel of him.

She wanted him. Emptying and aching as much as she

wanted this last time to last, she knew that a quick, hard coupling might be all her impatient body would allow.

She shoved her hand up into his thick hair and bit his tongue as he pulled it out of her mouth. Not hard, just a nip because the emotions he stirred in her were too intense to control.

Luna was horny, wanton, and a little bit angry at life that this could be the last time she had Nick under her body.

He lifted his head and looked down at her. Their eyes met and she wished she could read what was in them. He watched her so intently for a moment, she wondered if he felt the same thing she did.

Wanting something they both knew wasn't going to happen. And the heat between them was off the charts. There was no time to talk or contemplate what might happen later. He walked until she felt the wall against her back and then he brought his lips down on hers again, his mouth plundering hers. Taking things that she didn't know she could give.

His entire body moved against hers in one big caress that sent waves of heat through her. She was moist between her legs, and his cock rubbing against her through their clothes wasn't enough. She tried to wedge her hands between them, but he wasn't having it. Catching her wrists and drawing them up over her head. He held them in one of his as he raised his head and looked down at her again.

This time she had no trouble reading the feelings in his eyes. He'd taken charge, and she was happy to let him for tonight.

NICK WASN'T SURPRISED that Luna read him like an open book. There was a connection with her that he hadn't had with anyone else in his life. His friendships with Finn and Jack were deep and genuine, but he felt something different with Luna. And somehow she was stirring dreams of a future he'd never considered before this moment. This woman. In his arms for tonight, and he hoped for the future.

He knew he had to make something happen. Shake the attacker out and make them come for him. Nick had made up his mind when he'd entered the penthouse and seen Luna standing there in jeans and T-shirt like she lived there, and his heart had sped up. Emotions had washed over him. His life wasn't going to be worth living without her by his side.

Having her next to him while he'd played the piano had simply helped him to form his plan. He knew what he wanted. What he'd always wanted. But he'd been too afraid to push fate, to tempt it, by allowing himself to love. Or maybe he hadn't been ready to find love until she'd jumped across the room, covering him with her body as a gunshot hit the glass window of his conference room.

Maybe.

He didn't care why or how. He loved this woman. He was going to do everything in his power, use all of his luck, to keep her safe and put an end to the threat he was living under so he could find a way to make a life with her.

Holding her against the wall, her hands in his, her body pressed against his. The time for thinking was over. He held her wrists loosely with one hand while he pushed her T-shirt up. His hand moving over her until he could cup her breasts through the fabric of her bra. He undid the clasp at the back and then pushed the fabric off her breast and lowered his head to take her nipple in his mouth, sucking deeply on it.

Her hands slipped free of his grasp. They moved to the

buttons of his shirt, undoing them, and then her fingers were on his chest. They were a little cold, but he didn't mind as she caressed him, moving her hands lower on his body, her fingers dancing around his belly button and then lower still.

He lifted his head, toeing off his shoes as he undid his pants and shoved them down his legs with his underwear. Luna did the same with her jeans and panties before she tossed her shirt and bra onto the floor.

He shrugged out of his shirt. He pulled her back into his arms, savoring the feel of her naked body against his. He groaned, shifting his hips until he could get himself between her legs and then lifted her, slightly adjusting his stance until he felt the tip of his erection against the warmth of her body.

Nick drove himself up into her in one long thrust and she wrapped her legs around his hips. Her head fell back and he brought his mouth down on her neck, suckling against her as she clung to him.

He had forgotten how perfectly she felt around him, and he knew there would be time later to go slow, but right now, he needed her. Needed to drive himself harder and faster into her until she was calling his name. Her nails digging into his shoulders with her pussy tightening around him.

He wanted to make her come again. His body didn't care about anything pleasuring Luna.

He brought his head down and found her mouth, sucking her tongue deep into his as he drove up into her two more times until she orgasmed, hers triggered his and his body shuddered as his climax took everything from him. He continued thrusting inside her until he was empty. Then he turned, holding her in his arms, her legs still wrapped around him, her pussy still throbbing against his cock. He let the wall support them and just held her.

Wanting to believe that the love he had for her would be strong enough to overcome everything that life and fate could throw at them.

But then he looked down at her. Saw that bandage on her side and remembered the times she'd put herself in between him and danger. And that fear that had always kept him from letting anyone close to him stirred.

Why now, when he'd found the one woman who felt like the missing part of his soul, did he believe he could keep her? That he could keep her safe and never let her go.

His life hadn't changed…he'd changed. And fate might still be taking the people he needed and cared for from him.

He wouldn't let fate and his attacker take another person from him. He'd made up his mind. If fate demanded one of their lives, it would be his. He didn't want to live without Luna. Wouldn't be able to go on if she was killed in his place.

"Nick?"

"Hmm."

"I—"

He turned his head, kissing her to stop whatever she might want to say. He made himself stand back from the wall and carried her to the bathroom, where they showered together, and then he carried her back to the bed, made love to her again, and held her close to him. He wasn't sure if she'd fallen asleep or was simply pretending to be. But that suited him.

He couldn't talk right now. His emotions were too raw and his determination to make sure that Luna stayed safe was too strong. He'd made a decision that he might have been too cowardly to make in the past, and there was nothing that would stop him.

Not fate. Not Luna. Not the attacker who'd been threatening him for his entire life.

THE EVEN CADENCE of Nick's breathing indicated he was sleeping, even though he held his body too still to be convincing. But he wanted her to think he was, so she let him have it. Her mind was whirring too much for her to go to sleep herself.

The easier thing to think about was the investigation. She was reviewing the people and faces that she'd been analyzing with Lee earlier in the night. As much as she tried to make a connection in her mind, she only saw Nick. The way he'd looked when he'd sat down on the piano bench and taken a long swallow of his whiskey, and then the music he'd chosen.

Every song had a touch of angst or melancholy in it. Frankly, she didn't blame him for that. She knew the pressure he had put on himself for years believing that the accidents around him were more than coincidence. Finally having some validation had only brought more confusion into his world.

Luna wanted to solve this case, find the person attacking him, and give him the peace of mind he'd never had.

But she was too close to him to do it. She turned and put her arm around his stomach, squeezing him closer to her. He wrapped his arm around her, squeezing back for a moment. All the feels she had for him overwhelmed her and she turned her face into the curve of his neck, breathing in the scent of him.

She had to leave. There was no other way to find the attacker before Nick was injured again or someone else was killed. She'd indulged herself for as long as she could.

She felt his hand sweeping down her back as he held her closely and she opened her eyes, looking up at him.

Neither of them was sleeping and both were reluctant to talk. The hard conversations had never been the ones she'd avoided.

Until now.

Until Nick.

She took a deep breath.

"Don't."

"What?"

"Say whatever is on your mind."

"I have to," she said.

He sighed and then shifted away from her, sitting and resting his back against the headboard as he turned on the bedside lamp.

She crossed her legs as she sat up, facing him. She had put her T-shirt on after they'd showered.

"Okay then. What is it?"

"I have to stop being your bodyguard," she said.

"Good."

"What?"

"I can't bear it if you're hurt again," he admitted. "I hate that you were at all. I think you getting as far away from me as you can is the best idea."

She brought her knees up and wrapped her arms around them. "I think so too. But I'm going to stay on the investigation. I know there's still something I'm missing, and I want to solve this myself."

"Whatever it is, I'm not sure you or anyone will find it fast enough," he said.

"What makes you say that?" she asked. She, too, had a feeling in the pit of her stomach that another attack would happen soon. But she couldn't put her finger on why.

"Just my gut. Whatever it is that's kept me alive this long…"

He'd trailed off, and she realized there wasn't anything more for them to say. He'd agreed she should be replaced.

She rolled over and grabbed her phone from the nightstand, surprised to see it was almost six in the morning. The night had felt too short.

She texted Van that she needed to be replaced as Nick's bodyguard and that she'd explain later.

He answered her with a message that said he was sending Kenji to take over.

"That's done. Kenji's on his way. I'll get dressed and stay with you until he arrives," she said.

"You don't have to."

"I do. I can't let anything happen to you," she said.

He just watched her with that level stare of his and she wished there was a way to read his mind. To see what he was thinking. He'd been a little too agreeable for her. He'd been adamant that she not be replaced the last time they'd talked. She didn't blame him for changing his mind, but she didn't like it either.

"Are you sure you're okay?"

"No. Of course, I'm not okay. But as far as my life and this situation is, I think I'm as good as I can be."

She reached out to touch him and he took her hand in his, lacing their fingers together. "I don't want to talk about this. I want to find the bastard who's doing this and make them pay. Then I want to come back and—"

He broke off as they both got the signal that someone was in the penthouse elevator. She got out of bed and grabbed her gun, heading out of the bedroom and into the main area. Nick was behind her, his smartphone in his hand as he accessed the security cameras.

"It's just Kenji."

That was quick. He must have been nearby. She had hoped... For what? she asked herself. More borrowed time with Nick? Before this case and his life swept them apart?

"That's good. When he gets here, I'll get my stuff and leave," she said.

"If you can't pack it all, I'll have Finn send it to you," he said.

"I didn't realize you were in a big rush to get rid of me."

He didn't say anything, and she felt something she hadn't since she'd aged out of foster care at eighteen. Alone. Scared. Uncertain of her emotions and her worth.

Not as a bodyguard, she knew she was still very good at that. But as a woman and a person. She hated this. She should never have let her guard down and let Nick into her heart.

But, really, had there been any way to keep him out? She might be good at guarding everyone else, but she'd never had to protect herself from falling in love before.

Chapter Twenty-One

Luna left the penthouse without looking back. Leaving, she had down pat. She knew how to let go no matter how much she really didn't want to. She went back to the Price Tower and her apartment there, avoiding Van and Lee, who she knew from the team tracker app were both in the building.

She showered and then changed into clothing she preferred instead of the black suit that being a bodyguard to a billionaire demanded. Her jeans were faded and butter soft, and the T-shirt was from Inferno Brewing—one of the sponsors on Jaz's tour—and said Own Your Vices.

She'd never thought she had any vices, but Nick was making her rethink that.

Ugh.

She tried to shove all thoughts of him out of her mind and sat on the floor with her back supported by her bed as she spread her notes around her and started to run Nick and Everett's acquaintances through different databases, looking for any place where they overlapped.

While the search was running, she got up and went to make herself a cup of coffee. Seeing herself reflected in the mirror, she noticed she had a hickey on her neck. She touched it, knowing it would fade in time and that the mark from Nick would probably be the last vestige of him in her life.

There was a heavy knock on her door. That had to be Van.

She hurried to answer it, taking a deep breath before she opened the door.

"I'm sorry—"

"We can deal with that later. I just got off the phone with Detective Miller. Aldo Barsotti has been found dead in his car about two miles from the DeVere estate. Get dressed and into the briefing room."

"Has someone told Nick?"

"Kenji's doing it now," Van said.

"This is going to make him even more difficult," Luna said. "He'll take Aldo's death on himself."

"Is that why you asked to be replaced?" Van asked.

She shook her head and then shrugged. "I let it get personal. He needs someone with him who's focused on keeping him safe."

"And you weren't?" Van asked.

"Of course I was. But I was also worried about him for my own selfish reasons. You can't observe the situation while you're trying to make sure the client is emotionally okay, you know?"

Van nodded. "I've been there. For the record, I still don't think you needed to be replaced. I think you care too much about him to take the chance you might risk him somehow."

Luna didn't respond to that. Really, knew she didn't have to. That was the truth. She wanted—no, needed—Nick to be safe. She wasn't as sure of herself as she'd been in the beginning.

"Maybe."

"No maybe about it. Get dressed. I want to get a plan in place before the detective gets to Nick's building."

She closed the door and changed in record time, pulling her hair back into a ponytail. She contemplated covering the hickey with makeup for a split second, but left it. Everyone on her team had either been told or had guessed that she and Nick were together. Luna wasn't someone who liked to hide.

Rick and Luna piled into the back seat of the Hummer while Lee drove and Van kept them updated from the passenger side. She liked this part of the job, being surrounded by her team as they were briefed about a job.

She would risk losing this if she didn't figure out what to do with Nick. Would she still be as close with the Price team if she pursued a future with him? There was a part of her that was terrified to think of trying to make a life with him. She knew how to live on her own, to just make the job the only other part of her life.

But she also had the feeling that the job wasn't going to be enough for her. Not anymore. She wanted more with Nick. Now, if only she could believe that she deserved him, and actually take the risk.

"Kenji informed Nick. He took the news as best as can be expected, and Kenji said he's now in his workout room, waiting for us to get to there."

He'd need to work out, Luna thought. She knew how he had a hard time controlling that feeling of impotence that came from these deaths.

"Did Everett receive a letter?"

"No. He said normally the letter arrives within eight hours of an incident," Van said.

"Which means we've got a few hours until we get any more information. Detective Miller has a team going over the crime scene. Rick, do you think you could go over there and take a look?"

"I'll do it. Miller won't be happy. She found out I'd been talking to some friends to pull records, and gave me a friendly warning," Rick said.

"I can go," Luna said.

"I need you with Nick. He's going to need someone he can talk to and trusts. You're the only one who he confides in," Van said.

Her boss was right, but she wondered if he expected her to tell him everything Nick had said in confidence. "I can't betray his trust."

"I'm not asking you to. I think you might be our best bet to keep him alive," Van said.

All of a sudden, all the feelings she'd shoved down, pretended she wasn't experiencing, swelled up and she had to turn her head to look out the window instead of at the side profile of her boss.

Nick was reckless. This was going to drive him to do something dangerous. She wasn't sure she could convince him to give them a chance to get a plan in place.

And Van trusted her to keep Nick safe.

The man she loved. She had to do it. She knew herself well enough to accept that she wasn't going to fall for anyone else, and as much as they might not have a future, she needed him safe and alive so they could try.

That was the entire reason why she'd had Kenji replace her. "I'll do it."

"I know you will, kid. Rick, maybe talk to the detective and let her know that we need the information even if it's rough and unverified. We have an entire database of people from Nick's and Everett's lives that we might be able to find a connection with."

"I will," Rick said. "But you know cops don't like it when we tell them we have more sources than they do."

"You'll have to be charming when you do it," Van said.

Rick snorted. "That's not me. Maybe you should send Xander."

"She doesn't know him, she knows you," Van said.

They pulled into the underground garage and all got out of the vehicle and into the elevator to the penthouse. Luna ran the image of the garage through her head. Something was out of place, but she couldn't put her finger on it until they got to the penthouse.

NICK COULDN'T HELP but watch Luna leave. He knew she'd be safer away from him, but the minute the door closed, he wished he hadn't let her go.

Kenji noticed him eyeing Luna but said nothing. Instead he walked around the living area in the penthouse, familiarizing himself with it. Nick went to the grand piano and sat down. He started to put his hands on the keys and a flood of memories and emotions from last night washed over him.

He felt Luna's absence keenly and turned away from the keys to find Kenji watching him.

"So, what's your routine?"

"Weekdays, I run from six to seven, shower, breakfast, and at my desk by eight. Stay there until six or so. Then dinner and any social commitments. Tonight I'm quiet."

Kenji didn't sit but kept walking around the room, cataloging the entrances and looking out the windows. "Is there anything that Luna did that you didn't like?"

"No. She's really good at her job. That's not why I asked

to have her replaced," Nick said firmly, not wanting anyone to think she hadn't been performing her role.

"I know she is. So I'm not clear on why you axed her," Kenji said, coming closer to Nick, stopping a few feet away and putting his hands under his jacket on his lean hips as he stared Nick down.

He caught a glimpse of Kenji's shoulder holster and the faint outline of a bulletproof vest underneath his dress shirt.

"I'm not sure that concerns you."

That was all he was going to say about it. He was so tired of having to answer to Price Security. While a part of him knew that they were doing their best to keep him safe and alive, another part of him wanted all his yes-men back around him.

Kenji pulled his phone from his pocket, read something on it and then texted back quickly. He pocketed his phone and looked at Nick. There was a quietness to Kenji that hadn't been there before and that was telling because the man was eerily quiet at all times.

Even before the other man spoke, he knew that someone else had been killed. Luna? God, please don't let it be her. Don't let him have waited too long to send her away. He'd wanted one more night with her and he hoped his selfishness hadn't cost her life.

"Luna?"

"She's fine," Kenji said.

Nick felt weak with relief and, for a moment, closed his eyes. Grateful that she was okay. "Who?"

"Aldo Barsotti was found dead in his car. Detective Miller and her team are on their way to the crime scene. He was identified by someone he knew from the neighborhood."

Aldo.

No. Nick's gut churned with the pain of loss and anger that someone else he cared for was dead. The feelings that he'd had in the past stirred in him. A lifetime of grief that he had never been able to protect anyone. "Has someone informed my dad? Where was he found?"

"Detective Miller was going to send someone to speak with him. Aldo was found two miles from your father's estate," Kenji said. "I'll verify he's been informed. Do you want to call him?"

"I want to go and see him," Nick said. This was too close to his father. He knew that Aldo had been on Luna's list of suspects. Nick had never really thought Aldo would threaten him. He'd been too loyal to the DeVere family. And despite the fact that Aldo had never told him about the letters, Nick still loved him like a second father. This loss hurt.

Even more than Jack's had. Aldo was one of the few people who'd been in his world all of his life. Now there was only his father left. And his dad was dying. Whoever was doing this was intentionally chipping away at the people Nick cared about.

He felt isolated and alone.

"Of course. Van is on his way here with the team. We'll get a plan in place and then take you to see your father," Kenji informed him.

Nick just nodded and realized that merely making plans and regrouping wasn't working. Whoever had killed Aldo was taking a real risk doing it that close to his father's house. There was no time to figure things out. He needed to lose the security detail.

"Sounds good. I need to work out to work through this. I'll be in my dojo," Nick said.

"Let me check the room and then I'll leave you to it."

Kenji did a sweep of the dojo. Nick waited until he'd left before he went to the gun cabinet hidden behind a panel in the corner of the room. He took out the SIG-Sauer P220 that he used at the shooting range. Then he put on a bullet-proof vest that had once been Jack's. He covered it with his shirt and jacket and slipped out of the dojo. After checking the hall was clear, he made his way to the stairwell that he and Luna had used during the fire alarm. When she'd been shot at.

Hurrying down the stairs, he entered into his underground garage and got in his Bugatti. He hit the remote to open the exit and roared out onto the street, heading toward Malibu and his father.

He kept saying he wasn't going to let anyone else die in his place. Unless he was with his father, the killer was going to go after Everett next. Nick was the only one who could end this.

Whoever this was, it was time for them to stop with the pithy letters and homicides that took out people around him.

As he got on the freeway, part of him knew that Aldo's death was different. That was why he was concerned. This didn't feel like the other attacks. Whoever that man had been, he was responsible for Aldo's death, and he had some connection to the letters that his father had received. Nick was going to find out who he was and stop him from causing any more pain.

"HE'S GONE," KENJI said as they entered the penthouse.

The Bugatti had been missing from the garage. Damn. That was what had been wrong when they'd entered.

"Thoughts?"

"He was worried about his dad," Kenji said.

"I'll go," Luna said. It wasn't that she didn't trust anyone else to keep Nick safe, but she knew him better than they did and had been to the Malibu estate a couple of times.

"Make sure your tracker is on and put in your earpiece. Do you need a car?"

"I'll take one of Nick's," she said. She was already on her way out the door. Knowing the keys were all kept in a key-coded lock box in the garage. In the elevator, she couldn't help looking at her reflection and blaming herself for this. She'd known that he'd agreed too easily to her being re-placed and she shouldn't have gone.

But she'd wanted him safe. Or had she? It wasn't hard to see that she'd also been trying to keep herself safe. And now she was going to have try to catch up to him before he did something reckless.

And he would do precisely that.

Nick felt like he couldn't be killed. It didn't matter that she knew differently and had told him numerous times that he could be hurt. He didn't believe it. Not when he was put-ting others first.

She took the least conspicuous car in the garage, a classic Mustang stick shift with a heavy-sounding V-8, and drove like Nick always did. Fast, but carefully, toward Malibu.

Her mind needed to focus as she drove so that she didn't think of Nick possibly already dead or in the hands of a killer. These attacks were different from the "accidents" that had happened around Nick when he'd been growing up. Jack's death had been staged to look accidental, but the shot at his building, the knife attack in the club and Aldo's death were clear attempts at murder.

She activated her earpiece. "How was Aldo killed?"

"Gunshot, close range. Like the other person was in the car with him," Lee said.

"Thanks."

Luna pulled off the freeway and drove on the winding roads that led to the DeVere estate. When she got to the gated entrance, she waited for the security guard to clear her in. But the gates didn't budge. She parked the car on the side of the road and got out. She pulled her gun as she made her way to the gate, which she couldn't budge.

Great. She tucked her gun back into the holster and climbed up and over the fence. Her arms ached as she lifted herself over the top, which was what she got for skipping her arm workout since she'd been back in LA. She dropped to the ground, making her stab wound throb as she land in a crouch, and pulled her gun.

Sweeping the area before she headed to the guard booth. She approached cautiously. She saw the outline of a slumped body, blood oozing from a head wound. Luna rushed into the booth. The security guard was in a heap on the floor. She reached out to find his pulse and it was faint but steady. Unconscious, not dead.

She started to put her gun back into the holster when she heard footsteps behind her. She tensed, waiting until the person was close enough, and then sprang to her feet as she turned, dropped into fighting stance and used a front side kick to stop the other person.

Nick.

It was Nick sneaking up on her. She tried to stop the force of her kick as it connected with his body. He blocked it at the same time. So he wasn't hurt.

"What are you doing?" she asked him. Trying to stay focused on her anger and not her relief that he hadn't been killed.

"Trying to protect my dad. Now that Aldo is gone, he's vulnerable," Nick said. "There wasn't time to discuss it."

"I know. Van, Nick's with me. We are at his father's estate. The security guard is unconscious," she said, knowing Lee would inform Van via their comms.

"I'm going up to the house, I don't care what Price says."

Nick's voice was low with anger. She didn't have to relay that to Van.

Luna would go with Nick and keep him out of danger. Whatever it took.

"Keep me posted. I'm with Detective Miller at the crime scene," Van informed her.

She muted her earpiece after that and turned to Nick. Though it had only been a few hours since she'd seen him, it felt like a lifetime. "I thought you might be dead."

"I'm not. I told you—"

"Please tell me you have something other than fate to protect you," she interrupted.

"A gun, a bulletproof vest, and now you," he said.

"Now you want me by your side?" she asked, trying to get her head into that calm space it needed before they walked up to the house.

"I don't think I can keep you away," he said.

There was something in his voice she wanted to explore but that would have to wait. This was the moment she'd hoped wouldn't come but, as a bodyguard, had known it would. She was ready to put her life on the line for Nick as she had for all of her clients. But with him the stakes were higher.

She wanted the person who'd been torturing him for his entire life, stealing his sense of security and safety, to pay. And she wasn't going to let them get away with it.

"You can't. I'm in charge. You follow me when we get to the house. Is the housekeeper there?"

"She doesn't work every day. Dad's pretty low maintenance. So I'm not sure if she'll be there. Given that she was yesterday… I'm guessing no."

"Okay. We'll plan for her to be there," Luna said. "We'll go through and clear each room on the bottom floor before going up. You will stay where I tell you too, agreed?"

"I'll do what I have to," he said.

"Nick—"

He pulled her close and kissed her hard and quick. "I'm not going to take any chances with my life or yours, Luna."

He started walking toward the house and she moved quickly to keep pace with him. That embrace had raised questions that she wanted answers to. But later. After they made sure Everett was alive.

Chapter Twenty-Two

Entering the foyer of his father's house, Nick was very aware that Luna was in charge. He wanted to protect her and his father, and he knew his recklessness could put her in danger, so he held himself in check. She started to clear the rooms downstairs and Nick was impatient, wanting to get up to his dad.

All the security measures his father had put in place and none of it had ever really kept them safe. Not really.

"Is this necessary? Dad could be dead upstairs."

She didn't turn her head from scanning the last of the rooms downstairs. On the walk up to the house, she'd given him an earpiece so he could communicate with the Price team. Van and Kenji were on their way to them, and Rick and Detective Miller were still at Aldo's crime scene waiting for a backup unit before joining.

"Yes. We don't want any surprises. Let's go upstairs. Stay close to the wall and behind me. Can you use the gun you're carrying?"

"I can."

"Watch our back as we move up, just in case I missed something," Luna said.

He nodded and wanted to kiss her again. Right now his

mind and body was a jumble of thoughts and emotions. He was scared, angry, upset, guilty, worried, and the thoughts going through his head were ones that he didn't like. Mainly of his dad dead or injured in his bed. Luna injured again. He had promised himself no one else would be hurt in his place.

Only now did he realize how dumb that promise had been. He had no power to protect anyone. And being on the stairs behind Luna just reinforced that. He could watch their back and he could physically hold his own against someone else. But he couldn't control another person's agenda.

As they neared the top of the stairs, they heard voices coming from his father's room. One of them was a woman's. He started to move by Luna, but she grabbed his arm firmly, jerking him to a stop.

"No. We listen, we take a read of the situation, and then we go in. Aldo was shot, so there's a good chance whoever is in there with your dad has a gun," Luna said.

"All the more reason to get in there and protect him," Nick said in a low tone matching Luna's.

"Naomi, I never slept with you," he heard his father say. Who was Naomi?

"You don't remember. We were in love and you promised—"

"I didn't make promises. I was married and my wife was pregnant. You worked for me."

"I did work for you, and we spent a lot of late nights together," she reminded him.

"We did. But you were pregnant when you started working for me," his father said gently.

"I wasn't. That's just a story you've made up to make yourself feel better about what happened," Naomi said.

"Campbell is your son and rightful heir. He was born three weeks before Nicholas."

"Shit, that's Hazel," Nick said, recognizing the way she'd said his name. "What the hell?"

"That's not possible. Nick is my only son, and will remain my heir. You can point that gun at me all day and it's not going to change anything." His father was done coddling Naomi and his tone was firm. Nick knew from experience he meant business.

"Well, you can either change your will or die," Hazel said, "knowing that your son will be killed as well."

"With another accident?" his father said sarcastically. "You don't have a great record when it comes to actually getting Nick."

"I don't. But my son does. He stabbed him in the club the other night," Hazel said.

Nick moved around Luna, toward the bedroom once more. She tried to stop him, but he brushed her hands aside. "She's threatening my dad."

"Give me a second to just make sure there isn't anyone else here," she said, starting for the window at the end of the hall where she'd stood the first day they'd come here. She checked the lawn while he moved up quickly behind her, mimicking the way she held her gun near her shoulder, ready to aim. He'd only ever fired at targets at the shooting range and had no real-world experience with this.

Until this moment, he'd believed he'd be able to defend himself with the handgun. But he was sweating and the thought of firing at another person...unless he knew they were the one who'd killed Jack and Aldo, it would be hard. Could he shoot Hazel? He wasn't sure.

Before Luna got to the end of the landing hallway, a shot was fired and Nick tried to push her out of the way, but she leaped at him, shoving him to the ground. He felt her wince and knew that she'd been hit. He dragged them both back against the wall.

The sweats he'd had a moment ago gone, he lifted his gun, covering their rear. "Are you okay?"

"Yeah, just a graze. It's a good bet whomever is with your father knows we're here," she said. "Let's go."

She got up but stayed in a crouching stance and Nick did the same, following her as she moved down the hallway.

"Luna, you good? What direction were the shots fired from? Kenji and I are on the grounds," Van said. "Kenji spotted someone moving on the grounds."

"I'm fine. The shots came from the southwest. There are some trees."

"Situation in the house?" Van asked.

"It's Hazel."

"Nick's assistant?"

"Yes," Nick confirmed. "Price? Hazel's son is out there. I know he's a SEAL. Proably the sniper"

"She's gone silent," Luna added. "Do you think we're safe going into the bedroom?"

"Kenji and I aren't that far away. Wait until we get the sniper until confronting Hazel."

"Spotted the sniper. Going silent. You're good to move on Hazel. Watch your six."

"We'll be careful. You and Kenji stay safe," she said.

She turned to Nick. "I'll go first when we get to the door, I want to verify it's just Hazel and your father in there before we go in."

She moved toward the open door and Nick knew she was doing her job, but he also loved that woman and wasn't going to let her go in there first.

Luna was listening for the all-clear from Van as she put her head around the corner of the door. Hazel stood next to Everett's bed, holding her gun pointed at the older man. She had a two-way radio in the other hand. Hazel didn't look as calm as she had the other times Luna had met her.

The sweet grandmotherly-looking lady was gone. In her place was a woman wearing sleek, modern clothing and holding a weapon in her hand like she knew how to use it. She stared at Everett, not taking her eyes off the prone man.

Everett looked frustrated and scared out of his wits.

Hazel lifted the radio in her hand and spoke into it. "Campbell? What's going on out there?"

"Watch your six, Mom. Nick and his bodyguard are in the hallway. I shot Luna, upper arm or shoulder. She's not down. Nick has a gun as well," Campbell said.

Luna pulled her head out of the doorway as Campbell made that statement. But she could confirm there were only two people in the room. Hazel was on the left side of the bed and they were on the right. So Luna would have to move past the open doorway to get a good shot at her.

Nick looked furious, moving like he was going to enter the bedroom. Luna stopped and shook her head firmly no. "Not yet."

He held his gun like he was going to shoot and kill Hazel.

"Nicholas? I want you and your bodyguard to stay out of this room or I'll shoot your father," Hazel said.

"Talk to her," Luna said in a low voice, needing a few

minutes to figure out the best way to take out the threat to Everett and keep Nick safe.

"Why are you doing this?" Nick called. "Don't I pay you enough that you don't have to extort my dad?"

"He's the father of my son. Campbell deserves his inheritance. Everyone knows you two have a strained relationship. And you don't deserve DeVere Industries. You are a spoiled playboy," Hazel said, a note of derision in her voice.

Again, Nick tried to move and Luna stopped him. "Please just keep her talking," Luna whispered to Nick. "Try to distract her. I'm going to move to see if I can get a shot at her from here."

"I hate this. I want to confront her."

"We are going to get her. But we don't want your father hurt," Luna said.

"Okay," Nick responded then said to Hazel, "You know I'm more than that. You keep my calendar, and you have helped me set up work with charities. I'm not a bad man, Hazel."

"You're not a good man, either, are you? You lie."

"When did I lie?" he asked her.

Luna saw the way Nick held himself and knew that she was on borrowed time before he did something reckless.

He believed he was indestructible. More than once, he'd told her he couldn't be killed. That belief was so strong in him that she knew there was nothing he wouldn't do to save his father.

It didn't matter that he'd been upset with his father and Aldo because they'd kept things from him. Nick had only a handful of people he cared about, and Hazel had been responsible for picking them off one by one throughout his life. There was a limit on how long he was going to continue to talk to her.

Luna felt stuck, as well, trying to find a good position to get at Hazel.

"When you said you'd be at the beach house for your birthday..." Hazel said.

Luna body-crawled to the far side of the hall to keep her profile as low as she could. She had a glimpse into the open door of Everett's bedroom, but Hazel wasn't visible. She was going to have move into a better spot. She started to crawl toward the left of the door opening.

"Why did that matter?" Nick asked.

"You made me kill the bodyguard," Hazel said.

Luna wasn't sure their earpieces would pick up that confession, but she was sure that Van would get Hazel to repeat that to Detective Miller. She hoped they almost had Campbell because she could see the tension in Nick, and he wasn't going to wait much longer.

"Did that bitch just admit to killing Jack?" Van asked in the earpiece.

Hazel seemed tense. Her voice was getting tighter with each response to a question Nick asked her. She didn't sound hysterical, just really pissed.

"Jack Ingram. That was his name. I didn't make you kill him," Nick said.

"She confessed, but I don't know that we recorded it," Luna said under her breath.

"So you did that?" Nick asked her.

"I did. Once you walked into the office and I realized I hadn't killed you, I called Campbell and asked for his help," she said.

"So he just found out he's Dad's son?" Nick asked.

"He's not my son," Everett said.

"Shut up," Hazel said and they heard the sound of a punch or hit.

Nick was on his feet rushing into the room before Luna could stop him.

"We're moving in," Luna said, taking two large steps and getting to the doorway as Nick moved through it. Hazel turned toward them, gun raised. She fired a shot and Luna lunged for Nick, using the force of her body to knock him out of the way.

She felt the bullet hit her chest, the force of her lunge interrupted by the blow. God, that hurt. She felt the burning and then fell forward. Blood was running down her shirt. She felt light-headed and knew she was about to pass out. She wasn't going to be able to protect Nick.

That was her last thought as she blacked out.

DAMMIT. LUNA WAS on the ground, blood gushing from her chest. He blocked out the fear that she might be dead and leaped to his feet, running at Hazel, who seemed surprised and fired again. But the shot went wide. He knew he wasn't going to shoot Hazel. Maybe he could have fired at someone he didn't know, but this woman had sat in the office next to his for the last two years. She'd made him coffee, chatted with him and been a part of his team. This betrayal hurt more than Nick wanted it to. He put his gun back in his holster as he continued running toward her.

Hazel fired again and this time her bullet hit him in the chest. But he was wearing Jack's bulletproof vest and, while it hurt, making his breath catch, he didn't stop moving forward.

"Are you really going to kill me, Hazel?"

"I want to. You don't deserve—"

"To live?" he asked.

She fired again just as Nick jumped at her and tackled her to the ground.

He grabbed her hand holding the weapon, firmly gripping her wrist and slamming her arm down hard until her fingers opened. The gun fell to the floor. He used their joined hands to knock it away.

Hazel dropped the radio, bringing her leg up between his, kicking him hard in the balls. She reached for his shoulder holster, trying to get his gun. Pain spread up his body, but he was so pissed off, he shoved it aside, twisting his body so that she couldn't reach his gun.

She rolled, crawling away from him toward her own weapon. Grabbing her leg, he yanked her, pulling her off balance, and she fell onto her side, hitting her head hard against his father's solid walnut nightstand. Her body made a sickening thud as she fell to the floor, and he moved closer.

God, had he killed her?

He crawled over and checked her pulse.

"Is she dead?" his dad asked.

"She's still got a pulse, so, no. But she's unconscious," Nick said, standing as he handed his dad the gun. "Keep an eye on her. I want to check on Luna."

"We've got her," Van said, coming into the room.

Glad that the security expert was there, he rushed to Luna's side and was about to lift her into his arms when Kenji dropped down next to him. "Don't move her."

Nick held her hand in his and looked down at her face, tracing his fingers along the curve of her jaw and leaning low over her as Kenji ripped open her button-down blouse.

He took a pressure pad from a small bag and put it over the wound.

Nick rubbed his thumb against her knuckles, his heart in his throat. This was what he'd tried to keep from happening. This was the very thing he'd feared would happen to her. And he'd been right.

"Keep pressure on this—9-1-1 is on their way," Kenji said. "Detective Miller arrested the sniper. That's what took us so long to get up here."

"Glad he was arrested. I tackled Hazel. She's out," Nick said.

"Van's watching her. Are you okay?" Kenji asked, his dark eyes watching Nick.

Nick wondered if the other man could see the wildness still roaring through him. Holding Luna's inert body in his arms, keeping pressure on her bullet wound, made him regret not killing Hazel. She'd taken so much from him. And why? He still wasn't sure how she'd thought her son was his dad's.

"Dad, how did you know her?" Nick asked from where he was next to Luna. "How did this happen?"

His father had given his gun to Van and looked like he'd aged ten years since the last time Nick had seen him. "I'm not really sure. She worked for me at the office, but that's it. Aldo can—"

Emmett's voice broke off and Nick saw tears in his father's eyes. The first time he'd seen him cry. He wanted to go to his father but couldn't leave Luna.

Van put his hand on his father's shoulder and squeezed it. "I'm sorry about Aldo. If it helps, we're pretty sure he had figured out that Naomi was Hazel and confronted her."

"He did?" Nick asked.

"Yes," Van said.

"Will she live?" Nick asked.

"I think so. She's just knocked out. And I want her to pay for killing Jack and Aldo," Van said.

"Me too," Nick agreed.

The EMTs arrived, along with Detective Miller, and Hazel regained consciousness in time and was arrested before being taken to the emergency room. Luna was airlifted to the hospital. Nick wanted to be the one to go with her, but his father wasn't looking too good and Van had sent Kenji with Luna.

Nick couldn't get the image of her out of his mind. Pale, blood-stained clothing, and unconscious. That's what had happened to the woman he loved. And now that Hazel had been caught and had confessed, he should feel free. But he didn't.

He wanted Luna in his life, wanted a future with her. But she needed to survive. And even if she did, would she want to be with him? Her life would have to change, and he knew his would too. He wasn't sure a week with him was enough for her to believe they could have a future.

Nick stayed with his dad after they'd learned from Detective Miller that Naomi/Hazel's husband had been abusive, that after he'd died in a car accident, she'd convinced herself that her baby was actually Everett's. She'd raised Campbell to believe that he was the bastard son of Everett DeVere and that his "father" wouldn't acknowledge him.

Campbell hated Nick as much as Hazel did, and it was only when Everett was diagnosed with terminal cancer that she'd decided it was time to kill Nick and force Everett to accept Campbell as his heir.

Something that Nick knew his father would never have

done. He wasn't the kind of man who could be bowed to pressure. And until this moment, Nick thought he and his father were very different.

Chapter Twenty-Three

Luna woke up in a hospital room. Her chest felt like some-one was sitting on it and she heard the beeping of her heart-beat on a monitor. There was an IV port in the back of her hand and she was thirsty.

She looked around for either a bottle of water or the nurse call button, and the first thing she saw in the darkened room was Nick.

He was slumped over in a chair next to her, sleeping. Star-ing at him, she felt a wave of love rolling through her. But then she remembered that Hazel had been shooting at them. He was okay. He had to be if he was in the hospital with her.

She heard her heartbeat getting faster and took a few deep breaths to calm herself down. She shifted on the bed and Nick jerked upright. His hair was mussed from the way he'd been sleeping in the chair and stood up on one side. It was the first time she'd ever seen him not looking his best.

Their eyes met, and she realized that, no matter what, she wasn't going to leave him without telling him she loved him.

Just this one time she would take the risk that had always seemed too great for her. She was going to ask someone to stay in her life. She wanted Nick with her now and forever.

"How do you feel?" he asked, getting to his feet and coming over to her. She saw the bloodstains on his shirt and a hole in the center from a bullet.

"Thirsty. Are you okay?"

He was at her bedside now and put his hand on the side of her head, touching her so gently. "I'm fine."

He adjusted her bed so she could sit up and got her some water. She took a sip, slowly swallowing it.

"That looks like a bullet hole," she said, pointing to his shirt. "What happened after I went down?"

Nick told her everything that had happened and, while he was talking, Van poked his head in.

"Our girl is awake? Glad to see you, kid," Van said as he came into the room.

Nick stepped aside as Van walked over. She looked at her boss.

"You scared us," Van said. "I think Nick and I both wanted to kill Hazel for what she did to you."

"And Jack and Aldo," Luna said.

"Yes, but mostly you," Van said. "I'll let the team know you're awake. They are going to want to see you."

"I want to see them, too," Luna said. But she wanted some time alone with Nick. "Can you ask them to wait until the morning?"

"I will," Van said. He leaned over her, the scent of mint and his aftershave was strong. He kissed her forehead. "I'll be outside if you need me."

"Thanks, Van."

He turned on his heel, gave Nick a look that Luna couldn't read, and then walked out of the room. Nick came back to her side and stood there looking down at her as if he had something he wanted to say but wasn't sure.

That was so unlike him, she started to worry. Now that

the danger had passed and he had his life back, he might want her gone.

She would, of course, respect that. She wasn't going to try to stay in anyone's life who didn't want her. She never had. But this time she wasn't just walking away.

"I think we need to talk," Nick said.

"I agree," she said but, suddenly, with the moment this close, she knew she needed more time. So she went back over everything at his father's house. "You didn't listen to me."

"I just don't take orders well," he said, sitting down on her bed near her hip. "But you knew that."

"I did. I was scared when I blacked out. Afraid your luck wouldn't hold."

"I was scared you were dead and that she was going to kill my dad," Nick said. "I didn't need luck today, I just had anger and a need for retribution."

"Being ticked off is a dangerous time to attack someone," she said. He had been lucky. Somehow he'd managed to control his emotions enough to get the upper hand with Hazel and take her down. "Don't do it again."

"Considering that Hazel is in jail, I'm hoping I won't have to," he said.

"I hope so, too," she said. "Your safety is important to me."

"As is yours," he said. "Which is what I want to talk to you about."

"Before you go, can I?" she asked. She'd stalled long enough. She had to know if he was the man she thought he was.

"Of course," he said.

"I... I don't want to leave you, Nick. I'm sorry. I know

we live in different worlds and that, in reality, we might not work. But for the first time, I think I'm in love. I've never had that before." Crap, she was rambling, but he wasn't saying a single word. Just looking at her from that spot near her hip.

She had decided to take this risk but she felt more exposed than she had when Hazel had lifted her weapon and fired that shot at Nick. This was the one leap that was harder to take than putting herself between him and a bullet.

Luna almost started to call the words back. Tell him never mind, but she didn't. She had waited her entire life to fall in love and find a man who could love her. If it wasn't Nick, she'd be shocked. She'd come too far with him to back down now.

"So, there it is. I'm not sure what you wanted to say, but I love you and I want to spend the rest of my life with you."

She licked her lips and realized that this wasn't the hearts-and-flowers confession he was probably used to, but this was who she was.

SHE LOVED HIM.

He had been afraid to hope that she would. Not because he didn't feel like he deserved love but because Luna was so strong and so capable, she didn't seem to need anyone. He knew what it had cost her to say she loved him first.

Because he'd been almost afraid to say the words out loud to her. But those feelings had really blossomed once Hazel had been arrested. He'd been afraid to love and to lose Luna. Now he was free.

Hearing Luna say she loved him freed the last part of his soul that had been still chained to the past. He wanted to pull her into his arms, but she was fragile, injured because of the threat to him. They had a lot to discuss.

"I love you, too," he said. "I'm used to dancing through my life with no commitments, but since you jumped across that conference room, everything started to change."

"For me too. I thought you'd be just a typical CEO," she admitted, smiling over at him, but he knew she realized he wasn't jumping straight into a life together.

"I've never been typical." He was trying keep her smile, but the truth was she could sense he was holding back.

"Listen, I want to have that life together that you mentioned, but I'm not sure I'll be able to handle you putting yourself in danger. I don't think I can go through that again," he said.

When she started to speak, he held his hand up to stop her.

"I know I can't ask you to give up your job. I've never been in a situation like this before."

She took his hand in hers, lacing their fingers together. "Me either. This is the first time I've ever asked to stay with someone. I don't know how it will work either. But I do want to try. Do you?"

Nick took a deep breath. His entire life he'd drifted along, trying as a child to have close connections and a family of his own, finally finding that a few friendships were all that he could handle as an adult. "I guess this will be something new for the both of us. But, Luna, I can't see you like this again."

"This is only the second time I've been injured on the job," she said carefully. "So I don't think you have much to worry about."

"What was the first?"

"I twisted my ankle going for a morning jog with an ambassador I'd been hired to guard. I stepped off the curb."

He smiled because she was downplaying the danger of her job and he knew that the woman he had fallen in love with was a bodyguard. That asking her to give up her job wasn't something he could do. He was going to have to figure out how to accept it.

"That doesn't sound like you," he said.

"We were being chased by someone in a vehicle and I did push the ambassador out of the way," she said.

"See, that's what I'm afraid of. You are never going to keep yourself safe and I'll be worried every time you go to work."

She sighed. "I've never been in love before, Nick. I want this to work. Can we try six months of me on an assignment and us dating and see what happens?"

He moved closer to her and he knew that he'd do whatever he had to, to make this work. "Yes, of course we can. I've never loved a woman like I love you, Luna. I'd always thought I had a good life, and I do, but when we're together, I realize what I've been missing. And the thing is, I know I can't find that with anyone but you. We can take as much time as we need to figure this out."

He meant that. He wasn't saying what she needed to hear just to appease her. He would do whatever was needed to keep Luna in his life.

"You know I've never had anyone to come home to, Nick. I think that there were times when I was reckless because of that," she said.

"Me, too, but reckless in a different kind of way. Will you live with me and make a home with me?"

"Yes," she said.

He pulled her into his arms and kissed her gently. He wanted to get her home and make love to her. But for now he was happy holding her.

The nurse came in and checked on her, mentioning that Luna was doing well.

Nick sat next to her bed the rest of the night as she slept and when she woke up the next morning the Price Security team came in, Finn on their heels.

Luna was a like a little sister to everyone on the team. This was her family. He decided that he was going to make it a priority to get to know them all.

"I can't believe it was Hazel," Finn said. "I never suspected her. She and I even talked about how unfair it was that you never got a chance to just enjoy being a DeVere."

"In what way?" Nick asked him.

"Just living the good life without all of the trauma. But that doesn't matter. I'm just glad you're both safe," Finn said.

"Me, too," Luna said as the conversation she was having with Van paused.

Nick went back over to her side and took her hand in his again. "Luna and I are going to be living together when she goes home."

"Just what I was hoping to hear," Van said. "I think we can get her some assignments closer to home too."

Two days later, Luna was released from the hospital and Nick made love to her in his big bed. Afterward, they talked about the future and what their life might be like together.

Epilogue

One year later

The last year had been the best of her life, Luna realized as she stood next to her new husband on the lawn of Everett DeVere's Malibu mansion. It hadn't been all smooth sailing, but the good times outweighed the bad. And no matter what, they were both committed to each other.

Luna DeVere would never get used to seeing her name in the headlines—Bodyguard Tames Billionaire Playboy.

"You've been tamed," she said as she set her tablet down in front of her husband.

"Nice to see something can still surprise me," he said, pulling her off her feet and onto his lap and kissing her. They'd been married last night at his father's bedside with just Finn and the Price Security team around them.

As Luna sat on her husband's lap, she knew she had found something that she'd never expected to. Knowing she didn't have to keep her guard up all the time with Nick had given her a new vision of herself.

Everett was still on chemo and hanging on, but his doctors admitted they weren't sure how much longer he would be with them. He and Nick had gotten closer since Hazel and Campbell had been arrested. The trial had lasted for six weeks last September and had been in all of the headlines. Another scandal for the wealthy DeVere family. But Nick and Everett had ignored them and continued working to make DeVere Industries even stronger.

Finn had taken on the COO role within the company, allowing Nick to have more freedom in his schedule. Price Security kept her busy and, after a three-month bodyguard assignment away from Nick, Luna had decided she was ready to move into a different role.

Lee was tired of working in the office, so she and Luna switched roles. Luna realized that part of the reason she'd always wanted to be on the road for assignments was that she'd hated not having a home. Going home to Nick each night was perfect.

So when he'd asked her to marry him on Christmas Eve, she'd accepted. The wedding had been small and intimate, including only the people they loved.

"What are you smiling about?" Nick asked.

"Just thinking about how you thought it was luck that was protecting you all along, but once I became your bodyguard, you didn't need luck anymore."

"Not sure I agree."

"You don't?"

"I think you're my lucky charm," he said.

"And you're mine. Together we can face headlines, bullets, exes and the future."

"Yes. Together we're unstoppable."

* * * * *

COMING SOON!

We really hope you enjoyed reading this book. If you're looking for more romance be sure to head to the shops when new books are available on

Thursday 9th November

To see which titles are coming soon, please visit

millsandboon.co.uk/nextmonth

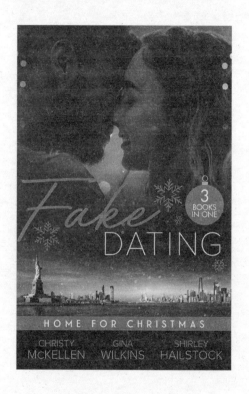

LET'S TALK
Romance

For exclusive extracts, competitions and special offers, find us online:

f MillsandBoon

🐦 @MillsandBoon

📷 @MillsandBoonUK

♪ @MillsandBoonUK

Get in touch on 01413 063 232